DEATH A

To my friend and brother Guillermo,

Wishing him a Happy Birthday

From Igor,
London, 2014

Writings from an Unbound Europe

GENERAL EDITOR
Andrew Wachtel

EDITORIAL BOARD
Clare Cavanagh
Michael Henry Heim
Roman Koropeckyj

MEŠA SELIMOVIĆ

DEATH AND THE DERVISH

Translated by Bogdan Rakić and Stephen M. Dickey

Introduction by Henry R. Cooper, Jr.

NORTHWESTERN UNIVERSITY PRESS

EVANSTON, ILLINOIS

Northwestern University Press
www.nupress.northwestern.edu

First published 1966 as *Derviš i smrt*. English translation copyright ©
1996 by Northwestern University Press. All rights reserved.

Printed in the United States of America

10 9

ISBN-13: 978-0-8101-1297-1
ISBN-10: 0-8101-1297-3

Library of Congress Cataloging-in-Publication Data

Selimović, Meša.
   [Derviš i smrt. English]
   Death and the dervish / Meša Selimović ; translated by Bogdan
Rakić and Stephen M. Dickey ; introduction by Henry R. Cooper, Jr.
      p.   cm. — (Writings from an unbound Europe)
   ISBN 0-8101-1297-3 (pbk. : alk. paper)
   I. Rakić, Bogdan. II. Dickey, Stephen M. III. Title.
IV. Series.
PG1419.29.E43D413   1996
891.8'235—dc20   96-17300
                                                                               CIP

∞ The paper used in this publication meets the minimum requirements of
the American National Standard for Information Sciences—Permanence
of Paper for Printed Library Materials, ANSI Z39.48-1992.

To Darka

CONTENTS

IX
Introduction

1
PART 1

241
PART 2

457
Notes

471
Select Bibliography

INTRODUCTION

Faintheartedness, or, more emphatically, moral cowardice, or, stronger still, pusillanimity—all rendered in Selimović's language by one word, *malodušnost*—epitomize Ahmed Nuruddin, the first-person narrator of *Death and the Dervish*. On one level at least, the novel is a case study of narrowness of spirit, emotional cowardice, and moral indecisiveness. One would be hard-pressed to find a better treatment of this particularly twentieth-century malady in any other modern literature. Meša Selimović, one of Bosnia's very best novelists, in his finest work, offers his readers an extraordinarily intricate examination of the anxious and incapacitated human heart, splayed against a backdrop of unsettling vagueness and mystery.

Death and the Dervish is set in Bosnia sometime during Ottoman rule, which lasted from the latter part of the fifteenth century to the latter part of the nineteenth. No specific date is ever mentioned (although the rebellions in the Krajina and Posavina suggest the seventeenth century), so that the reader is left with the feeling of timelessness, as if it had always been thus and would always continue to be. Islam is the established religion and no other faith is considered, let alone depicted, although ample reference is made to "Saint George's Day," an obviously Christian holiday that is treated in the novel as a moment of pagan relapse, an atavistic hearkening to a time before the "light of faith" (the meaning of Ahmed Nuruddin's name) arrived to impose its benevolent rule. Even the town itself, wherein virtually all the action of the novel occurs, remains obstinately anonymous (although, once again, the suggestion is Sarajevo; compare the references to the Sinan Tekke and Mount Igman). It is neither Tuzla (Selimović's birthplace) nor Travnik (Ottoman Bosnia's capital), for characters in the novel can be sent there. It is simply the *kasaba*, a generic term for any town with its market and institutions and homes. This *kasaba*, however, is more important than most, for it has its own fortress, in reality less a defensive construction than an enormously oppressive jail, the menacing presence of which plays an important role in the story. Indeed Selimović even called *Death and the Dervish*'s sequel *The Fortress*, to underscore the centrality that jails (and freedom) play in his Bosnian world.

Equally vague is the timing of the novel, despite the narrator's assertion early on that "it all began to occur two months and three days ago," on the eve of Saint George's Day (23 April, new style 6 May). As the novel progresses no further precision is offered regarding time, although the change of seasons, eventually moving from spring to summer to fall with forebodings of a severe winter to come, is mentioned. Lapses occur in the manuscript, which is what the novel claims in fact to be: Ahmed Nuruddin avers he has left off writing for a while, as other matters preoccupy him. Nonetheless the narrative flow is seamless, both beginning and ending with the same (mis)quote from the Koran; somehow, quite mysteriously, both beginning and end are on the eve of Ahmed Nuruddin's execution.

The characters are vague as well, more often than not they are called not by their names (if indeed they have any) but by their titles. So Ahmed Nuruddin himself, who makes so much of the meaning of his name, admits it was assigned to him; it is not really his own. In any event he is usually called the "sheikh," or head of a religious community. There is the kadi, or judge, and the kadi's wife; the musellim or sheriff; various tradespeople; guards; the miralay and his retinue; the mullah, the mufti, the defterdar, and so on (a Glossary has been provided at the back of this book.) Only two names figure at all prominently in the novel: Is-haq the fugitive, but then that is the name Ahmed Nuruddin capriciously gives him, without knowing his real name; and Hassan, the friend, active force, and moral and emotional counterweight to Ahmed Nuruddin. Only Hassan's then is a real name, only Hassan is unburdened by a title. All the rest are as vague and as shaky as their inauthentic names and insecure positions suggest.

Even the faith of Islam itself wavers in *Death and the Dervish*, though dervishes represent the most powerful, most severe, most pure witness among the various Islamic holy orders. The tekke, the order's home, is no safe haven. Its inhabitants are sick or scoundrelly or morally so indefinite that the regular performance of their religious rites imparts no piety to them, only an air of hypocrisy or at best meaninglessness. The administration of the town, and indeed even of the empire, is corrupt and unprincipled despite the omnipresence of Islamic structures and laws. And the sacred text of Islam itself, the Koran, a verse of which precedes each chapter, is unreferenced and often distorted. Thus, the surest guide itself can be used to contribute to the novel's unremitting air of spiritual ambiguity, confusion, and compromise. In other words, every feature of *Death and the Dervish*, its timing, setting, characterizations, and allusions, underscores Ahmed Nuruddin's own faintness of heart and soul.

The plot of the novel is based on an event in Selimović's own life. The confessional tone of the novel, from its first-person narration to its mention of Selimović's own executed brother, Šefkija, by name and in tandem with Ahmed Nuruddin's executed brother, Harun, is straightforwardly autobiographical. Meša (originally Mehmed) Selimović was born in Tuzla, northwestern Bosnia, in 1910, to a fairly well-to-do family. Though Selimović's mother was religiously observant, it seems the rest of the family was not. Selimović himself claimed to be a Communist and an atheist, and his brothers and sisters were active in the Yugoslav Communist Party before World War II and in the Communist-led partisan resistance movement during the war. In fact it was at the very end of the war in the Balkans that the episode occurred that would lead to the writing of *Death and the Dervish*. Šefkija Selimović, Meša's older brother, a Communist and partisan, was put in charge of a warehouse of property stolen by the Nazi and Ustaša occupiers of Tuzla. Needing some furniture to outfit an apartment for himself and his new wife after their home had been destroyed, Šefkija removed a few inconsequential pieces from the warehouse. Perhaps egged on by enemies he had made in the local party administration, or merely in a perverse streak of puritanism, the Communist authorities accused Šefkija of impropriety with the people's property and in very short order executed him as an example to others. Meša and his other brother, Teufik, also a Communist, were unable to prevent the tragedy; many felt that they had not tried hard enough to do so.

After the war, despite his activities as a Communist and partisan, Selimović was expelled from the Communist Party for abandoning his wife and newborn daughter for another woman, who was in fact a "bourgeoise" (this was Darka Božić, daughter of the former royal Yugoslav commandant of Sarajevo; it is to her that *Death and the Dervish* is dedicated). Though he was eventually reconciled with and readmitted to the party, and he found a very stable and important partner in Darka, the decade of the 1950s was difficult for Selimović: essentially he made his living at odd writing and scripting jobs, and the little fiction that he published was not received with critical acclaim. It was only in the 1960s that stability—a job as editor of a major Sarajevo publishing house—and success in writing, first modestly with *Tišine* (Silences), and then spectacularly with *Death and the Dervish* (1966), finally caught up with him. By the end of the decade Selimović had been awarded all the most prestigious Yugoslav literary prizes and even been nominated for the Nobel Prize in Literature. He did not win: the only Yugoslav ever to have done so, in 1961, was Ivo Andrić, Selimović's fellow Bosnian, with whom he is often compared and even more often contrasted. Failing health in the 1970s and the cooler reception for his later work, *Tvrdjava* (The fortress) and *Ostrvo* (The island), made the last decade of Selimović's life somewhat mournful. A move to Belgrade at that time, both to escape Bosnian provincialism and to enter Yugoslav and especially Serbian literary "high society," provided him no significant relief from the aftereffects of fading glory, although he continued officially to be honored by both state and public.

In his autobiography, *Sjećanja* (Memoirs), and his other public pronouncements toward the end of his life Selimović developed with increasing insistence the idea that he was a Serb by nationality, a Bosnian merely by birth. Such self-identification was no idle semantic game in Yugoslavia, as has become painfully clear in the aftermath of that country's breakup. Notwithstanding the claims of the nationalists, the difference among Serbs, Croats, and Slavic Muslims is neither linguistic, nor ethnic, nor, as religious practice fades, confessional. The essential difference derives from a sense of community: Which set of national myths will an individual choose to celebrate as his or her own? Which group of people will he or she celebrate them with? Despite contemporary appearances, movement among these groups has been appreciable over time, and the boundaries until recently have remained porous. How else could Ivo Andrić, born of Croatian parents, baptized a Roman Catholic, raised and educated in Bosnia, be hailed at his death as Serbia's greatest writer? How else could Selimović, so closely identified with the Bosnian Muslim milieu, expect acceptance as a Serb? Many have speculated on the motivations underlying both Andrić's and Selimović's adoption of Serbian cultural citizenship, and the unkindest have often posited mean self-interest. In both cases, however, it seems clear that the writers saw Serbdom's tent to be larger, more inclusive, more varied and inviting than the far smaller tents into which they had been born. In the context of the Slavic-speaking Balkans, the Serbs had the most cosmopolitan culture; the rest were more provincial and (consider the Croatian laureate Miroslav Krleža) even stifling. One way or another, Selimović insisted on his Serbian identity at a time when it was not particularly fashionable (or even politically astute) to do so. Whatever his motive, it seemed particularly important to him to join the ranks of Serbian writers, and to understand his Bosnian Muslim ways as a subset of the larger Serbian cultural heritage.

Selimović died at home in 1982: in his will he left everything to his beloved Darka and the two daughters he had by her, failing even to mention the daughter he had had by his first wife. As with Andrić, the Yugoslav literary establishment eulogized him upon his death, and he, and especially his greatest novel, have been the subject of considerable scholarly interest to the present.

The plot of *Death and the Dervish* is simple: Ahmed Nuruddin's brother, Harun, has been arrested by the corrupt establishment of the town on fabricated charges. In fact he knows something he should not, and to prevent his making use of it he is quickly and quietly put to death. As a pillar of the local order, Sheikh Ahmed Nuruddin agonizes over an appropriate response to his brother's incarceration, until it is too late. Then, wracked with guilt for his indecisiveness, he concocts a plot that brutally disposes of the powers that ordered his brother's death, eventually taking over in their place. But hatred engenders hatred, and soon he is the victim of an even more devious scheme to hurt him by targeting his one and only faithful friend, Hassan. In a monumental repetition of the pusillanimity that had allowed his brother to go uncontested to his death, Ahmed Nuruddin even signs the papers that order Hassan's execution. The final scene, with its radical change of tone and complex denouement, is as depopulated as a Shakespearean tragedy's—*Hamlet* comes to mind for more than one reason—and indeed the drama of the plot, though worked out slowly over some four hundred fifty pages, is as intense and inexorable as *Hamlet*'s.

In many ways it is remarkable how popular *Death and the Dervish* has been with the Yugoslav reading public (eventually, a film was made of it as well). It is not an easy read: it is long; it is full of meditations, reflections, and flashbacks; only one voice narrates throughout the whole novel; the dialogue is so sparse that on occasion the reader might have to check back to see who is speaking; the colorful Bosnian milieus that Andrić had so popularized are completely absent; even exotic vocabulary is kept to a spare minimum (though to the outsider this might not seem the case). Episodes do occur, small side trips are made, but they seem lush only in comparison to the austerity of the main plot: *Death and the Dervish* is a hard book to extract freestanding passages from; virtually every line and paragraph in the book derive their power not so much from the charge they carry within themselves as from their inextricable relationship to everything that precedes and follows them. One very astute critic, Thomas Butler, has called the novel's structure *poetic*; this is indeed the case, and not just in the prose's rhythmicity, its repetitions, its similes becoming metaphors, and its polysemous language. *Death and the Dervish* is in effect one very long poem, circular in fact, with its end becoming its beginning, and with every part interconnected to all the others. Moreover, it is a holy poem, or at least the text partakes of the essence of a holy text: each word is intentional, weighty, meaningful, unchangeable, and consequential. It is not an easy read, but it is a worthwhile and rewarding read, and that might in part account for its popularity.

But critics have also suggested another reason for its unusual success, one even more important for its universal appeal wherever it has appeared in translation (and this first full English translation is probably the last into a major world language, the others having been done decades ago).

Selimović's Bosnia is extraordinarily uniform. In this regard it bears no resemblance whatsoever either to the colorful variegatedness of Andrić's Bosnia, or to the reality of the country, which once was celebrated as a multiethnic, multicultural, multireligious society and now is being punished for it. Selimović's Bosnia is precisely what the ethnic cleansers, the sectarians, the fundamentalists, the dogmatists hope to achieve: one people, under one code, bowing to one authority. It is a nightmare (how much of the novel takes place at night!), it is darkness at noon, it is a twentieth-century horror set in a past age that mercifully lacked many (but not all!) of the means to impose such rigidity on living human beings. Ahmed Nuruddin is the pillar that supports this society, and he is the instrumentality that brings it down, by taking the fundamentalism he professes to its logical conclusion. Professing love, he experiences fear and nurtures hate. He is capable of sacrificing his brother and his friend, but, unlike Abraham sacrificing Isaac (the fugitive is named Is-haq—Isaac!), there is no loving God to stay his murderous hand. Murder begets hate, and hate more hate. And the only one to survive is the one who can escape this vicious circle. Some, of course, do escape, but at a price, as the finale of the novel sadly suggests.

Selimović's Ottoman Bosnia is a microcosm of post–World War II Yugoslavia, and postwar Yugoslavia was (it is no more) a microcosm of life in this century. *Death and the Dervish* was received in Yugoslavia as an antitoxin against the fears and hatreds of both the war and the postwar regime, and it can function that way as well for those who do not know Yugoslavia at all. The point, made slowly, in a complex, poetic way, and coming only at the very end of the novel, is disarmingly simple: the love of brothers, as between Ahmed and Harun; the love of parents and children, as between Hassan and his father; the love of friends, as between Ahmed and Hassan; and finally erotic love, whose absence in his life sends Ahmed down the road toward death—all will indeed remove fear, destroy hate, exorcise the past, generate new life, allow the sun in, bring peace. None of that is actually depicted in *Death and the Dervish*. It had been Selimović's fond hope to do so in the two following novels of the trilogy he had planned, and indeed, in *The Fortress*, the second and only other complete volume of the trilogy, he did move in this direction. But the suggestion may have been more important than the depiction: *Death and the Dervish* remains Selimović's masterly and most successful expression of an ancient wisdom that may prove salvific yet.

Henry R. Cooper, Jr.

TRANSLATORS' NOTE

Death and the Dervish has its fair share of stylistic and linguistic idiosyncrasies, complicating the task of remaining faithful to the original while producing a fluid translation. Selimović uses numerous words and expressions of Arabic, Turkish, and Persian origin, which give the original subtle stylistic and sometimes semantic nuances. As many have no simple equivalents in English, we have kept them if they preserve the flavor of the original and do not affect the translation's readability. Generally our criterion for inclusion was whether these words occur in the *Oxford English Dictionary*; however, we have taken into account their meanings specific to the local vernacular in Bosnia and Herzegovina. We have provided a Glossary at the end of the volume; terms marked with an asterisk may be found here. Since the word *dervish* itself is among them, we were faced with a problem at the very outset, as we obviously could not footnote the title. We assume, though, that the term, which refers to a member of any of various Muslim religious orders, is familiar to the English-speaking reading public—at least through the notion of "whirling" dervishes, to whose very order the novel's hero in fact belongs.

The novel's Koranic language and references to Islam deserve special comment. The motto at the beginning of each chapter is based on a text of the Koran. Other quotations and quasi-quotations occur in various places. Many of Selimović's quotations are less than exact, others are taken out of context, and some consist of lines from different chapters (*suras*), grafted together. Therefore we have in general followed his versions instead of relying on any English translations of the Koran itself. We have footnoted all the quotations we could identify.

We would like to express our gratitude to Henry R. Cooper Jr. and Vasa D. Mihailovich, who reviewed the manuscript and provided many helpful comments, and to Yusuf Nur, whose assistance with quotations from the Koran proved invaluable.

The preparation of this work was made possible in part by a grant from the National Endowment for the Humanities, an independent federal agency. We acknowledge their support with gratitude.

Finally, we dedicate this translation to Mirna Dickey, with whom it all began, and to the memory of Nikola Rakić.

PART I

1

■ □ ■ □ ■

Bismilâhir-rahmanir-rahim![1]
I call to witness the ink, the quill, and the script,
which flows from the quill;
I call to witness the faltering shadows of the sinking evening,
the night and all she enlivens;
I call to witness the moon when she waxes, and the sunrise
when it dawns.
I call to witness the Resurrection Day and the soul
that accuses itself;
I call to witness time, the beginning and end
of all things—to witness that every man always suffers loss.[2]

I BEGIN MY STORY FOR NOTHING, WITHOUT BENEFIT FOR myself or anyone else, from a need stronger than benefit or reason. I must leave a record of myself, the chronicled anguish of my inner conversations, in the vague hope that a solution will be found when all accounts have been settled (if they may ever be), when I have left my trail of ink on this paper, which lies in front of me like a challenge. I do not yet know what will be written here. But in the strokes of these letters at least some of what was in me will remain, no longer to perish in eddies of mist as if it had never been, or as if I had never known what happened. In this way I will come to see how I became what I am—this self that is a mystery even to me. And yet it is a mystery to me that I have not always been what I am now. I know these lines are mud-

PART I

dled; my hand trembles at the task of disentanglement that I face, at the trial I now commence. Here I am everything: judge, witness, and accused. I will be as honest as I can be, as honest as anyone ever could be, for I have begun to doubt that sincerity and honesty are one and the same. Sincerity is the certitude that we speak the truth (and who can be certain of that?), but there are many kinds of honesty, and they do not always agree with one another.

My name is Ahmed Nuruddin. It was given to me and I took what was offered with pride. But now, after a great many years which have grown on me like skin, I think about it with wonder and sometimes with a sneer, since calling oneself *"Light of Faith"* evinces an arrogance that I have never felt and of which I am now somewhat ashamed. How am I a light? And how have I been enlightened? By knowledge? By higher teachings? By a pure heart? By the true path? By freedom from doubt? Everything has been cast into doubt and now I am nothing but Ahmed, neither sheikh* nor Nuruddin. Everything has fallen from me, like a robe or a suit of armor, and all that remains is what was at the beginning, naked skin and a naked man.

I am forty years old, an ugly age: one is still young enough to have dreams, but already too old to fulfill any of them. This is the age when the restlessness in every man subsides so he can become strong by habit and by the certainty he has acquired of the infirmity to come. But I am merely doing what should have been done long ago, during the stormy flowering of my youth, when all the countless paths seemed good, all errors as useful as the truth. What a pity that I am not ten years older, then old age would protect me from rebellion; or ten years younger, since then nothing would matter. For thirty is youth that fears nothing, not even itself. At least that is what I think now that thirty has moved irretrievably into the past.

I have just spoken a strange word: rebellion. My pen hesitates above this straight line, upon which a dilemma has been impressed, but all too easily uttered. This is the first time I have so named my anguish, and I have never before thought of it in this way. Where did this dangerous word come from? And is it only a word? I have asked myself if it might not be better to stop writing, so as not to make everything harder than it already is. What if writing, in some inexplicable way, draws from me even things that I do not want to say, things that I have not intended, or that have hidden in the darkest depths of me, just waiting to be stirred up by my present agitation—a feeling that is hardly likely to obey me? If that happens, then writing will be a merciless interrogation, a hellish affair. And maybe it would be better to break the reed that I have so carefully sharpened at the tip, and toss the ink out on the stone tiles in front of the tekke.* That black stain would remind me never again to take up the magic that wakes evil spirits. Rebellion! Is it only a word, or a thought? If it is a thought, then it is my thought, or else my delusion. If it is a delusion, then woe to me! If it is the truth, then woe to me even more!

And yet I have no other path to take, I can tell all of this to no one except myself and the paper. Therefore I will continue to write these irrepressible lines, from right to left, from margin to margin, from thought to thought as if from one chasm to the next. The long rows of these lines will remain as a testimony, or an accusation. But whose accusation, almighty God, you who have abandoned me to the greatest of all human miseries, which is to face oneself? Whose accusation is it? And against whom? Against me or against others? No matter, there is no longer any way out, this writing is as unavoidable as life or death. What must be will be, and my guilt lies in being what I am, if that can be guilt. It seems that everything is changing completely; everything in me is shaking right down to my very foundations. And the world sways with me, because it cannot be in order if there is no order in me. But still, everything that is happening and has happened has one and the same cause: what

I want, and what I must do, is respect myself. Without that I could not find the strength to live like a man. It might seem absurd, but yesterday I lived like a man. I want to live like a man today, which is a different day, perhaps even contrary to the old one. This does not disturb me, because a man changes constantly, and it is a sin to ignore your conscience when it speaks.

I am the sheikh of a tekke of the Mevlevi[3] order, the most widespread and purest of orders. The tekke in which I live stands at the edge of the kasaba,* between black, gloomy cliffs that block out most of the sky and leave only a blue fissure above me, like a meager act of mercy or a remembrance of the endless expanse of the sky in my childhood. But I do not like that distant recollection—it torments me more and more, like a missed opportunity, though I do not know which. I make a vague comparison between the lush woods above my father's house, the fields and orchards around the lake there, and the rocky gorge where the tekke and I are trapped, and it seems that there are many similarities between the narrow confines inside me and those around me.

The tekke, pleasant and spacious, overlooks a river that makes its way down from the mountains and through the rocks of the gorge. There is a garden, a plot for roses, and a veranda covered by an arbor. Upstairs there is also a long porch where the silence is as soft as cotton, and seems all the more silent because of the soft gurgling of the river below. This building was formerly the harem* of the ancestors of the wealthy Ali-aga* Janich, who donated it to the order to serve as a meeting place for dervishes and a shelter for the poor, "since they are brokenhearted." Through prayer and incense we cleansed the house of its sin and the tekke acquired the fame of a holy place, although we never rid it entirely of the shadows of young women. At times it seems that they pass through the rooms, leaving their fragrances to linger behind.

The tekke, its fame and holiness—that was me. I was its foundation and roof. Everyone knew this, and therefore I make no effort to hide it. Otherwise these lines would contain a conscious lie (no one is to blame for lying unwittingly and thereby inadvertently misleading himself). Without me the tekke would have been just another five-room house, but with me it became a bastion of faith. Since there were no houses beyond it, the tekke seemed like the defense of the kasaba against all evil, known and unknown. Thick wooden lattices over the windows and a massive wall around the garden made our seclusion more impenetrable and secure. But the gate was always open, so that those who needed comfort or purification from sin could enter. We received them with kind words, although our words were scantier than their troubles, scantier still than their sins. I am not proud of my service, that was just how one really serves his faith—sincerely and wholeheartedly. I considered it a duty and a blessing to shield myself and others from sin. Yes, myself as well; there is no point in hiding that. Sinful thoughts are like the wind—who can hold them back? And I do not think this is a great evil. What is the purpose of piety if there are no temptations to resist? Man is not God, his strength is the ability to restrain his own nature, so I thought, and if he has nothing to restrain, then what are his merits? Now I think somewhat differently about this, but I should not bring up anything before I need to. There will be time for everything. The paper rests on my knee and waits quietly to accept my burden, although without taking it from me, without feeling its weight. There is a long, sleepless night ahead of me, many long nights—I will come to everything. I will do everything I must, I will accuse and defend myself; there is no need to hurry, although I see that there are things that I can write about now and maybe never again. When the time comes, when I wish to talk of other things, they will also have their turn. I can feel how they are piled up in the stores of my brain, all connected, all pulling

PART I

at one another. None of them exists independently, and still there is a sort of order in that turmoil, and one of them always leaps out from among the others, I do not know how, and comes to light either to hurt or comfort me. At times they jostle and assail each other, impatient, as if afraid of remaining untold. No hurry, there will be time for everything; I have allotted it to myself. A trial consists of confrontations and testimonies; I will not circumvent them, and in the end I will be able to pass a verdict on myself, since this is about me and no one else. The world has suddenly become a secret to me, and I a secret to it. We have come face to face and look at each other in amazement. We no longer recognize each other, no longer understand each other.

Let me return again to myself and the tekke. I loved it, and still love it. It is quiet, clean, mine. It smells of tansy in the summer, and of harsh wind and snow in the winter. I also love it because I made it what it is, and because it knows secrets that I have never revealed to anyone, that I have hidden even from myself. It is warm and peaceful; in the early morning pigeons coo on the rooftop, and rain drums lightly on the tiles. It is raining now as well, persistently, perpetually, even though it is summer. The rainwater drains away through wooden gutters into a night that has descended ominously on the world. I fear that this night might never be lifted; at the same time I hope that the sun will soon rise. I love the tekke because it protects me with the peace of my two rooms, where I can be alone when I wish to rest from people.

The river resembles me: sometimes turbulent and foaming, more often calm and inaudible. I was sorry when they dammed it up below the tekke and diverted it into a trench to make it obedient and useful, so it would run through a trough and drive a mill wheel. And I was happy when it swelled, destroyed the dam, and flowed free. I knew all the while that only tamed waters can mill wheat.

But the rain is still pouring down, as it has for days, and the pigeons coo in the attic, since they cannot go out from under the eaves. They announce a day that has not yet come. My hand has become stiff from holding the pen, the candle spits and sparks a little to stave off its death. I look at these long rows of words, the tombstones of my thoughts, and I do not know whether I have killed them, or given them life.

PART I

2

> If God were to punish every evil deed, not a single
> living creature would remain on earth.[1]

EVERYTHING BEGAN TO GET COMPLICATED TWO MONTHS AND three days ago. It seems I should count time from the night before Saint George's Day,[2] because this has been my time, the only time that matters to me. My brother had already sat imprisoned in the fortress for ten days.

Toward dusk on Saint George's Eve I walked the streets, embittered and upset beyond words. Yet I appeared calm (one gets used to doing that) and my gait did not betray any agitation. My body attended to my disguise by itself, leaving me free to be as I wanted in the unseen darkness of my thoughts. I would have gladly left the kasaba in that quiet, late afternoon hour, so that night might find me alone, but my duties led me in the opposite direction, among people. I was taking the place of the ill Hafiz*-Muhammed, who had been summoned by Janich, our aging benefactor. I knew that Janich had lain sick for months, and that maybe he would ask one of us to come to him before his death. I also knew that his son-in-law was the kadi* Aini-effendi,* who had signed the order for my brother's arrest. For that reason I had gladly agreed to go, filled with a vague sense of hope.

As I was led through the courtyard and house I walked as always, used to not seeing what did not concern me—I kept closer to myself that way. Then I was left alone in a long corridor, where I waited for the news of my arrival to reach wherever necessary, and I listened to the silence. It was absolute, as if no one lived in that great edifice, as if no one moved through its corridors and rooms. In the quiet of that muffled life, beside the dying man who still breathed there somewhere, in the silence of steps fading on the carpets and in soft, whispered conversations, the old wood of the ceilings and window frames split with a faint, creaking noise. As I watched evening surround the house with silken shadows and the last reflections of daylight quiver on the windowpanes, I thought about the old man and what I would say to him at this last meeting. I had spoken with the sick more than once; I had sent a dying man on that long journey more than once. Experience had taught me, if any experience were necessary, that every man feels fear at what awaits him, at the unknown that already knocks, unrevealed, in a terror-stricken heart.

To comfort them I would often say:

Death is a certainty, an inevitable realization, the only thing that we know will befall us. There are no exceptions, no surprises: all paths lead to it. Everything we do is a preparation for it, a preparation that we begin at birth, whimpering with our foreheads against the ground. We never move farther away from death, only closer. But if it is a certainty, then why are we surprised when it comes? If this life is a short passage that lasts only an hour or a day, then why do we fight to prolong it one more day or hour? Worldly life is treacherous, eternity is better.[3]

I would often say:

Why do your hearts tremble with fear when in your death-agony your legs twitch and squirm? Death is a move from one house to another. It is not a disappearance, but a rebirth. Just as an eggshell bursts when the chick inside is fully developed, there comes a time for the soul and body to part. Death is a necessity in the inevitable passage to the other world, where man makes his full ascent.

I would often say:

Death is the decay of matter, but not of the soul.

I would often say:

Death is a change of state. The soul begins to live by itself. Until it parted from the body, it held with hands, saw with eyes, heard with ears, but it knew the heart of the matter on its own.

I would often say:

On the day of my death, when they carry my coffin,
do not think that I will feel pain for this world.
Do not cry and say: it is a great loss!
When milk sours, the loss is greater.
I shall not vanish when you see them lay me in the grave.
Do the sun and moon vanish when they set?
This seems like a death to you, but it is a birth.
The grave seems like a prison to you, but the soul has been freed.
What grain does not sprout when it is put into the ground?
So why do you not believe in the grain of men?

I would often say:

Be thankful, O House of Dawud,[4] and say: the truth has come. The hour has come. Because every man travels his path until the appointed time. God creates you in the womb of your mother and he changes you from one form to another in a threefold impenetrable darkness. Do not grieve, but rejoice at the paradise that has been promised to you. O my slaves, do not fear for yourselves today, you will not be sorrowful. O peaceful soul, return to your master satisfied, because He is satisfied with you. Join my servants, come into my paradise.[5]

I had said these things countless times.

But now I was not sure that I should say them to the old man who was waiting for me. Not for his sake, but for mine. For the first time (how many times these days will I say: for the first time?) death did not seem as simple as I had believed or had made others believe. It happened that I had a terrible dream. I stood in an empty space above my dead brother; at my feet his long coffin was covered with a piece of blue broadcloth, and around me there was a distant circle of people. I saw no one, recognized no one, the only thing I knew was that they formed a ring around us and left me alone, above the corpse, in a painful silence. Above a corpse to whom I could not say: Why does your heart tremble? because my heart also trembled, and I was afraid of the dead silence. A secret pained me, one that I did not see any purpose for. There is a purpose, I said, shielding myself from terror, yet I could not find it. Arise, I said, arise. But my brother was hidden in darkness, vanishing in mist, in a greenish gloom, as if underwater, a man drowned in an unknown void.

How could I now tell the dying man: follow the path of your Lord obediently, when I shuddered at that hidden path, of which my minute knowledge did not have the slightest notion?

I believed in the Last Judgment and in eternal life, but I also began to believe in the horror of death, in the fear of its opaque blackness.

I had not yet made a decision when I was led into one of the rooms. A young maidservant showed me the way. I walked with my eyes lowered, so I would not see her face and could think up something, anything. I'll lie to you old man, God will forgive me; I'll tell you what you expect to hear, and not these muddled thoughts of mine.

He was not there. Without raising my eyes I noticed that the room was free from the heavy odor of the sick, which, after a prolonged illness, cannot be removed by cleaning or airing, nor by the burning of incense.

PART I

When I looked up and searched for this man who had long been ill but did not smell of death, I beheld a beautiful woman on a divan, a reminder of life more powerful than could be good for me.

Maybe it is strange for me to say this, but it is true: I felt uncomfortable. There could have been a number of reasons. I had prepared for a meeting with an old, dying man, and was oppressed by dark thoughts myself, but I came before his daughter (although I had never seen her, I knew who she was). I am unskilled in conversations with women, especially with women of her beauty and age. Around thirty, it seemed to me. Young women merely imagine life and believe words. Old women fear death and listen to tales of paradise with a sigh. But women like her know the value of everything they gain and lose, and they always have their own reasons for what they do, reasons that might be strange, but are rarely naive. Their mature eyes are free even when lowered, and unpleasantly open even when hidden behind their eyelashes. Most unpleasant of all is our awareness that they know more than they show and measure us by their own strange standards, which are beyond our understanding. Their undeceivable curiosity, which emanates even when concealed, is protected by their inviolability, if only they want it. And as we stand before them we are protected by nothing. They are certain of their strength, which they do not use but keep like a saber in its sheath, always with a hand on the hilt, and they see in us potential slaves or despicable creatures who are proud of our useless strength without reason. Their foolish self-confidence is so convincing that it affects us even as we detest it. We remain fearful despite our faith in some unknown possibility, some spell, some secret power of the devil.

This woman also had a special power that did not belong to her, but rather to her lineage. Her posture and gestures, self-assured and commanding (that is how she motioned for me to sit down) appeared tempered, softened by something

I could not determine, by a habit, by a soft gleam in her eyes, which were shaded with kohl in the slit of her veil, by an arm, curved like a swan's neck, that held one end of the thin fabric, by a strange allure that effused from her like a magic spell.

The daughter of the devil, cursed the dervish and thought the peasant in me, both of them astonished.

Darkness drifted into the room; all that showed white were her veil and hand. We sat at almost opposite ends of the room, with only its insufficient width and an uneasy expectation between us.

"I called for Hafiz-Muhammed," she said, secure in the half-darkness.

She was not satisfied, or it seemed so to me.

"He asked me to come in his place. He's ill."

"No matter. You're also a friend of this house."

"Yes, I am."

I wanted to say more, something more ceremonious: that otherwise I would not have earned such warm, friendly words and would not be worthy of our benefactor's attention, that their house had a special place in our hearts, and so on, like in a song. But it all came out muddled.

Some maidservants brought in candles and refreshments.

I waited.

The candles burned between us on a table standing to one side. She appeared closer and more dangerous. I did not know what she had in mind.

I thought that I had been summoned on account of her father. I would have come even if I had not been hoping for a miracle, some hidden opportunity, some stroke of luck that would help me try to save my brother. Somewhere among my words of death and paradise I would slip in a word seeking mercy for him. Maybe it would help, maybe the old man would perform a good deed before his great journey, of which we know nothing. Maybe he would thus raise a memorial to himself. Maybe. Because shortly before death we remember that two angels sit on our shoulders and record our bad and good deeds, and we are eager to improve our accounts. It is hard to die more profitably than with an act of kindness that remains fresh and unsoured after us. And he could have easily helped me as well as himself. Aini-effendi would be more concerned with not displeasing his rich father-in-law than with keeping some poor wretch in prison, if Ali-aga decided that simply releasing him, without any sacrifice or worry, would serve as a stepping-stone on his path to heaven. He could not earn anything more easily, and I did not believe he would refuse.

But I knew nothing about her. She would not be able to talk with me about anything, and I could not be of any use to her. I failed to see any connection between us.

We faced each other like two warriors with their weapons hidden behind their backs, like two adversaries hiding their intentions within themselves. We would reveal ourselves when our combat began. I waited to see what she wanted to capture, what she wanted to take away, and hope still lived in me, although it was not so strong as it had been a few moments before. This woman was too young and too beautiful to think of the angels that record our deeds. This was the only world that existed for her.

She did not search for words or hesitate very long; she was indeed like a warrior who marched into battle without faltering or turning back. That was due to her status, as well as to mine. If she had ever wavered, she did not in front of me. At first I followed her deliberately soft voice, which had the timber of a zurna,* and listened to her speech, which resembled embroidery or a string of pearls, words and phrases completely different from those of the townspeople, somewhat withered yet ornate, with the aura of those old chambers and something enduring.

"It's not easy for me to say this—I wouldn't tell it to just anyone. But you're a dervish. You've certainly seen and heard everything, and helped people as much as you can. And you know that in every family things happen which aren't pleasant for anyone involved. Do you know my brother Hassan?"

"I do."

"I'd like to talk about him."

Thus as she began, she said all that was necessary: she flattered me, showed her confidence in me, cited my title, and prepared me for the unpleasant things she was going to say, thereby including everyone, so I would not forget that disagreeable affairs befall all families, and not only theirs. Although the evil was thus greater, the disgrace was smaller, since it was universal, and could be discussed without shame.

This uselessly nice introduction was followed by a fairly well known complaint about the black sheep of the family and great hopes that had been shamefully betrayed. The family's stray sheep was not bothered by its blackness, while for the others it was sorrow and grief, disgrace before the world and fear before God. People would recite this lovely lament in front of us, sometimes sincerely, hoping for assistance, which we would promise but rarely give, but most often so we would witness to others that they had done everything in their power, approached even the clergy, and that it was not their fault that the evil was ineradicable.

I knew this story by heart; it had been told to us for a long time now, and my interest dwindled as soon as I heard it. I listened with a feigned attentiveness, and covered that up with an insincerely watchful expression. With no reason, I had expected something that would astonish me. But nothing could. She would say what was appropriate, complain about her brother and ask me to talk with him, to try to bring him to his senses; I would listen to this allegedly melancholy confession with sympathy, and promise to do everything in my feeble power, relying on God's help. Nothing would change, but she would be at peace because she had fulfilled her duty and everybody would know it. I would talk with Hassan, trying not to appear silly, and Hassan would continue to live as he pleased, glad that his family was furious about it. And no one would receive any harm from any of this. Or benefit. Least of all my imprisoned brother and I. For she spoke without a real need, without any prospects for benefit or success, from a weak feeling of social obligation that was intended for the ears of those outside the family. And I was supposed to proclaim it. But that was only polite behavior, a posture that suited the reputation of the family, a justification for other, unafflicted families, a disassociation from the culprit, his expulsion. She gained little, not nearly enough for me to seek mercy for my brother in return. Those family renegades such as Hassan occurred more and more, it seemed that they had become fed up with the order and reputations of their fathers. Hassan was only one of many, so it was not even a particular disgrace, but an occurrence like many others, which human will could hardly control.

Her story was of no interest to me, for I knew the end as soon as I heard the beginning, and I was not moved at all by her complaint, since it was insincere. But she also knew how to show restraint; she did not want to exaggerate. For her it was enough to state it. There was a certain acceptable insensitivity in this fulfillment of a duty that her heart had not sought.

As I no longer had any reason or ability to listen to her attentively, I concentrated on observing her. This I did with interest, and she might have thought that it was on account of her words. Thus, we both appeared polite.

I had in fact been watching her from the very first moment of our encounter. She surprised me with the beauty of her smooth face, which gleamed through the thin fabric of her veil, and with the subdued light of her large eyes, which revealed a passionate rashness and deep shadows within. But that was a hasty glance, anxious, insecure, in expectation of what she would say, and it told more about me than about her. And when her spell wore off, when I entrenched myself in the safety of my ostensible attentiveness, she enticed me to view her with my eyes and without uneasiness.

This was not ordinary curiosity for a better glimpse of these strange creatures, so foreign to our world, a curiosity we rarely satisfy. We might not even feel it in our encounters with them, out of understandable considerations. I suddenly found myself in a position to observe her secretly, without disturbing anything in our relationship, since in front of her I remained a dervish who respected her will and dignity. I felt somewhat superior, as I knew what she was thinking, and looked at her freely, but she could not see me. She saw nothing of me and knew nothing about me. This was an advantage we might often desire, but seldom receive. It was man's ancient desire to be invisible. Yet I did not do anything improper, I watched her, calm and composed, and I knew I would not have a single thought that I would remember with shame.

First I noticed her hands. While she held the veil with prescribed, fixed gestures that restricted their possibilities, they were separated and unexpressive, hardly perceptible. But when she let go of the fabric and put them together, they suddenly came to life and became a single entity. They would not begin their movements rashly or move briskly, but in their silent motionlessness and slow wandering there was a strange meaning and so much power that they drew my attention again and again. It seemed that at any moment they might do something important, something decisive. Thus an air of expectation arose, constant and exciting. They rested together on her lap, in an embrace, as if smothering each other in quiet yearning or keeping each other from wandering off, from doing something unreasonable. They remained motionless in an incessant, barely perceptible rippling, like a restless shiver, or a light spasm of excessive energy. Then they parted, without haste, as if by agreement. They hovered for a moment, looking for one another, and then alighted tenderly on a satin knee like amorous birds, embracing again, inseparable, happy in their silence together. This lasted for a long time, then one moved and began to stroke the satin under it, and the skin under the satin, with fingers that contracted slowly and passionately. The other lay nestled on top of it, silent, listening to the smooth silk rustle inaudibly on her round, marble knee. Only occasionally would they tear themselves away, and one would embark upon a journey of its own, to brush softly the earring on the edge of an ear hidden timidly under black hair with a reddish tinge. Or it would pause in the air as if to hear a word or two, and then withdraw without much interest for the conversation to meet the other, which was silent, offended at that small lapse in attention.

I followed them, surprised by the expressiveness of their independent existence. They were like two small creatures that had their own realm of life, their own needs and love, their own jealousy, longing, and lewdness. At one moment I was delighted, at the next frightened by the crazy thought of the isolation and senselessness of that petty life, so similar to every other. But that was a quick and harmless thought, a single, momentary beat of another life in me, which I did not want to awaken.

I also watched them for their beauty. They began at her wrists, which were enclosed in bracelets and the embroidered cuffs of her silken shirt. Their joints were tenderly oval and inconceivably slender, their knuckles limpid. Most beautiful of all were her fingers, long and supple; their fair skin was perfectly smooth, with shadows at the joints. They seemed strangely alive as they slowly opened and closed into a transparent calyx, like petals.

But if at first I paid attention to those two little creatures, two small animals, two octopi, two flowers, they were not the only thing I noticed, not even at the beginning when I had been mostly watching them, nor later on as I discovered her like an unknown land. Everything about her was harmonious and inseparable: the look of her eyes, lightly shaded with kohl, which merged with the gestures of her arm, barely hidden by the transparent fabric of her shirt; the slight tilt of her head and the glimmer of an emerald set in gold on her brow; the unconscious quiver of her foot in its silver-embroidered slipper; her smooth, even face, along which a tender light effused from somewhere within, from her blood, which changed into a warm glow; the moist flash of her teeth behind seemingly lazy, full lips.

She was only a body; everything else was supplanted by it. She did not awaken desire in me; I would have not allowed myself that. I would have stifled it at the very beginning, with shame, with the thought of my age and title, with the awareness of the danger that I would have exposed myself to, with the fear of an unrest that could be more serious than disease, with my habit of self-control. But I could not hide from myself the fact that I watched her with pleasure, with a deep and peaceful enjoyment, with which one watches a calm river, the evening sky, the moon at midnight, a tree in bloom, the lake of my childhood at dawn. Without a desire to possess her, without the possibility of experiencing her completely, without the strength to leave. It was pleasant to watch her lively hands chase one another, forgetting themselves in the game. It was pleasant to hear her speak. No, she did not have to say anything, it was enough that she existed.

Then it occurred to me that even this joyous observation was dangerous, and I no longer felt superior or hidden. Something unwanted came to life in me. It was not passion, but something maybe worse than that: memory. Of the one and only woman in my life. I did not know how she had emerged from underneath the sediment of years; she had not been so pretty as this woman, not even similar to her. Why did the one recall the other? I was more concerned with that distant one, who no longer existed, whom I had been forgetting and recalling for twenty years. She surfaced in my memory when I neither wanted nor needed her, bitter as absinthe. She had not appeared for a long time, so why did she come now? Was it because of this woman, whose face came right out of sinful dreams; was it because of my brother, to make me forget him, was it because of everything that had happened, so I would reproach myself? So I would blame myself for all of the missed opportunities which I could no longer bring back?

I lowered my eyes. A man must never think that he is secure, or that his past is dead. But why did it awaken when I needed it the least? She was not important, that distant woman, the memory of her replaced the hidden thought that everything might have been different, even the things that hurt me. Go away, shadow; nothing could have been different, and there would have always been something else that hurt. Nothing would improve if things were different in our lives.

The woman who had sent me adrift brought me back to herself.

"Are you listening?"

"I am."

Had she noticed that I had become preoccupied?

"I'm listening, go on."

I actually listened now; that was safer. And as I did, I heard with surprise that she was not telling an utterly ordinary story. It was not truly unusual either, but it was not boring, and listening to her was worth more than watching her. My hope suddenly lifted its head.

She told me what I already knew about her brother's strange lot: that he had finished school in Constantinople[6] and attained a position that corresponded both to his knowledge and the reputation of the family (she overemphasized the former and underemphasized the latter, as his position was not high, but in this way she balanced everything out). They were all proud of him, especially his father. But then something unexpected happened, that no one could explain, that no one knew the real reason for, not even Hassan: he changed completely. As if that wonderful young man had never lived, she said. And everyone wondered in utter bewilderment where his knowledge had gone, which even the muderrises* had recognized, how so many years had disappeared without a trace, where the origin of the evil lay. He left his post without telling anyone, returned home, married inappropriately, and began to associate with common people. He took to drinking and squandering his fortune, doing unheard-of things around the kasaba with his companions and with tavern-dancers (her voice lowered, but did not break), and at other places that should not even be mentioned. Then he became a caravan driver (there was disgust, almost horror in her voice): he brought cattle down from Wallachia[7] and Serbia and drove them to Dalmatia and Austria, working for other merchants as a middleman, as their servant. He lost a great deal, ruined himself. His estate was dwindling; he had sold half of what his mother had left him. Hassan's father went out of his mind, and even fell ill because of him. He implored him and threatened him, all to no avail: no one could turn him from his path. Now his father would not hear of him, he would not even allow Hassan's name to be mentioned in his presence, as if his son did not exist, as if he had died. She had cried her eyes out in front of her father, but nothing helped. Then she said something that aroused my attention; the zurna began to play an interesting tune. Her father had decided to deprive him of his inheritance, to compose a will before respected people and publicly disown him. And to keep this from happening, to keep things from getting worse than they already were, she was asking me to talk with Hassan so that he would renounce his inheritance himself, voluntarily. In that way his father's curse would fall from him, and the shame of the family would be lessened. She added that her husband, Aini-effendi, knew nothing about any of this, he did not want to come between father and son. Everything she was doing to lessen the misfortune was of her own account, and we could help her greatly, Hafiz-Muhammed and I, because she had heard that Hassan visited our tekke, and she was glad that at least sometimes he talked with good and sensible people.

I was thankful that she had thus revealed herself before me. She had indeed showed that she did not respect me very much, because she had not hesitated to say any of this. But it did not matter; more important things were at stake.

May Hafiz-Muhammed's alleged illness be blessed, I thought. It had created an opportunity for me that I could not have even dreamed of. Not even her dying father could have had more of a reason to help me. It was clear to me that Aini-effendi knew about all of this; maybe he had even thought up the words that his wife now spoke with such satisfaction. He would have known that it was not easy to deprive one's only son of his inheritance without sound reasons. And if he had been sure of himself, if they had been sure of themselves, they would not have worried much about the family reputation or have called for our help. Well, all right, I thought, watching her with the attention that I had owed her from the beginning, trying to keep the expression of my face from looking too cheerful: you and I are both in trouble, because of our brothers. You want to destroy yours, I want to save mine. These are our greatest desires, only mine is honorable, and yours filthy. But be that as it may, it doesn't matter to me. I don't know anything about you, although it seems I see clearly how much you can dominate your lifeless kadi, who respects your strength and your wealth because he has neither one nor the other. One humiliating night for him, one decisive demand by you could change my brother's fate. We invest so little, yet gain so much.

I was almost ready to tell her openly: very well, we no longer have any reason to conceal ourselves. I'll give you Hassan, you give me my brother. You don't care about yours; I'd do much, much more for mine.

I said nothing, of course. She would have taken offense at my openness: they never like it in others.

I assented to her request and said that Hassan in fact came to our tekke, that he was a friend of Hafiz-Muhammed (which was true) and of mine (which was not true), and that we would try to persuade him to do what she wanted, because I was moved by her sisterly grief and her concern for the family reputation. I mentioned that if they were defamed, then we were all defamed, and so we had to help prevent blemishes from falling upon the best among us, to avert malicious sneers when misfortunes befall people of reputation. Moreover, I was bound by gratefulness to the benefactor of our tekke (I mentioned her father on purpose, since she, his own daughter, would not do it). I added that I thought that not only her intentions, but also her plans were good, because everything else would be uncertain: it was difficult to disinherit one's eldest heir without sound reasons.

"There are sound reasons."

"I'm speaking about the courts. It's true that Hassan trades cattle, but that's not a dishonest profession. He does spend money, but money he's earned. He didn't sell half of his estate, but rather gave it to his former wife. It's hard to see any reason for this, let alone a sound one."

I felt secure, more secure than she. I had altered our relation within myself. We were not what we had been in the beginning, she an upper-class woman with beautiful eyes, and I a humble dervish, an eternal peasant. Now we were two equals discussing business. In this I was stronger than she. When I agreed with what she said, she watched me approvingly; this seemed completely reasonable to her. But when I said something that did not please her, the curves of her eyebrows began to twitch and her look sharpened. My resistance seemed awkward and spiteful to her.

"Father will undoubtedly disinherit him," she said threateningly.

PART I

I worried little about whether Hassan's father would disinherit him. And I was hardly disturbed by her anger. I wanted to shatter her confidence, to accomplish what really mattered to me.

"He may disinherit him," I said calmly. "But your father is old and has been sick for a long time. Hassan might contest the will in court, and prove that your father was weak and feeble, that he wasn't in his right mind when he made the decision, or that someone had persuaded him to do it."

"Who could persuade him?"

"I'm speaking about a lawsuit. It doesn't matter who. I'm afraid the verdict might fall in Hassan's favor. Especially since the case wouldn't be tried here, on account of Aini-effendi. And we shouldn't forget that Hassan also has connections."

She watched me in silence. Her veil had been lowered for a long time now, ever since the candles had been brought in and she had begun her ugly tale. On her beautiful face, made of moonlight, in the corners of her eyes the reflections of the candles glimmered like restless, quivering sparks. She did not quiver herself, but it seemed so to me. I felt somewhat malevolent. I knew that I had upset her; she had not believed that I would burden her scheme with so many obstacles, although she had certainly known about some of them.

She stared at me, as if trying to find the trace of a joke on my face, a lack of conviction, a possible dilemma. But she saw only certitude, and a regret that it was so. It seemed to me now that her anger was swelling, as if fed by an underground river, growing ever fiercer, since it was unable to offer any effective resistance. I deliberately waited for the swell to overcome her, but I prevented it from breaking out. I agreed to everything she wanted, but my well-founded objections remained.

"He needs to be persuaded so everything will pass without being brought before the courts."

I thought that she would persist in her defiance, that she would deny any possibility of a lawsuit or change in her father's decision, and that she would then enter into another conversation which I would suggest.

However, she abandoned her resistance immediately. She was in a hurry.

She revealed her doubts with a question: "Will he consent to it?"

"Sound and sensible reasons must be found, so he won't get angry or offended. Stubbornness doesn't work very well with him."

"I hope you can find sound and sensible reasons."

That was scorn or impatience. She had thought that everything would be easier.

And I had thought so as well.

"I'll try," I said.

I did not know if she had sensed any insecurity, hesitation, or doubt in my voice. I did not know. But my enthusiasm had indeed sagged.

"Don't you believe he'll consent?"

"I don't know."

If I had only endured a moment longer, if my love for my brother had been a little stronger than my moral considerations, everything might have turned out better. Or worse. But I might have saved my brother.

I did not give up so easily as it might have appeared. In a single moment I saw countless reasons both for and against her plan, both for accepting and rejecting it. The reasons were often the same, and during the short time that she waited, long enough only to catch one's breath, a storm raged in me. I was making a decision about the lives of both me and my brother. I would give her guileless brother over to her; he would be taken in by the counsel of a friend. I would collect payment for my efforts and betrayal, which was not such a great betrayal, since they would do as they pleased even without me. And I could help them to make

PART I

everything seem more proper. Why should I have been ashamed of myself? Why should I reproach myself? I was trying to save my brother!

But I should have cried louder and more convincingly. I should have shouted down another voice that was warning me. I did not know what my brother had done. Nor did I know how guilty he was. I did not believe it was anything serious; he was too honest and young for graver misdeeds. Maybe they would release him soon. And even if they did not, even if I had been certain that they would not, could I agree to this dishonest scheme against a man who had never spoken an unkind word to me? It was not a matter of his fortune, I had none and had little respect for that of others. It was a matter of something else—of an injustice, a vile act, dishonesty, a flagrant violation of someone's rights. I did not have a high opinion of her brother: he was superficial, impetuous, strange. But even if he had been worse than he was, how was I to justify myself if I helped this ruthless woman in her highway robbery?

What had I been saying to others for so many years? What would I say to myself after all of this? If he lived, my brother would constantly remind me of this ugly deed, which I would no longer be able to redeem. The only thing that I had was my conviction that I was honest. If I lost that as well, I would be ruined.

That was indeed what I thought. It might seem strange that I could waver between those two unequal things, that I could hesitate to commit this small betrayal in order to free my brother. But when one has learned to measure his actions by strict standards of conscience, fearing sin perhaps even more than death, then it does not seem so strange.

Aside from that, I knew, I was absolutely certain that if I only went to Hassan and told him to renounce his inheritance for my brother's sake, he would do it immediately.

But I could not, I did not want to tell her anything before I talked to him.

She pressed me, dispelling my hesitation: "I wouldn't forget the favor you've done me. It matters a great deal to me that no trouble arise concerning our family."

How would she return the favor, almighty God!

Get up, Ahmed Nuruddin, get up and leave.

"I'll let you know," I said, thus making way for another meeting.

"When?"

"As soon as Hassan returns."

"He'll be back in a day or two."

"Then in a day or two."

We stood up at the same time.

Her lovely hand did not rise to cover her face: we were plotting together.

Something shameful had happened between us, and I was not sure that I had remained completely clean.

3

My God, they do not believe![1]

ANXIETY WAS WAITING FOR ME PATIENTLY, AS IF I HAD LEFT IT in front of that house and picked it up again when I came out.

Only now it was more complex than before; it had become more intricate, oppressive, and vague. I had done nothing wrong, but my thoughts were assailed by memories of the dead silence, of the impenetrable darkness and strange, glimmering lights; of the ugly tension and the time I had spent anxiously waiting; of our shameful secrets and thoughts disguised by smiles. I felt as if I had missed something, as if I had made a mistake somewhere, although I did not know where, or how. I did not know. But I was not at peace. I could hardly bear this feeling of uneasiness, this anxiety whose source I could not determine. Maybe it was because I had not mentioned my brother, because I had not insisted that we talk about him. But I had done that on purpose, in order not to spoil my chances. Or was it because I had taken part in an shameful conversation and heard shameful intentions without opposing them, without protecting an innocent man? Only I had had my own reasons, which were more important than all of that, and it would not be right for me to reproach myself too much. For each of my actions I found an excuse, yet my distress remained.

The moonlight shone frail and silken, and the tombstones in the graveyards gleamed warmly white. Broken night whispered between the houses as young people moved excitedly in the streets and courtyards. Giggling, a distant song, and murmurs were heard, and it seemed that on this Saint George's Eve the whole kasaba trembled in fever. Suddenly, for no reason, I felt separated from all of it. Fear crept into me unnoticed, and everything around me began to acquire strange proportions—the people and their movements, the kasaba itself no longer seemed familiar. I had never seen them like this before, I had not known that the world could become so disfigured in a day, in an hour, in a moment—as if some demon's blood had begun to boil and no one could calm it. I saw townspeople in couples, heard them, they were behind every fence, every gate, every wall. Their laughter, talk, and glances were not like on other days; their voices were muffled and heavy. A scream cut through the darkness, like lightning in an impending storm. The air was permeated with sin, the night full of it. On this night witches would fly cackling above rooftops wet with the milk of the moonlight, and no one would retain his senses. People would burn with passion and fury, with madness and the need to destroy themselves, all of them in a single moment—where would I turn then? I would have to pray, to seek mercy from God for all of those sinners, or for punishment, to bring them to their senses. Anger came over me like a fit of fever. Is everything we do really useless? Is the word of God that we preach made of mute clay, or are their ears simply deaf to it? Is the true faith in them so weak, like a rotted fence trampled under a stampede of wild passions?

From behind the fences one could hear the torrid voices of girls who were putting lovage[2] and red-colored eggs in cauldrons full of water, so they could wash themselves at the break of dawn. They believed in the spells of flowers and the night, like savages.

Shame on you, I said to those behind the wooden fence,

shame on you. In whose faith do you believe? To which devils are you surrendering yourselves?

It would have been useless to do or say anything that night, a night more frenzied than others. At midnight those girls would go to water mills and bathe naked in the mist sprayed by the water-wheels. At that time devils would rise up from their lairs, and their hairy hands would slap the girls on their wet thighs, which gleamed in the moonlight.

Go home, I said to the unruly young men who were approaching. Tomorrow is Saint George's Day, an infidel holiday, it is not ours. Do not commit sin!

But it was all the same to them, all the same to the kasaba, no one could take this night away from them.

There was an old right to sin on the eve of Saint George's Day. They kept it without regard to the faith, even in spite of it. They defiled themselves during these twenty-four hours full of the lustful scent of lovage and love, of lovage that smells sinfully of women and love that smells of the lovage of women's thighs. In this span of day and night sin spewed from the sealed bellows of desire, lavishly, as if spilled from a giant bucket. A strange, ancient time is lumbering behind us, stronger than we are, showing itself in a rebellion of the body, which, although short-lived, is remembered until the following rebellion, thus perpetuating itself. Everything else is an illusion, everything else that might occur between these primal victories of sin. But the trouble is not so much in lustfulness as it is in this foreign evil that has lasted for ages, stronger than the true faith. What have we done, what have we achieved, what have we torn down, and what have we built? Are we not struggling in vain against these instincts, which are stronger than anything offered by reason? Are the things that we promise in exchange for an earthly, primal rampage not too arid and unattractive? How can we resist the allure of these ancient calls? Will our distant, savage ancestors vanquish us and return us to their age? I wanted nothing more than for my apprehension to be worse than the truth, but I was afraid that the vision of my anguished soul was clearer than that of my brothers, who were more concerned with this world than with the other. I accuse no one, O Lord, you know everything. Be merciful to me, to them, and to all sinners.

I remembered that night. Even if nothing else had happened, I would have remembered it for the heat with which it choked me and for the emptiness that the passion of these people carved inside me. But it was God's will that this night should be different from others, that on this night some event would split my life in two, as at a carefully pre-arranged meeting, and that it would separate me from all I had been for forty peaceful years.

I made my way back to the tekke, lost in thought, dejected. Perhaps I was the only unhappy man in the kasaba that night, exhausted by the turmoil of those altered streets, by the subdued moonlight, by fears that had been revived without reason, by an uncertainty the world had thrust upon me. It was as if I were passing between burning houses, and the quiet, sleepy tekke appeared like a desired refuge, whose massive walls would return me to a silence that I needed and to a peace that would not fill me with disgust. I would recite the yasin,* and that prayer would calm my shivering soul, which was suffering more than was pleasing to God. For a true believer must never fall into despair and faintheartedness. But I, a sinner, was so fainthearted that I kept forgetting the cause for distress that I had discovered on the way back, and had to invoke it with a conscious effort, so that my anxiety would have something to hold onto. I wanted stubborn, heathen sin to be the single cause of my distress, so I could leave any others in the darkness.

I did not need to chase witches through the streets that night, I did not care about the sins of others. I had wanted to turn my thoughts from my brother and from the temptation that had been put before me. But all I accomplished was to come back anxious and bitter.

On other nights I would often stand in the moonlight above the river, letting vague desires and the quiet flickers of my memory overcome me. I knew when that was allowed to me—whenever I felt a serene calm that did not portend a storm. But when I sensed even a hint of commotion, I would confine myself to the four walls of my room and force myself to follow the hard, familiar path of prayer. There is something intimately protective in it, as there is in old heirlooms that become a harmless part of our very selves. Those prayers are a recognized and accepted solace; they soothe and deaden any dangerous thoughts that might emerge in us against our will. We trust them unquestioningly, and place our weakness under the protection of their ancient strength. Thus we belittle our human worries and nightmares through the habit of measuring them against eternity, and by putting them into such an inferior position we reduce them to insignificant proportions.

That night I could not stay in the garden. I needed to isolate myself, to forget, but everything rose up there, like a challenge. The moonlight was chilling, and seemed to reek of sulphur. The scent of flowers was too strong, irritating. They should have been torn out and trampled down, so that only thistle and barren ground would remain, a graveyard without any markers, which would not remind anyone of anything, so that an abstract human thought would be all that was left, lacking images and scents, lacking any connection to the things around us. Even the river should have been stopped so that its scornful gurgling would cease, and the birds in the treetops and under the eaves should have had their necks wrung, so that their senseless twittering would end. All the water mills where the naked girls bathed should have been torn down, all the streets closed, and the gates nailed shut, all life silenced by force, to prevent evil from sprouting.

O God, bring me to my senses.

I had never thought about people and life with such

senseless fury. I became frightened. Where did the wish to annihilate everything come from?

I wanted to go into my room, I had to, but I lacked the strength to do so. The night, which I hated, was stronger than I, and held me back with a strange power. Yet when I surrendered I felt that it calmed me. It overcame me with the mild violence of its soft sounds, drowsy and important only to themselves, with a shimmering darkness that quivered in barely perceptible motions, with its strange shadows and forms, with scents that penetrated deep into my blood and became a part of myself. Everything smelled of a life that is woven out of little voices and movements into something powerful, more powerful than anything I might have wished for. It was inseparable from me, the same as my very self, which was still undiscovered and yet desirous of discovery. I forgot that the moonlight had been so chilling a moment before, and how it had reeked of sulphur. That had merely been my fear of it. Now the fear was gone, and there was a peaceful light above me and the world, a trace of something in me, of something that might have been and had been, something that would be if I continued in this empty state, with neither defense nor protection since the floodgate of my habits, consciousness, and will had been opened. Or else unknown desires would burst out of the dark cellars of my blood. It would be too late when they came out; I would no longer be able to believe that they had died or been tamed, and I would never again be what I had been. And it seemed to me that I did not have the power to hold those desires back, to return them to their dark confinement. I did not even want that. Their true nature was not clear to me, I knew only that they were very powerful. They were certainly not innocent, or they would not have gone into hiding.

In that moment of weakness and expectation, which I wished would last longer, God saved me from near destruction. I say God, because chance could never have been so punctual, so calculatedly attentive as to come exactly in the elusively small span of time when those unknown forces began to grow—unknown and still unillumined by my inner light, but already massing and half-free. Afterward, as I spoke with Mullah*-Yusuf, I was glad they had not broken away, although I was sorry that I had not been able to see their essence. For that reason I was shaken inside. But I had learned to conceal myself in front of others.

He approached quietly, I heard him only when the gravel crunched beneath his cautious feet and his hushed breath singed my skin. I knew who it was immediately, without even turning around, since no one else could step so silently. He had adopted a cautious gait too early in life.

"Have I disturbed you in your meditation?"

"No."

Even his voice was quiet and disguised, although clumsily—birds still sang in it. His eyes also betrayed him, bright and restless as they were.

I asked him nothing, he needed to tell it himself. He had agreed not to keep any personal secrets other than those that no man could learn. The order of the tekke was strict, and I would have remembered it if he did not say where he had been for so long.

"I was in the Sinan Tekke.[3] Abdullah-effendi was discussing cognition."

"Abdullah-effendi is a mystic. He belongs to the Bayramiyya order."[4]

"I know."

"What did he say?"

"He spoke about cognition."

"Is that all you know? Don't you remember anything?"

"I remember the verses he interpreted."

"Whose verses?"

"I don't know."

"Let me hear."

"'Ahriman[5] knows not

The secret of God's unity.
Ask Asaf,[6] he knows.
Can a sparrow swallow the mouthful of the Anka-bird?[7]
'Can a single jug take in
The waters of a great sea?'"

"Those are the verses of Ibn Arabi.[8] They say that the perception of God's wisdom is possible only for the chosen, only for a few."

"And what remains for us?"

"To comprehend what we can. If a sparrow cannot swallow the mouthful of the Anka-bird, it will still eat as much as it can. You cannot scoop up the whole sea with a jug, but whatever you scoop up is also the sea."

I began my fickle refutation of Ibn Arabi's mysticism hastily, passionately, and with pleasure, realizing maybe for the first time that the heavens and the secrets of the universe, that the secrets of death and existence were the most convenient region into which one could escape from the cares of this world. If they did not exist, one would need to invent them as a refuge.

But this young man was not a suitable interlocutor. People in fact talk most often for their own sake, and with a need to hear the echo of their words. And he stood before me, with his face illuminated by the moonlight so clearly that its every feature was visible. He stood obediently, he could not leave until I released him, but his thoughts left without him, only God knew where to or how far away. I could not hold them back, and they left his body there to express the due obedience with its empty presence. Verses and mysticism and cognition were so far from his thoughts and from the capability of his understanding that he surely listened with his eyes only, watching the movements of my lips. It would have made more sense for me to shout words into an empty well, at least then their echo would have come back. He did not even try to understand. He had not listened to verses in the Sinan Tekke for very long.

He was inexperienced. He exposed himself to the moonlight; he still did not know how to hide himself with darkness and feigned expressions. His eyes were wide open, as if he were listening, but the gleam of something he had seen earlier bore witness against him, said that he was not listening to me, betrayed him. What was in them? What image or recollection, what word still resounded, what sleepy memory, what sin? The pallor of the moonlight had not extinguished the healthy color of his cheeks, which were shaded by the manly features of a young peasant, ripe for marriage, and by the strength of his robust blood. What did he seek in the silence of this holy place, in the hard shackles of a dervish order? He was of this world, of this Saint George's Eve, of this illuminated, tepid darkness, which summons us to sin. The scent of lovage was on him; he brought it on his hands, in his breath, he was pervaded by the spell of the intoxicated streets. He had heard the capercaillie's mating call, and had been deafened by it. Maybe the pulse of another young body's blood still beat in his numb palm. A flame, barely controlled, shot out of the ovals of his eyes. He had been defiled by this pagan night, soiled, singed, illuminated, purged. On this evening he should have been put under seven locks, so he would not be consumed by his own flame or the flames of others. The silence and solitude of the tekke would suffocate him; why did he not return into the night and remain what he was? It would be hard for him to wait out the distant dawn; this evening was filled with the scent of lovage; something was happening, something was terrible. The moon would not set for long; under the water mills and yew trees sparkling droplets of water would fly through the thick light, which was full of intoxicating shadows. The moon would shine all night long, the moon would beckon all night long. I needed to leave with him, or alone, to leave and wander, to leave and never come back, to leave and die, to leave and live, on this night that remained even as all else was lost.

So it all burst out.

Surely it lasted only an instant, as long as it takes for an eyelid to close, I knew because the young man was still standing in front of me with a frozen, absent smile. He heard nothing, felt nothing of the tumult within me, he was unmoved by the madness that had suddenly come over me. It came like rebellion, following my anguish and fear for my brother, after the doubts that had shaken me to my roots. The power of life, waiting for the foundations we had set to collapse, burst out and carried away the crops that we had cultivated for so long, like a flood, leaving debris and wasteland behind. In this moment of astonishment I could neither pass judgment on myself, nor feel remorse, nor pray; everything was still too fresh. It was as if lightning had struck and scorched me, taking away all my strength.

Go, I told him softly. Go, I said. Maybe I did not even say it, but he understood, from the movements of my lips, from the motion of my hand, because he wanted to leave. And he left, without haste, so as not to reveal the impatience that undoubtedly wanted for him to be left alone again with whatever he had brought in his eyes. Go, I said, for he was a witness of my weakness, unconscious, blind and deaf, but I knew he had been there, and I did not want to be ashamed of him. Or to hate him. I wanted to remain alone with myself.

I had felt anxiety and commotion inside myself earlier, but that came and went, like momentary lapses of consciousness, like an inexplicable defiance of my inner order. Those had been quick stumbles that left no trace. But on that night it seemed that utter confusion had come over me, that all the links inside me had snapped, and that I was not what I had been. I became aware of one of my possibilities, which could become destructive if it continued.

The first thing I felt was fear, still distant, but deep, certain, like an awareness that I would pay for that moment. God would punish me with pangs of conscience, and I would not have to wait long for them to appear. Maybe that night, maybe the very next instant.

PART I

But nothing happened. I stood in the same place, my feet firmly planted on the gravel of the garden path. I was perplexed and tired, the fire that had flared up in me had all but died out. Forgive me, God, I whispered unconsciously, mechanically, without remembering the prayer that could have helped me at that moment.

I moved away from that spot, as if in flight, and stopped at the fence above the river.

I felt as if there were not a single thought inside me, as if my senses had been numbed with shock. But surprisingly, I was aware of everything, more responsive and receptive to everything around me than I had been a moment before. My ear caught the resonant noises of the night, they were clear and purified, like echoes bouncing off glass. I could hear each of them separately, and yet they all merged into a larger drone of water, birds, a light wind, voices lost from afar, the soft murmur of night swaying slowly under the beat of unknown, invisible wings. And none of that bothered me, or disturbed me, I wished for more of those voices, sounds, droning, wingbeats, I wished for more of everything outside of me; maybe I heard it all with such clarity so I would not listen to myself.

That was probably the only time in my life that voices and noises, that light and shapes appeared as they really are, like sound, noise, smell, form. Like a sign or a manifestation of things beyond me, because I listened and watched as one detached and uninvolved, with neither sorrow nor joy, neither damaging nor mending them. They had lives of their own, without my involvement, unaltered by my feelings. They were thus independent, true, not recast into my concept of them, and they left a somewhat insipid impression, like something foreign and unrecognized, something that happens and exists despite everything, futile and useless. I had withdrawn and had been withdrawn, separated from everything around me. The world seemed rather ghostlike, alive but indifferent. And I had become independent and impenetrable.

The sky was empty and deserted. It offered neither a threat nor consolation: I saw it thus disfigured, upside down, and shattered in the water, like a close reflection rather than a mysterious void. The sparkle of pebbles could be seen through the clear water, like the bellies of fish asleep or dead on the shallow bottom, concealed and motionless, like my thoughts. But my thoughts would float to the top; they would not remain deep within me. So let them be, let them rise when they came to life, when I could accept their meaning as more than a mere hint. For now they were calm, and maybe my senses, independent and free, were celebrating mildly in this quiet, which was of uncertain duration. Surprisingly, my senses seemed pure and innocent, as long as I did not burden them with the violence of my thoughts and desires. They freed me as well, returning me to peace, to some distant time that might never have existed, a time so beautiful and pure that I did not believe in its previous existence, although it still remained in my memory. The most beautiful thing would have been the impossible—to return to that dream, to naive childhood, to the secure bliss of that warm and dark primeval spring. I did not feel the sadness or foolishness of such a longing, which was not a desire, because it was unattainable, even as a thought. It hovered in me like a dim light, turned back toward something impossible, nonexistent. Even the river was flowing backward, the tiny ripples of water overlaid with the silver of the moonlight did not drift downstream; the waters were flowing again toward their source. The stone fish with the white bellies swam up to the surface; and the river was flowing again to its source.

Then it occurred to me that my thoughts were coming to life and beginning to turn everything I saw into pain, memories, and unattainable desires. The empty sponge of my brain began to soak itself full again. The time of separation had been short.

4

Do you really believe that man can achieve what he desires?[1]

IN THE STREET, NEXT TO THE TEKKE WALL OVERGROWN WITH ivy, there were footsteps. I paid no attention. I barely even noticed them, and did so only because of something about them that might have seemed strange. But that impression remained entirely superficial, unchecked, and my absent-mindedness did not allow me to connect the occurrence with its possible cause. I did not care who at that late hour might be passing by the tekke, the last building on the edge of the kasaba. Nothing stirred within me, no presentiment, no foreboding; those footsteps meant as much to me as the flight of a moth, and nothing warned me that they could be decisive in my life. What a pity and what a wonder it is that man cannot sense even the most immediate threat to him. Had I known, I would have shut the heavy bolt on the gate and gone into the tekke, so the fates of others would be decided without my involvement. But I did not know, and I continued to watch the river, trying to see it in the way I had seen it a moment before, it alone, apart from myself. I did not succeed, it would soon be midnight, and a little superstitiously I went to meet that hour when all kinds of dark spirits awaken. I expected something to emerge, good or evil, even from this silence of mine.

The footsteps returned, silently, more silently than before.

I had no idea what they were, but I was sure they were the same ones. A part of me knew this; my ears detected something unusual, something that I thought nothing about, and recorded it: one foot was cautious, the other made no sound. Maybe I heard it only because it was impossible to imagine someone walking on one leg, creating the impression of that other, nonexistent foot myself. I could not hear the night-watchman—had some one-legged spirit arrived early?

The footsteps stopped in front of the gate, one of them real, quiet, and wary; the other, imagined, unheard.

I turned around and waited. They had begun to concern me, and this intrusion made me shudder. I could still have gone up to the gate and pushed the bolt, but I did not do it. I could have leaned against the worm-eaten wood of the door, to hear whether that someone was breathing, whether he had flown away or turned to darkness. I waited, aiding chance with my inaction.

In the street there were more footsteps, at a run, in a hurry, out of breath. Would the one-legged one join them, or had he disappeared?

The gate opened and someone entered.

He stepped onto the stone tiles of the doorway and leaned with his back against the wide door, as if he had collapsed or were trying to hold it shut. This was an instinctive and futile act—his small, fragile body could not have kept anyone out.

Two trees cast shadows on the gate, and he stood in a crevice of light, as if condemned, isolated, exposed. He would surely have liked to hide in the thickest darkness, but he did not dare to move. The footsteps ran past the gate, clattering on the cobblestones, and faded away at the bend in the gorge, where there was a post of Albanian guards. The pursuers were certainly asking about this man who stood as if crucified on the door. Both he and I knew that they would return.

PART I

We looked at one other, each motionless where he stood, and said nothing. From the other side of the garden I saw his bare foot on the stone tiles of the doorway, and his face, whiter than the tekke wall. In that white face, in those feebly outstretched arms, in that silence there was the terror of waiting.

I did not move, I did not speak, so as not to disturb this exciting game of pursuit and flight. As our situation became more difficult, the wait became even tenser. I sensed that I had been drawn into something unusual, grave, and brutal. I did not know which one of them was cruel—the fugitive or his pursuers—it was not important to me then. The chase smelled of blood and death, and everything was happening before my eyes. It dawned on me that life itself had been tied into a bloody knot, maybe a little too snugly and tightly, maybe too closely, too crudely expressed, but always the same in all of its endless chases, both great and small. I was not on either side, but my position was extremely important. It excited me that I could be the judge and decide everything with a single spoken word. The fate of this man was in my hands. I was his fate, and I had never felt so much power in anything that I could do. An innocent greeting or a soft cough could destroy him. Yet I did not give him away, not because his eyes, which I could hardly see from where I stood, were certainly begging for mercy, not even because it might have been unjust to do so, but because I wanted the game to continue: I wanted to be a spectator and a witness, horrified and excited.

The pursuers returned. They were not running any more, but walking, confused and furious, because everything had gone awry. Now they were not only the pursuers, but also the pursued: his escape would mean their condemnation. Here nothing could end peacefully; the outcome, whatever it might be, would be ugly.

Everyone involved in this game kept silent, I, the pursued, and the pursuers. Only the Albanian guards on the dam in the gorge were singing a drawling song from their homeland, and that foreign lament, which sounded like wild sobs, made our silence even more oppressive.

The footsteps drew near, hushed and indecisive. I began to follow them, straining my senses, part pursuer and part fugitive, since I was neither. I passionately wished for him both to be caught and to escape, fear for the fugitive mixed strangely with the desire to shout out where he was, and all of this turned into a torturous pleasure.

The pursuers stopped in front of the door. I held my breath, and with heartbeats full of impatience I lived through that moment, which was to decide my own fate as well.

The fugitive was certainly not breathing, either; the thin boards of the door were all that separated him from his pursuers. They stood less than a few inches apart, and yet they were far away from each other; their ignorance and his hope separated them like a mountain. His arms were still outstretched, and his face glowed like phosphorous. I was so excited that the forks of his arms and legs blurred in my eyes; but the white blot of his face remained, like a symbol of his terror.

Would his pursuers open the gate and enter? Would his foot slip on the smooth stone and draw their attention? Would I clear my throat from anxiety and summon them? Their two forms of despair would struggle, but there were more of the pursuers, he would be able to hold them back only for a moment. Then they would find themselves face to face, and that would be his end. They would fall on him brutally, because of their fear and rage at having lost him, and because of their joy at finding him again. I would only watch, sickened by the outcome, praying for them to leave the tekke garden. But at that moment I felt like the pursued, accidentally, because I could just as well have felt like the pursuers. But maybe that was not accidental. Him I could see, and I wanted the unseen men in front of the gate to leave, so I would not also have to see his ugly end. It seemed that my wish aided this man who was fighting so helplessly for his life, that it gave him some prospects for survival.

And indeed, as if my concentrated will had some effect, the footsteps moved away from the gate. Then they stopped again in confusion, one of them was not sure that they should not try it: they could still come back. But they did not; they set off down the street toward the kasaba.

The man was still standing in the same position, but the stiffness of his muscles had surely slackened, and the farther away the footsteps moved, the more his strength gave out.

It was good that everything had ended this way. If they had caught him or beat him in front of me, the brutal image would have lingered in my memory long afterward. And I might have even begun to feel remorse at having for a moment been ready to hand him over, and at having taken pleasure (painfully, but still taken pleasure) in that human hunt. Like this, if I felt any remorse at all, it would be weaker.

I did not think about who was wrong and who was right. I did not even care: when people settle their accounts, guilt is easy to find, and justice is the right to do whatever we think must be done, and therefore justice can be anything. The same is also true with guilt. As long as I did not know anything I could not take either side, and I would not get involved. Indeed, I had already gotten involved, by my silence, but that was an involvement that did not contradict my beliefs, and I could always justify it with the reason most convenient for me, if I ever learned the truth.

I started toward the tekke, leaving the man to himself. Now he could do whatever he wanted. The chase was over, he could go his own way. I looked in front of myself, down at the gravel of the path and the green grass on its edges, to shut him out, to sever even those thin ties that had connected us only a moment before. I wanted him to remain what he was, a stranger, whose path and eyes would never cross mine. But even without looking I saw the whiteness of his shirt and the paleness of his face, maybe only in my imagination, in an image I later remembered. I saw that he had lowered his arms and put his legs together. He was no longer tense, no longer tied in a knot of trembling nerves, living solely for an instant that would decide between life and death, but a man relieved from a momentary worry so he could be free to think about what awaited him. For I knew that nothing had been resolved between him and those who were after him, it had only been prolonged, postponed for an unknown length of time, maybe only until the next moment, since he was condemned to run, and they to chase him. And then I thought that he lifted an arm, indecisively, barely moving it away from his body, as if he wanted to stop me, to tell me something, to induce me to take part in his fate. I do not know whether I actually saw this, whether he really did it, or whether I imagined the motion that he might have, that he must have made. I did not stop. I did not want him to concern me any longer. I went into the tekke and turned the key in the rusty lock.

When I got to my room I could still hear the creaking sound that had separated us. For him it meant freedom, or maybe even greater fear, absolute solitude.

I felt the need to take a book, the Koran, or some other, about morality, about great men, about holy days. I would be soothed by the music of familiar sentences that I trusted, that I did not even think about but carried inside myself like the flow of my blood. We are not aware of it, but it is everything to us; it enables us to live and breathe, keeps us upright, and gives its own meaning to everything in our lives. Those processions of beautiful words about things I knew always lulled me in a strange way. In this familiar circle, in which I moved, I felt secure, safe from any traps that men and the world might set for me.

But it was not good that I wanted to take a book, no matter which, that I sought the protection of familiar thoughts. What was I afraid of? What did I want to escape from?

PART I

I knew, the man was still down there in the garden; I would have heard it if he had opened the gate. I did not make any light; I stood in the yellow darkness of my room, with my feet in the moonlight, and waited. What was I waiting for?

He was still down there; that was all that mattered. It was enough that the tekke had saved him; he should have left. Why did he not leave?

The room smelled of old wood and leather, of forgotten life. Only the shadows of young women, long dead, occasionally passed through it: I had become accustomed to them; they had lived here before me. But an unfamiliar man, a stranger with a white blot for a face and forked arms and legs, had taken up residence in this ancient sanctuary and crucified himself on the door in anguish. I knew that he had changed his position; I saw that his body had grown limp, as if all of his bones had suddenly been broken. This was something new, more important and more painful, but I remembered his previous stiffness and effort, his tension, which lived and fought, surrendering to no one. I remembered the taut springs of his muscles, capable of miracles. I preferred that image to the newer, broken one; I had hoped for more from it, it released me more easily from any responsibility, promising that he would rely on his own powers. The other was dependence, hopelessness, a need for support. I remembered the movement that I had seen, or not seen, with which he had wanted to draw my eyes to his. He had hailed me, begged me not to pass by him and his fear as if none of it concerned me. If he had not done it, if I had only imagined that inevitable movement of a life struggling and calling for help, then he had lost all of his strength, and now even his hope. It was a pity that I knew nothing about this man. If he were guilty I would not think about him at all.

I went up to the window, and was frightened by the moonlight that struck my face. It was as if it had given me away. I looked down, askance—he was not at the gate any more, he had gone away. I looked more freely around the garden, hoping to find it empty. But he had not left. He was standing under a tree, in its shadow, up against its trunk. I saw him when he moved: his feet were also in the moonlight; the edge of a shadow cut across his legs above the knees.

He did not look at the tekke or my window; he did not expect anything more from me. He listened attentively toward the street; he certainly could have heard even the footsteps of a cat, the movements of birds, his own silent breath. I followed his eyes as he raised them to the treetop: it was swaying slightly in the midnight breeze. Did he beg it to be silent or curse its rustling, since he could no longer make out the noises beyond the tekke walls, noises that could be worth as much as life itself to him?

He went around the tree with his back against its trunk, moving his silvery feet in a circle, and then stepped away from it and approached the gate with silent, weightless steps. He carefully locked the bolt. Then he returned and, keeping in the shadows of the trees, crept up to the fence, leaned over the river, looked up into the gorge and downstream toward the kasaba, then retreated and disappeared among the dense bushes. Had he heard or seen something? Did he not dare to come out, or did he have nowhere to go?

I would have liked to know if he was guilty.

And so, I had walked past him, with my eyes lowered to the ground. I had locked the tekke door and shut myself in my room, but I had not yet separated myself from the man who had burst into this peace and compelled me to think about him, to stand by my window and watch his growing fear. He made me forget about the sins of others on this Saint George's Eve, about the beginning of my own sins, about the two wonderful hands at dusk, about all of my worries. But maybe it was precisely because of them that this happened.

I should have turned away from the window, lit a candle, and gone into another room, if I did not want my lighted window to torment him unnecessarily. I should have done anything except what I actually did. Because that meant concern, a morbid interest, a lack of resolve in me. It was as if I no longer trusted in myself and my conscience.

This hiding was childish, or even worse: it was cowardly. I had nothing to fear, not even myself. Why was I acting as if I did not see the man, and why did I give him an opportunity to leave when he did not want to? Why was I pretending not to be sure whether he was in the tekke garden, whether he was hiding a crime or fleeing from one? Something was happening that was not at all innocent. I knew that grave and cruel things happen all the time, but this was before my own eyes, and I could not brush it away into what I had not known or seen, like everything else. I did not want to be an outlaw or an unwilling accomplice. I wanted to be free to make my own decision.

I went down into the garden. The moon shone near the horizon, it would soon set. The oleaster was beginning to bloom, and the air was heavy with its scent. It was obtrusive, too strong, and the tree should have been cut down. Sometimes I am oversensitive to smells; the whole earth will reek unbearably and stifle me. That happens suddenly, when I am excited, it seems, although I do not know what the connection is.

He stood in the thick bushes, I would not have found him if I had not known where he was. His face was featureless, blotted out by the half-shadows; he could see me better. I was exposed by the light, and felt naked, but I could not cover myself. He had turned into bushes, grown into branches, and would soon begin to sway in the night breeze that descended from the mountains through the gorge.

"You have to go," I said in a whisper.

"Where?"

His voice was firm, deep, as if he were not this small man in front of me.

"Away. No matter where."

"Thank you for not giving me away."

"I don't want to get involved in other people's affairs, that's why I want you to go."

"If you make me leave you'll be getting involved."

"Maybe that would be best."

"You helped me once. Why spoil that now? You might need a nice memory sometime."

"I don't know anything about you."

"You know everything about me. They're after me."

"You must have done something to them."

"I've done nothing wrong."

"What are you going to do now? You can't stay here."

"Take a look, is there a guard on the bridge?"

"Yes."

"They're waiting for me. They're all around. Are you really going to send me to my death?"

"The dervishes get up early, they'll see you."

"Hide me until tomorrow evening."

"Travelers might stop in. Unexpected guests."

"I too am an unexpected guest."

"I can't do it."

"Then call the guards, they're there behind the wall."

"I don't want to call them. And I don't want to hide you. Why should I help you?"

"For no reason at all. Now go away, this doesn't concern you."

"I could've destroyed you."

"You didn't have the strength, not even for that."

He caught me off-guard, I had not been prepared for this conversation. As I listened to his words I was surprised, mostly because I had expected to meet a completely different kind of man. The image of those outstretched arms and legs on the gate had deceived me. The white blot of his face, the scant protection provided by the thin boards, the pity that I felt had formed my impression of him. I imagined him to be a poor, frightened, lost man, and I even thought that I knew what his voice sounded like—trembling, insecure. But everything turned out differently. I had believed that a single word from me would soften him, that he would look at me humbly: he was in a hopeless situation, and depended on my good or bad will. But his voice was calm, not even angry. I thought that it sounded almost cheerful, mocking, challenging, that he did not answer gruffly or humbly, but rather indifferently, as if he were above everything that was happening, as if he knew something that made him feel confident. He flouted my expectations so much that I must have also exaggerated in my estimation of his composure. I was also astonished by the manner in which he requested that I hide him: as if that were something totally natural, a favor he would appreciate but that was not crucial for him. He did not repeat his appeal, or demand; he gave up easily. He was not angry that I refused it. He did not even look at me, he listened attentively, his head slightly raised, no longer expecting my help anymore. He no longer expected anyone's help. He knew that now no one dared to offer him a hand, that he did not have family, friends, or acquaintances, that he was condemned to be alone in his distress. An empty space had been left around him and his pursuers.

"You must think I'm a bad man."

"No, I don't."

"I'm not. But I can't help you."

"Everyone knows himself."

That was not a reproach, or reconciliation to his misfortune. It was merely an acceptance of what is, an ancient, bitter recognition of the refusal of people, all people, to help a condemned man. He counted me among them, and was not surprised at all. That realization did not break him or take away his strength; he did not look around desperately, but very calmly and purposefully, determined to fight alone.

I asked why they were pursuing him. He did not give an answer.

"How did you escape?"

"I jumped from the cliff."

"Did you kill anyone?"

"No."

"Did you steal anything, did you rob anyone, did you do anything shameful?"

"No."

He did not hurry to justify himself, he did not try to convince me, he answered my questions as if they were superfluous and bothersome. He no longer judged me according to good or evil, no longer regarded me either as something dangerous or as a source of hope: I had not given him away, but I was not going to help him. Surprisingly, that neglect, as if I were a tree, a bush, or a child, wounded my vanity; it somehow depersonalized and belittled me, deprived me of value not only in his, but in my own eyes as well. I did not care about him, I knew nothing about him, I would never see him again, but his opinion had become important to me, and I was offended because he was acting as if I did not exist. I would have been pleased if he were angry.

I was deserting him, but his independence upset me.

I stood there, and kept standing, in the stifling scent of the oleaster, on Saint George's Eve, which had a life of its own, in the garden, which had become a world of its own. We stood there, face to face, joyless that we had met, incapable of going our separate ways as if we had not. I tormented myself trying to decide what to do with this man who had turned into branches, without doing anything evil or sanctioning his sin when I did not know what it was. I did not want to sin against my conscience, but I could not find a solution.

That was a strange night, not only because of what happened, but also because of how I perceived it. My reason told me not to get involved in something that did not concern me, but I had already gotten involved so much that I could not see any way out. My old practice of self-control had led me into my room, but I returned, driven by a new need. The discipline of a dervish and of the tekke had taught me to be firm, but I stood in front of the fugitive not knowing what to do, which meant that I was already doing something I should not. I had every reason to leave the man to his fate, but I was following him down his slippery and dangerous path, a path not meant for me.

And while I was still thinking about this, searching for the right word to pull myself from this dilemma, I said suddenly:

"I can't bring you in the tekke. It would be dangerous for both of us."

He did not respond; he did not even look at me. I had not told him anything new. There was still time for me to go back, but I was already starting to slip, and it was difficult to stop.

"At the far end of the garden there's a shed," I whispered. "No one ever goes there. We keep old junk in it."

Then he looked at me. His eyes were lively and distrustful, but they showed no fear at all.

"Hide there until they go away. If they catch you, don't tell them I helped you."

"They won't catch me."

The certitude with which he said that sickened me. I again felt that unease at his self-confidence, and regretted having offered him a place to hide. He was utterly self-sufficient; he thrust all others aside: I felt as if he had struck me, pushed away the hand that I offered him, disgustingly sure of himself. Later I was ashamed of my irritability. (What else could he do but believe in himself?!) I caught myself feeling that vile need for others to be grateful to us, to show themselves as small and dependent, because that is what creates our favor, nurtures it, and heightens the importance of our deeds and kindness. But his behavior made them seem trivial and unnecessary. At that moment, however, I was not ashamed, I was angry. It seemed to me that I had become involved in something utterly senseless, but I started through the garden toward the dilapidated shed hidden in the bushes and alder trees. I went without joy, without any justification, without a definite inner need, but I could do nothing else.

The door was open, bats and pigeons lived there.

He stopped.

"Why are you doing this?"

"I don't know."

"You already regret it."

"You're too proud."

"You didn't need to say that. And a man can never be too proud."

"I don't want to know who you are or what you've done; that's your affair. Stay here, this is all I can do for you. Let everything be as if we had never met, never seen each other."

"That's best. Go into your room now."

"Should I bring you some food?"

"No. You're already sorry you've even done this."

"Why do you think I'm sorry?"

"You hesitate too much; you think too much. Whatever you do now, you'll regret it. Go to the tekke, don't think about me anymore. If you think anymore, you'll turn me in."

Was this derision, mockery, scorn? Where did he get the strength to act like that?

"You don't trust people very much."

"Dawn will break soon. It wouldn't be good if they found us together."

He wanted to get rid of me. He looked impatiently at the sky, which was changing with the pale light of oncoming morning. Yet I wanted to ask him countless questions, I would never see him again. No one could give me the answers but him.

"Only one more thing: you're alone. Aren't you afraid? They'll catch you and kill you. You don't have a chance."

PART I

"Leave me alone!"

His voice was rough, muffled with anger. It was really unnecessary to tell him what he already knew himself. Maybe he thought that I was indeed a bad man who took spiteful pleasure in his troubles. And he paid me back in full measure:

"Something is troubling you," he said with his sudden sagacity, which stunned me, catching me in my own hidden turf. "I'll come to talk sometime, when there's no danger. Go now."

He had not told me what I wanted to know; he left me rather to face myself. And what kind of answer could he have given me? What could we have had in common? What could he have taught me?

I opened the window; the room was stuffy. I would have gone down into the garden if he had not been there, to wait out the dawn without sleeping, just as I would up here. It was not far off, the first birds were announcing it with ever louder song as the sky above the dark hills raised its eyelid, showing its blue iris. The trees in the garden were still sleepy, covered with the hazy, thin darkness. Soon, at the first rays of the sun, fish would begin breaking the water's surface. I loved that morning hour of awakening, it was as if life itself were just beginning.

I waited in the middle of my room with a feeling of unease, but I could not determine its cause. I was bitter, because of what I had and had not done. I had failed on this night filled with danger and unfounded fear.

I strained to hear every rustle, every flutter of birds' wings, I listened to the even flow of the river, but I was expecting to hear him, or them coming after him. Would he escape, would he stay, would they catch him? Had it been a mistake not to give him away, or not to hide him in my room? He had told me: whatever you do, you'll regret it. How had he guessed what had not been altogether clear even to me? I did not want to be either for or against him, so

I found a middle position, which was no position at all, since it solved nothing and only prolonged the suffering. I would have to take a side.

There were countless reasons to do both, to destroy him and to save him. I was a dervish, a defender of the faith and of my order, and to help him meant to betray my convictions, to betray what had been an unblemished part of my life for so many years. If they caught him it would be bad for the tekke as well, and it would be even worse if it became known that I had helped him. No one would forgive me, and it was almost certain that someone would find out; he would tell them, either out of spite or fear. It would also be bad for my brother. Both for my brother and for me. I would have worsened both of our positions; some connection, some consistency would be found in such an act. It would look as if I were avenging my brother, or helping another man since I could not help him. There were also enough reasons to hand him over to the authorities—let him settle his dispute with justice the best he could.

And yet, I was human, I did not know what he had done, and it was not for me to judge him. Even justice can err; why should I have taken responsibility for him and burdened myself with possible remorse? There were also enough reasons to help him. But they were somehow pale, not convincing enough; I devised them and gave them importance only so that they would serve to protect me from the real reason, the only reason that mattered: that I had tried to absolve myself through him. He appeared at the very moment when he could have tipped the scales of my indecisiveness. If I condemned him, if I gave him over to the authorities, I would circumvent the dilemma and remain what I had been, in spite of everything that had happened, as if nothing had happened, in spite of my imprisoned brother and the sorrow I felt for him. I would sacrifice the fugitive as an unfortunate victim, forget about my wounded self, and continue on the trodden path of obedience,

PART I

unfaithful to my own suffering. But if I saved him, that would be my final decision: I would be crossing over to the other side and rising up against someone, against my former self, unfaithful to the peace within me. But I could do neither, my shattered confidence kept me from one, and the power of habit and my fear of returning into the unknown kept me from the other. Ten days before, when my brother had not yet been imprisoned, it would have been all the same to me. I would have been calm regardless of what I did. Now I knew that I was taking a side, and thus stopped halfway, undecided. Everything was possible, but nothing happened.

And he was in the garden, in the old shed in the bushes. I kept looking over there, but nothing moved, nothing could be heard. I was sorry that he had not gone, in that way he would have solved everything himself. He could not escape anymore, he would stay there all day, and all day long I would think about him and wait for the night to save him, or me.

I knew how the tekke woke up. Mustafa got up first, if he had not slept at home. His heavy shoes knocking on the stone tiles of the ground floor, slamming doors, he would go out into the garden and perform the abdest.* He blew his nose loudly, cleared his throat, rubbed his broad chest, bowed and prayed hastily, then lit a fire, and took dishes out and put them back, all with such a racket that he woke even those who were not used to rising early. He was deaf, and in his empty world devoid of sounds and echoes noise was but a desire, and when we occasionally succeeded in telling him about his excessive knocking, slamming, crashing, and banging, he was surprised that it could even disturb anyone.

Almost at the same time one could hear Hafiz-Muhammed's quiet coughing. Sometimes he coughed all night long, and in the spring and fall his cough would become heavy and choking. We knew that he spat blood, but he got rid of the red flecks himself and came out with a smile, with faint red stains on his cheeks, talking about usual things, not about himself or his illness. It sometimes seemed to me that he had an arrogance of a special sort, striving to rise above us and the world. He performed the abdest with special care, rubbing his thin, translucent skin for a long time. That morning he coughed less, and not so hard as usual; it happened that the mild spring air soothed him, the same air that would devastate him sometime else. I knew that today he would be agreeable, quiet, distant. That was how he took revenge on the world, by not showing his bitterness.

Then Mullah-Yusuf went down. The slow clatter of his wooden shoes showed restraint, it was too measured for his vibrant health. He paid more attention to his bearing than any of us did to ours, because he had more to hide. I did not trust his composure; given his ruddy face and his youthful twenty-five years, it seemed like a lie rather than an affectation. But this was not a firm belief, it was merely a suspicion, an impression that changed according to my mood.

Although we lived together, we knew little about one another, since we never talked about ourselves, never openly. We only talked about what we had in common. And that was good. Personal matters were too subtle, murky, and vain; we were to keep them to ourselves if we could not suppress them entirely. Our conversations were largely reduced to general, familiar phrases that others had used before us, phrases that were tried and safe, because they protected us from surprises and misunderstandings. A personal tone is poetry, an opportunity for distortion, or arbitrariness, and to leave the realm of general thought is to doubt it. Therefore, we knew each other only according to what was unimportant, or what was identical in each of us. In other words, we did not know each other at all; nor was that necessary. To know each other meant to know what we should not.

But these general thoughts were not at all peaceful, because with them I was attempting to entrench myself in something firm and secure, so that no turmoil would tear me out of our common circle. I was walking on the very edge, and I wanted to return to anonymity. This morning I envied everyone, because their morning was an everyday morning.

There was a sure and simple way for me to reduce, or even to eliminate my anguish: to turn it into a common problem. The fugitive now concerned the whole tekke, and it was not for me to make a decision by myself. Did I have the right to hide what had become theirs as well? I could express my opinion, I could appeal on his behalf, but I was not allowed to hide him. That would be the very decision I was trying to avoid. And the decision should be ours, not mine. It would be easier and more honest that way. Everything else would be dishonesty and lies, and I would know that I was doing something forbidden when I had no reason for it. Not even the certitude that it was what I needed to do.

But whom could I talk to? If we acted together, the fugitive would be sacrificed in advance. We would be afraid of one another and speak for those who were absent, and in that case the most acceptable decision was the most severe. It would be easier and more honest to talk with one man; the others would not influence him; reasonable arguments would receive more consideration before fewer ears. But whom was I to choose? Deaf Mustafa was surely out of the question. We were equal before God, but everyone would have thought it funny if I talked to him about it, and not only because he was deaf. He was so preoccupied with thoughts of his common-law wife, from whom he often ran away, sleeping in the tekke for nights on end, and of his five children, both his own and adopted, that he himself would have wondered why I would ask something he knew nothing about. And there were all sorts of things that he was totally unaware of. In this respect he resembled his numerous children.

Hafiz-Muhammed would listen to me absently, with a smile that said nothing. He lived hunched over his yellowed books of history. For that strange man, and I envied him because of this then, it was as if the only time that existed has already passed, and even the present was only a time that would pass. Rarely is there a man who is so happily excluded from life as he was. For years he had wandered in the East, searching for historical works in famous libraries, and when he returned home with a great bundle of books he was poor and rich, full of knowledge that no one needed except him. Knowledge flowed from him like a river, or a flood; he submerged you in names and events; you would be taken by a fear of the throngs that lived within that man as if they still existed, as if they were not spirits and shadows but living people who acted ceaselessly in some terrible eternity of existence. In Constantinople a military officer had even tutored him in astronomy for three full years, and because of these two sciences he measured all things by the vast expanses of the heavens and time. I thought that he was also writing a history of our times, but had my doubts, since for him events and people could acquire magnitude and significance only when they were dead. He could only write a philosophy of history, the hopeless history of superhuman dimensions, indifferent to ordinary life, which still continues. Had I asked him about the fugitive, he would certainly have felt uncomfortable because I was bothering him with such unpleasant matters on this beautiful morning, which he had met without a fever, and because I was making him think about something so trivial as the fate of a man in the tekke garden. And he would have answered so vaguely that everything would have still depended on my decision.

I decided to talk to Mullah-Yusuf.

He had just finished with the abdest. He greeted me and wanted to leave quietly. I stopped him and said that I would like to talk with him.

He gave me a quick look and lowered his head at once. He was afraid of something. But I did not want to derive any kind of advantage by making him wait, and told him everything about the fugitive: how I had heard and seen him from my room when he entered the garden and hid in the bushes. He was certainly still there somewhere, and it was just as certain that he was on the run, otherwise he would not be hiding. I told him the truth, which was that I had been, and still was, at a loss as to what to do, and that I did not know whether to report him to the authorities or to leave everything to chance. Maybe he was guilty, the innocent are not chased at night, but I also realized that I knew nothing about him, that I might do something unjust, and God keep me from that. And now we needed to decide whether it was wrong to get involved or not. Was it worse to cover up a crime, if it was a crime, or not to act mercifully?

He looked at me apprehensively, trying to conceal the attention and interest that my confused story had called forth in him, but his ruddy, smooth face, fresh with water and the morning, became lively and restless.

"Is he still in the garden?" he asked softly.

"He didn't leave before dawn, and he won't dare during the day."

"What do you think we should do?"

"I don't know. I'm afraid of sin. If he's guilty, people will eventually reproach us, and that wouldn't be good for the tekke. But if he's not guilty, sin will fall on our souls. And only God can know where a man's guilt lies; men cannot."

It was the hour when all colors are brighter, all random noises louder, the hour of a roseate half-light still heavy with the night's shadows, the hour of the clarity of incipient day. But on this day I felt no joy at the fresh morning, I joined the previous day with a new one, without having alleviated my worries with sleep.

When I returned from the mosque, still upset in spite of the morning prayer, I found guards in the garden with Mullah-Yusuf. They had searched through every corner and looked through the shed, but the fugitive was not to be found.

"Maybe I was mistaken," I said to the dissatisfied guards.

"You weren't mistaken. He escaped yesterday and hid somewhere."

"Were you the one who called them?" I asked Yusuf after the guards had left.

"I thought it was what you wanted. Otherwise you wouldn't have told me."

In any case, it did not matter; that was best. I had freed myself from responsibility and guilt, and no one had been caused any harm. I should have felt relieved and stopped thinking about the night before.

But I kept thinking about it, more than I could justify in any way. I walked around the garden. The footprints were visible on the sandy path, side by side, one of them shoeless. That was all that remained of him, that and some broken branches of snowberry, an image of his outstretched arms and legs on the door, and the presence of something unusual that hovered under the boughs of the old trees—a new tinge, an absence of emptiness and desolation, freshness after a storm. Now that he was out of reach and there was no danger to me from him nor to him from me, I thought about that stranger in a very peculiar way, as if he were a torrent, a brisk wind, as if he had come in a dream. He began to dissolve, my experience renounced him, a living man could not have gone away from here unnoticed. The footprints did confirm his presence, but those tangible traces did not eliminate a strange sense that I felt but did not completely understand. He had escaped from the guards, through a window in his house when they came for him; he had smashed through the prison wall and jumped from the cliff and entered an unfamiliar gate without respect for the property of others; he had disappeared, but his step had not been heard by the sentries that were waiting all around, as if he were a spirit. He had not trusted me, he no longer trusted anyone, he was running from others' fear as much as from the cruelty of the guards, sure only of himself. I was sorry that he had lost all his faith in people, he would be unhappy and empty inside. That was why he was still alive and free, to be sure, but I would not have liked for him ever to learn that I could have been to blame for his doom. This man did not concern me, we owed nothing to each other, and he could do me neither harm nor good; yet I would have been glad if he could carry a nice thought of me into his solitude, if in his utter distrust of people he remembered me differently than the others.

Later I watched Mullah-Yusuf copy the Koran, outside, in front of the tekke, in the dense shade of a branchy apple tree; he needed even light, without flashes or shadows. I observed his full, rosy hand as it drew in the complex curves of the letters, an endless row of lines across which the eyes of others would roam without even thinking of how long that difficult task had taken, or maybe without even noticing its beauty. I had been surprised the first time I saw this young man's inimitable skill, but after so long I still marveled at it. The refined curves, ornate loops, the balanced wave of lines, the red and gold beginnings of the verses, the floral designs in the margins—everything was transformed into a beauty that perplexed the beholder, that was even slightly sinful, as it was not a means, but an end into itself, important in and of itself, a dazzling play of colors and forms that diverted attention from what it was supposed to serve. It was even somewhat shameful, as if from those ornamented pages a sensuality emerged, maybe because beauty is in and of itself sensual and sinful, or maybe because I did not see things as I should have.

I could smell the oleaster, the same tree as the night before, which had stifled me with its heavy scent; a song echoed from one of the mahals,* the same song as the night before, which had astonished me with its bare shamelessness. A black rage came over me, the same as the night before, which had filled me with fear. I had left the fold, fallen from the circle; nothing sustained me anymore, nothing protected me from myself and the world, not even daylight shielded me. I was no longer the master of my thoughts and deeds, I had become an accomplice to a crime. I needed to leave, to go somewhere, I needed to get away from this young man who irritated me with his questioning glances. I needed to say something to keep from revealing myself; he knew a lot about who I was that morning. There was something dark in him, cruel but peaceful. I had never seen eyes so passionate yet so confident.

I turned away from him, from the ugly image that I saw in him, and from the absurd hatred that flared in me, choking me like smoke, like something rotten. How calmly he had gone to fetch the guards so that they would capture the fugitive! Not for a moment had he pondered his fate, his life, or his possible innocence. I had tormented myself all night long, he had made the decision in an instant. Now he wrote out his splendid, sinful letters calmly, spinning his miraculous fabric as skillfully, cruelly, and insensitively as a spider spins its web.

I went to the uneven footprints in the sand and rubbed out the traces.

"One of his feet was bare," Yusuf said.

He watched me, followed my movements and my thoughts. I was overcome by a mad desire to be open with him, so that he would not wonder or guess. I wanted to tell him everything about the fugitive, and everything I thought about him, it would not be nice at all, to tell him about them, about myself, about many things, and to tell him even what I did not think, only so it would be ugly.

"Maybe they've already caught him . . ." I said in a daze, almost losing consciousness.

A moment was enough for my caution to warn me and to change my words. This young man frightened me because of what I had wanted to say, because of what I could have become, because of what he might have done.

What I said was unexpected, contradictory to the passion

of my angry decision, which I could barely hide, and the tone of my voice would have been better suited for abuse. He looked at me surprised, as if disappointed.

And then it became clear to me that I had known from the first moment what he would do. When I decided to tell everything to someone in the tekke, when I rejected all the others in advance and chose *him*, when I said that it would be best for us not to get involved, I had been certain that he would call the guards. So certain that after the prayer in the mosque I went for a walk in the neighboring streets in order not to see them catch the fugitive and take him away. I had counted on Yusuf's heartlessness. I had known that he would do it, but I nevertheless felt disgust and scorn for him when he did. He was the perpetrator of my secret wish, which had not been a decision, the decision had been his. But even if it had been mine, the deed was his.

But maybe I was being unfair toward him. Had he really thought that I wanted to hand over the fugitive to the guards, his guilt lay in his obedience, and that was not guilt. Even the day before I would have called his willingness to be cruel resoluteness. Today I reproached him. It was not he who had changed, but I, and with me everything else.

I wanted to repay him with kindness for a possible injustice of which he was unaware, but that bothered me nevertheless. Although I changed my opinion of him little, my hate had not yet subsided, and maybe I could not hide it well.

I told him that his Koran would be a real work of art, and he looked at me surprised, almost frightened, as if he had heard a threat. Maybe this was because real kindness is rare among us, and if it occurs then it is serving some end.

"You should go to Constantsa[2] to perfect your calligraphy."

Now his face showed real fear, he could hardly conceal it.

"Why?" he asked quietly.

"You have hands of gold; it'd be a pity if you didn't learn everything there is to know."

He lowered his head.

He did not trust me. He thought that I wanted an excuse to send him away from the tekke. I calmed him, as much as his distrust could be soothed in a moment, but a strange feeling of awkwardness persisted in me. Had his distrust existed the day before, the year before, and always? Was I discovering it only now? Was he also afraid of me, as I was of him?

I had never thought like this before: everything changes when a man loses his bearings. And that was exactly what I had wanted to avoid; I did not want to lose my bearings or to change my point of view, because I would cease to be what I had been, and no one could know what I would be then. Maybe I would be someone new and unknown, whose actions I would not be able to determine or foresee. Discontent is like a wild animal, powerless at birth, terrible when it grows stronger.

It was true, I had wanted to hand the fugitive over to the guards, and this did not trouble me. He had been a challenge, an incitement, an enticement into the unknown; his deeds were the heroism of fairy tales, a dream of courage, foolish defiance. And he was even more dangerous if all of this were true in my mind only. I needed to kill this irresponsible thought, to entrench myself, with his blood, in a place that was mine, mine according to reason and conscience.

The tekke rested in the sunlight, green with ivy and lush foliage. Its old, thick walls and dark, red roof emanated a sense of security; under the eaves the soft cooing of pigeons could be heard, and it succeeded in reaching my previously closed senses. That was tranquility returning; the garden smelled of the sun and warm herbs. A man needs a place that is dear to him because it is his and because it is protected; the world is full of traps when you have nothing to sustain you. Slowly, I stepped in the high millet with the soles of my feet, touched the pearly snowberries with my hands, and listened to the gurgling flow of the water. I was settling into my old peace again, like a convalescent, like a returned traveler; I had wandered in my thoughts the entire night, but now it was day, and sunlight. I had returned, and everything was nice again, it had been regained.

But when I came to the place where we had parted before dawn, I saw the fugitive once more: an obscure smile and a mocking expression hovered before me in the heat that was taking over with the day.

"Are you satisfied?" he asked, watching me calmly.

"I'm satisfied. I don't want to think about you; I wanted to kill you."

"You can't kill me. No one can kill me."

"You overestimate your strength."

"It's you who overestimate it, not I."

"I know. You can't even speak. Maybe you don't exist any more. I'm thinking and speaking instead of you."

"Then I exist. And so much worse for you."

I tried to smile to myself, feebly, almost defeated. Only moments before I had rejoiced at my victory over him, and over everything he could have meant, but he was already revived in my memory, more dangerous than before.

5

Have padlocks been put on their hearts?[1]

THE LONG CORRIDOR THAT RINGED THE OLD INN LIKE A square hoop was so jammed with people that one could not pass. They were waiting in front of a door, excited, crowded together in an irregular circle, in the empty center of which there stood a guard. Others kept coming, and the corridor filled like a clogged conduit. There was the rustling sound of whispers, angry and astonished. The crowd had its own language, different from the language spoken by each of those people. It resembled bees buzzing, or growls. Words were lost, leaving a collective noise; individual moods were lost, leaving a collective, dangerous one.

A traveler had been murdered the night before, a merchant, and now the murderer was to be brought in. They had caught him that morning while he was sitting and drinking peacefully, as if he had not killed anyone.

I did not dare to ask who the murderer was, although his name would not have meant anything to me. I feared that I would recognize it, no matter which name I heard, because I had only one man in mind. I imputed the murder to my fugitive almost without thinking. He had done it the previous night. They had chased him and he had hidden in the tekke; in the morning he went off to drink, thinking he was safe. I was surprised at how small the circle is that closes

PART I

around men's lives, how intertwined the paths are that we follow. Chance had led him to me the night before, and now it led me to see his end. Maybe it would have been best to go, with this discovery and proof of God's swift justice as a sign and a comfort for me. But I could not leave, I waited to see his face, which had perplexed me the night before, to see his lost confidence or criminal impudence, to reject him. Listening to the hushed conversation around me as to how the murder had been carried out, with a knife to the neck and heart, I thought of how I had been involved in a shameful affair, how I had spent a troublesome night tortured by my conscience, in no way suspecting that the fugitive was a murderer. I was defiled by that encounter, degraded by his words, guilty for his escape and that he could have chosen not to stop foolishly at the café.

But I tried in vain to imagine everything graver than it was, accusing myself and pretending to feel disgust. In fact, I felt better; the painful burden was lifted from me, and the nightmare that had been constantly oppressing me gradually disappeared. He was a murderer, a vile and cruel man who brought death to others on the quick blade of his knife, for no reason, for a word or some gold. With all my heart I wished for it to be true; in that way I would rid myself of him. That was why I felt relieved: I would now expel him from my thoughts and forget about the previous night of madness, which had seared everything within me that I considered sacred. But the murderer was only a wretch, and it did not matter whether I spat upon him or grieved for him, since in me he could stir only a sense of sorrow, or disgust with humanity.

I knew they were bringing him in from the quiet, excited voices that rustled like a light wind (it could produce anything, storms or calm weather). These voices were full of hatred and excitement; they quivered with curiosity and smelled of blood; they revealed a secret admiration, and a readiness for violence and revenge. His arrival was announced by livelier movements in the crowd, by anxious, slight shuffles of feet shifting in place, by a curious turning toward those who were approaching, by a spasm that seized them and took their voices away, and probably their breath as well. Footsteps sounded in the complete silence of the cobblestone passageway, and without looking up I tried to determine whether there was an uneven one among them. Then I saw his feet between the two guards. He had both of his shoes on. I raised my eyes higher, unable to remember anything from the previous night except his white shirt and sharp face. His arms were tied crosswise, they had turned blue, their veins were swollen. I could not remember anything of his arms, either. My gaze stopped at his slender neck; I should have already left. And without haste, apathetically, I shifted my gaze to his face. He was not the man from the night before.

I had known that even before I saw him.

He stood in the circle, pale and calm. It seemed to me that he even smiled in one corner of his thin mouth: he did not care what happened to him, or he was satisfied that people were watching him. The guards cut a path through the crowd and led him into the room where the dead merchant lay.

I went down the corridor; this did not concern me. I was not surprised that he was not the same man; that would have been truly unbelievable. But I had wanted it to be so; I had expected a miracle. I had linked external appearances with one another, while forgetting everything that I had thought about him that morning and the night before. Maybe I thus did him an injustice, or maybe not. But he was not who was important: I was. I wanted to free myself from him, just as I had that morning. This was my second attempt to destroy him, to punish myself and to erase the trace that he had left. I had been too preoccupied with him, he had charmed me so much that I wavered within myself, even desiring for him to escape and remain free, like an untamed river. His presence had offered a rare and unusual opportunity, one that needed to be preserved. That was what I thought, and I regretted it immediately. He had burst into my life in a moment of weakness, and was the cause and witness of a betrayal, short-lived but real. For this reason I wanted him to be the murderer; everything would thus have been easier. Murder is less dangerous than rebellion. Murder cannot be an ideal or an incitement; it evokes condemnation and disgust; it happens suddenly, when fear and conscience are forgotten. It is unpleasant, like an ugly reminder of the permanence of our base instincts, of which we are ashamed, as we are ashamed of our ignoble ancestors and criminal relatives. But rebellion is contagious; it can incite dissatisfactions that are always present. It resembles heroism, and maybe it is heroism, because it is resistance and dissent. It seems beautiful because it is borne by fanatics who die for beautiful words, who risk everything since they have nothing. Therefore it is attractive, just as anything that is dangerous can sometimes appear attractive and beautiful.

My father stood in the middle of a room; he had opened the door and was waiting.

I knew what I should have done; I should have gone up to him and embraced him, without hesitating or taking a moment to look at him. In that way everything between us would have been resolved in the best and simplest manner; I would have removed all of our inhibitions, and we would have been able to act like father and son. But it was difficult to reach out and embrace that gray-haired man, who was not standing for nothing in the middle of the room, fearing this encounter. We both felt awkward; we did not know how to behave or what to say to each other. Many years had passed since our last meeting, and we wanted somehow to conceal the fact that life had led us apart. We looked at each other for a few moments. His face was furrowed with age, his eyes fixed on me. He was not what he had once been. I had to reconstruct everything—his sharp, strained features, his powerful voice, the simplicity of a strong man who knew how to work with his hands—and for some reason I needed to imagine him younger and healthier, as he had long been preserved in my memory. God knows how he saw me, what he sought and what he found. We were two strangers who did not want to act as such. And most painful of all was the thought of how things should have been between us, and what we could and could not do.

I bent down to kiss his hand, as all sons do, but he did not let me. We grabbed each other by the arms, like acquaintances, and that was best—it seemed intimate, but not overdone. Yet when I felt his arms, still strong, on mine, when I saw his gray, moist eyes from up close, when I recognized his hale scent, dear to me from childhood, I forgot about our awkwardness and leaned my head on his broad chest with a childlike gesture, suddenly moved by something that I thought had disappeared long ago. Maybe this very gesture excited me, or maybe hidden feelings were awakened by the old man's nearness (he smelled of the lake and the wheatfield), or maybe the reason lay in his excitement, but I felt his collarbone tremble when I laid my forehead against it. Maybe my nature had taken control of me, or the miraculously revived remnant of what might have been my nature, surprising myself with an abundance of tears. That lasted only for a moment, and even before they began to dry I grew ashamed of that silly, childlike act, because it corresponded neither to my years nor to the garb that I wore. But surprisingly, long afterward I remembered that shameful weakness as an infinite relief: for a brief moment I had been separated from everything and returned to my childhood, under someone's protection, freed from years, events, and painful decisions. Everything had been placed in hands stronger than mine, and I was wonderfully feeble, with no need for strength, protected by omnipotent love. I wanted to tell him how I had rushed through the mahals the night before, frightened by the sinful excitement of the people, poisoned by strange thoughts myself. I always felt that way when I was upset and unhappy, as if my body were searching for a way out of my torments, and it was all because of my brother. And he, my father, had come because of him. I knew that, and wanted to tell him how the fugitive had hidden in the tekke and how I had not known what to do, how everything inside me had been pulled out of joint, so that I had wanted to punish both the fugitive and myself, that morning, and moments before, although it did not matter, nothing was in its place any more. And so I sought refuge on his chest, like the small child that I had once been.

But this feeling of tenderness passed quickly, like a flash of lightning. Then I saw an old man before me, confused and frightened by my tears, and I knew that they had been foolish and unnecessary. They would kill any hopes that he might have had, since there was only one thing on his mind; or they would convince him that I had failed in life, and this was not true. It was also clear to me that he would not understand anything I meant to say, things that I did not merely want but rather passionately desired to say, like a child, or a weakling: his horrified eyes and the watchful guards of my reason would have stopped me immediately. We wanted the same thing from one another, each placing his faith in the strength of the other, both of us powerless, and that was the saddest part of this pointless encounter.

I asked him why he had not come to the tekke. Even strangers stay there, and he knows how happy he would have made me. And people will wonder why he wanted to spend the night somewhere else, since we haven't quarrelled or forgotten one another. The inn is a disagreeable place, everyone stays there. It's only convenient for someone who has no place to go, you never know who's coming or leaving—there are all sorts of people around these days.

To all of my entreaties, with which I tried to delay what was to follow, he gave the same answer: he had arrived late the previous night and had not wanted to bother me.

He waved me away when I asked whether he had heard about the murder in the inn. He had.

He did not agree to come over to the tekke. He was going to leave that afternoon, and would spend the night in a village with friends.

"Stay for a day or two. Get some rest."

He waved me away again and shook his head. Before, he had talked well, slowly, he had had time for everything, arranging words into harmoniously composed sentences. There had been a certain peace and confidence in his soft, unhurried manner of speaking; it seemed that he was above all things and that he was in control of them. He had believed in the sound and meaning of words. And now this feeble gesture with his hand meant surrender in the face of life, an abandonment of words, which could neither prevent nor explain his misfortune. He shut himself up with this gesture, and hid his confusion before his son, with whom he no longer knew how to speak. He hid his horror at the town that had met him with a murder and darkness, and his helplessness in the face of the troubles that had ruined his old age. He wanted only to conclude the affair that brought him here, and immediately to flee the kasaba, which had taken all that he had, his sons, his confidence, his faith in life. He looked around, looked at the floor, pressed his knotty fingers together, hid his eyes. I was sorry and depressed.

"We're scattered all over," he said. "Only trouble brings us together."

"When did you hear?"

"The other day. Some caravan drivers came through."

"And you came at once? Are you afraid?"

"I've come to see what this is all about."

We talked about the imprisoned man who was my brother and his son, as if he were dead, without mentioning his name. He, who had disappeared, brought us together. We thought about him even as we talked about everything else.

My father watched me with fear and hope now, anything

PART I

that I said would be fateful for him. He did not mention his fears or expectations; he superstitiously avoided saying anything definite, fearing the evil magic of words. He merely added a last reason, the one that had in fact brought him here:

"You're respected here, you know all the important people."

"It's nothing serious. He said something he shouldn't have."

"What did he say? Can you really be imprisoned for a word?"

"Today I'll go to the musellim.* To find out why and to ask for mercy."

"Should I go as well? I'll tell them that they've made a mistake, that they've imprisoned a most honest man, that he couldn't have done anything bad. Or I'll fall on my knees, let them see paternal sorrow. And I'll pay them if need be; I'll sell everything I own and pay them, only let them release him."

"They'll release him; you don't need to go anywhere."

"Then I'll wait here. I won't leave the inn until you return. And tell them he's all I have left. I'd hoped that he would come back home, so the fire of my hearth won't die out. But I'd still sell everything, I don't need anything."

"Don't worry. Everything will be all right, with God's mercy."

I made up everything except the part about God's mercy. I did not have the heart to leave him without hope, and could not tell him that I knew nothing about my brother. My father lived in the naive belief that my presence and reputation would be a possible shield for him. I did not want to mention that my presence had not only not helped him, but that my reputation had been cast into doubt as well. How could he understand that a part of my brother's guilt had also fallen on me?

I left the inn, burdened by the duty that I had accepted

out of consideration for my father, without knowing how to perform it, oppressed by the careless words that he had blurted out in sorrow. He never would have spoken them had he been in control of himself; in this way I saw how great his sorrow was. And I also saw that he had written me off: I no longer existed for him, it was as if I were dead and my brother were all that he had left. That was what I should tell people: I'm dead for my father; my brother is all he has left, give him back to him. I no longer exist. Peace to the soul of the sinful dervish Ahmed, he's dead, he only appears to be alive. If my father had not been so stunned by his sorrow, I never would have learned what he thought about me. And now I knew it, and saw myself differently, through the eyes of someone else. Was the path that I had chosen so worthless for my father that he would bury me alive because of it? Did my calling really mean nothing to him, were we so distant from each other, so different, on such totally opposite paths that he did not even recognize my existence? He did not even regret losing me; so long ago, so thoroughly had he recovered from this loss. But maybe I was exaggerating, maybe my father would have also come as quickly on my account, if something had ever happened to me. And maybe then he would have thought only about me, because one feels closest to whoever has it the worst.

What is it that suddenly happens, what stone slips from our foundations, leaving everything to collapse and crumble? Life had seemed to be a solid edifice, without a single crack, but an unexpected tremor, meaningless and unprovoked, demolished that proud edifice as if it were made of sand.

From the hills, from the Gypsy mahal rising up at the edge of town, a drum beat deafeningly and a zurna wailed. The festivities of Saint George's Day poured down on the kasaba like rainfall, continuously, and there was nowhere one could go to escape it.

PART I

Fools, I thought, distraught, angry like the day before. They did not know that there were more important things in the world.

But my anger was not so fiery as it had been the previous night. It was not even anger, but rather indignation. That foolish celebration was a disturbance and an injustice. It deepened my anxiety, which had completely engulfed me, which had become my life and my world, so that nothing existed outside of it.

Everything I could have done was insurmountably difficult, and resembled misdeeds, or the first steps in life. But I had to do something, for myself: I was his brother. And for him: he was my brother. I would have been content with such conventional reasoning, so obvious and appealing, if there had not been this unrest in me, this restlessness full of dark foreboding, that drove me to think about my imprisoned brother with bilious anger: Why had he done this to me? At first I had tried to fend off that selfish thought. I told myself: this isn't right; you're viewing his misfortune only in terms of your own troubles. He's the blood of your blood; you should help him without thinking of yourself.

It would have been nicer that way. I would have been able to take pride in such noble thoughts, but I did not succeed in getting rid of my worries about myself. And I answered to those feeble, pure thoughts: Yes, he's my brother, but this is precisely where the difficulty lies; he's cast a shadow on me as well. People looked at me with suspicion, scorn, or pity; some turned their heads so our eyes would not meet. I tried to comfort myself, and said: This isn't possible, it only seems so to me, everyone knows that my brother's deeds, whatever they might be, are not mine.

But that was futile, people did not look at me as they had before. Those looks were hard to endure, and continually reminded me of what I wished no one knew. It is hopeless to try to stay pure and free; someone close to you will always make your life miserable.

I left the bazaar and turned onto a path beside the river, walking along its current, between the gardens and its shallow bed. People only passed by that way; no one ever stopped there. It would have been best to follow its waters far beyond the kasaba, into the plain between the mountains. I knew that it is bad when one wants to escape, but one's thoughts free themselves whenever they are troubled. Small, silvery loaches swam in the shallow water; it seemed that they never grew large, and that was good. I kept walking and watched them. I wanted to stay near them, because I did not feel at home on that path. I was supposed to be going in another direction, but I did not turn around. There is always time for things that are unpleasant.

It would be nice to be a vagabond. He can always search out good people and pleasant places, and he carries a cheerful soul that is open to the wide sky and free roads that lead nowhere and everywhere. If only men were not rooted in their small domains.

Go away from me, vile weakness; you deceive me with false images of relief, which are not even my real desire.

On the path behind me I heard a dull rumbling that almost seemed to come from underground. A large herd of cattle was moving along the river in a cloud of dust.

I stepped into a garden gate to let it pass, a monster of a hundred horned heads, blind and mad, rushing ahead of the cattle drovers' whips.

Hassan rode on horseback at the front of the herd. He was dressed in a red cape, upright, cheerful. He alone was calm and smiling in that drove, amid the angry lows, shouts, and curses that resounded in the river valley.

The man never changed.

He also recognized me, and leaving the herd, the cattle drovers, and the billowing dust, he rode up to the gate where I stood.

"I wouldn't want to ride *you* down," he said, laughing. "If it were someone else I wouldn't care."

PART I

He dismounted easily, as if he had just started out on his journey, and gave me a vigorous hug. It was strange and awkward for me to feel the grip of his hands on my shoulders. He always showed his joy openly. And it was just this joy that surprised me. Was that because of me, or was it some extravagant generosity, bestowed equally upon all? An empty vitality that overflows like water, worthless because it belongs to everyone?

He was returning from Wallachia; he had been on the road for months. I asked him although I already knew, just to say something. The night before I had been prepared to deliver him to his sister.

"You don't look well."

"I'm troubled."

"I know."

How could he have known? For almost three months he had been wandering in foreign lands; he had traveled thousands of miles trading, and as soon as he returned he heard everything. All the while I had not thought that everyone in the kasaba knew. People always find out about misfortune and evil, only good things are kept secret.

"Why is he in prison?"

"I don't know. I don't believe he could have done anything wrong."

"You'd know if he had."

"He was quiet," I said, without understanding him.

"Our people live quietly and perish suddenly. I'm sorry, for him and for you. Where is he now?"

"In the fortress."

"I greeted it from afar; I forgot what's in it. I'll come to the tekke this evening, if I won't be disturbing you."

"How would you be disturbing me?!"

"How is Hafiz-Muhammed?"

"He's well."

"He'll bury us all!" he said, laughing again.

"We'll be waiting for you this evening."

His empty, sterile kindness could neither help nor hinder me. Everything in him was empty and useless—his peaceful temperament, his cheerful disposition, his quick mind—everything was empty and superficial. Yet he was the only man in the kasaba who had offered me a word of sympathy, which, while useless, was surely sincere. I am ashamed to say, though, that it resembled alms given by a poor man; it neither warmed nor moved me.

He left ahead of the bulls' horns, which were lowered as if in attack, riding in clouds of dust that drifted above the cattle like gray bubbles, hiding them.

I had kept him at a distance, because of what had happened the night before and because of what I was expecting.

In my thoughts I crossed over the wooden bridge to the other bank, into the silent, peaceful streets, where footsteps wandered alone and houses were hidden in tree branches behind high fences, as if all things were avoiding each other, withdrawing into solitude and peace. I had no business there, but I still wanted to go, to delay everything before I attempted anything. And I might have gone to the other side, into those dead, hidden streets, where things would have been easier. But at that moment I heard the frightened beating of a drum from the direction of the bazaar, it was different from the Gypsy drums, and the shrill sounds of a trumpet from the clock tower at the wrong time. Confused, indistinct voices called out in a common distress; the scene resembled an upset beehive. People swarmed like bees, flew off in escape and returned to its defense, shouting curses and calling for help. A gray thread of smoke rose slowly above the kasaba, and it seemed as if human cries had woven themselves into that skein and become visible. Flocks of pigeons flew around it, frightened by the screams and the heat.

Soon the pillar of smoke gained strength and began billowing over the houses, thick and black. The flames spread out of control, unabated, violent, and rampant; they leaped with unconcealed joy from roof to roof, blazing over the screams and fears of the people.

I shuddered instinctively at this tragedy. We are always in some danger; something ugly is always happening somewhere. Then my own troubles distracted me; they were graver and more important than that. I even began to watch the fire with satisfaction, hoping that it would leave the people helpless, and that in this way all our misfortunes, even mine, would be resolved. But that was a momentary fit of madness, and afterward I thought nothing of it.

And so, when I already had enough reasons to turn from the path and not to do what I intended, I decided not to delay it any longer. I had not given it much thought, but maybe hope came to life in me, hope that it would be easier to speak of mercy in this tragedy, which reminded people of their fragility and helplessness before the will of God.

And I had the right to find out as much about my own brother as they were obliged to tell me or anyone else. I was bound to help him, if it were possible. It would have been unseemly for me to stand aside; I would have been reproached by everyone. Whom did I have besides him? And whom did he have besides me?

I tried to encourage myself, to justify and affirm my right, and also prepared a path of retreat. I did not forget what I had thought before, that I was afraid for myself and that I felt sorry for him. I did not even know what was more important, nor could I easily separate one from the other.

In front of the musellim's office there stood a guard with a saber at his hip and a small gun in his wide leather belt. I had never been there before; I had never thought that armed guards might stand in the way.

"Is the musellim in his office?"

"Why?"

I secretly hoped that the musellim would not be in, there was a fire in the town, and he had all sorts of other affairs to look after. It would be strange if he were there just when I came to see him. Maybe that hidden thought, that I would not find him, had induced me to come in the first place. And I would leave, putting off my visit for another day. But when the guard, with his hand on the handle of his gun, impudently asked me something that was not his business, anger flared in me, as if a vent had been found for my restlessness, which could hardly wait to escape, no matter how. I was a dervish, the sheikh of a tekke, and a soldier could not address me in such a manner, with his hand on his gun, not even because of the garb that I wore. I was truly insulted, but later it occurred to me how we avenge our fear where we can. His question was rude; it emphasized his authority and importance and indicated my worthlessness, showing me that even the order to which I belonged did not command any respect. But all of this could not serve as an excuse to leave. If he had said that the musellim was out, or that he was not seeing anyone that day, I would have been grateful to him and left with a feeling of relief.

"I'm the sheikh of the Mevlevi tekke," I said softly, quelling my anger. "I need to see the musellim."

The guard looked at me calmly, not in the least impressed by my words, suspicious, offensively indifferent to what I had said. I was frightened by his vicious composure, and it seemed that he might easily draw his flintlock and shoot me dead, without joy or anger. Or that he might admit me to see the musellim. It was he who had been after my fugitive the night before; he had taken my brother to the fortress; he was guilty before them. And they were guilty before me. It was on their account that I was there.

Without haste, expecting something more from me, a rebuke or an appeal, he called another guard from the corridor and told him that some dervish wanted to see the musellim. I did not protest at this depersonalization; maybe it was better that way. Now the musellim would not be refusing me, but some nameless dervish.

We waited for that message to pass through the corridors

and for the answer to come back. The guard returned to his post, without looking at me, with his hand on his flintlock. It did not matter to him whether I would be admitted or refused. His dark, lean face radiated a tranquil arrogance, with which that place nurtured him.

As I waited, I began to regret that I had stubbornly insisted on overcoming this obstacle, thinking that it was trivial. Instead it turned out to be the same as the musellim, an extension of his hand. I could no longer leave. I had nailed myself to that spot, I had put myself in a situation where they would either have to let me in or turn me away. I did not know which was worse. I had intended to pay the musellim a visit, since we knew each other, and to start a conversation about my brother in a casual manner. Now this was impossible. I had set a whole string of people in motion and demanded that he see me. Our conversation could no longer be casual; it had acquired an official character. And if I talked in a low voice, humbly, it would be an admission of cowardice. I wanted to maintain both my dignity and my caution. Impudence would not help me, and it was not one of my traits; humility would have degraded me, although I felt it in every fiber of my being.

It would have been better if he refused me, I was upset and unprepared. I tried in vain to think of what to say, tried in vain to imagine the expression that I would wear into his room. I saw the contorted features of a flustered man who did not even know what had driven him to take such a step. Was it love for his brother, fear for himself, regard for his father? I saw the man fearful, as if he were doing something forbidden, as if he were risking everything. What was I risking? I did not know, and therefore I say: everything.

They called me in.

The musellim stood at the window, watching the fire. When he turned around, I saw that his face was blank, and I did not detect even a flicker of recognition in his eyes. That motionless face did nothing to encourage me.

For the brief moment that I looked into his inhospitable eyes, which were waiting to pass judgment on me, I felt like a guilty man. I stood somewhere between him and an unknown crime that I had committed, and his eyes put me at a distance, pushing me toward that offense.

I could have begun the conversation in a number of ways had I not been so nervous. Calmly: I haven't come to defend my brother, but to inquire about him. Magnanimously: he's guilty because of the very fact that he's in prison; may I know what he's done? Moderately offended: he's in prison; very well, it would've been proper for you to let me know. I needed to begin with some intention, with some definite aim, showing more firmness in this affair, but I chose the worst way. I did not even choose it, it imposed itself.

"I wanted to ask about my brother," I said confusedly, beginning as I should not have, without confidence. I immediately exposed my weak spot, without succeeding to prepare a more advantageous reception and impression. That face, heavy with sleep, forced me to say something, anything, all at once, so that he would recognize me, so that he would notice me.

"Brother? What brother?"

In that deaf question, in his dead voice, in his surprise at my assumption that he should know something so trivial, I felt that my brother and I had been reduced to the size of grains of dust.

May I be forgiven by all honorable people who are more courageous than I, by all good people who have not experienced the temptation to forget their pride, but I must say this, since it would not help if I hid the truth from myself: his intentional rudeness did not offend me, nor did the terrible distance that he kept between us. It frightened me, because it was unexpected; I felt restless and threatened. My brother did not serve as a possible bond between us; he had to be revived, to be brought before the musellim for the first time, and therefore his guilt would have to be determined for the first time. But what could I say without also inflicting damage on my brother and insulting the musellim?

I said that I regretted what had happened. This misfortune had hit me like the death of a close relative, fate had not protected me from the pain of seeing my own brother taken to the place where sinners and criminals go, or from the pain of being watched with surprise, as if I also bore a part of the guilt, I who for years had been serving God and the faith honorably. And as I said this I knew that it was loathsome. I was committing a betrayal, but these words flowed easily and sincerely, and this lament of my fate unfolded by itself, right until my conscience spoke so strongly and so loudly that I became disgusted at the sweet tears that I was shedding for myself, at the cowardice that I could find no real reason for, at the selfishness that stifled all of my other thoughts. No! something cried in me, this is shameful, whom did you come to defend? Yourself? From what? It's your brother who is in danger, afterward you'll be ashamed, you'll worsen his position, be quiet and leave, speak and leave, speak and stay, look him in the eye, it's only his phantom face that frightens you, silence your groundless fear, you have nothing to be afraid of, don't disgrace yourself complaining to him and yourself, say only what you must.

And I said it. That my brother, *as I have heard*, has done something that *maybe* he shouldn't have, I don't know, but I don't believe that it's anything serious, and therefore I'm appealing to the musellim to look into the matter so the prisoner won't also be accused of something that he hasn't done.

What I said was not enough, it lacked both courage and honesty. But it was all that I could do. A heavy fatigue came over me.

His face said nothing. It revealed neither anger nor understanding; either condemnation or kindness could have issued from his lips. Later I recalled with uncertainty how it occurred to me then that everyone who begs is in a terrible position: he is necessarily small and insignificant, squirming beneath someone's foot, guilty, humiliated; threatened by the whims of others and vulnerable to their power, he wishes for some inadvertent good will; nothing depends on him, not even an expression of fear or hatred that might ruin him. Under that dull gaze, which hardly saw me, I ceased to expect kind words or mercy, I wanted only to leave, to let everything end as Allah wished.

Finally the musellim spoke, in a voice as dead as his silence, but I no longer cared. Over the years he had grown accustomed to this attitude of impenetrability and scorn. But I did not care about that either. I felt slightly nauseated.

"Your brother, you say? In prison?"

I looked through the window. The fire was out. There was only some smoke, black and sluggish, drifting above the bazaar. It was a pity that it had not destroyed everything.

"Do you know why he's in prison?"

"I've come to ask."

"So, you don't even know why he's in prison. And you've come to beg, regardless of what he's done."

"I haven't come to beg."

"Do you want to accuse him?"

"No."

"Can you bring witnesses for him or against him? Can you point to any other guilty parties? Or accomplices?"

"No."

"Then what do you want?"

He spoke lazily, interrupting himself and turning his head to the side, as if he were insulted, as if he were displeased that he had to explain such obvious things and waste his time with such an unreasonable man.

A feeling of shame came over me: because of my fear and cowardly selfishness, because of his scorn, because of his right to rudeness, because of the boredom that he did not try to hide, because he had humiliated me, and talked with me as if I were a servant, a softa,* or a criminal. I was used to listening without objecting and to bowing my head. This inquiry about my brother even seemed like a transgression to me, but my old habits were stifled by the arrogance of this cruel man, or maybe more so by his vulgar impoliteness. I felt myself turning livid with rage, although I knew that this could not help me. It did not matter to him, but it did to me, and that was exactly what he wanted, what he was trying to do. No, he did not even have to try, he simply radiated a feeling of disgust at people. I did not know why he insisted on creating enemies, and it was not my concern, but how did he dare to behave like this toward me? I was still deceived by my ideas about the importance of my calling and the order to which I belonged.

People live quietly and die suddenly, Hassan had said, that strange cattle drover who never acted rashly or suffered because of his imprudence. And I had also believed that I was immune to any surprises that might come from within me.

"What do I want?" I said, startled at myself, aware that what I was saying was inappropriate. "You shouldn't have said that. Is it a crime to inquire about one's brother, whatever he's done? That's my duty, according to the laws of both God and men. People would spit on me if I neglected my right to do so. And we would all deserve to be spit upon if that right were ever questioned. Have we become animals, or worse than animals?"

"Your words are serious," he said in the same calm manner, only his heavy eyes narrowed somewhat. "Who's right in this affair? You're defending your brother, and I the law. The law is strict. I serve it."

"If the law is strict, must we then act viciously?"

"Is it vicious to defend the law, or to attack it, as you are?"

I wanted to tell him that it was vicious to be cruel in any circumstances. Men perish suddenly. It was good that I did not answer his challenge. He felt a need to drive people insane; it pleased him.

Afterwards I felt dejected. My anger passed quickly, and was replaced by regret at such rashness—it was not typical of me. I had responded to him sharply because I was too tense, unable to restrain my impulses. Everything done at such moments is usually harmful: it is a form of stupid heroism, a suicidal defiance with no purpose, which lasts but for a short time, leaving behind only discontent with itself. And a belated hindsight that does no one any good.

What I had feared most had happened, I had been told that my defense of my brother was in opposition to the law. If that were really true, or, since I knew that it was not, if it only seemed so to someone, if people thought that I considered a personal loss more important than anything around me, then everything had ended in the worst possible way, and my vague fears had been justified. And worst of all was the fact that I had not really defended my brother, I had only rebelled against terrible cruelty in a moment of irrationality. I had not been on either side, not on my brother's, not on the musellim's. I had been nowhere.

I was glad that it was almost noon and that I would not be alone. My prayers would sequester me from this day, and I would leave my painful thoughts at the gates of the mosque. They would certainly wait for me, but I would be away from them for at least a while.

When I took my place before the few believers gathered there and began the prayer, I felt more acutely than ever the protective peace of that familiar place, of the thick, warm odor of melted wax, of the healing calm of its white walls and its sooty ceiling, of the motherly tenderness of sunlight gleaming on golden motes of dust. That was my domain—the threadbare rugs, the copper candlesticks, the prayer-niche where I bowed in front of people humbly on their knees—that was my silence and security. I had belonged there for years: I knew the spot in the carpet where I placed my feet; its patterns were worn and faded. In performing my sacred duties there from day to day, I had left my trace on something that endures longer than we do. That place had become mine, ours, and God's, although I denied, maybe even to myself, that it was mostly mine. But that day, at that noon, freed from my nightmare, returned to that tranquil silence from a strange world I was not accustomed to, I did not actually perform my duties. I was sure that I served no one, and that everything served me, that everything shielded me and brought me back, erasing my murky, bad dreams. I dove into the pleasure of that familiar prayer, and aided by everything that had been mine for years, by familiar odors, by the indistinct murmur of the people, by the dull thud of their knees on the floor, by unchanging prayers, and by a circle that closed like a line of defense or a fortress, affirming and justifying me, I felt that my lost balance was returning. Performing the prayer by habit, without interrupting it, I watched a ray of sunlight that shone through a windowpane and reached from the window to my hand, as if at play, challenging me. I could hear the cheerful, twittering banter of the sparrows outside the mosque, the unceasing tones of their voices. They seemed brightly yellow, like wheat, or the sun. Something warm and serene hovered around me, separating me, waking memories of something that had once existed, I knew not when or where, but it had, and I had no need to revive it. It was vibrant, strong, and precious as it had once been, like it had never been, shapeless and therefore all-encompassing. I knew it had existed, maybe in my childhood, which no longer remained in my memory but rather in my grief, maybe in my desire that it become and be, translucent, weightless, like a soft movement, like the silent flow of water, like the silent rush of blood, like sunny joy at nothing. And I knew that it was sin, this absorption in prayer, this delight of the body and mind, but I could not tear myself away, I did not want to end this peculiar oblivion.

But then it ended on its own.

It seemed to me that the fugitive from the night before was standing behind me, among the people in prayer. I did not dare to turn around, but I was sure that he was in the mosque. Maybe he had come in after me, or I had not seen him. His voice sounded different from the others, deeper and more masculine; his prayer was not an appeal but a demand; his eyes were sharp, his movements supple. His name was Is-haq, or at least that was what I called him, since he was there and I did not know his name. But I should have known it. He had come on account of me, to thank me. Or on account of himself, to hide. We would be left alone after the prayer, so that I could ask him what I had not had the chance to ask the previous night. Is-haq, I repeated, Is-haq. That was the name of my uncle, whom as a child I had loved dearly. Is-haq—I did not know why I made a connection between them, how and why I so persistently yearned for my childhood. It was surely an escape. An escape from everything that was, an attempt to save myself with an unconscious memory and a mad, impossible desire to deny reality. If I had really believed it, I would have been driven to despair. But like this, it even became reality, at moments of warped, hazy rapture, when my body and unknown inner powers searched for my lost peace. At that moment I was not aware that oblivion lasts only for a short time, but when the thought of Is-haq appeared, I knew that my peace had been disturbed. For Is-haq also belonged to that world which I did not want to think about, and maybe for that very reason I wanted to relegate him to the distant realm of dreams, not to think about him when we were not meeting face to face. I wanted to turn around; my prayer was empty for him, reduced to words without meaning, longer than it had ever been.

What would I talk about with him? He did not want to say anything about himself, I had become convinced of that the previous night. We would talk about me. We would sit there, in the empty space of the mosque, in the world and yet outside it, alone. He would smile with his confident, distant smile, which was not a smile but a piercing coldness, a look that saw everything but wondered at nothing. He would listen to me attentively, absorbed in the pattern in the carpet in front of him or in a ray of sunlight that stubbornly penetrated the sparkling, dusty darkness. And he would tell me the truth, which would ease my burden.

Imagining that conversation, I revived his face, and was not surprised that I remembered so much of it. I waited for us to be left alone, like the night before, to continue that unusual conversation openly. In a moment of utter inconsistency that restless, rebellious man, whose ideas contradicted everything that I could believe, seemed to me like someone whom I could rely on. Everything he did was mad, everything he said was unacceptable, but I could confide only in him, because he was unhappy yet honest; he did not know what he wanted, yet he knew what he was doing; he could kill yet would not cheat. And while in my heart I counted the good features of that completely unknown renegade, I failed to notice how far I had come since the previous night. In the morning I had wanted to hand him over to the guards, but at noon I was on his side. But I had not even been against him in the morning, and although I might have still turned him in right then, these two matters had nothing to do with each other. Or maybe they did, but in a bizarre way, very intricately. In fact, the only thing I was sure of was that Is-haq the rebel could explain some things that had been tied into a knot inside me. He alone. I did not know why, maybe because he had suffered and gained experience in his distress; because his rebellion had freed him from established ways of thinking that bind us, and he had no prejudices; because he had purged himself of fear and taken a path that led nowhere; because he was already condemned and was only delaying his death heroically. Such people know a lot, more than those of us who stagger from learned rules to fear of sin, from habits to worries of possible guilt. And although I would never have taken the path of a renegade, not even in my thoughts, I would gladly have listened to his truth. But what was his truth?

I did not know.

I would tell him this:

I went off to school when I was a small child and have been a dervish for twenty years, but I know nothing more than what they wanted me to learn. They taught me to be obedient, to endure, and to live for the faith. Some were better than I, but few were more faithful. I always knew what I should do. Although the dervish order thought for me, the principles of its faith are firm and thorough, and nothing of mine existed that couldn't fit into them. I had a family, which lived its own life; it was mine according to my blood and distant memory, according to a childhood that I've been trying to bury ever since, mistakenly believing it to be dead. It was mine because that is how it should be. I cherished that love from a distance, without benefit, although for this reason it was even cold. My family existed, it was mine, and that was enough for me. And it was probably enough for them. Three visits in these twenty years have neither harmed nor helped anything; they've neither disturbed nor aided my service to the faith, although I felt more pride in finding a larger family than sorrow because I'd strayed from my original one. And now, it happened that my brother was struck by misfortune. I say this word because I don't know the right one, since I can't say whether it was just or unjust, and that's the source of the trouble. I don't like violence, it's a sign of weakness and bad judgment, a means by which people are driven to do evil. And yet, when it was exercised against others I kept silent and refused to condemn it. I either shifted the responsibility onto someone else or refused to think about what wasn't my fault, even admitting that it's occasionally necessary to commit evil for a higher and greater good. But when the rulers' whips struck my brother, they drew my blood as well. I somehow think that this action is cruel: I know that boy; he's not capable of crime. And so, I'm not doing enough to defend him, but I'm not justifying them, either. It only seems to me that they've all inflicted evil on me, almost equally, they've disturbed me, forced me to confront a life beyond my own. They've forced me to take a side. What am I now? Some twisted kind of brother, or an unsteady dervish? Have I lost my love for mankind, or weakened the faith, thus losing everything? I'd like to weep for my brother, whatever he is, or to be a firm defender of the law, even if my brother is in question, even regretfully. But I can do neither. What is it, Is-haq, you rebellious martyr, who have taken one side, and don't know indecision? Have I lost my human face, or my faith? Or both? And what, then, is left of me—a shell, a grave, a tombstone with no inscription? Fear has settled inside me, Is-haq, fear and confusion; I no longer dare to do anything for either side. I'll lose my way and perish.

I did not turn around to look at him, I did not believe that he was still there, nor did I know what I could tell him of all this pain, which did not even have a name. And the thought, that I would entrust him with what I would not tell anyone else, was dangerous. I had not chosen a dervish or any of the people whom I knew, but a renegade, a fugitive, a man outside of the law. Did I believe that only he would not be surprised if he heard it? Did I believe that only he would not look upon me with reproach? Help me, O God, to emerge from these trials the same man that I was. And the only way out that I really saw was for nothing to have happened.

> Salvation and peace to Ibrahim,
> Salvation and peace to Musa and Harun,
> Salvation and peace to Ilyas,[2]
> Salvation and peace to Is-haq,
> Salvation and peace to the unhappy Ahmed Nuruddin.

People went out, coughing and softly whispering. They

left me, and I remained alone on my knees before my pain. Fortunately and unfortunately, I was alone, afraid to abandon this place where I could torture myself with indecision.

A commotion began outside; someone was shouting, someone was making threats—I did not want to hear those words; I did not want to know who was shouting and who was making threats. Everything that happens in the world is ugly. O God, receive the prayer of my weakness; take away my strength and my desire to leave this silence; return me to peace, either the first or last. I thought that something existed between them, a river that had once flowed, its surface covered with the sun's reflection, shrouded in mist at dusk. It still existed in me; I thought that I had forgotten it, but it seems that nothing is ever forgotten; everything returns from the drawers in which we lock it, from the darkness of apparent oblivion, and everything that we thought belonged to no one is ours. We do not need it, but it stands before us, shimmering in its former existence, reminding and tormenting us. And taking revenge for our betrayal. It is late, O memories, you have come in vain, your powerless solace is useless, as are your reminders of what might have been, since what never happened was never even possible. And what never happened always seems beautiful. You are a deception that gives birth to discontent, a deception that I cannot and do not wish to drive away, since it disarms me and protects me from suffering with a quiet grief.

My father was waiting for me, distraught because of his son, who was all that he had left. I did not exist, and neither did his son: the old man was alone; he waited for me in the inn, alone. Once we had thought that we were one, now we thought nothing at all. First his eyes would ask me, and I would respond with a smile. I would still have that much strength, because of him: I have been told that my brother will be released soon. I would send him away with hope: Why should he leave heartbroken? He would receive no benefit from the truth. And I would return saddened.

I breathed in the fresh May night; it was young and effervescent. I love spring, I thought, I love springtime, it is unwearied and unburdened, it wakes us with a cheerful, lighthearted call to begin anew. It is the deception and hope of each new year; new buds sprout on old trees. I love springtime, I shouted inside myself stubbornly. I forced myself to believe in it; for many years I had hidden springtime from myself, but now I was calling it, offering myself unto it. I touched the blossoms and smooth, new branches of an apple tree at the side of the path; sap rushed in its countless veins. I felt their pulsing, I wished that it would enter me through my fingertips, so that apple blossoms might sprout from my fingers and translucent green leaves from my palms, so that I would become the tender scent of fruit, its silent carelessness. I would carry my blossoming hands before my astonished eyes and extend them to the nourishing rain. I would be rooted in the ground, fed by the sky, renewed by the spring, laid to rest by autumn. How good it would be to begin everything anew.

But there could be no new beginning, nor would one be important. We are not aware when new beginnings arrive; we only discover them later when they have already engulfed us, when everything merely continues. Then we believe that everything could have been different, but it could not have, and so we rush into springtime, so as not to think about nonexistent beginnings or unpleasant continuations.

I walked the streets in vain, trying to pass time that would not pass. Hassan was waiting for me in the tekke. That morning my father had waited for me in the inn, and now in the evening Hassan in the tekke. They were on all paths and at every corner; they did not allow me to leave my worries behind. "Let me know as soon as they release him," my father had said as he left. "I won't rest until I hear it. It'd be best if he came home."

It would have been best if he had never left home.

"Go to the musellim tomorrow," he reminded me, so I

would not forget. "And thank him. Thank him in my name."

I was glad that he left; it was hard to look him in the face. He sought a solace that I could offer only with lies. He left with both of them, and all that remained was an ugly memory. We stopped at the edge of the field, I kissed his hand and he kissed me on the forehead. He was my father again. I watched him as he went, stooped, leading his horse almost as if he were leaning on it. He kept turning around, constantly. I felt better when we had parted, but I was sad and lonely. We had parted for good; there could no longer be any mistake about it. We buried one another the very moment that we saw each other for what we were—our last, useless bit of warmth could no longer help us.

I still was standing in the middle of the wide field when my father mounted his horse and disappeared behind a cliff, as if he had been swallowed by the gray rock.

A long afternoon shadow, the somber soul of the hills, crept over the field, darkening it. It passed over me and surrounded me on all sides, the sunlight fled from it, retreating toward the opposite hill. Night was still far away; that was only one of its early signs, but there was something ominous in those dark forerunners. There was no one on this field split by shadow: both halves of it were empty; I alone stood in that divided place as it grew dimmer. I was small in the space that was closing around me, preoccupied by a murky anxiety that I carried in my ancient soul, foreign yet mine. Alone in the field, alone in the world, powerless before the secrets of the earth and the expanse of the sky. But then, from somewhere in the hills, from the houses on the slopes, a song rang out. It penetrated the sunlit area of the field right up to my shadow, as if coming to my assistance, and indeed set me free from that brief, absurd spell.

I did not escape Hassan's unsolicited attention. He was sitting with Hafiz-Muhammed on the terrace upstairs, above the river. His soft beard neatly trimmed, he was dressed in a blue mintan,* and wore the aroma of fragrant oils. He was fresh and smiling; he had cleansed himself of three months of travel, of the smell of cattle, sweat, inns, dust, and mud. He had forgotten about curses, mountain passes, dangerous fords through rivers; now he resembled a young aga spoiled by life, which demanded neither effort nor courage from him.

I found them in the middle of a conversation. This cattle drover and former muderris was goading Hafiz-Muhammed into expounding upon his knowledge, so he could contradict him, jokingly, attaching no importance to what he heard or answered. I always wondered at his ability to arrive at clever arguments in casual conversations, disguising them as foolish remarks.

When we had greeted each other, he asked me: "Have you learned anything about your brother?"

"No. I'll go again tomorrow. And you, how was your trip?"

That was best. My worries should be left to me.

He made a few ordinary remarks about his trip, joking about how it always depended on God's will and the cattle's temper, and how he changed his will and temper according to theirs. Then he suggested that Hafiz-Muhammed continue his exposition, which was very interesting and very dubious, about the origin and development of life, a question of significance as long as living beings would exist, and suitable for debate, especially at a time when there were no debates and we all died of boredom agreeing with each other about everything.

Hafiz-Muhammed, who for three months had either kept quiet or only talked about the most ordinary things, continued his exposition on the origin of the world, which was strange and inexact, and unsupported by the Koran. But the picture that he developed was interesting. Taken from one of the many books that he had read (God only knows which one), and enlivened by his imagination, it glittered with the fire of his lonesome fevers, when in delirious visions he saw the beginning and end of the world. It seemed like blasphemy, but we had already become accustomed to it. We hardly considered him a real dervish: he had won the right to be irresponsible, the most beautiful and rarest right in our order, and the things that he sometimes said were not considered too harmful, since they were mostly incomprehensible.

It seemed to me very unusual, almost unimaginable, that a naive scholar would discuss the origin of the world with a clever wag, a good-natured joker, a former alim* turned cattle drover and caravan escort. It was as if the devil himself had worked to bring those two totally different men together and to engage them in a conversation that no one could have foreseen.

This young man surprised me again and again with something unexpected that was not easy to explain or justify. Although he was intelligent and educated, everything he did was odd, and none of it predictable. He had finished school in Constantinople, wandered in the East, he had taught as a muderris in a madrasah,* worked as an official at the Porte* and as a military officer, but he left all of that behind. He went to Dubrovnik for some reason, and returned to the kasaba with a Dubrovnik[3] merchant and his wife. People said that he was in love with that fair-skinned Catholic woman with black hair and grey eyes, who now lived with her husband in the Latin mahal.[4] He brought a suit against a distant relative who had taken over his estate and then dropped it when he saw how many children that wretched man had to feed. He married one of the man's daughters, whom they had thrust upon him as payment for the estate, but when he realized what they had bestowed upon him, fled without looking back. He left all of them in his house and became a merchant, traveling in the East and West, to the horror of his family. It was hard to say how he had combined so many trades, or which one of them was his real line of work. None of them, he would say laughing; a man has to live from something, and in the end it is all the same. He was too talkative for service at the Porte, too tempestuous for a muderris, too educated for a cattle drover. People said that he had been driven out of Constantinople; just as many stories circulated about his honesty as did about his dishonesty, about his exceptional abilities as about his utter incompetence. People said he was heartless when he took up the suit about his estate, and that he was a fool when he dropped it; some said that he was shameless because he lived with the lady from Dubrovnik, along with her idiot husband, and others said that he was the idiot because the woman and her husband were taking advantage of him. He was passed again and again through the fine sieve of kasaba gossip, a convenient subject for hundreds of nosy rumors, especially in the beginning, before they grew accustomed to him. But he dismissed everything with a wave of his hand, it was all the same to him, as was everything else in life. He associated with everyone: he conversed with muderrises, traded with merchants, drank with ruffians, laughed with journeymen. He was everyone's equal in anything he did, but still a failure at everything.

I did not want to talk with Hassan about my brother. He would have been saddened, but not for long; embittered, but not for long. And I was troubled by the previous night's conversation with his sister. I would have preferred for him not to have come.

Fortunately, he was not pushy. And fortunately, he was interested in their conversation. In that way I was able to delay everything for a while.

Hafiz-Muhammed said that moisture and warmth were the sources of life. The first living creatures sprang up in a rotten dankness, where they had been developing for a long time, without real form, without limbs, tiny round and oblong shapes glowing with the power of life. They swam in their dark blindness, roaming aimlessly, living in water, crawling ashore, burrowing in the mud. Thousands of years had thus passed . . .

"And God?" Hassan asked.

That was a jocular, yet serious question. Hafiz-Muhammed ignored it.

"Thousands of years thus passed and those small, helpless creatures changed. Some of them adapted to dry land, others to water. They were born deaf and blind, without arms or legs, without anything, and everything developed slowly, according to necessity and after many failed attempts."

"And God?"

"God wanted it so."

He had to say that, although it did not sound convincing. But with this inviolable, general assertion Hafiz-Muhammed was removing an inconvenient obstacle more than he was responding to a challenge.

I was surprised at how they both behaved. Hafiz-Muhammed truly denied the role of God in the creation of the world, and Hassan only referred to it in jest, without desiring to pursue the issue or to exploit an advantage that he could easily have gained.

I knew that what Hafiz-Muhammed was saying was only a slight modification of the teachings of the Greek philosophers, which had been adopted by Avicenna[5] in his works in Arabic. According to those teachings, man gradually became what he is, adapting to nature slowly, subduing it, the only creature with an intellect. For this reason nature was no longer a secret to him, the space around him no longer a mystery; he conquered and overcame it after his long ascent from worm to master of the earth.

"A bad master," said Hassan, laughing.

That was how the argument and their whole conversation had begun: man had set up the world badly, as Hassan had asserted, although he was not angry that it was so. But Hafiz-Muhammed did not agree, and sought his proof as far back as the beginning of the world.

PART I

A hundred objections could be made against what Hafiz-Muhammed was saying, from his view of the origin of life, which had occurred spontaneously, to his assertion that man was master of the earth, almost independent of God's will. But when I joined their conversation, I did not reproach him for these transgressions; it seemed silly to argue about such familiar issues. Something else was more important to me: was it not naive to think that man was comfortably settled on earth and that this was his true home?

Space is our prison, I said, listening to the echoes of my unfamiliar thoughts, thus bringing an unexpected verve into that dead and unnecessary conversation. Space owns us. We own it only as much as our eyes can pass over it. And it wearies us, scares us, challenges us, pursues us. We think that it sees us, but we don't matter to it; we say that we've overcome it, but we only make use of its indifference. The earth isn't friendly to us; lightning and the waves of the sea aren't here for us; rather, we exist in them. Man has no true home, he can only wrest one away from those blind powers. And the earth is a foreign domain; it could be a dwelling only for any monsters that might be able to come to grips with its abundant plights. Or else it's no one's. Certainly not ours.

We haven't conquered the earth, but only a clod to put our feet on; we haven't conquered mountains, but only their image in our eyes; we haven't conquered the sea, but only its resilient firmness and the reflection of its surface. Nothing is ours but illusion, and therefore we hold onto it firmly.

We're not something in the world, but nothing in it; we're not equal to what's around us, but different, incompatible with it. In his development, man should strive for the loss of his self-consciousness. The earth is uninhabitable, like the moon, and we only delude ourselves thinking that it's our true home, since we have no other place to go. The earth is good for those who are irrational or invulnerable. Maybe mankind will find a way out by going back, by becoming sheer strength.

Yet when I had said all of these absurdities, I became fearful that I had exposed everything that I wanted to conceal. I had responded to the present day and to my own bitterness. I had put both myself and them in an awkward situation.

Hafiz-Muhammed looked at me with surprise, almost frightened, but Hassan smiled absentmindedly. Only in their eyes could I see the full weight of these words that I had not thought about beforehand. But my conscience did not reproach me, and I even felt better.

The expression on Hassan's face became unexpectedly composed. No, he told me, slowly shaking his head, as if to excuse himself for speaking seriously. Man shouldn't become his opposite. Everything of any value in him is vulnerable. Maybe it's not easy to live in this world, but if we don't think that we belong here, so much the worse for us. And to wish for strength and insensitivity is to take revenge for our disenchantment. Therefore, that's not a way out; it's giving up on everything that man might achieve. Denial of all responsibility is a primeval fear, the ancient essence of man, who wishes for power because he is afraid.

"We're here, on the earth," said Hafiz-Muhammed, flustered. "To deny that this is our place is to deny life. Because . . ."

He started coughing, and went on waving his hand to show that he did not agree with me, but did not manage to soothe his agitated illness.

"You should go to your room," Hassan suggested to him. "It's cold and damp. Do you want me to help you?"

He refused with a wave of his hand; it was not necessary. And he left, coughing. He did not like for people to witness his illness.

Hassan and I were left alone.

It was a pity that we could not part without explanation or further words. It would have been best to get up and leave. Our discussion was one that was hard either to interrupt or continue, and Hafiz-Muhammed was no longer there to serve as a link between us and as a reason for general conversation. We were awaited by matters that concerned only him and me.

But Hassan did not feel uncomfortable; he always found a way to make everything natural. As Hafiz-Muhammed walked away he shifted his eyes to me and laughed. His laugh was his path to people. It expressed understanding and put them at ease.

"You frightened Hafiz-Muhammed. He looked astonished."

"I'm sorry."

"Do you know what I was thinking while you spoke? That some people can say whatever they want, and whether you agree or not, it doesn't upset you. Others throw themselves into a single word, and suddenly everything glows red-hot and no one can keep calm. We sense that something important is happening. That's no longer conversation."

"Then what is it?"

"Readiness to set everything on fire. Your brother's misfortune has hit you too hard."

Normally I would not have allowed anyone to speak with me like that; I would have forbidden it angrily. But he stunned me with his ability to guess the essence of my rebellion, and still more with his good intentions. They were not conveyed so much by his words as they were by his eyes, his deep sincerity, understanding, and concern, in the entire attitude that he projected, as if he had seen me only then, a side of me that was usually hidden. But I did not forbid him, I still wanted to turn the conversation to other things. I did not like anyone prying into my life.

"What did you mean when you spoke of the primeval fear that we've been carrying since ancient times?"

"Is this really the first time that we've met? I'd like to talk about your brother. If it's not unpleasant for you."

I could have told him: this isn't your concern, leave me alone, stay out of my secret places, I'm sick of people giving me advice. That would have been most sincere. But I could not stand rudeness, not mine or anybody else's. I felt ashamed when it got the better of me and remembered it for a long time when I encountered it in others. Excusing myself, I said that my father had come to see me today and that I was not in the best of moods.

"This is the second time that you've refused me," he said laughing.

"What can I tell you? I haven't found anything out."

"Not even why he's in prison?"

"Not even that."

"Then I know more than you do."

He was not easy to refuse.

He told me a strange tale, one that I could barely comprehend with my narrow and limited experience, which was childlike because of my unfamiliarity with the world that I lived in.

Near the town there used to live a small landowner, Hassan said, he lived, and now he's dead. It's hard to say whether he had a real reason, because something had hurt him, or whether he was naive, or honest, whether he was hot-tempered, a ruffian, an idealist, whether he had someone backing him or had proof, whether he was crazy, or whether he didn't care what happened to him; it's hard to say and now it's not important, either, but that man began to say the worst things about certain people in power, accusing them loudly and openly of what everyone knows but no one ever mentions. They let him know nicely that he should straighten up, but he thought they were afraid of him and kept doing things that didn't do anyone any good. Then they sent soldiers after him, tied him up, and brought him to the kasaba, locked him in the fortress, wrote out interrogations in which this unfortunate man admitted to many sins and himself quoted his own words against the faith, the state, the sultan, and the vali,* explaining that he had spoken in anger and rage. He admitted that he had even maintained contacts with rebels in the Krayina,[6] that he had aided them, and that his house had been a meeting-place for their messengers and confidants. They sent him along with all of the transcripts to the vizier* in Travnik,[7] but on the way they sabered him to death, because he tried to escape. Now regarding that attempted escape, people can think what they want; maybe he tried to escape or maybe not; it was all the same to him anyway, because the vizier would have killed him if the soldiers hadn't. And Hassan wouldn't be telling me about him, that man wasn't the first or the last, if my brother hadn't been mixed up in all of it. And my brother didn't even know him; he probably never even saw him, and that man probably never even knew of my brother's existence; his fate would have been the same even if my brother hadn't become involved. They didn't know each other, they were different and yet somehow similar: there was something suicidal in each of them. Unfortunately, my brother worked for the kadi. Unfortunately, he says, because being close to powerful men is dangerous and difficult. As a trusted clerk he had access to secret documents. How he came across them no one will ever know; they certainly didn't show them to him, he must have found them by accident, and they were the most fateful thing he could have found.

"What did he find?"

"He found the transcripts of the man's interrogation, written before he was interrogated, before he was imprisoned, before he was even brought to the kasaba, and in that lay their fatefulness and danger. Do you understand? They knew in advance what he would say, what he would admit, what would kill him. Very well, it's not that unusual; they were in a hurry; they needed to finish everything quickly and safely, and everything would have remained the way it was if the young clerk had left that prepared interrogation where he had found it. And forgotten what he had seen. But he didn't. I don't know what he did; maybe he showed it to someone, maybe he said something about it, maybe they caught him with the documents—anyway, they imprisoned him. He knew too much."

I listened with disbelief. What was this? Madness? The terror that seizes us in bad dreams? The dark side of life, of which most people never get a glimpse? It seemed unbelievable that a man could be unaware of so much. Had people been silent before me? Had this been whispered too softly for me to hear? Had I been ready in advance not to believe it, since this discovery would have jolted me out of the calm that I had achieved and ruined the image that I had created of a fairly balanced world, in which I had a place? Even if I had not thought that it was perfect, I had believed that it was bearable, so how could I now accept that it was unjust? Someone might have doubted the sincerity of my words and asked me: How is it that a grown man who has lived for so many years among people, in the belief that he is close to them and can see what they hide from others, and who is not stupid, does not know what is going on around him, all of which is anything but trivial? Was that hypocrisy? Or blindness? If it were not sinful to take oaths, I would swear firmly that I had not known. I considered justice a necessity and guilt a possibility. And all of this was too complicated for my naive ideas about life, which had been formed in isolation and obedience; a lot of dark imagination would have been necessary to enter those intricate relationships, which I accepted as a difficult and honorable, though rather vague struggle for divine knowledge. Or had people hidden this from me, careful not to mention what I would not want to hear? That was hard to believe. And even then, when I had heard, I was prepared not to believe it, at least not entirely: to believe this was to be deathly afraid, or to take action—I did not even have words to express the unknown duty that my conscience would thrust upon me. I admit, and I am not ashamed of it, the sincerity of my thoughts justifies me, that Hassan's very character diminished the importance of the information he passed on. He was well intentioned but superficial, honest but reckless, and his irresponsible imagination could invent God-knows-what kinds of tales, adding a load of conjecture onto a grain of truth. He had just returned from his trip, how could he know?

I asked him, searching for some solid ground to stand on: "How did you find out?"

"By accident," he said calmly, as if expecting that question.

"Maybe it's all just speculation, empty talk?"

"It's not speculation or empty talk."

"The man who told you this, is he in a position to know?"

"He knows only what I've told you."

"Who is he?"

"I can't tell you, nor is it important. He wouldn't tell you any more than this. What else do you need to hear?"

"Nothing."

"He was so scared that I felt sorry for him."

"Then why did he tell you?"

"I'm not sure. Maybe to rid himself of the burden. So what he knows won't choke him."

I was so upset by what I had heard that I could not collect my thoughts at all. They fled like birds from a fire; they hid in dark holes like partridges. A terrible image of omnipotent evil appeared before my eyes.

"This is terrible," I said. "So terrible that I can hardly believe it. I'd have preferred for you not to tell me."

"And I as well. Now. Well, let it be as if I hadn't said anything, if it's of no use to you."

"That's not possible. Nothing exists until it's told."

"Nothing can be told until it exists. The only question is whether anything should be told. If I'd known how much I'd upset you, I'd have kept silent. Why are you afraid of the truth?"

"What use is it to me?"

"I don't know. And maybe it's not the truth."

"It's too late for you to retreat. We can't take back what's been said. Do I know the man who told you this?"

He looked at me with surprise.

"I wanted to help you. I expected that you would think about how to save your brother as soon as possible, as quickly as possible. But it seems that you can only think of that wretch, who surely doesn't sleep at night out of fear. It's as if you don't care to know about anything else."

Maybe that was true, maybe he was right. Maybe I eased my horrible burden with the thought of something trivial. Only, we should not have been talking like this, and it seemed to me that I knew how we should have. On the tip of my tongue there was a silly, childlike question: What am I to do, good man, you who've ignored the warnings of your reason and gone to meet another man, tell me, what should I do? I'm astonished by what you've said; it's as if I've been brought to the edge of an abyss, and I don't want to look. I want to return to what I was, or not to return; I want to save my faith in the world, but that is impossible until this terrible, murderous misunderstanding has been removed. Tell me, where should I begin?

At that time I was not aware that I had not agreed to this rupture, that I had persistently tried to maintain connections established long before, not knowing that I thus laid the blame on my brother, since someone had to be guilty. If only I had begun to speak, I would have stopped hiding from Hassan and myself. I did not know what would happen; maybe he could not tell me anything, maybe he could not help me at all, but the cramp in my soul would have eased, and I would not be alone. And maybe I would have avoided the direction that my life later took, had I accepted his greater and more bitter experience, had I not shut myself inside my pain. But even that was not certain, because our intentions were completely opposite; he wanted to save a man, while I was trying to save an idea. At least that was what I thought afterward. But at that moment I was perplexed and bitter. I unconsciously resented him because he had told me what I did not know. I was conscious that I had to do whatever it took for the truth to come out. Now I had to. If I had not known I could have waited; my ignorance would have protected me. But now there was no longer any choice, I was condemned by the truth.

Preoccupied by worries of what was to come, tomorrow, in a couple of days, in the near future, I still thought of how painful it would be for us to part. Should he leave without a word? Should we say something too ordinary? Should we part coldly and angrily? I could not find the proper words and proper attitude since my own affairs were in question: until that moment I had always known what to say and how to act. After this conversation I felt a certain unease, a heavy foreboding and a dissatisfaction that not everything had been said. But I unwittingly restrained myself from showing coldness and anger, because I did not know whether I might need this man again. I say: unwittingly, because I was not maneuvering consciously; I had no idea how he might be useful to me, since I had not figured him out, but my sense of caution warned against losing him. And I might need his goodwill for the arrangement that I had made with his sister. Therefore I concluded our conversation in such a way that it could be resumed again, or maybe not, according to the will of God.

I spoke, trying my best to make my voice sound casual and kind:

"It's late. You must be tired."

He surprised me with an answer and an act that were unexpected but natural, so simple that they were even strange.

He put his long, firm fingers on my hand, which rested on the back of the bench, barely touching me, only enough for me to feel the pleasant freshness of his skin and soft fingertips. He said calmly, with a soft, deep voice, with which, for all I know, people usually declare love:

"It seems that I've hurt you; that wasn't what I wanted. I thought that you knew more about people and the world, much more. I should've spoken with you differently."

"How could you have spoken with me differently?"

"I don't know. As with a child."

These words might have meant nothing, but I was struck by the way in which he spoke them. His voice sounded like the deep notes of a clay flute, clear, without overtones and fitful breathing. He smiled sorrowfully, because of something that should have happened but had not. His smile was tender, intelligent, and assuasive; for the first time I thought with surprise that something very mature and full lived in him, which revealed itself only at times, when he lowered his guard. In that moonlight which flooded us with anxiety. In difficult moments. I remembered his full voice, which inspired confidence, his calm smile, and that hour before midnight, when secrets are revealed. All of this remained in my memory, because of something powerful, yet not entirely tangible. Maybe because it suddenly seemed to me, quite unexpectedly, that I saw a man show a side of himself that no one before me had seen. I did not know whether he had just been born, or was just emerging, shedding his skin like a snake. I did not even know what he had revealed to me, but I was convinced that the moment was extraordinary. I also considered the possibility that my own excitement could have distorted each word, each movement, each sensation. But the memory persisted.

Then he got up, having deftly untied the knots of awkwardness between us. He had found the right word, which had a pleasant and lasting sound, and now he could leave. My absurd emotions of a few moments before were gone. They were replaced by shameful intentions, peculiar not because they had appeared at all, but rather because they followed immediately upon such enthusiasm.

As he left, he took a small bundle out of his pocket and put it on the bench. "This is for you," he said.

And he left.

I saw him to the gate. And when he went around the corner I started after him. I stepped quietly, close to the walls and fences, ready to stop if he turned around—he would think that I was only a shadow. He disappeared in the darkness of the streets. I followed him by the noise of his footsteps; mine were silent, soft, and secret. I had never walked like that before. At each moonlit corner I caught a glimpse of his blue mintan and his tall figure. I followed him, in circles it seemed, and then, with disappointment, I realized that these deceptive circles narrowed around a familiar place. I stopped at the mosque. He struck the door of his yard with its knocker, and someone opened it, as if they were expecting him. If he had gone into some other house, I would have thought that he was visiting the man whose name he had refused to tell me. As it was, I knew nothing.

I returned to the tekke, weary, but with something that was not physical fatigue.

Hassan's gift lay on the bench: Abu Faraj's *Book of Tales*,[8] in an expensive morocco binding with four golden birds in the corners. I was surprised that four golden birds were also embroidered on the silken kerchief that contained the book. This was not something that he had merely picked up on his way.

In a conversation I had once mentioned Abu Faraj, recalling my youth. I had mentioned it and I forgotten it. He had not.

I sat down on the bench with the book in my lap, caressing the smooth morocco leather with my fingers. I watched the river, which was deadened by the moonlight; I listened to the striking of the hour from the clock tower and, strangely calmed, I wanted to weep. This was the first time since that distant Bairam* of my childhood, already lost from memory, that someone had given me a gift, the first time that someone had thought about me. He had taken note of something I had said and remembered it somewhere in a distant land.

The feeling was quite unusual: as if it were a fresh, sunny morning, as if I had returned home from a long trip, as if an irrational but powerful joy had come over me, as if the darkness had vanished.

The clock struck midnight, and the night-watchmen could be heard calling out, like birds of the night. Time was passing, but I sat in amazement. Because of Abu Faraj's book and the four golden birds. He had seen them on a thin cotton kerchief, which was all that I had from our house. Long ago, my father had brought me some hard pastries in a peasant cloth, and a much nicer kerchief spread over the coarse linen. And Hassan had remembered it.

It is hard to believe, but it is true: I was deeply moved. Because someone had remembered me. For no reason, not out of any need, from the goodness of his heart or maybe as a joke. So you see, then, how even an old hardened dervish, who thought that he had overcome his small weaknesses, can be bought with attention. But it seems that such weaknesses do not die so easily. And they are not small, either.

The night passed and I sat joyous, silly even to myself because of an excitement that I could not explain. But I did not want it to leave.

6

> He who seeks is paltry,
> and what he seeks is paltry as well.[1]

IN THE MORNING I WENT OUT INTO THE FIELDS AND CLIMBED a hill that was in full bloom. I stood beside a low fruit tree, with my face next to its cluster of flowers, calyxes, leaves, petals—a thousand living wonders ready for insemination. I felt the intoxicating sweetness of that growth, the rush of juices through innumerable, invisible veins, and like the night before I wished that my arms would grow into branches, that the colorless blood of trees would flow into me, that I would bloom and wilt painlessly. And it was just this repetition of my strange desire that convinced me of the weight of my burden.

The forest echoed with the resonant strokes of an axe, at regular intervals, in time to the swing of strong arms, and each stroke was followed by a brief silence. Even at that distance I could tell that the axe was sharp and had a large blade; it bit into the wood, snapping angrily, chopping furiously into the pith. A cuckoo sang its two-syllabled lament, which was gloomily indifferent, like fate. Someone—a woman—was calling out, cheerfully, shrilly, unintelligibly; she was young, tanned by the spring sun, laughing. I could not see her, and turned toward that young voice, as if it were the kiblah.* But I knew everything about her. Only those three sounds in the silence of the spring morning, in the vast space of a foreign world. I closed my eyes, savoring the sweet scent of pollen, listening: three utterly simple sounds. And then I experienced an extraordinary moment of forgetfulness. It was not memory, but rather existence in another time, long since passed; nothing of my present self had existed then. It was a light, joyful awareness of life, a trembling concord with everything around me. I knew that the axe was my father's; those were his strong arms swinging it in the forest above our house. I recognized the voice of the cuckoo as well; I had never seen it, but its song always echoed from the same place. And I knew the girl; she was sixteen years old. I saw her across so much endless time, it was as if centuries had passed, but I had forgotten nothing, not the fine, golden down above her smiling lips, not her waist, so slender that it fit between your two hands, not the aroma of lovage on her, unfaded after so many years. To whom was that girl calling through time? I could not answer her call, I could not go back.

A lively encounter woke me from this spell of distant time. A boy was approaching on the path toward me, plucking flowers and tossing them over his head, throwing clumps of dirt at birds, and yelling unintelligible words in some language of his own. He was joyous and carefree, like a kitten. When he saw me, he quieted down and went to one side, serious. I did not belong in his world.

Many years before I had met such a boy, on another path, at another place. There was no reason for me to remember this and to compare the two boys. But I remembered it anyway. Maybe because that day had been destined for recollection, or because I had also been at a crossroads in my life then, as I was now; or maybe because both of them were chubby, carried away, content with themselves in the empty landscape, and because they both walked past me seriously, as if I had stifled their happiness. I asked the boy, who had eyes like hemp flowers, the same thing that I had asked the other one long before, a question that was old and sounded gloomy, although he was not aware of that.

Fortunately, our conversation went quite differently from that earlier one. I wrote it down for refreshment, not out of any other need, just as a tired traveler stops in front of a cool spring.

"Who are you, little one?"

He stopped and looked at me, not at all in a friendly manner. "That's none of your business."

"Do you go to the mekteb?"*

"I don't go any more. Yesterday the hodja* gave me a thrashing."

"He gave it to you for your own good."

"If that's true, then I should give loads of them to everyone else. But the hodja deals them out across our behinds. For our every word they turn blue as eggplants."

"Don't say bad words."

"Is 'eggplant' really a bad word?"

"You're a little devil."

"Don't say bad words, effendi."

"Did you speak so freely yesterday?"

"Until yesterday I was the hodja's drum. Today I'm like that bird. Come on, let someone hit me now."

"What does your father think?"

"He says 'You'll never be an alim anyway. And you can plow with or without reading and writing. The land's waiting for you; I won't give it to anyone else. And if it comes to giving thrashings, I can do that, too,' he says."

"Do you want me to talk with your father? I'll take you to the kasaba; you'll go to school, and become an alim."

I had said that to the other boy, long before; now he was a dervish in the tekke. But this one was different. The cheerful expression disappeared from his face and was replaced by one of hatred. For a moment he looked at me with hostility, in angry confusion, then suddenly bent down and picked up a rock from the path.

"My father's over there, plowing," he said threateningly. "Go and tell him that, if you dare."

Maybe he would have really thrown the rock at me. Or run into the hills crying. He was smarter than the other boy.

"No," I said, placating him. "No one can force you to go. And maybe it's better for you to stay here."

He stood there, confused, but did not drop the rock.

I went on and turned around a few times. He did not move from the spot where he stood, like a barrier between his father and my offer, frightened and distrustful. Only when I was far away, when he no longer had any reason to be afraid, did he throw the rock far out into the wheatfield and run off toward his father.

I returned in a somber mood.

A small woman opened the gate, pretending to hide her face with her veil, and sent me into the yard. They're over there, she said, the three fools are trying to catch a rabid beast, and I can go watch, if I want, or I can wait there and she'll talk to Hassan and tell me what he says, if he says anything at all, because today he's not very talkative.

I'll go there, I said, and the woman shut the gate and went inside.

In a large yard behind the house, an open, grassy area surrounded with plum trees, two of Hassan's stablehands were trying to catch a young stallion. Hassan stood just inside the fence and looked on calmly, saying nothing or spurring them on with quick shouts and curses.

I did not enter the grassy arena, where clumps of earth flew from the hooves of the untamed horse.

His stablehands approached the horse in turns; the older one was short and stocky, the younger one tall and slender. It was strange that they did not try to catch it together, they would have overcome it more easily. And it was just as strange that Hassan kept quiet, letting them wear themselves out.

The stallion, with its shiny, black coat, stout croup, sinewy legs and slender joints, stood in the middle of the yard, furious, its pink nostrils flaring, its eyes rolling, its firm skin twitching, rippling in minute waves.

The older hand approached the horse from the side, with his head tucked between his broad shoulders, his entire body tensed. He did not try to calm it with words or gestures; he accepted that they would be enemies. He jumped unexpectedly, trying to grab its neck and mane, confident of his own strength. The horse looked as if it would stand there calmly, but all of a sudden spun around with lightning speed. The man dodged, as if he had been waiting for that, and rushed in from the other side, grabbing it by its long mane. The horse stopped in surprise and then began to drag him around, trying to free itself, but his grip was firm and his strong hands would not let go of its slender neck. It appeared that he would subdue it; it seemed like a miracle that human strength could tame that knot of tensed muscles. Both of them stood motionless, as if they were exhausted, as if now inseparable, as if neither of them knew what to do next. And then, with an unexpected jerk, the animal threw him clear of itself.

The same thing happened with the younger one. He approached the horse more cautiously, more slyly, trying to deceive it with his open palm, even with his kind face and the meaningless smile hovering on it. But when he got within arm's reach of the horse, it spun around and knocked him away with its body.

Hassan shouted an obscenity. The younger one laughed; the older one cursed the wild rogue.

"You're the rogue," Hassan told him.

I watched how he followed this struggle calmly, as he would a wrestling match or a duel. He did not care whether they caught the horse, although the blacksmith was waiting by the fence, as I was. He only wanted to see them try and fail; he did not give them any advice, or interrupt the dangerous game. But I was more surprised by his unusual seriousness. He was even somber, discontent with something, and I did not believe that it was on account of the clumsiness of his stablehands. It was strange that he would let all of this go on for so long; it seemed like unnecessary cruelty, which might be common among them, but still appeared senseless to me. And such behavior also changed my impression of him. He was not the gentle and cheerful man that I knew; maybe he was like that only when he was with equals, but like others when dealing with his servants. And even when he saw me and greeted me tersely, he did not change. He did not end their torment, and they did not protest, either.

Fortunately the horse hit the older man in the thigh, and he paid it back with a harsh blow to the ribs.

"You're as crazy as the horse! Get out, both of you!" Hassan yelled, and without a word the older hand limped clear of the horse.

He waited for them to reach the fence, and then started slowly toward the horse, moving around it, approaching its head, changing position carefully, without haste, without making sudden movements, without trying to trick it, right until the horse stopped, calmed by something, maybe by Hassan's steady movements, maybe by his soft, indistinct words, which gurgled constantly, like water in a stream, maybe by his concentrated gaze or his lack of fear and anger, and it waited for him to come close. It still looked distrustful, snorting through its wide nostrils, but Hassan was already next to it, and, still calming it with soft whispers, reached out and began to caress its brow. And again, without haste or impatience, as if he did not notice the horse shaking its head, he ran his hand slowly down on its snout, back onto its brow, onto its neck, and finally grabbed its mane and led it toward the fence.

"Here he is," he told the hands. "Maybe now you'll be able to do it."

And he came up to me.

"Have you been waiting long? I'm glad you came. Let's go inside."

"You're not in a good mood today."

"I've been in worse."

"I can leave if I'm bothering you."

"Why? I'd have gone looking for you if you hadn't come."

"Did your stablehands anger you?"

"Yes. I was hoping one of them would die."

I did not answer.

He laughed: "A real dervish answer: silence. Yes, I'm in a bad mood, and I'm talking nonsense. Forgive me."

I had offered to go, but wanted him to stop me: I would not have been able, nor would I have dared to go back out in the streets. I had not been wandering that morning without reason, either. I had wanted to see him, I needed to hear his soothing words and feel his gentle confidence, which would calm the storms in me, just as one is occasionally taken by the desire to sit beside a quiet, mighty river and to be soothed by its peaceful strength and steady current. But as it was, I found a different man, a stranger; I was sorry, I felt betrayed, and I had no idea what two upset people might be capable of.

Fortunately, he could control himself, or his cheerful nature could not endure rage for long, and he became more and more the man that I had been hoping to find.

He led me into a large room with windows along one entire side, which exposed one-half of the sky to view. The size of that summer chamber surprised me, with its divans, its framed inscriptions from the Koran, the carved wood of its closet doors, its abundant carpets: a whole collection of dusty riches and luxuries that no one took care of. Like him, I thought. I preferred the strict order of a dervish: each thing must have its place, like everything else in the world; man must create order so that he will not go mad. Surprisingly, this negligence did not bother me, it resembled a lavish willingness to use things without serving them, without respecting them too much. But that was something that I was not capable of.

He laughed, putting away his mintan, boots, and weapons; he had grown accustomed to disorder in inns, and noticed it only when someone else saw it, when someone came. But I was certain that he had always been that way—that was a part of his irresponsible and dishevelled nature. And I told him jokingly that this was what was nice about him, and that he must have always been this way. He listened to the joke with a laugh: exactly, he had always been careless, although at times he respected the order that others had created. But he himself did not feel any need for it, and no longer gave it any thought. At one point in his life he even tried, forcing himself, but to no avail. It was as if objects were his adversaries, as if they did not respect him, and refused to submit to him: he was unable to exercise power over anything. In fact, he even feared order somewhat. Order is finality, a firm law, a reduction of the possible ways of life, the false conviction that we can keep life under control. But life keeps slipping away, and the more we try to keep hold of it, the more it eludes us.

It was truly unusual how that crude horse trader of a few moments before could jump so easily into a conversation so unsuited to his profession, but I took part in it with pleasure. I asked him:

"But how should we live? Without order, without purpose, without any conscious goals that we try to accomplish?"

"I don't know. It would be good if we could determine a purpose and goals for ourselves, if we could create rules for all of life's circumstances, if we could establish our imaginary order. It's easy to invent general principles, looking over men's heads into the sky and eternity. But try to apply them to the lives of real people, whom you know and maybe love, without harming them. You'll hardly succeed."

"Doesn't the Koran determine all relations between people? We can apply the spirit of its principles to each individual case."

"Do you think so? Then solve this riddle for me. It's not rare, it's not unusual, it's not foreign to us. We encounter it whenever we decide to open our eyes. Let's say that a man and his wife live together, and are apparently in love. But wait, let's talk about people we know; that'll be easier. Let's suppose that they are the two whom you saw, the woman who opened the gate for you and my older stablehand, Fazli, her husband. They live here, in the servants' quarters, they live comfortably. He travels with me and earns more than they need; he brings her gifts from our trips and enjoys her happiness, and she knows how to be happy, like a child. He's silly, clumsy, strong as an ox, somewhat childish, but unusually considerate of her. He loves her, and would be lost without her. He steals from me a little for her, but he also loves me, and would die for me. I'm glad that they get along, I can't stand couples that fight. I care about them, because I helped bring them together, and maybe I've even become attached to them. But the point is this: What would happen if the woman found another man and secretly gave him what belongs to her husband, according to the laws of both God and men? And what should be done if that happened?"

"Has it?"

"Yes. And you've seen him, the younger one. Her husband doesn't know. The Koran tells us: an adulteress is to be stoned. But you must admit, that's rather old-fashioned. So what should I do? Tell her husband? Threaten her? Get rid of the youth? None of that would help."

"But you can't just stand by and watch sin being committed."

"It's more difficult to prevent it. They both love her; she's afraid of her husband and loves the youth. He also works here. He's a little cunning, but he's smart, so skilled in business matters that I worry about his honesty. But I need him.

He lives here, with them, her husband brought him here himself; he's one of his distant relatives. Her husband is such a good-natured man; he suspects nothing. He trusts people, and is content in his happiness. His wife doesn't want anything to change; she's afraid that everything might go wrong. The youth keeps silent, but doesn't want to leave. I could quarter him somewhere else, but she'd go there, too; she told me herself, and then things would only be worse. I could send him to another town, but she'd follow him there. It wouldn't be good if anything changed from the way it is now. Her husband would kill both of them if he found out, because the fool has built his life around her. Those two steal their happiness, thinking that they're entitled to it, but don't dare to go the full way. And it's not easy for them either: not for her, because she has to be a wife to a man she doesn't love, not for the youth, because every night he gives her up to another man. Her husband has it the easiest, because he knows nothing and none of this exists for him. And all the while we think that he is hurt the most. He no longer has any right to her; he lives only by her fear. And I wait, I let everything go on, I don't dare to do anything, it's all so fragile. If I did anything, I'd break the delicate threads that hold them together, I'd hasten the tragedy hanging over them. So there you have it, find whatever rule you like, solve this for me, set up your order! But without destroying them. Because then you've done nothing."

"This can only end in tragedy; you said that yourself."

"I'm afraid so. But I don't want to rush it."

"You're talking about consequences and not about causes, about the impotence of principles when something happens, and not about the sin of people who don't adhere to them."

"Life is larger than any principle. Morality is an idea, but life is what we live. How can we fit it into this idea without damaging it? More lives have been ruined in attempts to prevent sin than because of sin itself."

"Should we live in sin then?"

"No. But prohibiting it doesn't help at all. It creates hypocrisy and spiritual cripples."

"So what should we do?"

"I don't know."

He laughed, as if that made him glad.

The woman brought in sherbet.*

I was afraid that Hassan would start a conversation with her. He was too open and rash to hide what he thought. Fortunately, surprisingly, he said nothing. He looked at her with a barely visible smile, not at all malicious, and even with a certain scornful kindness, with which one might watch a loved one, or a child.

"You were looking at her as if you were on her side," I said when she had left.

"Yes, I am on her side. Women are always intriguing when they're in love, then they're more clever, determined, and charming than ever. Men are absentminded, crude, impulsive, or tearfully compassionate. But I'm also on his side, or rather on the side of both men. To hell with all of them."

At that moment I both felt sorry for him and envied him. But neither of these emotions was very strong. I felt sorry for him because he had deliberately destroyed a thorough and safe way of thinking, with which he might have served the faith; I envied him because of an uncertain freedom that he possessed, which I could only sense. It was not mine, it was contrary to me; on the other hand it seemed like a breath of fresh air. I thought that way because of his effect on me, and made such concessions since I could not hide from myself how glad I was to see him. I liked his light, limpid smile, which blossomed all on its own, I liked his face, tanned by the wind, and his bright, blue eyes; I took pleasure in a serenity that surrounded him like a light, and maybe even in his unassuming recklessness. In his unusual attire, his blue trousers, his yellow boots made of goat's leather, in his white, wide-sleeved shirt and his Circassian hat, with his skin clean and smooth as pebbles in a stream bed, with his broad shoulders, and strong chest showing its healthy tan through the triangular cut of his shirt, he resembled an outlaw leader relaxing with his trusted cohorts, or a cheerful bandit who fears neither himself nor others; he resembled a deer, a tree in bloom, a brisk wind. I tried in vain to see him differently, as I had in the beginning. And I exaggerated the contrast between him and myself.

Once he had been the same as I, or similar to me. But at one point something happened, and he changed the course of his life, and his very self. I tried to imagine the sheikh Ahmed Nuruddin thus transfigured, traveling the highways, carousing in inns, taming wild horses, cursing, and talking about women—but I could not, it was ludicrous, impossible. I would have to be born for a second time and not learn any of the things that I knew now. I wanted to ask him, maybe because I also sensed a change in myself, a different one. I sensed it and was afraid, but I did not know how to ask. It would have seemed very strange, he could not see my train of thought or the reasons for my curiosity.

I began in the wrong way: "Are you satisfied with your work?"

"Yes."

He laughed, looking me in the eye cheerfully, and refused to beat around the bush: "Admit it, that wasn't what you wanted to ask."

"You guess other people's thoughts, like a wizard."

He smiled and waited, freeing me from my inhibitions with his openness and a calm, encouraging look. I took advantage of that opportunity, an opportunity for me: he always gave them to others. I told him: "You used to think as I do, as we do, or similarly. It's not easy to change oneself, one must reject all that one has been, all that one has learned, everything that one has grown accustomed to. And you changed yourself completely. It's as if you learned how to walk all over again, to say your first words, to acquire basic habits. The reason must have been very, very important."

He watched me for a moment with a strange attentiveness, as if I had taken him back into his past, or some forgotten pain; but that alert expression soon subsided. He acknowledged calmly:

"Yes, I've changed. I used to believe in everything that you do, maybe even more firmly. But then in Smyrna,[2] Talib-effendi said to me: 'When you see a young man reaching for the sky, grab him by the leg and pull him back down to the ground.' And he pulled me back down to the ground. 'You are destined to live here,' he scolded me. 'So live here! And live as nicely as you can, but without shame. It is better that God ask you: why did you not do that? rather than: why did you do that?'"

"And what are you now?"

"A wanderer on wide roads where I meet good and bad people, who have the same worries and troubles as people do here, who have the same trivial joys as people do everywhere."

"What would happen if everyone took your path?"

"The world would be happier. Maybe."

He was trying to bring our conversation to an end.

"And now nothing matters to you. Is that all that you've achieved?"

"Not even that."

As I sat and talked, my attention dwindled and my interest waned; I had expected much from his confession, but had gotten nothing. His case was exceptional. He was a bit of an eccentric, or a clever man who hid his thoughts, or a wretch who defended himself with spite; and to do that one needs to be either too weak or too strong. I was neither. The world keeps us in fetters—how can we break them? And to what end? How can a man live without beliefs that grow on him like skin, that become inseparable from him? How can you live without your self?

And then I remembered my brother. I remembered where I was going to go that day. I remembered that I was afraid of being left alone.

"I've come to thank you for your gift."

"I'd have liked it if you'd come for no reason. To talk about nothing, not on account of anything."

"For a long time I've not been as excited as I was last night. In this world good people are precious."

This was a pleasantry that demanded nothing, not from the man who said it or from the man who heard it. But I remembered the night before, and it seemed to me that I really thought this way, and that what I had said was inadequate. I felt a desire to say more, to satisfy a need that was growing inside me, to fill myself with tenderness and warmth. Hassan tried in vain to stop me with his laughter, but that was no longer possible. I held onto him like an anchor. I needed him right then, at that moment, and I needed for him to be dear to me, to be the best possible friend. I told him that I was going to do everything in my power for my brother, soon, either the next day, or maybe even that afternoon. I believed that I was in the right, and I would seek justice to the extent that I could. Maybe it would not be easy, as I had imagined, maybe there would be difficulties (these I had already encountered: that morning I had gone to the musellim again and he had refused to see me; they said impudently that he was not in, although he had entered his office just ahead of me), maybe I would be alone and in danger, and so, that was why I had come to him; I felt that we were close, and I sought nothing except kind words. I wanted to tell him that, to get it off my chest.

What I said was true. It was an unusual, inner truth, and it was what had brought me there, although I said it to myself only then, in front of him. I felt as if I were setting out on a perilous journey, or marching into a deadly battle; I looked at my only friend, who had appeared along with my misfortune so that it would not be absolute. Although he

PART I

could not help me, and I did not need his help, a deep, indistinct fear kept me from letting him go. Maybe only then, before that composed man who listened to me quietly, drawn by the seriousness of my voice and a hidden anxiety that he could sense, maybe only then, I say, did I become completely aware of the emptiness that I had felt that morning in front of the musellim's office as I listened to the soldiers lie to me calmly. I had been humiliated, but did not have the strength to feel insulted. I was astonished by the realization that I had been irrevocably associated with my condemned brother. Saving my brother meant saving myself as well. But I could not conceal from myself the cold emptiness that had seized me. I knew that the musellim's door was not the only one that I would have to knock on; he was not the only man who would have to hear my request. There were others, some better and stronger than this bully who was crazed with power. But I had still shuddered from fear and felt a sudden weakness, like a man who loses his way at night. That was the reason why, in a moment of confidence and desire for support, I tried to tie Hassan to myself with the bonds of friendship and love; I was surprised at myself, at this new need, which was as senseless as it was strong. I succeeded, I did it in the best possible way, led by the subconscious cunning of genuine helplessness, by a heightened desire to quench some great thirst that had certainly been in me for a long time, hidden and suppressed. Long afterward I remembered that moment, and how moved I was then.

I upset him as well. His blue eyes were wide open, watching me as if they recognized me, as if removing me from anonymity and giving me a face and features. His usual expression of scornful joy changed into nervous tension, but when he began to speak he was again a calm and collected man who could control his feelings, who made sure that they were not too strongly expressed, as happens with people who easily forget their enthusiasm. His ardor was longer lasting, it was not a flame that burned out in passionate words. And that impression of him was also new. Earlier that day, just moments before, I had considered him superficial and empty, although somewhere inside myself I must have thought differently—otherwise why would I have come to him and no one else when I needed to hear a kind word? That was my new love defending him, my enthusiasm, which I connected with him in my fear of isolation. Anyway, it did not matter, let him be superficial, let him be reckless, let him squander his unusual talents however he wanted: he was still a good man, and he knew the secret of being a friend. I did not, and he would reveal it to me. Maybe this was a prayer that resulted from a deep fear, or maybe a talisman against evil powers, prophecy before the beginning of a pilgrimage of suffering.

But we never know what our words, which have a definite meaning only for us and therefore satisfy only our needs, might call forth in other men. I had, it seemed, awakened in him a well-hidden desire to meddle in other people's lives. It was as if he could hardly wait for my outburst of friendship, so he could offer me his hand and assistance. For him words were never enough.

"I'm glad that you have confidence in me," he said readily. "I'll help you in any way I can."

Suddenly everything in him came to life and readied itself for something, for action, for danger. He needed to be stopped.

"I'm not looking for help. I don't think I need it."

"You can never have too much help, and now you'll need it more than ever. We need to get him out of the fortress as soon as possible and take him away from here."

He got up, restless, looming over me, his eyes glowing with an evil fire. What had I awakened in him?

I had not expected such an offer or such haste in making a decision. I will continue to meet people as long as I live, but I will never really figure them out; they will always baffle me with their inexplicable deeds. I thought for a moment,

PART I

caught by this rashness, afraid of it, in danger of being drawn into a shameful endeavor. And without giving the real reason, not even myself knowing exactly what it was, I refused:

"Then he'd still be guilty."

"He'd still be alive! Saving him is all that matters."

"But I'm saving more: justice."

"All of you will suffer: you, your brother, and justice."

"If it's fated to be so, then that's the will of God."

Those calm words of mine might have been sorrowful, bitter, or helpless, but they were sincere. I had nothing else left. I do not know why my words provoked him so much, as if they were mud that I had slung in his face. Maybe because I had thwarted his enthusiasm, prevented him from showing his kindness. A fire had ignited somewhere within him, different from a moment before, more distinct, closer; his eyes glowed hotly, his face flushed a deep red, he grabbed his right hand with his left, as if to keep it from striking me. I have rarely ever seen such excited strength, such rage. I thought he was going to lose control of himself, to explode, to swear at me. Surprisingly, he did not shout, but I would have preferred it; he spoke in a low voice, unnaturally softly, contracting his vocal chords, suddenly so upset that even his appearance changed. For the first time I heard him speak passionately, saying his angry thoughts out loud, without softening any hard words or insults.

I listened in amazement:

"O wretched dervish! Will you all ever stop thinking like dervishes? You act according to destiny, which is determined by God, and you try to save justice and the world! How is it that you don't choke on such pompous words?! Can nothing be done by the will of man, without trying to save the world? Leave the world alone, for God's sake; it'll be better off without your concern. Do something for a man whose first and last names you know, who also happens to be your brother, so he won't perish completely innocent in the name of the justice that you uphold. If your brother's death were a guarantee of future paradise for the rest of us, very well, let him die; he would redeem much suffering. But he won't, nothing will change."

"Then that's the will of God."

"Can't you find any other, more human words?"

"No. And I don't need them."

He went up to the window, and looked at the half of the sky above the kasaba and the surrounding mountains, as if in that clear expanse he sought an answer or some consolation. And then he began shouting to somebody in the yard, asking whether the horse had been shod and telling them to hurry up and get the musicians.

It was no use, I could not figure him out. As soon as I saw one side of him another, unknown one, surfaced immediately, and I did not know which one of them was real.

When he turned around he was calm again, but his smile was not serene as it had been before.

"Forgive me," he said, trying to sound cheerful. "I've acted rudely and stupidly. Those are the manners of a cattle drover. It's good that I didn't start to curse."

"No matter. That's not important now."

"And maybe I'm not even right. Maybe your approach is better. Maybe it's better to adhere to the standards of heaven than to those of this world. Failure doesn't upset you, since you can always rely on eternity; you find your justifications in reasons beyond yourself. Personal loss is less important. And pain. And men. And the present day. Everything continues into eternity, faceless and vast, sleepily torpid and solemnly indifferent. Like the sea: it cannot lament the innumerable deaths that continually occur in it."

I was silent. What could I say? Those anxious words revealed insecurities and dilemmas that are endless. What was there to dispute or condone when he himself did not know where he stood? All he did was doubt everything. I did not. I really thought that the will of God was the supreme law, that eternity was the measure of our deeds, and that the faith was more important than people. Yes, the sea had existed forever and would exist forever, and it would not stir up at every tiny death. He had said that bitterly, meaning something else, without believing it. And I would have liked to rise to that idea, even when my own happiness was in question.

I did not feel like explaining that I would not agree to free my brother with a planned escape or bribery, because I still believed in justice; he would not have understood, he thought differently than I did. If I ever became convinced that there is no justice in this world of mine, the only thing left to do would be to kill myself, or to turn against the world, since I would no longer be able to be a part of it. Hassan would have said again that this was the logic of a dervish, and blind obedience of rules. Therefore I said nothing, although I did not understand how men could live otherwise.

Or could they?

I looked at the buds on a branch under the open window. I should have left.

"It's springtime," I said.

As if he did not know. He certainly did not know the way I did. It did not occur to me that what I said might have seemed strange to him. It was as if it had interrupted our conversation and thoughts. But it had not.

I remembered the white and pink abundance that had been repeating itself endlessly, that morning, and long before. There were many light shadows under the trees, the fragrant earth was awakening, and I thought of how nice it would be to go out into the world with my wooden dervish bowl in my hands, led only by the sun and any river, any path, not desiring anything, except to be nowhere, to be bound by nothing, to see a different place every morning, to lie down somewhere else every night, to have neither obligations nor regrets nor memories, to give free rein to hatred only after I had gone on and it had become meaningless, to distance the world from me as I passed through it. But no, that idea did not belong to me. I attributed to myself the desire that Hassan had just expressed; it seemed so beautiful to me, so liberating that I adopted it, and for a few moments I even thought that it was mine. In my mind I even heard it as he would have said it. It suited the desolation I felt that morning and I later embraced it in retrospect, as if it had existed then. But I was sure that it had not.

I told Hassan about my encounter with the boy after the humiliation that the musellim had bestowed on me.

"Why did you ask if he wanted to come to the tekke?" Hassan asked, laughing.

"He looked bright."

"You felt bad, you were running from your troubles, you wanted to forget how the soldiers had turned you away at the musellim's office, and then, in a moment of great personal hardship, you noticed bright boys and thought of future defenders of the faith. True or not?"

"If I feel bad, have I ceased to be what I am?"

He shook his head; I did not know whether he was laughing at me or feeling pity for me.

"Say that it's not true, please, say that your brother is more important than everything. Say that everything else can go to hell as long as you save your brother. You know he's not guilty!"

"I'll do everything I can."

"That's not enough. We have to do more!"

"Let's not talk any more about it."

"Fine. As you wish. I hope you won't regret this."

He was persistent. I did not know why he wanted to get involved in the dangerous and risky business of saving a man whom he hardly knew; that was strange, because it contradicted everything I knew about him. But he was not lying, he was not only offering words because he knew that I would refuse: he would really have done it, without a moment's hesitation.

Maybe someone will think that I was touched by his readiness to run to my assistance, that I accepted that unusual sacrifice of his with tears in my eyes. But I did not. Not at all. At first I hoped that his offer was only a lie, empty talk that did not bind him to deeds. But since I could not reduce it to that, since his sincerity was obvious, I felt anger and indignation. His keen interest seemed inappropriate and intrusive; it was unnatural. It threatened to surpass my own efforts, and indicated that my concern was inadequate; he was offering to sacrifice himself in order to show my lack of love, to chide and punish me. This conversation had worn me out, and I wished it would end, we could not understand one another. When he made his remark about my story of the boy, he caught me off-balance and revealed something I had not given any thought to. It was without a doubt true, but rebellion was lurking in everything that he said. When I reached that conclusion I shut myself up, like a besieged fortress that arrows strike to no avail. Whoever severs my roots or undermines my foundation is not my friend, or is a very strange kind of friend. No true friendship can exist between people who think differently.

This bitter realization (one that I needed like fresh air, or medicine) helped me to refuse him more easily, and to begin the unpleasant conversation that I had been delaying constantly, although it was always on my mind.

I could have asked him as a friend, I had a right to that, but my thoughts took another direction, and prevented it. I could have passed it on to him like a message from someone else, which was allegedly not my concern, but in that case I would have had difficulties expressing my request and everything would have gone wrong. This way was best: he was not my friend, that was certain, and I would present a demand made by others, from which I also expected some benefit. Maybe it was for this reason that I had not shown my anger a moment before: I would have turned him against me and reduced my chances for success.

I prepared to leave and told him, as if I had just remembered it, that I had visited his sister, that she had summoned me (I know, he added, thus warning me that I would have to tell more than I might have wanted to) and that she had asked me to tell him that his father was going to disinherit him (I also know that, said Hassan, laughing), and that it would be best if he renounced his inheritance himself, before the kadi, because of what people would think, so that there would be no scandal.

"No scandal for whom?"

"I don't know."

"I don't want to renounce it. Let them do whatever they feel like."

"Maybe that's best."

There is no point in hiding it, I trusted that my mediation in this shameful affair would help me and my brother. When he refused, it seemed that he was acting rudely and stubbornly, and it took great effort for me to support his decision. It was hard, the words burned in my throat like poison, but I could not do otherwise: I could not have forgiven myself if he caught me in such a game. I had begun badly, everything had come out wrong, it should all have been said in a simple way, without mincing words; it would not have even been inappropriate for him to refuse me, but now I had ruined everything. A long-awaited opportunity was irrevocably lost, and I was left helpless.

But just then, when I had lost all hope, when I had begun to think that my visit was pointless, he said: "If I renounce my inheritance, would my brother-in-law, the kadi, help your brother?"

"I don't know, I haven't thought about it."

"Let's do that! If he'll help you, I'll renounce everything. I'll shout it from a minaret if I have to. It doesn't matter anyway, he won't leave me a thing no matter what I do."

"You could raise a lawsuit. You're the first heir, and you haven't offended your family; your father is sick, it would be easy to claim that he's doing everything under pressure from someone."

"I know."

I strained to say that, forcing myself with effort to act honorably, for a second time already. I wanted to be his equal, I wanted to have an answer for myself, later, whenever I remembered his generosity: I had done what I could, to my own detriment; I had not deceived him, I had left him to make his own decision.

"I know," he said. "Let's do this for now. My brother-in-law is also afraid of a lawsuit: he's not stupid, just dishonest. And fortunately, he's greedy. Maybe he'll help, because he cares more about the estate than about some unknown, petty clerk. Let's rely on human vice, since we can't do anything else."

"You're too generous. And I can only pay you back with my gratitude."

He laughed, and immediately denied the value of his gift:

"I'm not very generous; they'd take it anyway. Why should I drag myself from court to court?!"

Now, no matter how much I might try to dissuade him, he would not give up. But I no longer wanted to play with fate.

I thanked him and began to take my leave. My good mood, my hope had returned; he had won me over with his irresponsible generosity. Fortunately, he had renounced everything himself; he had not hung his sacrifice around my neck, or burdened me with expectations of gratitude, and was no longer my adversary (he could have turned out to be anything in those early days; he still had not become anything definite; I adjusted to him from one moment to the next, like one does with his first, uncertain love, which can easily turn into hatred).

"It's a pity you're a dervish," he said suddenly, laughing out loud. "I'd invite you to a party; my friends are going to be there."

And he added cunningly, openly: "I won't try to hide it, since you'll find out tomorrow anyway."

"So you don't like order?"

"No, I don't. I know, you'll reproach me, but 'You do your work, and I'll do mine.'[3] It's not important if we do not do good; it's important that we do not do evil. And this is not evil."

Thus, he even joked about the Koran, but without malice or mockery. He did not like order or anything sacred; he was indifferent to such ideas.

Suddenly, the cheerfulness left his voice. His smiling lips puckered into a cramped circle, and a barely perceptible paleness shot through his wind-leathered face. I looked through the window, following his eyes: the slender woman from Dubrovnik and her husband had entered the yard.

"Have they also come to your party?"

"What? No, they haven't."

He was overcome by excitement, and lost control of himself, but that lasted only for a moment. His eyes froze in the wide openings between his eyelids, and his hands fidgeted. But only for a moment, then everything was over, as if it had never happened. His smile returned, he was again unruffled and confident, calmly happy at the arrival of his friends. But although his look did not reveal it, he was still agitated. I knew because his eyes no longer saw me, as if I no longer existed. He was not unkind, he did not quit looking at me, he told me to stop by again, and reminded me to go see his sister. On the surface everything was as usual, but his thoughts were not with me: he was down there, in the yard, with the woman who had come to visit him.

We went out to see them. We met at the door and greeted each other; I took a quick, stealthy look at her face. She did not seem especially beautiful from up close, her cheeks were thin and pale, there were traces of fever or sorrow in her eyes, but there was something in her expression that was not easily forgotten. Her faint fragrance drifted past me and

I left, thinking how everything between them defied a solution. That was why he had spoken with such interest about the servant-woman and her two men! Did he have the same problem, was he at the same dead end? If he had not been in love, everything would have been easier and simpler. But his sudden pallor had not lied. Did she know? Did her husband know, the good-natured Dalmatian who bowed low before me, with the pleasant smile of a kind man, slow at everything? He could not have known; he was not torn by passion. And he would not have killed anyone, even if he had. His wife knew; women always know, even if nothing is said, and they are more likely than not to think that something is going on. What was happening between them, unsaid, unarticulated, in front of her husband whose presence kept them apart, and whose lack of suspicion encouraged them, her husband who was always ready to ease their dangerous silence with cheerful talk about nothing? What passionate, raging desire had those two young people tasted, or failed to satisfy, what enchantment had they been nourishing in their thoughts, which could grow into a dangerous obsession?! Or was it just that Hassan had fallen under the spell of her figure, which swayed like tall reeds, and of the quiet clarity of her glistening eyes, marked with illness? Had he become an outcast for that reason, to become irrevocably entangled in a passion that could not be consumed and that would not disappear? During the months that they were separated he would think of her, and meet her upon his return. Her beauty was enhanced by the longing he felt in his travels in distant lands, and he would drink her in with his thirsty eyes so he could remember her when he left on a new journey. How long could they move in this circle, nourishing their passion, but unable to sate it?

If he ever thought about me, he certainly forgot about me then; she had displaced me long before, me and everything that was not her. And if I hated her then it was because her long velvet dress, full girlish lips, and mature, seductive voice were more important to him than I and my troubles. She reduced me to nonexistence; she undermined my only support—which had not existed either, although I would have liked for that illusion to continue.

I was alone again.

Maybe that was best, then you expect no help and fear no betrayal. Alone. I would do everything I could, without relying on support that was not there; then everything I achieved would be mine, both the good and the bad.

I passed by the mosque on the corner of Hassan's street, passed along the wall that hides the madrasah, went down the street where the cobbler's shops are, and came to the tanneries. The Catholic woman's fragrance had vanished, and my thoughts about Hassan faded. I walked by workshops and craftsmen quietly going about their work; I was entering the realm of my own troubles again and starting out on a journey into the unknown. But why was it into the unknown? I did not doubt that I would succeed; I did not dare to doubt it, because then I would not have had the strength to take even one more step. But I had to; it was a matter of life and death, or of something even more important. At that moment I longed for peace. I walked past the storefronts with my head lowered; exhausted, I breathed in the smell of leather and the bark of alder trees; tired, I watched the feet of the passersby and the round cobblestones in front of me; tired, without even a shred of strength. I wished for my closed room and a long deathlike sleep, that of a drowned man, to lie behind a locked door and closed windows, like an invalid. But that weakness, fear of unimagined difficulties, and desire to lie down and die, to give up and accept fate—I did not dare to let them stop me now. I could not let any weariness or fatigue keep me from performing this duty. My remaining peasant stubbornness and the mercilessly clear realization of the need to defend myself urged me on. I had to. Go forward, die later.

PART I

What was the source of my fear and sense that trouble was imminent, when there was nothing in my experience that could have warned me?

When I heard the clatter of hooves in the street, I raised my eyes and saw two soldiers on horseback, armed, riding abreast, yielding to no one. People passing through the narrow street pressed themselves up against the storefronts and walls to avoid being struck by the horses' crops or caught by the soldiers' sharp stirrups. They rode slowly, and people were able to move out of the way, to wait without a word until they passed. The soldiers did not try to hit anyone on purpose, but they did not alter their path, either. It was almost as if they saw no one.

I wondered whether I should go into a shop to let them pass, or stand up against a wall like everyone else. I decided to stay outside, like all the others; I would let them humiliate me. The street was narrow; there was just enough space for them. A stirrup would catch me and tear my gown, and I would not even turn around; they could do whatever they wanted. I would do the same as the others, who said nothing and waited. What were they waiting for, what were those people along the storefronts waiting for as the soldiers rode toward me? To see them humiliate me, or to hear me shout at them (my rank and garb gave me the right to do that). At that moment I wanted both to happen. It suddenly seemed to me that what I would do was important, even decisive. I was upset that they watched and waited: Were they on my side, were they against me, or were they indifferent? I did not even know that. I did not dare to shout; the soldiers would mock me, and I would end up looking silly. The people would not feel sorry for me because of that defeat. No, let them humiliate me, everyone would see that I had moved out of the way, that I was the same as them, powerless; I even wished for my disgrace to be as great as possible, to be greater than that of the others. I stood with my back against a wall, barely feeling the uneven bricks, with my eyes lowered. I was not upset by the disgrace that awaited me, and chose the narrowest place in the street on purpose. I even waited with painful pleasure for it to come—people would hear about it, and pity me. I was turning into a victim.

But what happened was not what I had predicted: one soldier rode out ahead and they passed by me in single file. They even greeted me. At first I was surprised, their actions caught me off-guard, all my efforts had been unnecessary, and everything seemed somehow ridiculous: my feeble heroism, my needless steps toward the wall, my readiness to accept insult. Without raising my eyes I walked on, among the people standing in the street and watching me silently. I had been tricked and humiliated. I had been on the verge of becoming one of them, but the soldiers had singled me out.

When I had passed through the gauntlet of their eyes, not daring to look at them, when I had gone into another street where there were no witnesses of my failed sacrifice, my tension abated, and I felt more at ease. I raised my eyes toward people, greeted them and returned their greetings, calmed and quieted, and it became clearer and clearer to me that this outcome was best. They had recognized me, paid me respect, and refrained from using violence against me. And that was what I had wanted, I had even thought to myself superstitiously, standing against the wall: if they pass by in single file, everything will be all right, everything that I intend to do will turn out well. Or maybe I had not, maybe it occurred to me later, when everything had already happened, since before I would have been too superstitious to connect the outcome that I desired with a miracle, with such an impossible condition. But anyway, a miracle had happened—or maybe it was not a miracle, but a sign and proof. How could I have faintheartedly believed that I had been cast out or stripped of my rights? Why would that have happened? Whom would that have benefited? I remained what I had been, the dervish of a distinguished order, the sheikh of a tekke, a confirmed defender of the faith. How could I be cast out, and why? I had no desire to be anything else, I was not able, I did not want it, and everybody knew that, so why would they prevent me from it? I had imagined everything, I had confused everything within myself unnecessarily; I did not know where the source of my cowardice lay. I had stood in the face of death a hundred times without flinching, and now my heart was like a pebble, dead and cold. What had happened? What had become of our courage? Was it now a cowardly shudder at the hooting of an owl, at a voice stronger than ours, at nonexistent guilt? Such a life is worth nothing. I had swum across rivers with my saber in my teeth, I had crawled on my belly through reeds, listening eagerly for the enemy; I had rushed at guns without faltering, but now I was afraid of one wretched soldier. O misery of miseries, something has happened to us, something awful, we have shrunk to nothing and not even noticed it. When did we lose our way, when did we allow this to happen?

It was still daylight, dim and weary. Shadows were already gnawing at it, but it had to last long enough for me to meet the night without pain or shame. I had known where I was going even before I made the decision to go there. My thoughts were subconsciously directed at him and I hoped that his wife had told him of her conversation with me; we could both pretend that we knew nothing, keeping an apparent secret. We would not discuss Hassan, but my cheerful expression would tell him everything. And even if she had not told him, I had nothing to fear. Maybe it would be better if I went to see her first, to bring her the news of Hassan's agreement, like a gift. Then it would be easier to talk to her husband.

But it was no use. Cowardice pervades us, it forms our thoughts. May it be damned, it speaks from our mouths even as we are ashamed of it.

I took advantage of that moment of resentment and went immediately, so that I would not put it off forever.

Surprisingly, Aini-effendi received me at once, as if he had been expecting me. No word of my arrival had preceded me, although a hidden presence of people and eyes made itself felt in the corridors.

He met me kindly, with a greeting that was neither eager nor indifferent, without pretending that he was glad or surprised to see me. He was measured in everything he did, wearing a vague smile, and did not try to frighten or encourage me. That was honest, I thought, but I felt ill at ease.

A cat stole in from somewhere, looked at me with its yellow, evil eyes, and went up to him, sniffing him. Without shifting his indifferently kind gaze from me, he stroked the pampered animal, which squirmed with pleasure under his hand, rubbing its neck and sides against his knee, and then climbed into his lap, curled up there, and began to purr, squinting at me menacingly. Now two pairs of eyes were looking at me, both of them yellowish, cautious, and cold.

I did not want to think of his wife, but she emerged from the dark, from far away; I did not want to think of her because of him, stiff and guarded, his hidden hands surely were suffocating in his long sleeves, his face transparent, with thin lips, his shoulders narrow. He was pallid, fragile, as if only water flowed in his veins: What were their nights like in that large, silent house?

He was unbelievably calm, he felt no need to move at all (his stillness reminded me of rigor mortis or a fakir's* power of self-control), and his face wore the same expression that I had met when I came in, with a smile that said nothing deceptively stretching across his lipless mouth. That smile wore me out more than it did him.

Only from time to time, and it always happened unexpectedly, one of his hands would come to life, treacherously, emerging from its sleeve like a snake (hers were like birds). And his eyes would come to life as well whenever they looked into the eyes of his cat, which were the same as his, and softened only then, only for a moment.

I did not know how long I sat like that. Dusk came, then darkness. The phosphorous eyes glowed in his lap. And strangely, his did as well, or so it seemed to me. He had four gleaming eyes. Then candles were brought in (just as they had been on that night, but I was no longer thinking of her, I did not dare) and that was even worse. His dead smile unnerved me, his dead expression frightened me, as did the darkness behind him and the shadows on the wall; I was unsettled by a soft rustling, as if rats were crawling around us. But maybe most troublesome of all was that he never once raised his voice, or changed the way he spoke. He did not get excited or angry, and did not laugh. Words fell slowly from him, yellow, waxen, foreign. Again and again I wondered at his ability to arrange them so well and put them in the right places, because it seemed that they were amassed somewhere in the cavity of his mouth, about to spill out of him and flow away in disorder. He spoke patiently, persistently, confidently; he never once doubted himself; he considered no other possibility, and the few times that I contradicted him he seemed truly surprised, as if his ears had deceived him, as if he had met a lunatic. And he continued to reel off phrases from books, adding his dank lethargy to the centuries of their existence. I was disturbed, and asked myself: Why is he speaking? Does he really think that I don't know these familiar phrases, or that I've forgotten them? Is it his high position that speaks, his prominent office? Does he speak from habit, or to keep from saying nothing? Is he mocking me, or doesn't he have any words other than those that he's learned by heart? Or is he trying to torture me, to drive me insane? Is the cat there to claw out my eyes at the end?

Then it occurred to me that he had indeed forgotten all ordinary words, and that was a terrible thought: not to know a single word of your own, not to have a single thought of your own, to be unable to say anything human, to speak without need or meaning, to speak in front of me as if I were not there, to be condemned to speak by rote. And I was condemned to listen to what I already knew.

Or was he a madman? Or a corpse? Or an apparition? Or the cruelest of torturers?

At the beginning I could not believe my eyes and ears; it seemed impossible that a living man before him and a living prisoner in the fortress could not induce him to speak even a single real word, one relevant to the present moment. I tried to draw him into a human conversation, to make him say something, anything at all, about himself, about me, about my brother, but it was all in vain; he only spoke through the Koran. And alas, he was also speaking about himself, about me, and about my brother.

And then I, too, dove into the Koran. It was mine as much as his, I knew it as well as he did, and there ensued a duel of thousand-year-old words that replaced the ones we usually spoke and that had been created on account of my imprisoned brother. We resembled two broken fountains that spilled stagnant water.

When I said why I had come, he answered with a passage from the Koran:

Those who believe in God and the Last Judgment do not associate with the enemies of Allah and His prophet, even if they are their fathers, or their brothers, or their kindred.[4]

I cried out:

"What has he done? Will anyone tell me what he has done?"

You who are faithful, do not ask about that which might cast you into distress and despair if it were told to you openly.[5]

"I'll be indebted to you as long as I live. I've come to have it told to me openly. And I'm already in distress and despair."

They walked the earth proudly and plotted wicked intrigues.[6]

"Whoever you're talking about, I can't believe he's my brother. God says that of the infidels. My brother is one of the faithful."

Woe to those who do not believe.[7]

"I've heard that he's in prison because of something he said."

There cannot be clandestine understandings or whisperings between three people without God being the fourth among them. Clandestine meetings are the work of Satan, for Satan wants to aggrieve the faithful.[8]

"I know my brother well—he couldn't have done anything wrong."

Do not help or aid the infidel.[9]

"He's my brother, for God's sake!"

If your fathers, sons, brothers, wives, and families are dearer to you than God, His prophet, and the struggles on the path to His righteousness, do not expect His mercy.[10]

O faithful ones, avoid suspicion and slander, because slander and suspicion are sinful.[11]

I was the one who said that.

I responded in the same measure, with the Koran; I could no longer keep to ordinary words, because in that way he was stronger than me. His arguments were those of God, while mine were those of men. We had not been equal. He was above everything and spoke the words of the Creator, and I tried to place my minute troubles on the scale of ordinary human justice. He drove me to apply eternal measures to my case, if I were not to deprive it of any value at all. At that time I was not even aware that I had lost my brother in those dimensions of eternity.

Even then he defended his principles, and I myself. He was calm and confident; I was upset, almost enraged. We both spoke the same words, but we each said something completely different.

He said: *Neither the skies nor the earth wept for the sinners.*[12] And I thought: Woe to the man whose standards are the skies and the earth. He said: *Verily, he who defiles his soul will be unhappy.*[13] And also: *O Zul-qarnain, Gog and Magog are causing discord all over the earth.*[14]

And I said: *O Zul-qarnain, Gog and Magog are causing*

discord all over the earth. And: *Verily, he who defiles his soul will be unhappy.* And: *There is truth, and there is also error.*[15] And: *Let people have forgiveness and mercy for one another, if they want God to forgive them.*[16] And also: *Indeed, man is a great tyrant, and tyrants are farthest from the truth.*[17]

To that he was silent for a moment, and then said calmly, still smiling:

Woe to you, woe to you, and woe to you again![18]

Allah is every man's refuge,[19] I said desperately.

Then we looked at each other. I was shattered by everything that had been said, thinking that I had forgotten my brother and incriminated myself. He was calm and stroked the raised tail of his repulsive cat, which squirmed behind him. I should have left; if only I had not even come. I had learned nothing, I had helped nothing, and I had said what I should not have. Because even the Koran is dangerous if you use God's words about sinners to refer to those who decide who the sinners are. You will regret a thousand times what you say, but rarely what you keep silent. I had known this wisdom when I had not needed it. It would have been better if I had only listened, and only said what would have been most useful. I had totally forgotten this, and I knew that it was important. It had been important the night before; it concerned him, and me; his wife had said that he knew nothing about it. And I remembered: I had betrayed a friend because of this.

And I told him quickly, trying to suppress the shame that came over me, how I had persuaded Hassan to renounce his inheritance. Nothing more, only that. I did not make any connection with myself, this visit, or my brother. But he would make it, he would have to, and he would not be able to answer with the Koran. There was also a certain spite in this sudden change in the conversation, and a malicious wish to defile him with his own greed.

But I was wrong, again. He did not show at all that he understood me. He was not surprised; I saw neither anger nor joy in his eyes, but in the Holy Book he found an answer for this occasion as well:

He who seeks is paltry, and what he seeks is paltry as well.

What he said could have meant everything and nothing. The end of the conversation, hidden anger, mockery.

It was useless; he was stronger than I. He resembled a corpse, but he was not: principles raged within him.

The eyes shone in his lap, under his hand, the cat's eyes. I did not dare to look into his; they scorched me with their icy, phosphorescent glow.

I lowered my gaze and said nothing, frightened by my unnecessary courage and his superior rebuttal.

"Come again," he said politely. "We don't see each other often."

7

> Do not grieve, rejoice at the paradise
> that has been promised to you.[1]

I WENT OUT INTO THE NIGHT. MY LEGS SEEMED WOODEN beneath me; an icy shudder rippled through my veins, and weariness, remorse, anger, fear. Everything crazy and helpless in me collected and turned into a sludge that buried my consciousness. He had seen me to the corridor politely. Candles had flickered in the hands of two servants (how had they known that I was leaving?), and I had thought that their glimmering would blind me in the lengthy darkness. He had invited me to come again any time I wanted. Maybe he was still waiting for me to return, maybe I should have gone back, to tell him that I had not meant anything bad, that I was troubled, confused, and restless, that he should forget everything that I had said. Maybe I should have gone back to kill him, to grab him by the neck and strangle him. Even then the smile would not have left his pale lips, and his yellow, phosphorous eyes would not have gone out.

I rubbed my sweaty hands together, as if I were carrying the dampness of his skin on my own palms. I held them open in front of me, to air them of that imagined touch, trying to rid myself of it.

I walked along the bank of the river for a long time, meeting only an occasional passerby. Most people shut themselves in their houses early, leaving the night to night-watchmen, drunkards, and the luckless.

Everything called me back into the tekke, to lock its heavy door and to be left alone. That desire was strong, like an impulse to escape. But I did not allow myself such weakness. I refused it in spite of myself, since I knew that such a desired withdrawal could never be more dangerous than at this moment; it would have belittled me, deprived me of any value. I would no longer have had any right to self-respect or ever been prepared to do anything at all, I would have waited for every blow with my head lowered, a wretch, I would have become nothing. I could not give up. I had challenged them, and I had to remain on my feet. If I yielded at any time I would have been giving myself the finishing blow.

I walked along the still bank, listening to the current, hoping for tranquillity: the vibrance of nature calms a man's soul, maybe precisely because of its indifference toward him. But the river did not help me, the tumult inside me was louder.

I did not expect to meet the renegade Is-haq; I had matured since that time in the mosque when I had vaguely hoped to hear his words. His opinions and advice would not have mattered to me today. He had some goal of his own and took misfortune like rain, or clouds. But I was not thinking of a particular misfortune. I knew that everything in my life had been called into question. *Everything*—that was very indefinite, but also very real. That meant desperation and waywardness, an erring from the path of life, but I knew of no other; it was a sense of nameless terror at the empty, silent void that can be created around you.

If someone distant and unknown reads these unusual notes, I fear that he will understand little of them, since it seems that we dervishes really do have a special manner of thinking about ourselves and the world, a world in which everything of ours depends on others. No one is so powerless and meaningless, no one can be so utterly ruined inside as we are, if they only decide to shut us out. And we realize this only with difficulty, only when it does indeed happen.

A night-watchman stopped me at the wooden bridge where the river bends. He stood hiding in the shadow of a tree, and whispered for me to hide as well. Until they leave, he said. Some youths were throwing rocks at a lamp by the path.

When the glass broke and the light went out, they left, without haste.

The night-watchman watched them go calmly, explaining that they had already gotten used to destroying something every night. But he hides, to save his skin. And the next day the people from the mahal will pay for the damage; it isn't right for him to pay out of his own pocket. And when I asked why he doesn't turn them in, he asked how he can turn them in when he doesn't know who they are. Night, the darkness, the distance: you might make a mistake. And when I told him that I wouldn't be lenient toward them if I were in his place, he said that he wouldn't either, if he were in my place. But as it is, he doesn't hear or see them; what else can he do, since in that job he's like a catkin: blow, and he's gone. And God only knows who they are, full of food and drink, well-dressed, plenty of money, nothing to worry about; idle, they carouse till dawn, looking for women, if I'll excuse him, looking for trouble. All night long he tries to avoid them, hiding so they won't meet, and if they find him he tells them to go off into some other part of town; and they say: no; and he says: so don't; and they say: you're an old fool; I know, he says, and I'm a bigger one every day; Do you want us to throw you into the river, they ask; No, he says. That's how their conversations go, and he tries to find a way to escape. That's his job, he says, you see and hear everything. Night was created for things that are done in secret, and walking around until dawn he even learns things that he doesn't want to, things that are none of his business, but he's not much for conversation, especially free of charge: Why should you waste your time for nothing? And he doesn't need what he knows; he can't eat or drink it, although it could be of use to someone. But it seems strange to him: he knows and doesn't care, while someone else cares and doesn't know. When he gives some information to someone the only thing that he, the night-watchman, cares about is whether he's giving it to someone who might have some use for it, and everything is out of love and friendship, as long as he doesn't go home to his children empty-handed. Indeed, he says "friendship" just like that, but you can't say that there's a lot of it around; he doesn't run into it at night, and during the day he sleeps, so he doesn't know. But what he does know hasn't made him happy. He's even begun to look at his wife with suspicion; she might be plotting against him. Now regarding his wife, he's exaggerating and making a mistake; she'd pluck out her eye for him if he needed her to (and she'd pluck out another one, his, if she heard what he's saying), and he mentions it only as an example.

I listened to this deranged, shrewd babble, this jocular openness from the neighborhood spy, who was always ready to sell the secrets of others. They did not matter to me, but I was not in a hurry to leave; I stood there for a while, to pass the time for both of us; he liked to talk and I liked to listen; it did not matter to what. I even became interested in the way that he apparently hid his thoughts and then revealed them completely, unable to persevere in his cunning. But then he began to act strangely and whimsically. He was old, at least fifty, and old people are either bored or afraid of being left alone. He invited me to go on his watch with him, I had probably never seen the kasaba so late at night, and a man should see everything. It was especially beautiful just before dawn, when bakers pulled hot bread from their ovens. If I wanted to we could go to the street where Hassan lived. He was celebrating; he had brought in musicians; we would stand somewhere near and listen; that was not a sin; it would gladden anyone's soul, even a dervish's. He was sorry when I refused. Do as you wish, he said, do as you wish, whatever you like, but it's a pity that you don't want to go. I wondered at this invitation; it sounded like a rude joke, or a childish wish. Now he would have to wait for someone else.

"Well, fine," he said as we parted.

Had something frightened him?

I left him in a covered doorway, invisible in the shadows.

A strange man, I thought as I walked through the empty streets.

Everything changes when darkness falls. No particular time of the day is reserved for sin, but night is the most natural time for it (at this time all children, the little, clever ones as well as the big, dull ones, are asleep, along with those who manage to work their evil during the day). Or whenever we cannot see well.

So that is what we have achieved: we have pushed sin out of our sight and made it more powerful.

I walked through the quiet town, the only thing that could be heard was the sound of a distant zurna; at times human shadows slipped past, restless like the souls of the damned; dogs barked in the different mahals, and the moonlight was leaden. Even if I had yelled, dying, not one of the doors would have opened. I could not remain in the present moment; everything in me strove toward either what had already happened or what was about to happen, but I did not succeed in stepping over the boundaries of the night. I saw it as if from far away, as if I were looking down from a hill into a gloomy landscape: I was outside of it, yet in it, separated from it, yet surrounded by it. Everything seemed trivial in my world—the many births taking place at that very moment, the many deaths, the many loves, the many evils. I say my world, because no other existed. There were only shadows and empty moonlight around it. And around us only the quiet dripping of time. And within me only powerless indifference and lifeless silence. I was like an infidel, I had no inner light.

O Lord, for what unknown sin are you punishing me?
I beg you, hear my prayer.

Salvation and peace to Is-haq, who is not here tonight.

Salvation and peace to Ahmed Nuruddin and his brother Harun, who seek each other tonight.

Salvation and peace to all those who are lost in the great silence between the earth and the sky.

I should have stayed with the night-watchman, so I would not be left alone with myself and my inability to resist or submit.

Empty and sadly indifferent. But I was still glad when I drew near to the tekke. Then I was neither empty nor indifferent, for it is good when a man is either happy or sorry, no matter what the reason. As soon as I noticed that slight glimmer of joy (and I looked into my soul and everything that was happening inside it, as a plowman checks the sky, clouds, and winds to see what the weather will be), I felt stronger because of that clear patch in the clouds. It is there even when we cannot see it; it is there even when we think that it is not.

When I entered my narrow street, which took me in like a kinsman, someone stepped out of the shadow of the tekke wall. Only his head was visible in the moonlight, as if he had surfaced in water, as if he had left his body somewhere else. He greeted me, trying to be polite, because of the fear that he must have assumed I felt: "You've been away for quite a while. I've been waiting for you for a long time."

I said nothing. I did not know if I should say or ask anything. His face looked familiar, although I did not remember that I had ever seen it; it was familiar in a special way, as when we discover some feature, some expression, some characteristic of someone that we have noticed somewhere, sometime, but forgotten, since it did not seem important.

I looked at the tekke, quiet and dead in the moonlight, and when I turned to him again, I had already forgotten what he looked like. I turned away once more, this time trying to remember his face, but it was futile; he disappeared from my memory as soon as I stopped looking at him. He was surprisingly faceless.

He noticed my movements and said hurriedly:

"Friends have sent me."

"Which friends?"

"Friends. I thought you wouldn't even come back tonight. They couldn't tell me anything in the tekke. You've been away somewhere for quite a while."

"I've been walking the streets."

"Alone?"

"I was alone, until now. And I was content."

He laughed, politely, kindly.

"Of course. I understand."

His face was flat, like two palms with a nose between; his wide, strong lips were spread into a cheerful smile, his lively eyes were attentively fixed on me. It was as if he were very glad that we had met, and was happy at everything I said and did. If it had not been dark and if we had not been alone, his appearance might have been pleasant. I was not afraid of this man; there was not a trace of fear in me, not even of the possibility of violence. I just felt awkward, everything was tightening around me. I was impatient.

"All right, friend, tell me what you want or allow me to pass."

"You've been walking the streets and wasting your time, but all of the sudden you're in such a hurry!"

I tried to pass, but he stepped in front of me.

"Wait a minute. Here's what I want . . ."

He looked confused, as if he were searching for the right words, or as if he did not like having to stop me, although he had done it without hesitation.

"You're making my task more difficult. Now I don't know how to begin."

"You've been waiting here a long time, you could've figured that out."

He laughed cheerfully: "You're right. You're not easy to deal with. Look here. But maybe it's best if we go inside the tekke."

"All right. Let's go."

"It doesn't matter, though. We can also do it here. My message is short. Who do you think it's from?"

"No one sends me any messages, and my friends tell me things themselves. You're playing a joke, or you're trying to anger me."

"Not at all! You learned people are really funny. So what if I'm joking? Can't we have a talk like reasonable men?! All right. Your friends think you should watch what you do a little more."

"You must have made a mistake; you obviously don't know with whom you're speaking."

"I haven't made a mistake, and I know with whom I'm speaking. So you be more careful. You're not thinking about what you're doing, and that could be dangerous. For you, I mean. Why are you hanging guilt around your own neck, and when no one is bothering you? What does a man need trouble for if doesn't already have any?! Isn't that true?"

So it was a threat, intended to humiliate me. It had been put into the mouth of this police thug, who was playing a joke on me at that, on his own account, giving me advice. Now I was interesting for him, like a rare animal caught in a trap. He even liked me a little: I could bring him some enjoyment.

"All right," I said, suppressing my anger, because I did not want to show it in front of him. "Tell your friends . . ."

"And yours . . ."

"Tell those friends that I thank them for their message, although they could've delivered it themselves. And I'll answer to God and to my conscience for everything I do. Can you remember all of that?"

"Of course I can! But I think you might have to answer to someone else, too. It's easy to answer to God. He'll forgive you. And it's even easier to answer to your conscience—you can always come up with a thousand excuses. But when you find yourself in the torture chamber, up there in the fortress, by God, it'll be more difficult. And especially when you know you're guilty."

"I'm not guilty of anything."

"Well, it's not quite like that. To tell the truth, who isn't guilty of something? Doesn't Hassan the cattle drover come to the tekke? He does. Don't you have conversations about all sorts of things? You do. And then . . ."

"You should be ashamed!"

"I'm not, effendi. And then, did a fugitive hide in the tekke garden? Yes, he did. Did he escape? Yes, he did. And who helped him to escape?"

"I sent for the guards."

"You sent for the guards too late. And I won't even mention what else you're guilty of. And you say: I'm not guilty! But again, has anyone asked you about all of this? No. So I'm telling you, stay clear of trouble. And if you don't care, it's your business, right? And it's mine to tell you this."

"Is that all?"

"What else do you want? Even this would be more than enough for reasonable men. But if need be, more can be found, don't worry. That's what all of them ask in the beginning: Is that all? Later they quit asking. I like brave men, but where are they? It takes years to find one who's really got any guts. Only one out of so many. This world's enough to make you sick! So there you have it. And don't say later: I didn't know. Now you do."

He was still looking at me with the same interest that he had had at the beginning, but he had already done what he was supposed to do, and wanted to see what he had achieved, to see whether he had inspired fear in me.

He upset me, but I did not feel fear. It was surpassed by my anger at this shameful act, this insult. I even felt defiant, I was determined to persevere, urged by a momentary thought of how they wanted to stop me from doing something that was my right. This meant, then, that they were not confident, that they were afraid. If that were not true, why would they be trying to warn me? They would do whatever they wanted, regardless of what I said or did. This strengthened my inner conviction, which I had been carrying for a long time, that I represented something here, in this place, in the dervish order, that I had not passed through the world unseen and insignificant. They were not that stupid; they knew it would not be good to attack me: in that way they would show openly that they respected no one, not even the most honorable or the most devoted. But they would not do that, they had no reason for it.

That was what I thought as I went toward the tekke. My confidence had increased, and I even thought it was good that they had sent this man: they had revealed that they were afraid, while their insults had only strengthened my resolve. But I knew that I could not give them much time to act against me, I had to reach the one man who could decide everything, before they did. If it had not been night then, I would have gone off that very moment. I was gladdened by this determination not to wait, not to give myself over to empty sorrow and feeble hope, but rather to do everything I could. I could not afford to walk the streets like a sleepwalker, with no will of my own, hobbling around as if I were crippled. A man is not what he thinks, but what he does.

Yet when I had closed the heavy oaken gate and pushed the bolt, when I found myself in the safety of the tekke garden, against all expectation and logic—since there I was protected by everything of my own—an unpleasant restlessness came over me. It happened all of a sudden, with almost no warning, as if while I was opening and closing the gate, pushing the bolt and checking whether it had settled in its wooden quarters, I let the thought that had been keeping up my spirits slip away. It disappeared, darted into the night like a wild bird, and in its place there appeared an unease, which resembled fear. It happened only then, belatedly; I did not know why. I did not dare to try to explain its source; maybe it was just that source that made me afraid, and so I left it in the darkness, unexplained, although I was aware of its existence. A thought overtook me, like heat; it struck me like a painful flash. I thought that it was what the beginning of a stroke must be like; it announced itself like deep, muffled thunder: they are surrounding me.

Neither then nor long after did it occur to me that human thought is an unsteady wave that is stirred and calmed by the capricious winds of fear or desire.

I knew only one thing; I had forgotten it, but it occurred to me again: presentiment is the herald of misfortune.

But at that moment it was clear to me that I must not give up. Early the next day I would strengthen my bulwark against the torrent already rushing toward me.

I will not give up.

May my arms wither, may my mouth go dumb, may my soul become arid, if I do not do what a man must.

And may God decide.

In the morning I carried out all my sacred duties, maybe a little more lively than usual, bringing excitement into those familiar gestures and words, remembering my unease of the previous night, thinking about the importance of what I had to do, as before a decisive battle, never doubting whether I should go. In battle men are wounded and even killed, and therefore my prayer was more ardent than ever; but there was no turning back, and so the curse and oath, with which I had offset my hesitation the night before, were unnecessary. I remembered, everything was indeed as it had been before that battle long ago. I bathed myself when I returned the previous night; I thought that the water would calm me down. I bathed myself the following morning as well. My shirt was clean; I had taken a fresh one, white as snow. As I had then. But I had marched into that battle along with others, in a line that was harder than stone, with an unsheathed saber in my bare hand, with passionate joy in my eyes. Now I was marching alone, O dear, distant time, in a black gown that got in the way of my feet, with empty, sagging arms, with a fearful soul.

But I walked on. I had to.

I went to see Hassan. I did not have much time, I was too impatient, but I still stopped in. I could not have gone without seeing him; it would have been like missing something very important. But I did not know why I needed to do it; he could not help me, he could not give me any advice. Maybe because he was closest to me, although even he was not very close. It resembled superstition a little, or a defense against a spell: his serenity could bring luck.

He was not at home. I knocked for a long time on the gate, I thought that he was sleeping. And when I had already given up, the small woman opened it, hiding her face again, adjusting her hair, strangely flustered. Hurriedly and stuttering, she explained that Hassan was not at home. He had left the night before and had not come back yet; her husband was out looking for him, and now they were waiting for both of them. They were waiting together for the two men, locked in, excited, satisfied that the troubles of others had brought them happiness.

I also told Hafiz-Muhammed where I was going, to hear what he thought. I would not have changed my mind no matter what he said, but I hoped that he would give me some encouragement. He was kind to me, as if I were the one who was ill, and not he. You should go, he said. You should have done this earlier. It's your duty to help even a stranger, to say nothing of your own brother. And don't hesitate, you're not committing any evil. That was what he said, sincerely and excitedly, but he did not encourage me very much, because that was what I had expected to hear. And he knew that. But a good man will always say what is expected—that is not sincere thought, but empty sympathy.

Hassan was not there. People are never around when you are looking for them.

Passing by a bakery, I inhaled the smell of hot bread and remembered that I had not eaten anything since the previous day. The night before the night-watchman had talked about those loaves of bread. I also had to find him today. How had I failed to realize that he wanted to tell me something? Not only about that man who had been waiting to threaten me. He had tried to keep me, almost by force, so that I would ask him. But I had been deaf and blind.

Then I forced myself to think about the kadi's wife, I would go again into her silent house; about Hassan, what he had done the night before, where he had gone; about my father, I would let him know immediately, as soon as all of this was settled; about the previous night, long and sleepless; about countless trifles, no one had trimmed the roses in the tekke garden, they would get thorny; about Mustafa's children, they sat in front of the tekke more and more often, his wife drove them out so that they would not bother her, while Mustafa grumbled and took them food—people would laugh at us, they already called them the dervish children, and I did not have the heart to drive them away; and I thought about God knows what else, only so I would not have to think about the conversation that I would have with the mufti.* It was not that I did not know what to say, but that afterward I would not be able to do anything else. Prior to a verdict there is hope for everything, and then there is only the verdict. If it is good, then hope was unnecessary; if it is bad, then there was no use in even thinking about it.

The mufti's house was on a slope, isolated, in a garden with a high wall. I had never been inside it before. And it seemed that I would not go in now, either.

A guard in front of the gate told me that the mufti was not at home. He had left the kasaba.

"When will he return?"

"I don't know."

"Where did he go?"
"I don't know."
"Who does know?"
"I don't know."

So, all of my fear had been for nothing. My hope had been prolonged, but it was growing weaker. Maybe soon I would not need it at all.

I did not know what to do. If I went away, I would never meet the mufti, or if I did, it would be too late. Where had he gone? To which of his houses? To which of his estates? Ugosko? Uglyeshichi? Gor? Tihovichi? To the plain? To the lake? To the river? He often fled, and from everything, from the heat, from the cold, from the fog, from the dampness, from the people.

Where was he now? Only there would they be able to tell me that.

"I don't know what to do," I complained to the guard. "The mufti told me to come; we have something important to talk about. I must find him."

The guard shrugged, thus repeating the only words he knew. And I could not make myself leave.

"Someone in the house must know."

Then the gate opened and a gaunt man, an old soldier, judging from the scars on his face and some of the clothes that he still wore (he must have regretted throwing all of them away), looked at me sternly. Until I justified my presence, I was a criminal to him.

I also told him what I had said to the guard.

From the suspicious expression on his face I thought that he doubted the truth of my words. His distrust offended me, but my desire that he really not believe me was even stronger. I had become involved in a lie. I had been forced to do it, but if the mufti found out, and he would, I would have to ask for forgiveness and not justice.

"Never mind," I said, trying to back out.

At that moment I noticed that the soldier's stern face was

changing, growing softer, widening into a smile. Why?

Then I recognized him as well. We had fought together for a while, only he had been in wars both before and after me.

We were both glad.

"You've changed," he said joyfully. "Who would recognize you in that dervish robe? But you see, I recognized you!"

"And you're the same. A little older, a little thinner, but the same."

"Well, I'm not exactly the same. Twenty years have passed. Come in."

He seemed to become less confident when he closed the gate behind us.

"So the mufti summoned you?"

"I need to talk to him. The guard didn't want to tell me where he is."

A clean, straight path cobbled with small river stones showed white through the garden. It was lined with a hedge of barberry and snowberry bushes that had tender, green leaves. The garden was skillfully arranged with fruit trees, birches, junipers, wild rosebushes; at places a single tree stood on the clear lawn, at others they were clumped together, thus creating a playful pattern that resembled nature, and nature that resembled a playful pattern. The flowery and leafy beauty of that large space had the effect of a miracle, mostly because of the thought that all of it had been created so that the feet of one man could tread the light green grass, and so that his gaze could rest on the tender treetops. It really seems that all beauty is superfluous.

The soldier lowered his voice. So did I. We almost whispered in that cleaned, raked, well-kept forest, which was deprived of wildness, but left with freshness, in that quiet place surrounded by a wall, where even the wings of storms were clipped.

The soldier looked along the path toward the white house,

which was hidden among the trees. I also looked. The eye caught sharp flashes of the sun on the windowpanes, alternating with the soft swaying of green tree branches.

The soldier's name was Kara-Zaim. Now he was just a shadow of the former Kara-Zaim, a shabby remnant of that fearless youth who had rushed with his saber drawn against the drawn sabers of the enemy, until an uhlan ran one through his rib cage. Until then he had been continually stabbed, cut, hacked, and maimed. One half of his left ear was missing, as were three fingers of his left hand; his face was furrowed with red scars where new skin had failed to grow in; he hid other scars under his clothes. He had always recovered easily and gone back into battle. His blood was strong and the deep cuts in his young flesh healed quickly. But when the uhlan's hideous saber cut through him, opening him up so that the sun's rays shone inside him for the first time, when the point and blade passed where they were not meant to, piercing his lungs, Kara-Zaim fell lifeless and was left behind as his fellow soldiers retreated. Only a medic brushed his cold hand and ran off after the other troops, intending to say a prayer for him when he reached a secure position. Kara-Zaim awoke at night, from the cold, among the corpses, exhausted, as quiet as they were. He had survived, but he was no longer fit for the military. He lost his strength, his agility, and his joy. Now he was the keeper of the garden, or the house, or just a wretch who took alms.

"I'm fine," he said looking at me cheerfully. I forced myself to look calmly at his scarred face. "My work isn't hard. And the mufti trusts me. I'm sort of like the head of the guards. I instruct them a little, watch over them, and that kind of thing."

"You could've become something else. The dizdar* of a fortress. An assistant to a kaimakam.* And they could've given you an estate, like they give the rest, so you'd have something of your own."

"Why?" he asked, disturbed. "They offered that, but I

didn't want it. I'm content. Not just anybody can serve in this place."

I felt offended and hurt that the onetime hero Kara-Zaim now had to look fearfully toward the house. If I went there, should I look at it the same way? What did he fear, this man who had never feared anything?

Not wanting to hurt him, I said:

"What a hero you were! Great God, what a hero!"

And regretted it immediately. Why should I have reminded him of his past? Why should I have woken him from his slumber? He had not forgotten (that was impossible), but he had calmed down, resigned himself, gotten over it, maybe. I should not have opened his old wounds.

Alas, I was talking about myself as well.

Now it was too late; I had said what I should not have.

He looked at me, astounded. Surely no one had mentioned his past for years; maybe he had mentioned it himself, trying to get others to say something, to remember him as he had been. Had even the memory of him died? Did he really no longer exist in anyone's recollection? But maybe even he did not talk about it any more. Why would he? Or maybe the more distant his past became the more he talked about it, losing hope that anyone would remember it. Everything was still alive in him, but for others he had died.

And so, some dervish had spoken of how he had been. And how he had spoken of it! Maybe he had dreamed that someone would say exactly what I said: Great God, what a hero you were! My words surely struck him in his heart, shooting through his blood like a hot wind, deafening his ears. Or he thought that those words were from his dreams; no one had uttered them, it was only his desire that heard them. But no! This old fool of a dervish had said it. He had remembered and spoken.

For a moment he looked at me, lost, like an epileptic. I did not know what he would do: maybe he would jump for joy and collapse on the stones, vulnerable, or embrace me in

PART I

order to stay on his weak legs, or laugh, or weep, and then die. But I did not know the brave Kara-Zaim well enough. I remembered a hero: How could he be any different now? Only his trembling voice and a soft wheezing in his pierced lungs betrayed him, because of his excitement.

"You remember? Do you really remember?"

"I do. Whenever I think about those times, I see you."

"How do you see me?"

He whispered softly, calling me from the darkness of time.

"Surrounded by light, Kara-Zaim. On a wide field. Alone. You're marching calmly, without turning around, without waiting for anyone. All in white. Your arms are bare up to the elbows. In your hand a saber, and maybe the light is from the sun on its blade. You're unstoppable, like the wind. You resemble a ray of sunlight that can penetrate anywhere. All the others have stopped and watch from afar. You alone."

"I didn't march like that."

"That's how I remember it. What might really have happened has been erased, and my memory is the only thing left."

"That's beautiful. More beautiful than it was in reality. Or maybe not. Surrounded by light, you say? On a wide field?"

He whispered drunkenly and then looked at me, searching for his image in my words, for his distant glory on my lips.

He thought that I was singing a song about his courage, but I only felt sorry for him.

And I could not any longer.

"I'm glad I saw you," I said, taking my leave.

"Wait."

He did not want to let me go, I was the one whom he had awaited for so long, the one who knew. I was a witness that memories do not die, an affirmation that he was more than just a shadow. My memory made up for his lengthy oblivion; it rewarded his long, patient wait.

The same words and two different moods. Both of ours had the same source, but his happiness was my sorrow. No matter, they were both a thousand years old. Even more. None of it was worth much bother.

"I have to go."

"Wait. The mufti is here, in the house. Come in, if it's something important. Tell him that I let you in. No, don't. Tell him that he called for you to come."

"He didn't call for me. I've come on my own."

"I know. You just say that: you sent for me to come. He's so busy that he won't remember. And if he asks you about me, if you get an opportunity to say it, tell him what you know. About long ago."

I had thought that the mufti was gone. I was sorry, but I had accepted it. It was almost easier for me to put everything off. And now things suddenly changed, and what I had wanted would now happen. I was confused and unprepared. I was not surprised that Kara-Zaim wanted me to mention him, but I was sorry that he had suddenly retracted his offer to let me rely on his position with the mufti. Still thinking about his image, in the light, on a heroic battlefield, he had offered to protect me. And refused in the same instant, as soon as he remembered how distant his past was. He flared up and burned out in the same moment. His scarred face still shimmered with happiness at what he had been, and with fearful insecurity at what he was now. Had two periods of time always collided in him? They were so different, and yet inseparable: he could not leave either of them.

As he whispered with some man at the entrance to the house, I thought, confusedly, regretting that his wretched support had slipped out of my grasp, that my insecurity was the same as his. It was pathetic how we expected help from one another, relying little on ourselves. We were trying to combine two weaknesses into one feeble hope. There was

PART I

still hope left in him, but it was worth as much as mine, which had been shattered.

When the man came out of the house and told something to Kara-Zaim with a sign, or a quiet word, he motioned to me with his hand: I've helped you, come on! And without saying anything, he sent me toward the entrance. Now that meant: go in, maybe everything will be all right. But I saw all of it only in passing, uncertainly, in the same vague way that I saw the stunted lemon tree in front of the house, and an even more stunted palm tree that had barely survived our harsh winter, dozing in the spring sun like an invalid. I do not remember where I went, or how many people followed me with their eyes; I was thinking the whole time about the first word that I would say. The first word! It was like a weapon or a shield. Everything depended on it, not because it would explain anything, but because I could lose all my courage if it were inappropriate. It could make me look ridiculous and impose itself like a judgment about me. I tested innumerable words in my head, and all the things that I imagined as my opening remark were truly amazing, as if I were suffering from a mental breakdown, or a concussion that shook up everything, leaving only confusion and nonsense. While I walked through that passage, which remained dark and unidentified in my conscience, everything came to mind, from solemn oaths to curses. I cannot even write down everything that wanted to come out at that first meeting, at that first encounter. What I, what my brain conceived then was incomprehensible; it was a madness that is difficult to explain. I was raging, and mocking everything sensible. It was as if the devil had taken hold of me, and whispered the most unseemly and repulsive words to me, the silliest and most undignified acts. I was shocked. How had he found me at that very moment when I needed the utmost composure? But he comes whenever you do not expect it, whenever you are feeling your worst. Because to consider going up to the mufti and calling him an Antiochian[2] ass, as I, a serious and peaceful man, did, could only be the work of the devil. Leave me alone, you renegade against God! I threatened, agitating him even more.

I was also upset by those tropical plants in their wooden coffins, the palm and lemon in front of the house. I knew that the mufti was from Antioch, and that he did not know our language, but I could not remember where that Antioch was, in which land, and what language was spoken there.

Fortunately, I did not need a first word. I did not need to say anything, I did not need to do anything.

In the room into which I was led, the mufti was playing chess with a man whom I had never seen before. Actually, the game was finished, or had been interrupted. At first I did not know what was going on, nor did I care. But the other man, whom I did not know, unhealthily obese, with a tired, patient and humble smile, agreed with everything the mufti said, and kept turning his head toward me, to divert the mufti's attention from himself. He certainly wished me success in all that I sought, just as long as the mufti noticed me.

But for a long time the mufti did not see that someone had come into the room (and yet he must have told them to let me in when they asked him), and did not respond to my greeting.

All winter he had languished in his overheated rooms, frightened by the harsh cold that lined the eaves with icicles a couple of feet long. He must have looked at them in amazement, weary and yellow, like his tropical plants that had barely lived to see the spring. He warmed himself in the sun, with his back toward the window and a fur coat over his shoulders, withered and irritable.

Both of them were obese; only their fat was distributed differently. They appeared colorless and shriveled, dried out by the inside air, as if they had been sitting since autumn over that black ebony table and ivory chess-set.

At first angrily, and then more feebly and apathetically, the mufti made objections and the other man agreed with him. It seemed strange how the mufti asked questions, how he argued, and how he answered. I could barely make any sense of it.

"Something's wrong."

"I can see."

"You can't see anything."

"Something's wrong."

"The whole time I was in a better position."

"I know."

"What do you see?"

"I made a bad move somewhere."

"How is it that I'm losing then?"

"It's not clear to me at all."

"You must have made a bad move."

"I must have made a bad move."

"How did your knight get here?"

"There, that's the mistake. I couldn't have moved there from where I was."

"Then, check."

"Exactly. Look, a sheikh has come."

"Why don't you watch what you're doing? I can't keep track of everything."

"It usually doesn't happen to me."

"If your knight's there I'll take it, right? I'll take it. Take it. It."

"And checkmate."

"Which sheikh?"

The man pointed to me, happily, and the mufti turned around. His face was yellowish-gray, sagging, with heavy bags under his eyes. Without getting up, he asked me:

"Do you play chess?"

"Not very well."

"What do you want?"

"You told me to come. I asked to speak with you"

"I said that? Yes, yes. To whom? What's it like outside?"

"Sunny. Warm."

"That's what they said last winter: it's not cold. Are the winters here always so harsh?"

"Almost always."

"A terrible land."

"One gets used to it."

"A boring land. Do you play chess?"

The fat man cut in softly:

"He doesn't. He already said so."

"What does he want?"

"He has a request."

"Who is he?"

I said who I was, that I was in trouble and seeking justice, and that if he did not give it to me no one would.

The mufti looked at the man in front of him without concealing his boredom, almost in despair.

Where had I gone wrong?

He got up, turned to the left and to the right, as if he were looking for some place to escape, then began to walk around the room, stepping carefully on the patches of sunlight. But then he stopped and became absorbed in thought, looking at me cheerlessly:

"I spoke with the Constantinople mullah about this. I used to like to talk to him, occasionally, not because he was intelligent, intelligent people can be very boring, but because he knew how to say something unexpected, that would surprise you and wake you up—do you understand, Malik? Surely you don't understand!—something that made it seem worthwhile to listen and answer. He said: human knowledge is trivial. For this reason, a clever man does not live from what he knows. But I wanted to say something different. . . . What was I talking about?"

"About the Constantinople mullah," Malik said.

"No. About justice. 'Justice,' he once said, 'We think we know what that is. But nothing could be more indefinite. It might be the law, revenge, ignorance, injustice. It all depends on one's point of view.' I answered . . ."

PART I

He began walking again, silent, but suddenly faltered. It seemed to me that there was a clockwork inside him, which kept him moving and gave life to his speech and body. And when that clockwork ran down he stopped as well, and was overcome by languor.

He did not offer me a seat, nor was he interested in what I had to say; the only thing left for me to do was to start speaking or leave. That way I might become a second Malik, one more shadow of the mufti, as useless as the first. I decided to speak.

"I've come with a request."

"I'm tired."

"It might interest you."

"Do you think so?"

"Let me try. You spoke of justice. Justice is like health, you think about it only when you don't have it. And it's truly indefinite; maybe more than anything it is the desire to wipe out injustice, something which is, on the other hand, very definite. All injustices are equal, but one always thinks that the injustice committed against him is the greatest of all. And if one thinks that way, then it must be true, because one cannot think with someone else's head."

The mufti's clockwork wound up again. He gave me a surprised look; his heavy eyes stopped on me with a recognition that was not very strong, but enough to encourage me. I had aroused his attention. And that was what I wanted: he had taught me that himself, with his ineffectual story about the Constantinople mullah. But I soon realized that it was easier to play with words about general matters than about particular affairs, which are ours and do not matter to anyone else.

"Interesting," the mufti said, waiting, and Malik looked at me with respect. "Interesting. But can several people think the same thought? And if so, would they then be thinking with someone else's head?"

"Two genuinely human thoughts are always different, just as two men's palms are."

"What's a genuinely human thought?"

"One that's usually not told to anyone."

"Nicely put. Maybe incorrect, but nicely put. And further?"

"I'd like to talk about my misfortune. I said that it seems to be the greatest to me, since it's mine. But I'd like for it to be someone else's, and if it were I wouldn't hurry to learn of it, just as I'm now hurrying to tell about it."

I hastened to move from general reflections to what pained me, while his clockwork still kept him going, while his eyes were more or less alive, since I feared his impending collapse, when my words would flutter around him uselessly.

It became clearer and clearer to me: he was tormented by ennui, and boredom. It draped him like a shroud, descended on him like a fog, covered him like loam, surrounded him like air, flowed into his blood, into his breathing, into his brain; it spread from within him, and from everything around him, from objects, space, the sky, it billowed like poisonous smoke. I would have either to fall into despair myself or struggle against it.

I am not exaggerating; had I thought that it would disperse the murky fog inside him I would have lifted the edges of my gown and begun a belly dance, or done other things that never occur to reasonable men. Maybe his attention, before it gave out, would make his yellow, colorless hand write out four decisive words: Release the prisoner Harun. And he would not know what he had written, he would never remember it. I would have done anything, I say, any madness, any despicable act, and I would not have been ashamed afterward. I would have even thought with pride how I had defeated one man's dead indifference, for a living man, for my brother. But I did not dare to change the game; I saw that he had been awakened for a brief moment only by some spiritual acrobatics. And it was like hashish; I had to give him more and more, so that he would not fall into a heavier state of motionlessness.

That was the weirdest struggle that I have ever heard of: against the lethargy in him, against the paralysis of his will, against his disgust for life. A difficult and torturous struggle, mostly because it had to be carried out with unnatural means, with distorted ways of thinking, with ugly couplings of incompatible feelings, with violence against words. But I was afraid, I was really afraid that his attention would dwindle the moment I stopped the game and turned toward my true goal, the reason why I was doing everything. I had to hover above my true intent, drawing near to it and yet concealing it, since his senses might close up by themselves as soon as he detected it.

Luckily, he was not insincere or opaque: he hid nothing, and everything could be seen on him, both his likes and dislikes. Thus, I guided my disturbed thoughts according to the shadowy or clear expressions that crossed his face; I was glad to have those landmarks, since I might also have been without them.

Everything in him said: surprise me, awaken me, warm me. And I kept trying to surprise, awaken, and warm him, waging a desperate battle to keep that dying man alive, always on the verge of fears that I would not succeed, though all my hope lay in him. I turned my mind inside out, I feverishly rummaged in its corners to find the droppings of the devil, struggling with that corpse so that there would not be yet another. And I had a momentary sense of relief only when he sat down, with some interest and liveliness showing on his sagging face. Then my hope spread its little wings.

"I have a brother," I said, sputtering and wondering whether the tone of my voice would be enough. "But if I don't tell you quickly enough, I might say that I *had* a brother, and having and had is the same as having and not having. And an instant of someone's good or bad will could decide that. He's my brother, not because I wanted him, since if I had I'd have created him, and then he wouldn't be my brother. I don't even know whether my father wanted him, but when he mated with my mother, when a drop of cloudy liquid entered her womb, from that pleasure of theirs, of which I was unaware, out of it grew the bond and obligation which is called a son and brother. He was a desired comfort, or a frequent problem; God bound him to us without asking, granting him joys that we couldn't share and burdening us with all of his troubles and misfortunes. And as your superior mind knows, misfortune is more common than joy, so we might say that brothers are a misfortune sent to us by God, which we therefore accept as His will and our destiny, thanking Him for all of it. So there, I thank God for this misfortune, but I wish that he were your brother so I'd thank Him for the happiness of listening to you, as you're listening to me now. In that case it wouldn't matter to me. But as he can't be your brother since he is mine, and I can't be you, because God destined me to be only an unworthy dervish, let's be what we are: I'll beg, and you decide. Or better yet: I'll talk, and you listen. It's harder for you, I know. You don't have to, I do."

I had awakened him, he had become alive, he watched, listened, comprehended and understood! I did not need a belly dance, my empty words were enough, let them fly like the wind, let them tumble like monkeys, let them rush headlong, as if gone mad, between the rays of the spring sun and the shadows of the room. And so, he settled in his chair, listening and waiting.

"And further?" he asked fairly energetically.

Malik, his first shadow, was staring at me, wondering, maybe learning from me. I could not see him well, I did not care about him. I looked at the mufti's face.

There is hope, brother Harun!

"And so I have a brother, or I have him halfway: I say his name, but he's imprisoned in the fortress. Half of his life is here, and half is up there. And if he loses this half, he might lose the other as well."

"Which half?"

"The one that I still have, telling you this."

"Which fortress?"

"The fortress above the town."

"No matter, go on."

"The fortress where they take bad people—thieves, criminals, outlaws, and the enemies of the sultan. Sometimes. But most of the time just fools. Fools, because they think they're not guilty, although you never know. They're always trying to make the world a better place, but that's not their job, and no one has asked them to do that. As they're proud of their folly, it's easy to catch them, and therefore they make up the majority of the prisoners. Accordingly, one might conclude that only clever people remain free, but it's not so: foolish men also remain free if they know how to hide their folly. And the clever ones are locked away if they show their cleverness. The others who remain free are those who have the right to be whatever they want. My brother was a nobody, a happy man, not clever enough to be feared and not foolish enough for no one to know what he might do; he was too cowardly to be an outlaw, too naive to be bad, too lazy to be someone's enemy. In a word, he was destined by divine providence to be greeted by people without respect, to be recognized for his value without being asked to show it."

"Why is he in prison?"

"Because he didn't listen to our father."

"Interesting."

"Our father is a simple man; he works as much as he can; he gives as much as he must; he's not concerned with anything except rain, clouds, sun, caterpillars, potato bugs, cockle on wheat, smut on corn, and peace in the family. Being utterly simple, of one piece, like a wooden spoon, like a linden bowl, like a plow handle, he didn't abandon the useless parental habit of saying what fathers always say and children never listen to. Our father advised him not to leave home: the land would become barren and towns crowded, with little space and many mouths, few possibilities and many desires; people would begin to choke each other for a bigger piece of bread. My brother didn't listen to him. And then our father said: remember, the trouble with us is that no one ever thinks he's in the right place, and everyone's a potential rival for everyone else; people scorn those who don't succeed, and hate those who rise above them; get used to scorn if you want peace, or to hatred if you agree to the fight. But don't enter the fray unless you're sure that you'll defeat your opponent. Don't point your finger at the dishonesty of others if you're not powerful enough that you don't have to prove it. And he didn't listen to that, either. Now our father has a reason for joy and says: that's what happens to disobedient sons."

As I spoke I noticed with horror that the weak light in the mufti's eyes was going out, they were becoming heavy and tired, and something lost appeared in his expression. Hardly opening his mouth, he asked:

"Who didn't obey that?"

O great God! I was moving forward continuously, but getting farther and farther away. As soon as I neared my real goal, he became frightened. As soon as I tried to make use of what I had built, he destroyed it. There was no end to my task!

I hurried onward, blindly. There was still at least a spark of life in him, otherwise he would not have even asked that. I had become uninteresting, I had wearied him with my philosophizing. I had not been playing the game, but mocking him; I had been carried away by my bitterness, and everything had begun to sound serious. Dizziness was coming over me: please, wait a little longer, don't go out, just a moment more.

The last gleam of sunlight faded, and I stood in an icy waste, with a long, dead night ahead of me. But I could not even scream.

PART I

I lost my confidence; the ease with which I had combined my words disappeared. I sensed that they would no longer fly or flutter, they would crawl along the ground like blindworms.

Only one more handful of crazy words, O God, you have to give them to me, I'm fighting for someone's life!—I prayed desperately, but the prayer did not help. I was crushed by my failure, I could see it in his face.

Where are you slipping away to, brother Harun?

Everything I said after that was useless and futile. I was forced to disclose my purpose.

The mufti sank more and more quickly into boredom, sank deeper and deeper into a pool of dead apathy. The world would begin to die out because of him.

Malik slept, with his head on his breast.

"I'm tired," the mufti said, almost as horrified as I was. "I'm tired. Go now."

"I haven't told you everything."

"Go now."

"Order them to release him."

"To release whom?"

"My brother."

"Come tomorrow. Or tell Malik. Tomorrow."

Malik woke up, afraid: "What happened?"

"God, how boring."

"Do you want to play chess?"

"Nothing happened."

He gave answers out of order, skipping over questions, miraculously remembering some word that would later receive an answer, and none of it seemed to make any sense at all.

He went out, without looking at us, dejected; maybe he had even forgotten that we were there. But maybe he was fleeing from us.

I had not defeated his boredom. It had overcome both of us. I could hardly wait to leave. If I had known what it was, I would never have even dared this attempt.

Malik gave me a murderous look, and, with bouncing steps, carried his sluggish body away, hurrying after the mufti.

"He told me to come tomorrow."

"I don't know anything. Ugh, you've ruined me."

So, now it was over. Maybe I should nevertheless have grabbed the mufti by both of his ears or given him a fillip on his yellow forehead. And I still did not know where Antioch was or what language we had spoken. The entire time it seemed to me that I was standing on my head, that I was hanging between the floor and the lamp, that I was holding the ceiling up with my shoulders, lost, driven insane by his boredom and my desire to overcome it. I had indeed spoken that strange language, but to no avail. Maybe it would be futile the next day as well, because I would already be discouraged by today's failure. I had to come again, but I would not come without faltering, and not only would I not know where Antioch was—damn that city!—but I would not even know my own name. We would again torture one another like an old couple on the second night of their wedding, after the first that had failed pitifully. Only none of it would last as long, since neither of us would hope for very much.

I had nowhere to hurry to now. His yellow, sluggish hand had not, in a fleeting moment of vitality, written the order: Release the prisoner Harun.

Was it because of this that Harun the prisoner sank into an even deeper darkness?

I went out; they led me out, pushed me out, and in front of the house the forgotten Kara-Zaim was waiting for me. People did not remember him after twenty years; I had forgotten him after an hour. He was the only one who did not forget—and that's how life is.

"You took a long time," he said, watching me with interest.

"Does a duel take less time?"

"They usually come out sooner. And they usually look confused."

PART I

"Do I look confused?"

"I wouldn't say so."

Kara-Zaim's eye was not exactly sharp. Let it be as he said.

"We talked about everything."

"But did you talk about me?"

"He told me to come tomorrow."

"I see. Tomorrow, then."

And we went once more along the clean path of river stones. And we would walk it again, tomorrow.

I thought that I would not have the strength to talk with Zaim, that I would not even hear what he was telling me, but I heard, and I answered, although everything inside me had been overturned, although I was still standing on my head. And I began to right myself slowly, slowly, certain that everything would seem even stranger when I came to myself. It would seem like drunkenness, or a bad dream. I would believe that I had been struck by a spell, and that nothing had really happened.

Zaim did not know what was happening inside me. He thought that I had been successful.

"It's good," he said, "that he called you to come tomorrow. Usually he doesn't do that. That means that he likes you; that means that you're in his favor."

You aren't particularly wise, you aren't particularly eloquent, my good Zaim. Yes, he liked me, so much that he went away almost breathless, and we'll continue the torture tomorrow.

Zaim looked at me confusedly, searching for words.

"Look, I'd like to ask a favor of you."

Did he also look at my face to see whether it was withering from his words? I encouraged him, listlessly, for old times' sake:

"Tell me, Kara-Zaim. Freely. Something's troubling you."

That was what the other one should have said to me, a little before.

"Well, nothing's really troubling me. But here they don't know who I am; they think that I've always been this short-winded and wretched. I'm not talking about the mufti, but about the others."

"Has something happened to you?"

"Nothing's happened. They say I'm no longer fit for the service."

"Are they going to let you go?"

"Yes, they're going to let me go. So I thought, maybe you could tell the mufti to keep me. I'm not for the military anymore, but I can guard gates better than most. I get a hundred piasters a year..."

"The mufti gets twelve thousand."

"The mufti is different. So I say, if a hundred piasters is too much, let it be less, let it be eighty. Let it even be seventy. Seventy a year, is that really too much? This is what I wanted to ask you."

Well, usually seventy piasters a year isn't much. You won't get fat from those seventy piasters, my dear Zaim, you who made a bad mistake by not dying on time. But forgive me if I can't pity you, I've been wrangling with the devil for a long time, and my entire body has been battered; not one of my bones is in its place.

"You aren't fit for the military," I said, thinking nothing. "But you can carry a gun. And you can carry a yataghan. How much would you want to help me free an innocent man? He's been imprisoned for no reason at all; he's done nothing wrong. Would you do it for a hundred piasters?"

He looked confused.

"I don't know whether you're just asking me this or talking about something that could really happen."

"Give me an answer."

"That's not easy. While I was still the real Kara-Zaim, I would have done it for nothing. But now, if it's an honest affair... a hundred piasters?"

"Two hundred."

PART I

"Two hundred piasters! O merciful God! I'd be able to live for three years on two hundred piasters. And an innocent man? Where is he?"

"In the fortress."

"So two hundred piasters. And an innocent man, in the fortress. I can't do it."

"But twenty years ago you would have? Even if he were in the fortress? Only if he were innocent, imprisoned for nothing?"

"I would have."

"But now you won't?"

"Now I won't."

"Then forget it."

"Is this a joke or are you serious?"

"A joke. I wanted to see how much you've changed."

"Well, I have. And if they let me go, should I look for you?"

"If they do, I'll find you some work."

"Thank you, I'll remember that. But still, say something to the mufti tomorrow."

He wanted to remain on this white path from the gate to the house, at any price. A reflection of the mufti's importance also fell on him, an insignificant man, and it certainly appeared to him that in this job he was closer to the old battlefield hero than he would have been kneading dough in a bakery or tending a garden bed. And that hero meant more to him than anything in the world.

He met me later the same day, around evening, in my darkest hour. As I was on my way to the gate of death, he rushed out of the fog, fell from the sky in front of me, in a place where there was no reason for us to meet, not for us, not for our eyes, not for our moods. I did not know what mine was, his was beaming with joy. His wheezing sounded victorious.

"They'll let me stay," he said, full of enthusiasm. "I won't have to go. That is, they'll let me stay. They asked me what I talked with you about, and I told them. Then they took me to Malik, and I told it again. That about the light and the battlefield, and your offer of two hundred piasters, and the rest, if I were out of work. Malik laughed, a good man, he said, that was about you, and I also said, it's true, he's a good man. And so, that is, you don't need to say anything tomorrow."

"All right."

He did not even know how I had helped him.

We should kill our pasts with each passing day. Blot them out, so that they will not hurt. Each present day could thus be endured more easily, it would not be measured against what no longer exists. As things are, specters mix with our lives so that there is neither pure memory nor pure life. They clash and try to strangle each other, continually.

8

My God, I have no one besides You and my brother.[1]

AFTERWARD I WENT TO SEE HASSAN, SEVERAL TIMES, BUT HE was not at home. One of his stablehands, the older one, had also been looking for him, and found out that he was with his friends, in prison. He said that they had gone out the night before, around midnight, and beaten up some youths in the Latin mahal, badly, hardly a one of them got away unhurt. It was the youths' fault; they had started it, and now they were getting their wounds tended with damp cloths while Hassan and his friends sat in prison. That's how their binges always end, he said; they lock them up whether they're guilty or not, and release them when they pay; Hassan and his friends never remember whether they're guilty, but they usually are. And they'll release them this time, too, only they want a lot, since the youths have been badly hurt and come from good families. Only Hassan won't pay so much; he yells and says that he's sorry he didn't hit them harder, and he'll do it when he gets out, because he's never met such impudent bastards. The stablehand said that he would bring the money; Hassan doesn't care about money, only about his spitefulness, but what's spiteful about sitting in prison? Of course, they aren't behind bars or in the dungeon, but, you know, in some room. Still, it's sunny outside and dark in there, and it's even hard to spend an hour there, let alone more, if one doesn't have to.

He'd tell Hassan that I was looking for him, and to come and see me immediately. That is, as soon as he's bathed and changed, because he always gets his robe so filthy and full of lice that he has to take it off in the yard, so he won't bring any of those nasty bugs into the house. And I ought to stay in the tekke, if it's important, so we won't go looking for each other like two idiots; but if it's not important, then no matter, we'll see each other soon enough. Maybe it's better if Hassan sleeps a little, because he hasn't had a wink of sleep since the previous morning, although he can go without sleep for three days and nights, and he can also sleep as long; you only wake him up to eat something in his slumber, and then he'll continue, like an animal, if I'll excuse the expression. Damn, when he was born they broke the mold.

It was not for no reason that I was trying to find him, and I did not want him to comfort or encourage me. I did not know why that idea had come back into my mind. In fact it had not been mine but Hassan's, although I considered it my own, and wanted to talk him into doing it. I had mentioned it to Kara-Zaim, and backed out when he refused. But it seems to me that it had occurred to me earlier, when I saw the light in the mufti's face go out, when I saw how futile everything was that I was saying and doing. We had to break Harun out, to bribe the guards so that he could escape, to send him to another country, so that he would never be seen again. This was the only way that he would ever leave the fortress dungeons: my shameful performances would not help him at all. With Hassan and Is-haq everything would be possible. With Is-haq everything would be possible. Maybe Hassan knew where he had hidden, and Is-haq would certainly have agreed to it. Unlike Kara-Zaim, Is-haq did not suffer from his memories; they could not stop him.

Thoughts of that rebel encouraged me, and I was overcome by an irresistible need to act, to do something. I felt a healthy restlessness and excitement: everything was possible, everything was within arm's reach, only one must not give up. It is difficult until you make up your mind; all obstacles seem impassable, all difficulties insurmountable. But once you shrug off your indecision, when you defeat your faintheartedness, then unimagined paths open up in front of you, and the world is no longer cramped and threatening. I imagined heroic feats, discovering many an opportunity for genuine courage, prepared tricks that would have deceived even the greatest caution. And I became more excited and agitated as I became more certain, in the depths of my heart and in the remote folds of my brain, that all of this was just empty dreaming. No, I did not think about it consciously; I was not dishonestly warming two opposite desires in my heart. My thoughts were undivided and sincerely tried to find the best way to free my brother. And the more sincerely and more energetically I did that, I say, the stronger the conviction became somewhere within me, like an indistinct whisper from the dark, like a certainty that is present but neither spoken nor thought about, that such an endeavor could not succeed. And I had only called Is-haq because he was unreachable. I could have hoped for him to come as much as my soul was able, and honestly, because this desire could not come true. My hidden instincts, which protected me even without my conscious will, generously granted me such beautiful, noble thoughts, without curtailing them: they knew that these thoughts were not dangerous, that they could not turn into deeds. But they helped me to take revenge for the shame that had filled me as I stood before the mufti.

If anyone considers this strange, or even unlikely, I can only say that the truth is something very strange, and we convince ourselves that it does not exist because we are ashamed of it, as we are of a leprous child, although in this manner the truth is not rendered less alive or less truthful. We usually beautify our thoughts and hide the vipers that slither within us. If we hide them, do they not exist? I am not beautifying anything, I am not hiding anything; I am speaking as I would before God. And I want to say that I am not a bad or strange man, but an ordinary one, more ordinary than maybe I would like to be, the same as most people.

A reader with good intentions might tell me: you're dragging things out too much; you're philosophizing too much. I would respond immediately: I know. I'm spinning this meager thought out to a great length, shaking it like an empty jug when you cannot get another drop out of it. But I am doing that on purpose, to delay telling about what upsets me even today, several months after it all happened. However, beating around the bush will not help. I cannot avoid it, and I will not stop.

I should also mention one other thing. I found the nightwatchman at home; he had been up for a long time and had already come back from the bazaar, but he met me grumpily, with a frown, as if he had just woke up. There was no trace of his earlier talkativeness and desire to keep me, no trace of his attention and kindness. He wanted to get rid of me as quickly as possible. He got angry when I asked him what he had wanted to tell me the night before:

"I said everything I had to say. Why would I hide anything?"

Was it possible that I had made such a mistake? I had thought about our conversation for a long time, and not so much about what we had said as about its meaning. He knew something about me; that was certain. I mentioned that to him, and he swore upon everything and everyone that I had misunderstood him. Night is one thing, but day is another. God knows what he might have thought while talking such nonsense, and what I might have thought listening to it. Now I had become obsessed by things that he had not even dreamed of. What does he know? And what can a man know—he wailed in a tearful voice—who roams

PART I

around all night long, tired as a dog, and who can hardly wait to get back to his poor shack and crawl under his torn blankets? He's got four mouths to feed besides his own, in such evil times, and he's had enough, more than enough, without having to worry about other people's affairs. But then his anger subsided, and he said in an unexpectedly calm, even kind voice that he would like to help me more than he would anyone; something is surely gnawing at me, since otherwise I wouldn't have come to hear him tell me what he doesn't know. And he doesn't even know what I want. And it seems that I don't, either.

Had I heard something the night before that had not existed in his words, or had something happened to him?

I left without having discovered anything, and—he was indeed right—without knowing what I needed to find out.

When the afternoon prayer ended I was weary and tense, tortured by thoughts about freeing my brother, a task that had become less and less likely due to obstacles that appeared in droves. I rejected the idea even in my thoughts. I was bereft of all hope, even my false hope, and began to reconcile myself to the torture that would be repeated with the mufti the next day. I was weak, broken, and exhausted by the difficulties that I had been imagining all day long, and it seemed that I would not have been so fatigued if I had actually had to deal with them, or if I had still expected them.

Mustafa's children came into the tekke garden. At first they played jacks on the stone tiles in front of the tekke; they also had lunch there, and then started running around, like puppies. They jumped over the roses, tore up the snowberry bushes, and broke branches off of the apple-trees; they shouted, laughed, screamed, cried; I thought that we would have to leave the tekke and the garden to them and move wherever we could. I shouted at them several times, then called Mustafa when he came out of the house and told him that the children were bothering me, that they were making too much noise.

"They're waiting for dinner," he said, without having heard me.

I said louder: "They're bothering me. Tell them to get out."

"Two are mine, three are hers, from before."

I gestured with my hand: get them out or I'll go crazy!

He understood and left angrily, grumbling: "Now even children bother them!"

When the racket died down I surveyed the damage, hoping that it would be greater. I wanted to be angry, I would have freed myself from thoughts that had not left me for days, and sat under the grapevines, above the water, which was still shimmering with the setting sun.

Maybe it was from an overpowering desire for tranquillity, maybe from the healing quiet that followed the children's screams, or because of the unchanging flow of the river, which gurgled barely audibly, but the tension inside me began to slacken. I even felt hunger; I did not know when I had last eaten. I needed to eat something; it would strengthen me, it would distract my attention, but I thought cheerfully that the time was not right. Mustafa was angry. I had driven out the children, and maybe that was something that I should not have done. Although I had calmed down—the silence was good for me—I was still sorry. Not very much, and that was good. But it was also good that I was sorry: I was returning to ordinary thoughts, to ordinary life, in which a man is part good, part evil, all with a moderation that is acceptable even if we think it is fairly boring. Perhaps it is bad when one does not feel that time is passing too slowly. War is not boring; neither is misfortune and trouble. Life is not boring when it is difficult.

So I reached that pleasant state of superficial thought that does not cramp up or clash with itself, but glides over the surface of things, finding easy solutions that solve nothing. And that is not reflection, it is daydreaming, wallowing in thought, a pleasant laziness of the brain. But nothing could have been better for me then. No, I had not forgotten anything of the greatest distress of my life: it weighed down my insides like a stone; my blood carried it on its long paths, like poison; it crouched in the folds of my brain like a polyp. But it abated at that moment, like a serious disease; a period of relief began, and it seemed as if the disease were gone. That brief absence of oppression, that momentary deliverance from suffering, precisely because it was so short-lived (and everything in me knew that), enabled me to see everything around me as something intimate and beautiful. I felt that my presence in this universal harmony was almost happiness.

Hafiz-Muhammed returned from somewhere, greeted me and went off to his room. A good man, I thought, still absorbed with the happiness of my shallow harmony and simplified thinking, it seems that life is unjust to him, but that's just a prejudice; life is life, one is just like another, everyone seeks happiness, but troubles come on their own. His happiness was books, just as for others it is love. His trouble was sickness, just as for others it is poverty, or banishment. We all walk from one bank to another, on the thin ropes of our lives, and each of our ends is known; they are all the same.

I remembered the verses of Hussein-effendi of Mostar[2] and recited them slowly, with a pleasure that I had not felt before. I heard them as a soft whisper, harmless, without dark overtones:

> Bareheaded and barefoot, Shahin the acrobat
> stepped onto the tightrope, over which
> the breeze alone passes without fear.
> Shahin, the falcon, feared no danger,
> asked for God's help and crossed over to the other bank.
> And the little falcons, his apprentices,
> passed over the chasm.
> Above the water, on which the sun glistened,
> they looked like pearls

strung on a thin thread.
The deep gorge beneath them,
the distant heavens above them.
And they on the unsteady tightrope,
on the dangerous path of life.

That image of a lonely, yet courageous man on the difficult path of life corresponded well to the sense of fate that I had then. If I had been in a different mood, I might have been upset by my hopelessness and condemnation to a dreary march, but at that moment it seemed like a sensible reconciliation, even like defiance. I did not know what the good Husein-effendi had really meant, but it seemed to me that he was laughing a little both at himself and others.

Hafiz-Muhammed came out of the tekke and stopped by the fence above the river. His face was pale, upset. He did not even look at me. Was he sick?

"How are you feeling today?"

"Me? I don't know. Bad."

I could sense that he did not like me, but I did not hold it against him. He was also walking the tightrope between two banks, the best he knew how. Sometimes he even tried to be kind.

I asked him, smiling, still in my good mood, ready to understand everything, ready to be thankful: "Tell me the truth: did you know what the kadi's wife wanted, and is that why you sent me to her?"

"Which kadi's wife?"

"There's only one kadi in town. And only one kadi's wife, Hassan's sister."

He got angry, almost disgusted. I was not used to seeing him like that.

"Don't mention their names together, please!"

"Then you knew. But you didn't want to get involved, right?"

"Forget that scum, for God's sake! I wanted to help you, that's why I didn't go. But don't mention them now."

"Why?"

"Haven't you found out?"

"About what?"

"Then I have to tell you."

From his troubled voice, from the painstaking effort that it took for him to look into my face, from his restless hands, which he continually thrust into his deep pockets and pulled out again, from everything about him that I had never seen before, that made him look like someone else, and from the fear that seized me, I knew that he had something very painful to say to me.

I asked him, rushing to immerse myself in the black waters:

"About my brother?"

"Yes."

"Is he alive?"

"Dead. They killed him three days ago."

He was not able to say anything else; nor did I ask.

I looked at him: he was crying, his mouth was contorted, he was terribly ugly. I know that I noticed this, and I know that I was surprised that he was crying. I did not cry. I did not even feel any pain. What he had said flared like a blinding light, and there was a calm.

The water gurgled peacefully.

I heard a bird in the trees.

Well, it's all over, I thought.

I felt relief: it's all over.

"So," I said, "I guess that's it. Above this water sparkling with the golden sun."

"Calm down," said Hafiz-Muhammed horrified, thinking that I had gone mad. "Calm down. We'll pray to God for his soul."

"Yes. That's all we can do."

I did not even feel pain. It was as if some part of me had been torn away, and it was no longer there: that was all. It was quite strange for it to be gone, quite unbelievable, quite impossible, but it had hurt more while it was there.

Mustafa also came, Hafiz-Muhammed had surely told him about my distress. He brought me something in a copper bowl, greatly moved, even clumsier than usual.

"You need to eat," he told me, trying not to shout. "You haven't had anything since yesterday."

He put the bowl in front of me, like medicine, like a sign of his concern; I ate, I did not know what. Both of them looked at me, one beside me, the other in front of me, like feeble guards against sorrow.

And then, between two mouthfuls, that absent part of me began to hurt.

I stopped eating, dumbfounded, and got up slowly, very slowly.

"Where are you going?" asked Hafiz-Muhammed.

"I don't know. I don't know where I'll go."

"Don't go anywhere. Not now. Stay here with me."

"I can't stay."

"Go into your room. Cry, if you can."

"I can't cry."

I gradually realized what had happened, and pain began to engulf me, like a river that rises quietly, and while it was still at my ankles, I thought with apprehension about my fear of the despair that was to come.

And then I felt a sudden burst of rage, as if my brother were standing guilty before me. It serves you right, my tearful anger hissed inside me, what were you trying to do, what did you want? You've brought misery on us, you foolish man! Why?

And that passed as well. It lasted only for a moment, but it set me back in motion.

From the hills, from the Gypsy mahal, came the deafening beats of a drum, at short intervals, and a zurna wailed, incessantly, without interruption; it had gone on all day, the entire previous night, and forever, the horrible madness of

Saint George's Day rushed down on the kasaba like defiance, or a threat. I listened to it and trembled, a big kettledrum was beating somewhere, sounding an alarm, summoning those who were no more, all our dead brothers above and below the earth. Someone had survived and was calling.

He was calling in vain.

There were still no thoughts or tears inside me, no direction. I should not have gone anywhere, but I was going somewhere; there must have been some trace of my dead brother Harun.

My river flowed beneath the small stone bridge, and on the other side there was dead land. I had never crossed that bridge, except with my eyes. That was where the bazaar, the kasaba, and all life ended, where the short road to the fortress began.

My brother had passed this way and never returned.

Since then I had often gone in my thoughts from the stone bridge to the heavy oak gates that split the gray walls. In those imaginary visits I had walked as in a dream; the road was always empty, cleared for my arrival (which was tortuous even in my thoughts), so that I would be able to pass more easily. The gates were the goal of everything: the road led from everywhere only to them; they were the meaning of fate, the triumphal arch of death. I saw them in my thoughts, in my dreams, in my fears. I sensed their dark calls and insatiable hunger. I always turned around and fled; they watched my back, luring me, waiting. Like darkness, like an abyss, like an answer. Behind them was a secret, or nothing. There all questions began and ended, began for the living, and ended for the dead.

For the first time I was actually walking through the street of my endless nightmares; for a long time I had been uncertain as to how I would meet it. And it was indeed deserted, as I had imagined and hoped then, but now it no longer mattered. I would even have preferred for it not to be so empty: it resembled a graveyard. It watched me, gloomily, darkly, viciously, as if it were saying: you have still come! This passage into nothing unnerved me, and killed even that small amount of pitiful courage called *indifference.* I did not want to look, in order to lessen my unease and shivers of everything inside me, but I saw everything, the hostility of the deserted street, the terrible doors into the unknown, and the eyes of the hidden guard in the small opening in the gate. I had not seen those eyes in my thoughts then, when I should have gone; I had seen only the gates and the street that led to them, the tightrope to the other bank.

"What do you want?" asked the guard.

"Has anyone ever come here alone?"

"You have. Do you have someone in the fortress?"

"My brother. They imprisoned him."

"What do you want?"

"Can I see him?"

"You can see him if they imprison you, too."

"Can I bring him some food?"

"Sure. I'll give it to him."

I tried to turn back time, like a lunatic, I tried to revive my dead brother. He had not yet been killed; I had just learned that he was in prison and come at once to inquire about him; it is human, brotherly. There is no reason for fear or shame, there is still hope, they will release him soon, and he will get the food that I sent him. He will know that he is not alone or abandoned; his own blood is at the gate. Neither turrets, nor guards, nor apprehensions have kept his brother from coming, he has come—I have come; he is fifteen years younger than I; I have always looked after him; I brought him to the kasaba. Hey, people! How could I abandon him in the hour of his greatest need? His miserable heart will cheer up when he learns that I've inquired about him. He has no one of his own except me, how can I, too, deceive him? Why? In the name of what? All of you may look at me askance, get angry, and shake your heads; I don't care, here I am, I won't deny these bonds. I have none that are closer; crucify me for this love if you will, I can't help it. I've come, brother, you're not alone.

It was too late. After everything that had happened, and everything that had not, I could only say the prayer of the dead for him, in the hope that it would reach him and be of some use to him.

That prayer was bitter, different from the one which I used to say over the corpses in coffins. It concerned only him and me.

Brother, forgive me, a sinner, for this belated love, I thought that it existed when there was a need for it, but it's waking only now, when it can't help anyone, not even me. And I no longer know whether it's love or a futile attempt to turn back time. Except for those family graves in our village you had only me. Now you and I no longer have anyone; you lost me before I lost you, or maybe you didn't. Maybe you thought that I stood in front of these ironbound gates just as you'd stand here for me; maybe up to the last moment you hoped that I'd help you, but if you had only not trusted in me so much, you'd have been spared the fear of final solitude, when everyone has abandoned us. And if you knew everything, then God help me!

"What are you whispering?" asked the man behind the gates.

"I'm saying the prayer for the dead."

"You'd better say the prayer for the living; they have it harder."

"You've seen a lot, you must know what you're talking about."

"What do I care whether you think I know what I'm talking about?"

"How many people have come through this gate?"

"More than have gone back out. And they're all accounted for."

"Where?"

"Up there, in the graveyard."

"It's bad to joke like that, my friend."

"They're joking. And you're joking. And now get out of here."

"Does one really have to be rude in your position?"

"Does one really have to be stupid in yours? Come inside, step over the threshold—it's only a few inches—and you'll start talking differently right away."

Only a few inches, that much, and right away everything would be different.

Everyone should go to see those few inches, so that they can hate them. Or no, they should be hidden from people; people should never go there before they are taken there, so that they will not conceal all of their thoughts or make everything they say repulsive.

I returned with my eyes lowered, searching for his footprints on the uneven cobbles where no grass grew, searching for the place where he had stood for the last time outside the fortress walls. There was no longer any trace of him in the world. Everything that remained was inside me.

I felt the greedy stone eyes in the slit of the gates piercing the back of my head: they would burn through me.

I had been at the edge of death, at the gates of fate, and had learned nothing. Only those who enter learn something, but they cannot tell it.

Maybe it will occur to people to make this the sole entrance to death and to herd all of us in, one after the other, in droves—why should we leave it to chance and our fated hours?

But this crazy thought was only a defense against the unspeakable horror that had seized me, an attempt to lose my own troubles in a common misery. I had gone to look for the last traces of my murdered brother, but I was at his funeral, without him, without anyone, all by myself. I had not meant to do it, I did not know why I needed to go to that place, to remember him who had died. Maybe because it was the saddest place in the world, and the commemoration of the dead was most needed there. Maybe because it was the most horrible place on earth, and there it was necessary to overcome one's fear in order to remember those who had been killed. Or because it was the most repulsive place on earth, and there the memory of one's former self could be a horrifying epiphany. I had sought none of this, but it happened; I had not needed it, but I could do nothing else.

At the entrance to the bazaar there were ten or so people, waiting, as if I were returning from another world. They watched me, motionless; their eyes were calm, but remained fixed on me. They were a burden to me; many of them pressed against my forehead, swarming around it. I would stumble and fall. I did not know why they had come; I did not know why they were blocking the way or what they were expecting; I did not know what to do.

I stepped out of the street leading to the fortress, as if stepping out of the night (I could hear the muffled beats of the kettledrum again; up there I had not), among the people who were waiting, protected by the sun and separated by the bridge from that path into nothing. And I saw Is-haq, the fugitive, wearing a shoe on one foot only—the other was bare. His face was hard, like those of the others. They were one; they did not differ in any way. I saw them like a multitude of Is-haqs, with many eyes and a single question. It seemed that it was because of Is-haq that I could tell why they were standing on that edge and what they wanted to find out. I knew it very vaguely; I sensed it, because of him, and I did not dare to raise my gaze from the cobblestones. Maybe the people would move apart; maybe we would somehow pass by each other. I would pretend that I was absorbed in thought and did not see that they were expecting something. No matter if they knew that it was not true, no matter if they thought that I was avoiding their eyes. Only I would have wanted for him not to be among them. They would not have been there if he had not brought them.

But when the wall of their legs prevented me from passing, I raised my eyes toward Is-haq's face; I needed to see what he wanted, I could not avoid it. He was not there. I knew where he had stood; he had been the third from the left. But from that spot a thin youth now looked at me, not at all surprised that I had stopped in front of him.

Their eyes were wide open, determined, waiting. Where was he? He was not to the right of the youth, or to his left, all the way to the end of the line. I did not count but I knew that there were nine of them now. My eyes passed along their faces; I inspected their closed lips and tensely knit brows. I forgot that they wanted something; I was searching for Is-haq. I did not know why I needed to see him, or what I would say to him, but I was sorry that he was not there. Yet I had seen him. From afar to be sure—I had gone twenty paces with my eyes lowered, and the sunlight glittered on the men, gilded them in that other world; they glowed like torches and deflected my gaze, but it did not matter. I would have pawned my soul to recognize him. To the others I did not need to say anything, even if I had known what to say.

I went on, and they parted to let me pass. For a few moments it was quiet; I was walking alone, but then I heard feet scraping on the cobblestones. They had started after me. I quickened my step, to keep ahead of them, but they hurried after me. They were not deterred by the distance between us. It seemed that their numbers were growing.

The spring twilight fell, and the streets were bluish, restlessly quiet.

I did not hear the muezzin,* I did not know whether it was time for the prayer. But the mosque was open; only one candle was burning, in a tall candlestick.

I went in and took my place at the front. Without turning around, I heard how people entered and sat down behind me, without words, without even a murmur. They had never been so quiet. And it seemed to me that during the prayer they were silent and solemn. I was moved by that earnest rustling behind my back.

While the prayers still continued, I began to feel that they were strange, different from any before, that they were more passionate and dangerous, that they were a preparation for something to come. I knew that they could not end as they usually did. *Amen* is a beginning, not an end: its sound was muffled, thick, full of waiting. But for what? What was going to happen?

In the silence, in the motionlessness, in their determination not to leave, although the prayers were over, I realized something that I did not want to know. They wanted to see me after I learned of this tragedy; they wanted me to show what I was at that moment.

I myself did not know what I was, and I did not know what kind of answer to give them.

Everything depended on me.

I could have got up and left, fleeing from both them and myself. And that would have been an answer.

I could have asked them to go out, so that I would be left alone in the silence of the empty mosque. And that would have been an answer.

But then everything would have remained inside me. Nothing would have reached anyone. In front of the fortress gate I had still been afraid of the pain and remorse that was to come, I might still have been consumed by fire, stifled by grief, or forever dumbfounded by unspoken rage and sorrow. I had to say something. For those who were waiting. I was a man, at least then. And for him, the undefended. Let it be a grievous brotherly prayer, the second already that day, but the first that people would hear.

Was I afraid? No, I was not. I was not afraid of anything, except whether I would do what I had to do well. I even felt a calm readiness for everything, a readiness that came with the inevitability of action, and a deep acceptance of it, more powerful than revenge, more powerful than justice. I could no longer oppose myself.

I got up and lit all the candles, carrying the flame from one to another, I wanted each of them to see me, I wanted to see each of them. For us to remember each other.

I turned around, slowly. No one would leave, not a single one of them. They watched me, sitting on their knees, excited by my silent movements and the flames that burned along the whole front side, releasing the thick smell of wax.

"Sons of Adem!"[3]

I had never called them that.

I did not know what I was going to say, nor had I a moment before. Everything happened on its own. My grief and excitement found a voice and words.

"Sons of Adem! I will not give a sermon, I could not, even if I wanted to. But I believe that you would hold it against me if I did not speak about myself now, at this moment, the darkest in my life. What I have to say has never been more important to me, but I am not trying to gain anything. Nothing, except to see compassion in your eyes. I did not call you my brothers, although you are that now more than ever, but rather the sons of Adem, invoking that which we all have in common. We are men, and think in the same way, especially when we are in distress. You have waited, and wanted for us to be together, to look one another in the eye, sorrowful about the death of an innocent man, and troubled by a crime. And that crime concerns you as well, since you know: whenever someone kills an innocent man, it is as if he has killed all men. They have killed all of us countless times, my murdered brothers, but we are horrified when they strike our most beloved.

"Maybe I should hate them, but I cannot. I do not have two hearts, one for hatred and one for love. The heart that I have knows only grief now. My prayer and my repentance, my life and my death—all of it belongs to God, creator of the world. But my sorrow belongs to me.

"Allah has commanded: remember your duties toward your kinsmen.[4]

"I did not remember them, O son of my mother. I did not have the strength to protect you and me from this misfortune.

"Musa says: O my Lord! Give me a helper from among my kin, give me my brother Harun, strengthen me with him. Make him my helper in my work.[5]

"My brother Harun is no more, and I can only say: O my Lord, strengthen me with my dead brother.

"With my brother who is dead but not buried according to the laws of God, who was not seen or kissed by his family before he embarked on the great journey, from which there is no return.

"I am like Qabeel,[6] to whom God sent a crow that dug up the soil, to teach him how to bury the body of his dead brother. And he said: 'Woe to me, can I not do as much as a crow, can I not bury the body of my dead brother?'[7]

"I, the unfortunate Qabeel, more unfortunate than a black crow.

"I did not save him while he was alive; I did not see him after he died. Now I have no one except myself and you, my Lord, and my sorrow. Give me strength, so that I will not despair from brotherly and humanly grief, or poison myself with hatred. I repeat the words of Nuh:[8] 'Separate me from them, and judge us.'[9]

"We live on this earth only for a day, or less. Give me the strength to forgive, since he who forgives is greatest. And I know that I cannot forget.

"And I ask of you, my brothers, do not hold these words against me, do not hold them against me if they have hurt or saddened you. Or if they have revealed my weakness. In front of you I am not ashamed of this weakness; I would be ashamed if I did not have it.

"And now go home, and leave me alone with my misfortune. It is easier to endure, now that I have shared it with you."

I was left alone, alone in the entire world, in the strong candlelight, in the blackest darkness, and felt no better inside, as the people had carried only my words away, and all of my sorrow remained for me, untouched, blacker still because my hopes that it would be lessened had been betrayed. I struck the floor with my brow, and knowing, alas, that it was in vain, recited in my desperation the words of the Baqara Sura:[10]

> Our Lord, we seek your forgiveness.
> Our great Lord, do not punish us if we forget, or commit sin.
> Our great Lord, do not place upon us a burden that is too heavy for us.
> Our great Lord, do not charge us with that which we cannot endure and accomplish.
> Forgive us, have mercy and give us strength.[11]

Maybe he forgave me, maybe he had mercy; he did not give me strength.

Weaker than I had ever felt, I began to weep like a helpless child. Nothing that I had ever known or thought had any meaning then; the night beyond those walls was black and threatening. The world was terrible, and I was small and weak. It would have been best to stay like that on my knees, to pour myself out in tears, never to rise again. I knew we must never be weak and sorrowful if we are true believers, but I knew that in vain. I was weak, and did not think about whether I was a true believer or a man lost in the deaf loneliness of the world.

And then there was an empty silence. Something was still rumbling somewhere within me, more and more distant; screams could still be heard, but fainter and fainter. The storm had worn itself out and abated, all on its own. Because of my tears, perhaps.

I was tired. I was an invalid who had just arisen.

I put out the candles, taking their lives one by one, without the solemn feeling that I had had when I lit them. Grief had destroyed me, and I was alone.

I feared that I would remain in the darkness for a long time. Alone.

But when I snuffed out the soul of the last candle, my shadow did not disappear. It swayed, heavy, on the wall in the half-darkness.

I turned around.

In the doorway stood the forgotten Hassan, with a live candle in his hand.

He had been waiting for me, silently.

9

> Everything that you can do against me, do it,
> do not give me even a moment of rest.[1]

AS IT HOLDS THE REED MY HAND STILL TREMBLES, AS IF THE things that I am writing were happening right now, as if a month had not passed since the moment when my life changed. I cannot exactly say what all I have gone through, or in which fires I have been burning (they have been my own as well as those of others), or all that I thought and felt when the storm hit me, because from this distance all kinds of things are obscured by the fog of my unrecognition, as if I were in a state of fever. But let me tell in turn everything that happened to me and around me. And I will tell, as much as I can, what went on inside me, as much as I myself know.

The day after my speech in the mosque, in the evening, they responded to my blow.

I did not suspect anything. I was not expecting anything. But I knew that they would spin their filthy web around me.

That afternoon Hassan stopped by the tekke. I thought that he looked at me differently than he had the night before, with respect and with a certain disbelief, as if he were surprised, as if he had not expected such an act of rebellion from me. Now that it had happened, I found reasons for it, in hindsight, bolstering my feelings of injustice and indignation. My brother is dead, I thought, and if I couldn't save him I can at least mourn him. I worried that Hassan would criticize me for not having done anything else, earlier, when it had not yet been too late; but he mentioned nothing, as if he had forgotten it. I was grateful to him for that forgetfulness. I paid more attention to what he thought than to what I did. His opinion had begun to mean a great deal to me, because he knew everything: he could have hurt me badly.

His surprised look was dear to me for another reason as well. Maybe I had never felt as I did then how much our moods, how much our decisions depend on those around us. If Hassan and Hafiz-Muhammed had been shocked, if they had condemned my speech as something imprudent, I would have also been upset. As it was, their approval of it relieved me of the burden of doubt, and I knew: I had done what I had to; what I had done was good. Maybe ill-advised, but necessary. Hassan was surprised; he had not thought that I was someone to be reckoned with. Well, I had showed that I was.

Such feelings of pride are pleasant; they protect us from remorse.

What I had said in the mosque was sorrow, astonishment, stifled sobs, and maybe even a stifled howl. But all of it had been mine. A sorrowful attempt at retaliation and defense. But when I had said it, it suddenly became something else. No matter how it had begun, no matter what it had been, it turned into a common burden and condemnation. And it bound me, for it was no longer mine alone, because of the words that I had spoken. Hassan also said this (he told it to Hafiz-Muhammed; I heard it from inside): he had not heard more sincere sorrow or more serious accusations for a long time. Like the others, he had been fixed to the spot where he sat, shaken by the moving simplicity of such ordinary words and by the grief of a man who wept, but also spoke. I felt that we're all guilty and miserable, he said.

Was I now supposed to forget everything that had happened and everything I had said? Words also bind us, they are also deeds; they bound me before others, and before myself as well.

But when I went out into the garden, they were already talking about something else. I was sorry that I was not the object of their thoughts for a longer time, but it did not matter. What is said in my absence means more than what is said in my presence.

"We're talking about Hassan's father," said Hafiz-Muhammed when I walked up to them.

As if he did not want me to begin another conversation. And I thought, magnanimously, that everyone has his own problems, and thank God that it is so.

Hassan spoke as usual, cheerfully, mockingly. He was easy and superficial in everything, in his thoughts, in his feelings, in his relationship toward himself and others (I forgot that the night before he had stayed with me until dawn, full of sorrow). My father is strange, he said, if that needs to be said at all, since everyone is strange except colorless and faceless people, who again are strange since they have nothing of their own. In other words, their character is precisely their lack of character. Except every one of us, of course, because we grow so accustomed to ourselves that everything that's different from us seems strange, so it could be said that whatever is not us is strange. So my father is strange because he thinks that I'm strange, and the other way around, and so on and so forth. There's no end to our strangeness, and maybe we should consider that in itself strange. The difference between them is that his father thinks that he, Hassan, has brought misery upon himself with his way of life. And Hassan is convinced that there are many ways for a man to bring misery upon himself, but the least likely way is to do what he wants as long as it doesn't disgrace him. And so, it turns out that his father is miserable because Hassan is content, and his father's idea of happiness, both his own and that of his family, would be for Hassan to be genuinely unhappy.

"Have you seen him since you've come back?" asked Hafiz-Muhammed, smiling.

"I've tried. I wanted to name for him all the ways that men can become miserable. And to ask him who is bothered by my way of life. I like it, as one does an unsightly, worn out shoe. Maybe it won't keep out water, maybe it looks funny, but it fits. You don't feel like taking it off in the middle of the street; you don't even know you're wearing it. Why shouldn't my life fit me? Why should it be a nightmare?"

"You wanted to tell him that? But you didn't want to see him."

"How could I tell him if I didn't see him? I wanted to see him first, since that comes first, but the first thing for him was that he didn't want to see me. And so neither of my wishes was fulfilled."

"Did he tell you that?"

"He spoke through the mouths of others. It sounded like my father, and I was so moved that I'd have gladly kissed the mouth that said it, which was so young and innocent that it didn't even know what it was saying."

"You should go again."

"For the girl?"

"Whatever you want," said Hafiz-Muhammed and laughed. "Just go."

"How many times do I have to go? How many times is a son obliged to go in vain?"

"One more time."

Hassan looked at him suspiciously and asked:

"Have you been to see my father?"

"Yes."

"So you've been there. But why? Do you want to bring two stubborn men together for one empty reconciliation?"

"Let whatever happens happen. I told him that you'd come today. Try to talk to him. Fathers are easily moved."

"Oh yes. Especially mine."

With unease I recalled my conversation with the mufti. It resembled this one a little, but I had been forced into it. So what was this?

I thought, somewhat saddened, that he might be reconciled with his father and, with a trace of envy, that he would forget me.

I performed the abdest and went to the mosque.

It was a dim, cloudy evening, I remember it well. I looked up at the sky, I did so according to an ancient peasant habit that I had not yet lost, although I had no need for it. And I was able to sense changes in the weather, days in advance. But this time a cloud deceived me, took me by surprise; I was too preoccupied with myself. And I was wishing for that cloud and bad weather. Maybe that was why I did not even see it coming. I had been nurturing the irrational hope that my father would not leave for the kasaba in rainy weather.

The day grew weary; in the west the sky was still red. I remember, against the red background of the sky I saw four horsemen at the end of the street. They were pretty, as if embroidered on red silk, as if sewn onto the blazing sky behind them. It seemed as if four solitary warriors were standing on a wide field, before a battle, calming their horses with movements that were barely perceptible.

When I started toward them, the horses lurched forward, spurred by blows that I could not see, charging abreast of each other, closing the narrow street from one wall to the other.

They were coming at me!

There was a time when I was not a coward; now I do not know what I am. But in that situation neither courage nor cowardice could have helped me. I looked back; the gate was too far—ten steps away but unreachable. I waved to the horsemen: Stop, you'll trample me! But they kept whipping their horses' crops, speeding them up, moving closer and closer. The earth shook with the most terrible rumble that I have ever heard, and the four-headed monster, furious and bloodthirsty, approached with unbelievable speed. I tried to run, or thought that I did, but there was no strength in my legs. I could hear the horses breathing down my neck. I shuddered along the length of my spine at the blow that was about to strike me: I would fall; they would trample me under. I pressed myself against the wall, flattening myself against it, but they could still reach me. I saw above me the gaping mouths of the four horses, huge, red, full of blood and foam. Four pairs of horse's legs flailing all around my head; four cruel, beastly faces and four open, beastly mouths, red and bloody like those of the horses; four pizzle whips, four vipers hissing at me, wrapping around my face, neck, chest. I felt no pain, I saw no blood, my eyes looked with horror at the countless legs and countless heads of that looming monster. No! something in me yelled silently, more terrible than fear, harder than death. I did not even think of God, or His name; all that existed was red, bloody, unfathomable horror.

Then they left, but I still saw them before me. They remained imprinted in the bloodstained cloth of the sky, and within me, even under my eyelids, as if I had been looking into the sun.

I could not, I did not dare to move. I was afraid that I would collapse onto the cobblestones. I did not know how I had kept standing, since I could not feel my legs under me.

Then Mullah-Yusuf came up to me, from somewhere, I did not know where. He looked frightened.

"Are you hurt?"

"No."

"Oh yes, you are."

"No matter."

His full, healthy face was pale. His eyes showed astonishment and sorrow. Was he grieving for me?

Luckily, he was the first one to see me; in front of him I

would act courageous. I did not know why, but I had to. I could have shown my fear in front of anyone else, only not in front of him.

"Let's go into the tekke," he said softly, and it occurred to me that I was still standing against the wall, for no reason.

"I'll be late for the prayers in the mosque."

"You can't go to the mosque like that. I'll go for you, if you want."

"Am I bleeding?"

"Yes."

I started toward the tekke.

He took me by my arm, to help me.

"I can manage," I said and freed my arm. "Go to the mosque, the people are waiting."

He stopped, as if ashamed, and gave me a gloomy look.

"Don't leave the tekke for a day or two."

"Did you see everything that happened?"

"Yes."

"Why did they attack me?"

"I don't know."

"I'll lodge a complaint."

"Don't do that, Sheikh-Ahmed."

"How can I not do it? I won't be able to face myself."

"Don't do it. Forget about it."

He did not look me in the eyes. He was pleading with me, as if he knew something.

"Why do you say that?"

He said nothing, averting his gaze. If he was afraid, he did not know what to say; if he knew something, he wanted to say nothing about it; if it occurred to him that it was not his affair, he regretted having said anything. My God, what had we made out of him?

It was because of him that I concealed my fear and weakness, because of him I wanted to go to the mosque covered with blood, because of him I said that I would lodge a complaint. I wanted to remain upright before this young man;

PART I

we had strange ties to each other. He pitied me, for the first time. And I had thought that he hated me.

"Go," I said, watching the color quickly return to his cheeks. "Go now."

It would have been more natural for me to go mad from the fear that this unbelievable event had caused. But miraculously, I lived through that first moment intact and, keeping everything inside of me, I succeeded in brushing it aside, suppressing it, blotting it out for the time being. Horrible, a naive memory said within me, but it was unable to bring anything to life. I was also proud that I had concealed my fear, and I still had a pleasant feeling of courage—not very certain though, but sufficient for me to delay everything.

While Mustafa and Hafiz-Muhammed, shocked and frightened, undressed and washed me I tried in vain to keep my arms and legs from trembling, although I still had enough strength not to feel shame or fear. It was as if a bed of dying embers flared up a few times and the terrible rumbling and fear would suddenly come to life; but I had succeeded in turning everything back to the time when it was still happening and nothing hurt yet. It's over, I said to myself, nothing has happened that should upset me too much. If only it doesn't get worse; if only it ends with this. And I listened avidly to their incoherent conversation, to Mustafa's inquiries about what had happened, since he could not understand any of it, and to Hafiz-Muhammed's astonished gasping, which alternated with awkward words of encouragement and angry snaps at Mustafa, and threats to someone indefinite, unknown, whom he called *they*. His stuttering disapproval supported a vacillating feeling I had of indignation at the insult that had been inflicted on me, and when Mullah-Yusuf returned from the mosque and stood by the door, silent, my desire to do something grew even stronger. I took advantage of it immediately, frightened by another desire, the desire to do nothing. I wrote out a complaint to the vali's mullah, and gave it to Yusuf to copy.

When I lay down I could not get to sleep. I was bothered by the complaint; I still had it, and was not sure whether to send it or tear it up. If I tore it up, everything would end there. But then everything that had been hidden would come to life, and the dying fire might flare up again. I would again hear the bloodcurdling rumble of hooves. If I sent the complaint I would preserve my conviction that I could defend myself, that I had the right to make accusations. I needed to be able to believe this.

It seemed that I had just fallen asleep when I was awakened by noisy footsteps and candlelight in my room. I saw above me the man with the flat face, the one who had brought the musellim's threat. Another man, someone I did not know, held the candle.

"What do you want?" I asked, frightened, jarred out of my sleep, startled by their impudence.

He did not hurry to give an answer. He looked at me scornfully, curiously, as he had the night before, in a cunning, friendly manner, as if he and I shared some joke that brought us closer and gave us occasion to be cheerful without saying anything. The other was holding the candle over my bed, as if I were someone's concubine.

"He wouldn't listen to me," the man said cheerfully. "But I warned him."

He took the candle and began to examine the room and rummage through my books. I thought that he would carelessly fling them all over the room, but he carefully returned each of them to its place.

"What are you looking for?" I asked, upset, eager to find out. "Who let you in? How dare you enter the tekke!"

My voice was very soft and very unsure.

He gave me a surprised look, and did not answer.

He found the complaint and read it, shaking his head.

"What are you going to do with this?" he asked, startled. And answered himself: "That's your business."

And he put it in his pocket.

PART I

When I again protested and said that I would lodge a complaint with the mufti about this, he looked at me with contempt and waved his hand, as if it bored him to argue with such a naive man.

"That's your business," he repeated. "Get up and get dressed."

I thought that I had not heard him correctly.

"Did you tell me to get dressed?"

"I did. But you can go the way you are, if you like. And hurry up, don't make any problems for either of us."

"All right, I'll go. But someone will pay for this."

"That's best. And someone always pays."

"Where are you taking me?"

"Oh! Where are we taking you?!"

"What should I tell the dervishes? When will I come back?"

"You won't tell them anything. And you'll come back immediately. Or never."

This was not a rude joke, but rather an honest remark about the possible outcomes.

Hafiz-Muhammed came into the room, flustered. Everything on him was white—his socks, shirt, face. He resembled a corpse risen from the grave; he was unable to speak. That could have been a bad omen. I expected him to do something, although I knew that the thought was absurd.

"They've come to take me away," I said, pointing at the men who were waiting for me relentlessly. "I'll come back soon, I hope."

"Who are they? Who are you?"

"Get moving!" the man said, rushing me. "Who are we?! What fools there are in the world! We can take you as well—then you'll know who we are."

"Take me!" the corpse yelled suddenly, since he was so bewildered. "Take all of us! We're all as guilty as he is!"

"Fool," concluded the policeman matter-of-factly. "Don't be in such a hurry. We might just come for you, too."

"Whoever boasts of violence . . ."

He did not finish the words that might have destroyed him. He was interrupted by a timely cough—it could never have been of more use to him. It racked him, as if all of his blood were rushing into his throat. That was from his excitement, I thought, feeling no sorrow for him, because he was going to stay here. I watched how he shook and squirmed, I watched and stood, alone, fearful at that unwanted departure into the night. But I did not want to show it.

I went over to help him. The policeman stopped me.

"Poor man," he said calmly; it resembled a reproach or scorn. And he gestured with his hand for me to go out.

In front of the tekke another man was waiting for us.

They walked abreast of me and behind me. I was pinned between them, barely able to breath.

It was dark. There was no moon or stars; the night had no light or life at all. There was only the barking of dogs in the yards, answering distant barks from the hills near the sky. It was past midnight and spirits were roaming the world. Men who still had their freedom were sleeping, dreaming nice dreams in the darkness. And the houses were in darkness, and the kasaba, and the whole world. This was the time of reckoning, the hour of evil deeds. There were no human voices, no human faces except those shadows guarding my shadow. There was nothing; my fiery excitement was the only thing alive in that dark waste.

Here and there, occasionally, a timid rushlight would flicker, because of someone who was sick, because of some child who, in the dead of night, had been awakened by my fear, by some ominous rustling. I was horrified by the thought of those peaceful lives, I pushed them away so that I would not see myself stepping through the darkness toward my unknown fate. I was going somewhere, with no purpose, nowhere, or it only seemed to me that I was going. I was losing my sense of reality, as if I were not in this world, as if I were not awake. That was because of the darkness, because of the formless shadows, because of my disbelief that this was me, that this could be me. This was someone else; I knew him and watched: maybe he was surprised, or frightened. Or I had gone astray. I did not know where I was; I was somewhere, at some time in my life, following paths that had been destined for me. I had never been in that place and I could not leave it, but right then someone would light a candle and call me into a sanctuary. Yet no one lit that candle, that desired voice did not send me in the right direction; the night continued, as did that foreign place and my disbelief. Everything was a bad dream. I would wake up and breathe a sigh of relief.

Why don't people shout when they're led to their deaths, why don't they make themselves heard, why don't they call for help? Why don't they run? Although they have no one to shout to, nowhere to run to, no one to appeal to: everyone else is asleep, their houses shut tight. I'm not asking this for my own sake, I'm not condemned to death; they'll release me, they'll send me back soon. I'll return alone, along familiar paths and not these foreign, terrible ones. I'll never again listen to the barking of dogs, their hopeless barking at death and desolation. I'll close the door, plug my ears with wax in order not to hear. Has everyone whom they've taken away heard it? Was this barking the last farewell they ever heard? Why didn't they shout? Why didn't they run? I'd shout if I knew what's waiting for me, I'd run. All the windows will open up and all the doors fly open.

Oh, no, they would not, not a single one. That's why no one ever runs; everyone knows it. Maybe they're hopeful. Hope is the pimp of death, a murderer more dangerous than hatred. It's deceptive; it knows how to win you over, to calm you and lull you to sleep, whispering whatever you want to hear, leading you to the blade. Only Is-haq had escaped. He was taken away that night, as I'm being taken now. No, there were more of them then; he was something else, he was important to them. I'm not important to anyone. He surely didn't listen to the dogs barking; he didn't think that he was dreaming and that he'd wake up; he knew where they were taking him, and he had no hope of staying alive. He did not deceive himself, as others do. He decided at once to run; that was his first and only thought. Therefore he walked meekly, afraid that his thought would call out on its own—it was so strong—and looked into the darkness continuously. There was moonlight, treacherous, hostile, but he looked for a shadow to hide in, searching for the thickest of them. And suddenly he decided to act, when it seemed to him that they were inattentive, and that he would not get another chance. For a single moment, only for a single, short moment, I was he, ready to spring away, ready to run. They were behind me, next to me; we were bound more closely than friends or brothers; now the bonds would break. There would be a violent and painful split between us. Without me they were nothing. They would suffer from this separation and everything would be resolved in imperceptibly small spans of time; we would not even be aware of them. We would know only about the moment of my jump, and again, and again. Every shadow was too transparent, every step too short, every hiding place too open. It was no use. Where could I run to?

My strength gave out at the very thought; I had not even tried. Because I had not made a decision, because it was not for me to decide. That was for Is-haq. This was happening to me; it was less than reality, or maybe more: an impossibility that was actually somehow happening.

They took me from one darkness to another. There were no shapes or places because I could see nothing and was preoccupied with myself, preoccupied with visions that deprived my senses of anything I might otherwise have recognized. The darkness changed; I knew because we were moving and time was passing, although I was not aware of it then.

Somewhere they met someone; they whispered something to each other, and I was again pinned between some others. I had become something valuable that must not be lost. I no longer knew who was with me, although it did not make any difference. They were all the same; they were all shadows; they were all out on this night errand because of me. All of them could be replaced; I could not be replaced by anyone.

When I hit my forehead on a low doorframe, I knew that we had arrived. I had arrived; they would go back. They would be replaced by walls.

"Give me light!" I shouted at the ironbound door, after I had gone in, unable to believe that such darkness could exist anywhere in the world.

That was the last remnant of my habits from outside, the only remaining word. No one heard it, or wanted to hear it, or could understand it. It might have seemed like raving.

Their footsteps disappeared into something that was probably a passageway. And this was probably the prison. And this was probably me. Or was it? Yes, it was, unfortunately. My thoughts were not lost in a dreamlike haze, I did not drift away and see myself from afar, as if I were looking at someone else. I was conscious, awake; everything was painfully clear to me. There was no mistake.

For a long time I did not leave the door and the sharp smell of rusted iron. This was the place where I first stepped into the darkness that had been destined for me. I had already known it for a few moments and thus it became less dangerous. Then I started to walk around, searching it, blind, relying on my fingertips, feeling everywhere the heavy dankness of uneven walls, as if I were at the bottom of a well. And the dankness was also under me, I felt it with my feet, which stuck to something ugly and slimy. Without finding anything, I soon reached the door again and the sharp smell of iron. It seemed more bearable than the stench of the dankness.

A confined emptiness, a walled-in desolation. I would see very little there, and did not know whether I needed what I had known before. Nothing of mine was of any use to me, neither my eyes, nor hands, nor feet, nor experience, nor reason. I could just as well have gone back to the state of Hafiz-Muhammed's first living beings.

All of my life and effort for these few feet of dankness and this complete sightlessness!

That new abode of mine was small, but it was large enough for me to lie down had it been dry. Walking around in that grave, I found a stone next to one wall and stood by it, but would not let myself sit down. I could still make decisions. It was as if I were waiting for the door to open and for someone to release me: Come on, get out! Maybe all the others had been so reluctant to sit down in the dankness and mud, hoping for something, waiting, giving up on waiting whenever they lost hope. It does not take long. Soon I, too, sat down on the stone—that was a transition—trying not to lean against the wall. But then I did, and I felt the dankness slowly seeping into me. That quiet decomposition into water and nothingness could begin; there was nothing else for me to do.

I did not know whether my wounds had hurt before then, without my being aware of it, or whether they had yielded before things that were more important. Now they made themselves felt, either because the time had come for them to hurt or my body had rebelled against my forgetfulness and reminded me of its presence. I unconsciously accepted this sudden help and began to rub my wounds with my fingers, spreading out the pain, evening it out so that it would not be in one place. I pressed the cuts so that they would not bleed, and felt my blood sticky on my hands. The previous evening they had washed my wounds in the tekke with camomile tea and clean cotton, but now I was rubbing the dirt from the walls into my torn flesh, and did not care. I did not think about what was going to happen; I thought only about what was happening then. The pain was strong, it began to burn in the darkness. It was my only existence; my body was returning me to reality. I needed that pain; it was a part of my living self, something I could understand, similar to the pain one feels in the outside world. It was a defense against darkness and the futile search for any answer at all, an obstacle that kept me from remembering my brother—he might appear on the black wall of this grave of mine, with a question that I could not answer.

I fell asleep covering one of my wounds with my palm, as if I were trying to keep it from disappearing, sitting on the stone against the damp wall. And I woke with it burning again under my palm, as if in a nest. It lived, it hurt. "How did you sleep?" I wanted to ask it. I was not alone.

I was glad when I noticed a small opening in one of the walls under the vault. Morning revealed it to me, and although daylight remained a desire and vague sensation, my darkness was no longer so complete. Morning had broken in the outside world, and shed a little light on me as well, although my night continued. I stared at that dark-gray spot above me, encouraged, as if I were watching the most beautiful roseate dawn on the broad hillsides of my childhood. Dawn, light, day—they existed, even if only as hints; not everything had disappeared. And when I turned my eyes away from that meager light, I was blinded. The darkness in my dungeon was again impenetrable.

Only when I grew accustomed to it did I realize that eyes were nevertheless necessary in this eternal night. I looked around, but I recognized only what my fingers had already seen.

The square opening in the door swung open with a creaking sound, but neither light nor air came in. Someone peered in from the other darkness. I went up to the opening and we looked at each other from up close. His face was bearded, featureless. There was nothing on it, neither eyes nor mouth.

"What do you want?" I asked, afraid that he would be unable to answer. "Who are you?"

"Jemal."

"Where have they brought me? What is this place?"

"We give out food once a day. Only once. In the morning."

His voice was hoarse, dark.

"Has anyone asked about me?"

"Do you want to eat?"

Everything around me seemed so dirty, slimy, and rotten that I felt sick at the very thought of food.

"I don't want to eat."

"That's how they all are. The first day. And then they want to. Don't call for me later."

"Has anyone come to ask about me?"

"No. No one."

"My friends will come to ask about me. Come and tell me when they do."

"Who are you? What's your name?"

"A dervish, the sheikh of the tekke. Ahmed Nuruddin."

He closed the little door, and opened it again.

"Do you know a prayer? Can you write an amulet? Against gout?"

"No."

"That's a pity. It's killing me."

"It's damp here. We'll all fall ill."

"You've got it easy. They'll let you go. Or kill you. And I'm here forever. Like this."

"Do you have any kind of mat or board? I can't lie down."

"You'll get used to it. I don't have anything."

The dervish Ahmed Nuruddin, light of faith, the sheikh of a tekke. I had forgotten about him, the whole night I had not had a title or a name. I remembered him, I brought him back to life in front of this man. Ahmed Nuruddin, preacher and scholar, foundation and roof of his tekke, glory of the kasaba, master of the world. And now he was asking for a

PART I

mat or board from Jemal the bat, so he would not have to lie down in the mud; he was waiting to be strangled and laid out dead in the mud that he refused to lie in alive.

It was better to be nameless, with wounds and pains, oblivious, with wounds and hopes for morning, but that dead morning without a dawn had awakened Ahmed Nuruddin, stifled his hope, driven his bodily wounds and pains into nonexistence. They had again become unimportant before a more severe and dangerous threat that was rising from within me to destroy me.

I tried to keep myself from going mad; anything, but not that. Once that started, nothing would be able to stop it, it would burn and destroy everything inside me. Only a waste would remain, more terrible than death. But I could feel it stirring, squirming. There was nothing for my thoughts to hold on to; I turned around in amazement, searching for something. It had been there until the day before, until the moment before. Where was it? I was searching, in vain. I had nothing to support me; I was sinking into the mud. No matter, it's all in vain, Sheikh Nuruddin.

But the wave that had welled up in me stopped, and did not grow. I was waiting, surprised: silence.

I got up slowly, holding on to the walls, leaning with my palms on the slimy bumps. I wanted to stand. I still had hope; they would come looking for me. The day had just begun. A moment of weakness would not kill me, and it was good that I was ashamed of it.

And I waited, waited, keeping the flame of my hopes alive as the long hours passed. I comforted myself with my pain and burning wounds. I strained to hear footsteps and kept expecting the door to open, a voice to reach me. And night fell, I knew because I no longer needed my eyes; I slept in the stinking muck, exhausted, and woke up without the desire to sit on the stone. In the morning I ate Jemal's food, and waited again. Days passed, dark dawns followed one after another, and I no longer knew whether I was waiting.

And then, drained of my strength, dazed from the fatigue of waiting, weakened by the moisture that my bones had absorbed, in a fever that warmed me and led me out from that grave for a while, then, I say, I spoke with my brother Harun.

Now we're equal, brother Harun, I said to him who was still, silent. I saw only his eyes, distant, stern, lost in the darkness. I followed them, placed them before me, or I went after them. Now we're equal; both of us are miserable. If I was guilty, there's no guilt now. I know how alone you were, and how you waited to hear from someone. You stood at the door, straining to hear voices, footsteps, words; you thought that they had something to do with you, time and time again. We've been left alone, both of us, and no one has come, no one has asked about me or remembered me, and my path is now empty, without a trace or a memory. I'd have preferred never to have seen it. You waited for me, and I waited for Hassan. We didn't wait long enough. No one ever waits long enough; in the end everyone is always left alone. We're equal, we're unhappy, we're human, brother Harun.

I swear by time, which is the beginning and end of all things, that every man always suffers loss. "Did anyone come?"

I asked Jemal by habit, no longer hoping for anything.

"No. No one."

I wanted to hope—no one can live without expectations—but I did not have the strength. I abandoned my sentry post by the door and sat somewhere, quiet, defeated, more and more quiet. I was losing my sense of life; the border between dreams and reality was disappearing. What I dreamed actually happened, I walked the paths of my youth and childhood freely. But I never walked the streets of the kasaba, as if they could take me into the prison even from my dreams. I lived with people that I had met long ago. And it was nice because I never woke up; I did not know about being awake. Jemal was also a dream, as was the darkness

PART I

around me, and the wet walls. Even when I would come to, I did not suffer very much; one has to have strength to suffer.

It became clear to me how men die. I saw that it is not so hard. Or easy. It is nothing. One just starts living less and less, being less and less, thinking, feeling and knowing less and less. The rich flow of life dries up, and only a thin thread of uncertain consciousness remains, more and more meager, more and more insignificant. And then nothing happens, there is not anything, there is nothing. And nothing matters—it is all the same.

And when, at one point, in that withering without time—because time had been interrupted before it could establish itself as duration—Jemal said something through the opening in the door, I did not immediately understand what he was saying, although I knew that it was important. I awoke and realized: my friends had brought me gifts.

"Which friends?"

"I don't know. Two of them. Take it."

I knew, I did not even have to ask, I had known that they would come. I had known for a long time, the wait had been a long one, but I had known.

I clawed at the door with my fingers, to get up. I had not been sitting there without reason.

"Two of them?"

"Two of them. They gave it to the guard."

"What did they say?"

"I don't know."

"Tell him to ask who they are."

I wanted to hear familiar names. Hassan and Harun. No. Hassan and Is-haq.

I took the food—dates and cherries—they had been like small green berries when I had gone in there, they had been pink blossoms. I had desired for their colorless blood to flow into me so that I would bloom without pain every spring, as they had then. That had happened once, a long time before, when life had still been beautiful. Maybe life had seemed difficult to me then, but when I thought about it in this place, I wished that I could go back.

I was afraid that I would drop the bundle. My hands were unsteady, joyous, crazy and weak; they pressed that proof that I was not dead firmly against my chest. I had known that they would come. I had known it! I lowered my head and breathed in the fresh scent of early summer, greedily, wishfully, more, more—the dankness would soon creep into the transparent red fragrance of the cherries. I touched their tender young skins with my soiled fingers. In a moment, in an hour they would shrivel and age. No matter, no matter. That was a sign, a message from the outside world. I was not alone; there was hope. I had shed no tears when I had thought that the end was near. And now they effused continuously from the revived springs of my eyes. They must have left their traces on the muddy coating on my face. Let them flow; I had risen from the dead. The least sign that I had not been forgotten was enough for my lost strength to return. My body was weak, but that did not matter; I felt a warmth within myself. I did not think about death, and I was no longer indifferent to everything. This happened at the last moment, to stop me on the slope down which I had been sliding, to keep me from dying. And I had indeed begun to die. (I realized, as I had many other times, that the soul can often hold the body together, but the body can never hold the soul together: it stumbles and loses its way all on its own.)

I was waiting again.

I said: they remembered, Harun.

And I thought about Hassan. And I thought about Is-haq.

They would start a rebellion and free me.

They would slip through secret passageways and smuggle me out.

They would turn into air, into birds, into spirits; they would turn invisible, but they would come.

PART I

It would take a miracle for it to happen, but they would come.

An earthquake would demolish these old walls, and they would be waiting for me, to lead me out of the rubble.

Hassan and Is-haq would be the first to open the door, no matter who came, no matter what happened.

There was not a single ordinary thought in my head; they were all beyond the usual and the familiar. I strained to hear the joyful roar of my deliverance. I waited for that rumble, as if it were vengeance for things that I had fearfully stifled inside myself whenever I sensed the slightest hint of them. There could be no ordinary end to all of this waiting. Maybe because of the grave in which I was shut and the nearness of death, the odor of which had already engulfed me; maybe because of the deep passageways and hard gates that could not be opened by a word or an appeal; maybe because of the horror that had befallen me and that might be eliminated by another, greater horror. I waited for a day of judgment and was sure that it would come. The two of them had announced it to me.

The next day I received gifts again. Time was beginning to flow again, uninterrupted. There had been two of them again, nameless. But I knew who they were and waited for the earthquake.

"What if there were an earthquake, a fire, or a rebellion?" I asked Jemal, puzzled that he did not understand. Or did he? And he asked me: "You're a dervish. Do you know the verse: 'When the great event comes to pass'?"

Were we really thinking the same thing?

"I do."

"Come here. Speak."

"No."

"A pity. You're not a good man."

"What do you want to hear it for?"

"I like it. I like to listen to it."

"How do you know about it?"

"From a prisoner. The one before you. A good man."
"That's from the Koran. The 'Waqiah' Sura."[2]
"Maybe."
"'When the great event comes to pass . . .'"
"Not so loud. Come here."
"'When the great event comes to pass, some will be exalted and others abased. When the earth is shaken by violent quakes, you will be separated into three classes.'"[3]

In the gray darkness, leaning with my chin against the sharp edge of the iron frame, I could discern his formless face in the rectangular opening, very close to my eyes. He listened to what I said with surprise, with an interest that I could not understand.

"That's not it."
"Maybe it's the 'Spider' Sura?"[4]
"I don't know. No matter. What three classes?"
"'One are the happy companions, equal in their happiness. They stood ahead of all men and preceded them. They approached near unto Allah, and dwell in the heavenly gardens of delight. This is the group of the first, and a few will also come later. They sit upon thrones adorned with gold, pleasantly reclining opposite one another. They are served by youths who never grow older, and who go round about with jugs, beakers, and cups filled with pure drink that flows from one spring. Their heads will not ache from that drink, nor will their bodies be weakened. And they will take fruits that please them, and the flesh of birds, whichever kind they desire. And they will be accompanied by fair maidens with large eyes, beautiful as pearls hidden inside their shells. This is their reward for their good services. They will not hear empty words or the speech of sinners. They will only hear the words: peace! Peace!

'And the companions of the right hand are companions in happiness. They sit under a bountiful lotus tree that has no thorns, and under banana tress whose fruit hangs in bunches, in shade that has spread along clear, flowing waters. And in an abundance of fruit that will never fail or be forbidden; they repose on lofty beds.'"⁵

"Nice. And for them, too."

His whispers were amazed, full of envy.

"'And how miserable are the wretches who have been struck by misfortune! Their place is in a glowing fire and scalding water, in the shade of dark, black smoke, which is neither pleasant nor beautiful. You will eat the bitter fruit of the tree of Zaqqum,* and you will drink boiling water. You will drink as a thirsty camel drinks. We have decreed that death will reign among you, and our power is great and it will be so.'"⁶

"But why? Are they guilty of something?"

"God alone knows that, Jemal."

"Is there any more?"

"'The unfortunate will tell the chosen: wait, let us take a little of your light! They will answer unto them: go back and find light for yourselves. Then a wall will be erected between them; mercy will be on the inside, and suffering will be on the outside of the wall. Those on the outside will shout: Were we not together with you?'"⁷

"O merciful God. Again. Without light."

After that he said nothing for a while, his excited brain was straining to think. His breathing was heavy.

"And I? Where will I be?"

"I don't know."

"Will I be on the right hand?"

"Maybe."

"'Heavenly gardens, through which rivers flow, await you.'⁸ That's what he said. Before you. And about the sun. Where will I be? That's for good service. Have I done any? Good service? Fifteen years like this. Here. And there the sun. Rivers. Fruit. For good service."

"What happened to that man?"

"He died. He was good. Quiet. He spoke to me. Like that. And you will too, he said. There. And all good people.

That's good. I said. Because of the sun. And the water. Clear. And because of gout. Mine."

"How did he die?"

"Slowly. His soul didn't want to. To leave. He resisted. I was there, too. Yes. I helped."

"What did you help with?"

"He was strangled."

"So you helped to strangle him?"

"He resisted."

"You didn't feel pity for him?"

"Pity. Because of the sun. What he talked about."

"What was his name? Wasn't it maybe Harun?"

"I don't know."

"What had he done?"

"I don't know."

"Go, Jemal."

"Maybe I will, too. On the other side. Of the wall."

"Certainly, Jemal."

He asked me whether I wanted to go to another cell. It was not so dark, and was not so damp as mine.

"It doesn't matter, Jemal."

"Will you tell it? Again? 'When the great event . . .' Only that. First. It's dark here, too. And bad. Fifteen years. It's not right. And there, too."

"Go, Jemal."

His crippled sentences staggered around me for a long time, cramped, mutilated; it seemed that they could hardly stay together, while lost, decapitated fragments miraculously clung to each other and even expressed human desires.

I was losing my senses again.

When once, afterward, that day or much later, or never, he opened the door of my cell, I was struck by two totally opposite feelings; fear that they would strangle me and hope that they would release me. They rushed at me simultaneously, like two impatient, spooked creatures pushing and jumping ahead of each other. Or maybe the distance between them was so small that I could hardly separate them in time. I probably rejected the first thought immediately, because Jemal was alone, and joy came at once: deliverance! Either could have happened; there did not have to be a reason. When they kill men without proof of their guilt, maybe they release them without explanation.

But it was neither one nor the other. I was to go to another cell.

I agreed, joyless.

I entered someone else's grave. It was mine now as well, and I stood by the door to get used to it.

"Pssst!"

This warning from the half-darkness seemed strange, but at that moment a pigeon fluttered away from a narrow window. I noticed it as it flew away.

"Now you can make as much noise as you want," said the man who had tried to quiet me so I would not scare the pigeon.

"I didn't know. Will it come again?"

"It isn't crazy. It wandered here accidentally."

"I'm sorry. Do you like pigeons?"

"No. But here you even begin to love bats."

"There weren't even any bats in my cell, probably because of the dampness."

"There aren't any here, either. They can't stand people. I caught one when it flew in accidentally, by mistake. I wanted to tie it with a cord from my waistcoat, but it made me sick. Sit down, wherever you want, it doesn't matter where."

"I know."

"How long have you been in prison?"

"A long time."

"Maybe they've forgotten you?"

"What do you mean forgotten?"

"Just like that, forgotten. A man told me, he was here. They had caught him somewhere in the Krayina, and led him for days and weeks from place to place, from prison to prison, until they brought him here. And here they forgot him. Months passed and he sat and languished here. No one called for him, no one asked about him, no one gave him any thought, and that was it. Just hope that doesn't happen to you."

"My friends sent me a message. They know where I am."

"That's even worse. That man's family also found out where he was and came, but he sent them a message not to look for him. As it was, he was at least alive; but if the authorities remembered him, something bad might happen. And indeed, one night they took him away. Into exile, it seems."

His voice was full of irony, as if he were trying to frighten me on purpose. But his story was not unlikely.

"Why are you talking like that?" I asked, surprised at his attitude and intentions. I had thought that everyone here was utterly dejected and unanimous at least in their desire not to hurt each other.

The man laughed. He truly laughed. It came so unexpectedly that I thought he was crazy. Although he laughed in a very ordinary manner, cheerfully, as if he were at home. And maybe for that very reason.

"Why am I talking like this? Here the key is to be patient. And to be ready for anything. That's how this place is. And if things turn out better than you expect, then thank God, you've come out ahead."

"How can you see everything so blackly?"

"If you don't think blackly, things can get blacker. Nothing depends on you. It doesn't help to be either brave or cowardly, neither to curse nor to weep; nothing can help you. So sit and wait for your lot, and it's already black since you're here. That's what I think: if you're not guilty, then it's their mistake. If you are guilty, then it's your mistake. If you're innocent, then misfortune has struck you, as if you've fallen into a deep whirlpool. And if you're not innocent, you've earned it, nothing more."

PART I

"Things are quite simple with you."

"They're not that simple. One has to get used to them—then they're simple. You see, I think I'm innocent, which is surely what you think about yourself. This, however, is not true, since it's impossible that you haven't, at least once in your life, sinned enough to have to atone for it. But no matter, at that point you escaped your punishment and now you're not guilty of anything. Of course, it seems to you that you should be released. Only how can they release you? Listen, try to think like they do. If I'm not guilty, then they made a mistake and imprisoned an innocent man. If they released me, then they'd be admitting to their mistake and that wouldn't be easy or useful. No one with any sense can demand from them that they act against themselves. Such a demand would be unrealistic and silly. So then I must be guilty. And how can they release me if I'm guilty? Do you understand? We shouldn't judge them too harshly. Everyone sees things from his own point of view. We think it's all right when we do that, but when they do, then it bothers us. You must admit, that's inconsistent."

"And if they forget about you, who's to blame then?"

That possibility was as bitter as poison: they have forgotten about you, darkness is falling around you, and no one even knows that you exist. People think that you are dead, or that you have wondered off somewhere in the world, that you are where you want to be, and that you are fine. Maybe they even envy you. And you wait in vain; you are not guilty but your guilt continues. You are not being punished, but your punishment is continuously meted out, more horrible than if it were pronounced.

"Who's guilty? Forgetfulness. That's human, it happens. And so, if you really think about it no one has even done anything wrong to you. That's your lot. Or you yourself are guilty of not being guilty. Because if you were guilty they wouldn't forget you. That's even an admission of your innocence."

He was joking; I realized it only then. What kind of man jokes like that? He would drive me to despair, I would have been better off if I had remained alone.

"That's a bad joke, friend," I said reproachfully.

"If it's bad, then it's not a joke. A joke is never so bad."

Then I recognized him. I lost my breath. I screamed, or thought that I did. I should have, I had to, I should not have met him here!

It was Is-haq!

Is-haq, the frequent object of my thoughts, my brightest memory, the vague aspiration of my unrealized and unfulfilled self, the distant light in my darkness, my human support, the long-sought-after key to mysteries, a sense of possibilities beyond the known, an admission of the impossible, a dream that could not be realized or rejected. Is-haq, admiration for a mad courage that we had forgotten because we thought that we no longer needed it.

They had caught the hero of fairy tales—the only real tales—who was created by pure imagination and remembered by adult weakness. They had destroyed human dreams. They were stronger than fairy tales.

He had also believed in fairy tales; he had said that they would never catch him.

"Is-haq!" I shouted, as if I were trying to call to someone lost.

"Who are you calling to?" the man asked, surprised.

"I'm calling to you. I'm calling to Is-haq."

"I'm not Is-haq."

"No matter. That's the name I've given you. How did you let them catch you?"

"Man was created to be caught at one time or another."

"You didn't think like that before."

"I wasn't imprisoned before. Then and now, those are two different men."

"Are you really giving yourself up to them, Is-haq?"

"I'm not giving up. I was given to them. It's beyond me.

It's not what I wanted but that's the way it is. I helped them because I exist. If I didn't exist, they wouldn't be able to do anything to me."

"Is that the only reason—that you exist?"

"The reason and the condition. That's always an opportunity. For you and for them. It's rarely left unexploited. Regardless of whether you're here or up there. The only thing I don't know is how long guilt lasts. Does it continue into the next world?"

"If you've done nothing wrong then you're not guilty. God makes amends for the injustices done here."

"You're answering too quickly. Think about it. Does authority come from God? If not, where does it get the right to judge us? If it does, then how can it make a mistake? If it doesn't, we'll destroy it; if it does, we'll obey it. If it's not from God, what binds us to endure injustices? If it is from God, are those injustices or punishments for a higher purpose? If it's not, then violence has been committed against you and me and against all of us, and then again we're guilty of putting up with it. Answer me now. Only don't give me the dervish answer that authority comes from God but that it's sometimes exercised by evil men. And don't tell me that God will roast the tyrants in the fires of hell, because we won't know any more than we do now. The Koran also says this: 'Submit to God and to His prophet and to those who direct your affairs.'[9] That's the divine prescription, for God's purpose is more important to Him than you and I are. Are they tyrants then? Or are we tyrants who will roast in the fires of hell? And are they committing violence or defending themselves? To direct someone's affairs is to rule; ruling is power; power is injustice for the sake of justice. Anarchy is worse: disorder, general injustice and violence, general fear. Answer me now."

I kept silent.

"You can't answer me? I'm surprised. You dervishes can't explain anything, but you can give an answer to everything."

"You're ready beforehand to disagree with me, no matter what I might say. It's hard for two men who think differently to come to an understanding."

"Two men who think will come to an understanding easily."

He began to laugh again. That laughter was not offensive, it was directed at him as much as at me, but it served as a reason for me to break off that conversation, in which I did not feel secure. It happened for the first time that I was puzzled by questions that had seemed clear. His reasons were arbitrary, superficial, even jocular, but it was still hard for me to give an answer. Not because I had none, but because he had rendered them unsatisfactory. He left arid land for any seeds that I might have been able to sow. He negated in advance everything that I could have said. He pinned me down, led me over the void with which he had surrounded me; any opinions that I might have had were deprived of their value by his mockery. He overcame me by imposing his logic on me, and bound me to consider all possibilities earnestly.

"You're honest," he said with seeming approval. "Clever and honest. You don't want to answer with empty words, and you don't have any real ones. And I've put answers into your mouth."

"Only so that you could refute them. You were mocking me."

"I just wanted to speak, for no purpose at all. But the problem is that you don't dare to think about anything. You're afraid; you don't know where your thoughts might lead you. Everything inside you is confused. You keep your eyes closed and stay on the old path. They brought you here, I don't know why and it doesn't concern me, but you won't accept my explanations of human guilt. You think it's a joke. Maybe it is, but maybe one could develop quite a nice philosophical idea out of it, not any worse than others, but it would at least have a good practical purpose. It would reconcile us with everything that happens to us. You're bitter; you think you're not guilty. A pity. If they don't release you, you'll die soon, from spite, and everything will be all right. And what would happen if they released you? That would be the strangest misfortune that I know of. What's above is yours as much as theirs, but they've excluded you. Would you become an outlaw? Would you begin to hate them? Would you forget? I'm asking, because I don't know which is more difficult. Everything is possible but I can't see a solution. If you become an outlaw then you'll commit violence, so how could you be angry with them? If you come to hate them, you'll be poisoned by your ill will unless you act against them, and against yourself, since you're the same as they are, and they'll catch you again. You might as well commit suicide. If you forget, you might make up for it somehow, thinking that you're generous. But they'll think that you're a coward and a hypocrite, and they won't believe you. You'll be excluded in any case, and that's what you cannot accept. The only possible solution would be this: for nothing to have happened."

"Those are my thoughts exactly!" I exclaimed in surprise.

"So much the worse. Because that alone is impossible."

Is-haq! Another, different, but the same as he was then. Everything was different and yet the same. The Is-haq who did not answer but asked questions, who asked questions in order to pose riddles, who posed riddles in order to mock them. Elusive. Go, he would have told me, as he had once, had it not been so silly, since I could not leave. He could. He would leave, if he decided to; a miracle would happen and he would disappear. They would search for him in vain; walls would not be able to hold him; guards would not be able to keep him; no one would be able to do anything to him. Elusive, like his thoughts. He would leave without an answer; although he knew it, he would not say it. He always left me shattered, unsettling everything within me that I knew. And it did not matter that afterward I knew what I should have said, since I had not answered him. I had not been able to; then I had believed him more than myself. It did not matter because I did not believe myself unless he was with me, because I was afraid that he would refute any of my opinions if he heard them. Therefore I said nothing. But I could maintain my opinions only if I defended them before him. And I did not dare to do that. He thought differently than I did: his thoughts took unexpected turns; they were casual, impudent, and did not respect what I respected. He examined everything freely, I hesitated in front of many things. He destroyed but did not build, saying what was not, but not what was. And denial is convincing; it sets neither boundaries nor goals for itself. It strives toward nothing; it defends nothing. It is harder to defend something than to attack it, because everything that is made reality constantly wears down, constantly deviates from the initial idea.

I said, trying to defend myself:

"Life always sinks downward. It takes effort to avoid that."

"The idea drags it down because it begins to contradict itself. And then a new idea is developed, an opposing one, and it is good until it begins to be turned into reality. What is, is not good; what is good is what is desired. When people come across a pretty thought they should keep it under glass, so it won't get dirty."

"Then there's no possibility of putting the world in order? And everything is only error and eternal attempts?"

He did not respond. The thought he had spoken was strange, strange at the beginning. Afterward I did not care.

"This is also the world. We're underground. To put it in order means to make it worse."

Then the nonsense began. It seemed to me that I was aware of it, but I could not escape. There was an irresistible pleasure in that nothingness, in that floating without effort or aim. A leaf floating down a careless stream. An unburdened and uncontorted thought. A capricious and pretty game with no purpose. Hovering without fear. A whim that you do not regret, a pleasant and unavoidable necessity, like breathing, like the flow of blood.

"For whom will it be worse?" I asked, unconcerned.

"For us. For them. We'll imprison one another. We'll get used to it. We'll turn into moles, into bats, into scorpions."

"We won't even get out. We'll come to love the silence and the darkness."

"We won't get out. We'll stay here forever. We can't live without eternity."

"We won't forget one another."

"We'll imprison our adversaries up above; we'll banish them to the earth. And we'll forget about them."

"'When they're pulled from hell, they'll be thrown into the river of life.'"

"They'll be unhappy up above. They'll cry: 'Give us a little darkness. We were together with you!'"

"And we'll say to them: 'Find darkness for yourself. Create it yourself!'"

"How unhappy they'll be! They'll cry: 'Release us! Let us come down below!' And we'll say to them: 'That's your own fault. You didn't believe us.'"

"That's your own fault. Remain up above."

"Occasionally I'll go up to the earth."

"You always rebel."

"You'll be a mole-dervish. You'll make sure that we never begin to see, that we never wander out of our dark world."

"We'll protect our world."

"I don't want to be a mole."

"We're growing claws. And fur. And snouts."

"I don't want to be a mole. Go."

I was squatting, with my forehead against the rough, wet wall, without the strength to move away.

Someone was standing above me.

He helped me to get up.

"You're being released. Your friends are waiting for you."

I reminded myself, with distant, anemic thoughts, that I should rejoice, but I did not even try. I did not feel any need for that.

"Where's Is-haq?" I asked Jemal. "He was here."

"Don't worry. About others."

"He was here, a moment ago."

An unknown man was waiting in the passageway. Three of them had brought me. Now I was not important.

"Let's go," he said.

We walked through the darkness silently. I kept running into the walls; the man held me up. We walked; in my thoughts I would flee, and would return only after a long time to wonder: Who's waiting for me? And I did not care. I would wonder: Did Is-haq escape? And I did not care. And then we staggered out of a greater darkness into a lesser one. I realized that it was night, transient: beautiful is everything that is not eternal, the night and rain, the summer rain. I wanted to stretch out my arms so that it would wash away the subterranean mud and extinguish the fire in me. But my arms hung powerless, useless.

PART 2

10

> He who defiles his soul
> will be unhappy.[1]

A CHILD SPOKE ABOUT HIS FEAR, LONG AGO. IT RESEMBLED A little song:

> In the attic
> there's a beam that hits you on the head,
> there's a wind that bangs the shutters,
> there's a mouse that peeps out of the corner.

He was six years old. His cheerful blue eyes watched the soldiers with admiration, and me as well, a young dervish-warrior. We were companions and friends. I do not know whether he ever loved anyone so much in his life as he did me, because I always met him joyfully and never acted as if I were older than he.

It was summer, and rain alternated with hot weather. We were bivouacked in tents on a plain full of mosquitoes and croaking frogs, an hour's walk from the Sava,[2] near a building that used to be an inn, where the boy lived with his mother and half-blind grandmother.

We had already been there three months since the spring, occasionally attacking the enemy, who had dug in along the bank of the river. At first we lost many men, and so we held back, as we knew that we could do nothing against them at such strength. The rest of our troops were tied down on God-knows-which other battlefields of the vast empire, and so both we and the enemy had gotten bogged down, each an obstacle and hindrance to the other.

That wearisome situation dragged on. The nights were steamy and hot, and the plain breathed quietly in the moonlight, like the sea; countless frogs in the invisible swamps cut us off from the rest of the world with their piercing voices, flooding us with a terrible drone that was calmed only by the misty dawns, while white and gray vapors drifted over us like at the very beginning of the world. Hardest to bear was the punctuality of these changes, their changelessness.

In the morning the mists turned roseate, and the most pleasant part of the day began, without the steamy heat, without the mosquitoes, without the tortures of nights spent half-awake. At that time we would fall into a deep sleep, as if into a well.

When it rained, it was even worse. The horizon narrowed around us. We squatted together and said nothing, tormented by the cold, as if winter were already setting in, or we just talked about anything at all, or sang, irritable and dangerous, like wolves. Our tents leaked and gray rain dripped down on us; water seeped up under our cots. The ground turned into an impassable quagmire, and we were trapped in our misery, as always.

The soldiers drank, played dice under canopies of blankets, quarreled and fought. It was a dog's life, which I led with outward calm, in no way showing that it was hard for me, sitting still, even when the rain drenched me, even when our tent turned into a madhouse, a cage of wild beasts. I forced myself to endure all that unpleasantness and nastiness without a word; I was young and thought that it was a part of sacrifice, but I knew that it was unpleasant and nasty. Both a peasant and softa, I flinched at every curse and vulgar word, until I realized that soldiers use them without even noticing that there is something indecent in them. But when they really wanted to curse, when they wanted to say obscenities on purpose and with pleasure, it was truly unbearable. They did it with a tranquil fury, with impudent relish, pausing and provocatively listening to the echo of an unnatural coupling of words. I could have wept from desperation.

I heard all sorts of things about life and people that I had not known before. Some of them I listened to with curiosity, some with astonishment. Thus I gained experience, and lost my naïveté without stopping to regret it.

I would sit with the soldiers to the point where I felt nauseated, but I allowed myself to leave only when I calmed back down, dulled my senses, and drifted away in my thoughts, accepting everything as a necessity called life, which is not always pretty. I rarely tried to bring them to their senses. A few times they ridiculed me so cruelly (since, except for my calling, I was no different from them, I had no rank to protect me) that, for their sake and mine, I gave up interfering in what they did. I limited myself to saying the prayers that were a part of my military duties, such as marches or sentry watches. At that time I was struck by the strange, discouraging thought of how a man who is spiritually more developed than others is in a difficult situation, unless he is protected by his position and the fear that position instills. Such a man becomes a loner: his standards are different, useless to others, but they still set him apart.

So most of the time I stayed alone with a book or with my thoughts. I did not succeed in finding a single one of the men whom I would have wanted to befriend. I saw them all together as a whole, as a multitude, odd, cruel, strong, and even interesting. As individuals they were unimaginably insignificant. I did not despise them when I thought of them as a group, I even liked that hundred-headed creature a little, cruel and powerful as it was, but I could not stand them as individuals. My love, or something less than that, was directed at all of them but not at any single one, and that was enough for me.

Once, while I sat in a field, on a rotted stump, in coarse bindweed up to my knees, alone, deafened by the crickets chirping under the hot sun (something was always chirping, screeching, or singing in that plain), troubled by what I had heard from the soldiers about the young woman in the inn, I saw the boy stop in the grass, which reached almost up to his neck. He addressed me trustfully. We already knew one another.

I would have preferred for him not to find me. I felt almost afraid that in my eyes he would read what I had heard about his mother.

The tale that the soldiers told was not unlikely. She was the only young woman nearby. The nearest villages could barely be seen on the distant edges of the plain. But they would go there as well, especially at night, I knew it, mostly because of the women, and no one is so inconsiderate as a soldier who knows that he can be killed at any moment but does not want to think about death, who does not want to think about anything and calmly leaves a trail of desolation behind himself. And women are kinder to them because of the old pity that soldiers always inspire, and because their shame leaves them, following the soldiers on their distant wanderings. Where armies pass, grass does not sprout, but children do. But this was hard for me to accept about the boy's mother. Any woman, only not a particular one. I had been generalizing about the world so much that I began to lose my grasp of it.

Small, seemingly weak, still young, she did not attract attention immediately, but her composed look, calm movements, and the confidence of her bearing did not let a man pass by her with indifference. Then he might discover her eyes, which did not gaze absently, her beautiful mouth, somewhat mocking and defiant, and the harmony of motion that only a healthy and supple body has. She courageously struggled with obstacles in her life. Widowed, she decided to keep the inn, somehow, and the land around it, which was gradually being destroyed by the war, so that it began to resemble a graveyard and wasteland. She did not leave; she protected her only possessions, trying to turn the misfortune to her advantage. She sold food and drink to the soldiers, let them gamble in the inn, and drew their meager pay from them, giving them what they did not have. She tried to keep her son from the house and the soldiers whenever she could. But she was not always able to. I talked to her about that. "It's because of him that I work," she told me calmly. "Life will be hard for him if he starts out with nothing."

And so, I had now learned that she slept with the soldiers. Maybe she had to, maybe she could not fend them off, maybe she had once agreed and afterward they kept pressuring her so that she got used to it—I do not know. I did not want to ask anyone, but I was bothered by what I had heard. Because of the boy. Did he know, would he find out? And because of myself. Until I heard I had admired her courage, but afterward I thought like any other young man, although I was ashamed of my thoughts. Now she was water that flowed freely, food that offered itself, within arm's reach. She was no longer protected by anything, except my shame, and I knew that shame is not such a great obstacle. Therefore I bound myself even more to the boy, to protect both of us.

I let him lead me on his childish paths; we spoke a childlike language, and thought childlike thoughts. I was happy when I succeeded in this completely, because I felt enriched that way. We made flutes from reeds and enjoyed the sharp, shrill sound that was produced when the green reed cut the air from our mouths. We carefully whittled an alder branch, carving out the moist pith in order to make a hollow full of hidden sounds. We wove wreaths of blue and yellow marsh flowers to take to his mother. But later I persuaded him to decorate poplar branches with them, so I would not think anything shameful.

"Will flowers sprout on the branches?" he asked me.

"Maybe they will," I said, myself even believing a little in that floral revival of the gray tree.

"Where's the sun?" he asked me once.

"Behind the clouds."

"Is it always there? Even when it's cloudy?"

"Always."

"Could we see it if we climbed to the top of that poplar?"

"No."

"And if we were on a minaret?"

"No. The clouds are above the minaret."

"And if a hole was made in the clouds?"

Indeed, why don't people make holes in clouds for boys who love the sun?

When it rained, I sat with him in one of the rooms of his spacious house; he also took me to the attic, and I actually hit my head on one of the beams. He told me his beautiful stories about the big-big boat, as big as his house, which sailed over the river-plain, about his favorite pigeon, which fluttered above his bed on steamy nights while he slept, and about his grandmother who could not see but who knew all the fairy tales in the world.

"Even about the golden bird?"

"Even about the golden bird."

"What's the golden bird?"

"Don't you know?" my little teacher wondered. "It's a bird made of gold. It's hard to find."

Later, I stopped going to the house so often. My thoughts were not pure, and it was hard for me to speak his language. And when I did go, I did not behave naturally. We sat in the kitchen, his mother came in and out, smiling at us, as at two children. I hid my eyes. And I did not want to eat or drink, I refused when she would offer it. I wanted to be different than the others, because I was the same.

"Stay with us," the boy suggested to me. "Why should you leave in the rain?"

The woman laughed when she saw how I blushed.

One morning, at the break of dawn, the enemy attacked and drove us out of our tents. Surprised, we offered weak resistance. We barely managed to gather our weapons and essentials, and fled over the plain in our white undergarments, our arms full of the meager possessions of soldiers. We stopped only when the sun was full and when there was no longer anyone behind us.

The enemy took our positions around the inn. They dug trenches and waited for us each time without fear.

We pushed them back to the bank of the river only seven days later, and occupied the positions around the inn again.

Then two of our soldiers came out of the house; the sudden attack had caught them in the inn, or they had taken shelter there, and they had spent all of the seven harrowing days hiding there, while the enemy roamed in and around the inn. The woman had fed them.

We were grateful to her up until they told us that she had also slept with the enemy soldiers.

There was a silence.

I requested from our commanders that the boy and his blind grandmother be taken in a cart to some neighboring village.

"And mother?" the boy asked.

"She'll come later."

They shot her as soon as the cart became a tiny speck on the vast plain.

He must have found out what happened to his mother, and his little song about the attic must have turned more bitter.

I remembered the boy and his fear as I sat in my room and returned in my thoughts to my own childhood.

There had also been an attic in my house. I would sit hunched on an old, discarded saddle, alone in that world of useless objects that lost their original forms and took on new ones according to the time of day and my moods, according to the varying shades of light, which transformed them, according to the sorrow or happiness within me. Riding out on the saddle to meet the desire for something to happen, something from my hazy childhood visions, which changed without rhyme or reason, unreal, just like the objects in the half-darkness of the attic.

That attic helped form me, as had innumerable other places and circumstances, encounters, and people. I developed in thousands of changes, and it always seemed to me that all of my former self disappeared with each new change, that it was lost in the mists of time that had passed and were now insignificant. But then, again and again, unexpectedly, I would find traces of everything that had been, like uncovered artifacts, like my own fossil strata; although they were old and unsightly, they became dear and beautiful. That rediscovered, recovered part of me, which was more than a memory, was beautified and returned from unreachable distances by time, which joined me with it. Thus, it had a twofold existence, as a part of my present personality, and as a memory. As the present, and as a beginning.

In that attic, learning about myself, where I sought solitude and a refuge from the open expanses of my homeland (though I loved it more than my own mother), I often thought about the golden bird of my grandmother's tales. I did not know what that golden bird was, but as I listened to the rain falling down on the shingle roof and the open shutters banging in the wind, as innumerable eyes peered from the corners, I would imagine finding my own golden bird, like the hero from my grandmother's sparkling tales, knowing that thus, in some strange, inexplicable fashion, happiness is achieved.

Later I forgot about that bird, which was conceived in inexperience. Life dispersed the daydreams of youth, which were possible in fiery, unhindered imagination, in the freedom of endless wishing. But it appeared again, as if to mock me, when I felt the worst.

Once upon a time there was a boy, in his father's house,

above a river, who dreamed golden dreams, because he knew nothing about life.

And there was another boy, in an inn, on a plain, who thought about the golden bird. They murdered his mother—she was a sinner—and drove him out into the world.

We were four brothers, and each of us sought his golden bird of happiness. One died in war, one of consumption, one was murdered in the fortress. I am no longer searching for mine.

Where are the golden birds of human dreams? Which countless seas and rugged mountains does one have to cross to reach them? Does this profound desire of childish irrationality appear for sure only as a sad sign embroidered on kerchiefs and morocco bindings of useless books?

I tried to read Abu Faraj, I forced myself, with little desire to do so, without any inner need. I wanted to hear someone else's thoughts, and not just my own.

I opened the book, picking a passage at random, and came across a tale about Alexander the Great. The emperor, as the story went, received as a gift some wondrous glass dishes. He liked the gifts very much, but smashed them all nonetheless. "Why? Are they not beautiful?" he was asked. "Precisely because of that," he answered. "They are so beautiful that it would be hard for me to lose them. And with time they would break, one by one. And I would be sorrier than I am now."

The tale was naive but it still astonished me. Its lesson was bitter: one should renounce everything he might ever begin to love, because loss and disappointment are inevitable. We must renounce love in order not to lose it. We must destroy our love so that it will not be destroyed by others. We must renounce every attachment, because of the possibility of regret.

This thought is cruelly hopeless. We cannot destroy everything we love; there will always be the possibility that others will destroy it for us.

Why are books considered to be clever if they are bitter?

No one's wisdom could have helped me. I wanted rather to return to my beginnings. I did that without effort or compulsion. I was not searching for anything; it sought and found itself on its own.

It rained for days on end; the rain drummed maliciously on the tiles of the tekke's old roof. The horizon was dark, unclear. In the attic above my head invisible feet scurried back and forth. There was a beam that hit you in the head, a wind that banged the shutters, and a mouse that peered from the corner. There was a childhood that watched from the darkness with sad eyes.

For a moment I succeeded in thinking like that distant, lonely boy, to feel his feelings and to fear his fears. Everything was a beautiful secret; everything had only a future or endless duration; everything was surrounded by vibrant reflections, profound happiness or profound sorrow. These were not events, but moods: sometimes they came on their own, like a breeze, like quiet twilight, like an indistinct glittering, like intoxication. Or disjointed images appeared—faces that in a split second flared in the darkness, someone's laughter on a sunny morning, the moon's reflection on a quiet river, a knotty tree at a bend in the road. I did not even sense that those particles of my earlier life existed within me, nor did I know why they lingered for so long. Was it possible that at one time they had meant a lot to me (that was why they had been ingrained in my memory), but were later put aside, like old toys? I had forgotten about my former self, sunken in time; now broken remnants and wreckage were floating to the surface.

I was all of that, fragmented, consisting entirely of pieces, reflections and shimmers. I consisted entirely of accidents, unknown reasons, of a purpose that had existed and been put aside. And now I no longer knew what I was in that chaos.

I began to resemble a sleepwalker.

I sat up late at night, motionless, with a candle lit on each side of the room, to eliminate the darkness. Calm, quiet, like the night around me, like the world at night, I watched the black windowpane that separated me from the darkness, and the gray walls that separated me from everything, not daring to look anywhere else, as if the walls would split asunder during a single short moment of inattention. Without getting up, without moving from the corner where I sat, so that I had the entire room in front of me, I listened to the driving rain, the gurgling of the flooded wooden gutter, the pigeons scratching with their legs and their sleepy cooing. And all those silent noises became part of a night that would not pass, part of a world that was not alive.

I was no longer looking for reasons, for a whole, for uninterrupted continuities.

At the end of everything that I had been trying to determine, to link, and give a sense to, there was a long, black night, and waters that were constantly rising.

And the boy from the plain was also there, like a painful symbol.

I had found him later and taken him into the madrasah and into the tekke. We barely recognized each other; our souls had changed so much.

His grandmother had died and he was alone in the world. He was a shepherd in the village where they had left him, an orphan whose mother had perished in the war, leaving her dubious merits in his memory. And a black burden in his soul.

He resembled a marsh flower transplanted into hills, a grasshopper whose wings had been torn off by children. He resembled a boy from the plain whose freedom from care had been taken away by people. Everything was his, his face, his body, and his voice, but it was not him.

I will never forget how he sat facing me, on a rock, lifeless, dumb, distant, without a trace of the birdlike joy that had once radiated from him, without sorrow even, without anything, shattered. You'll be with me, I'll take care of you,

you'll go to school, I said, although I wanted to shout: Laugh, run after a butterfly, speak of the pigeon that flutters over your dreams. But he never spoke about anything again.

Now, while it rained, while in the emptiness that had opened up in front of me I clutched like a drowning man at my childhood, at my books, at phantoms, he would enter my room quietly. Sometimes I even caught him in front of the door, when it seemed to me that the silence had changed.

He would stand by the wall, speechless.

"Sit, Mullah-Yusuf."

"That's all right."

"What do you want?"

"Do you need me to copy something?"

"No."

He would stay a little longer. We did not know how to talk, it was awkward for both of us, and he would leave without a word.

I am not really sure what it was that came between us, which bonds still tied us together, and which painful tensions kept us apart. I had loved him once, and he had loved me, but now we looked at each other with lifeless eyes. What tied us to each other was the plain, before the tragedy, and the joy that had shone on that time like sunlight. And yet we continually reminded each other that joy can never last for very long.

He never spoke about his childhood, the plain, or the inn, but whenever he looked at me I thought I saw the memory of his mother's death in his eyes. As if I had been inseparably linked with his most painful recollection. Maybe he had forgotten what actually happened, and thought that I was guilty as well, since I was no different from the others. Once I tried to explain to him, but he interrupted me, frightened: "I know."

He did not allow anyone to approach that forbidden part of him, or to disturb the gloomy order that he had created within himself. And so, we drifted farther and farther apart, secretly resentful; he because of his suspicion, rancor, and misfortune, and I because of his ingratitude.

Hassan made up with his father. He spoke jokingly of how he had gained a guardian, a mother-in-law, and a spoiled child all in the same man, but he gushed with joy. He made an agreement with his father to turn both of their portions of the estate into a wakf,* for the salvation of their souls and for their memory, for the benefit of poor people and the homeless. He ran around all day long, taking care of business concerning the contract and legal documents, looking for a man suitable to be caretaker, someone honest, intelligent, and skillful. If there is such a man, he said laughing. I was not sure whether he was happier that he had made up with his father or that such an estate had slipped through the fingers of his brother-in-law, Aini-effendi. "If his heart doesn't burst," he would say cheerfully, "then it's made of stone."

He bought the copy of the Koran that Mullah-Yusuf had been working on, as a gift for his father. Yusuf did not want to take any money, but Hassan's reasons were convincing:

"One doesn't give away two years of work easily."

"What'll I do with the money?"

"Give it to someone who needs it."

He marveled at Yusuf's Koran: "He's an artist, Sheikh-Ahmed, but you keep silent and hide him; you're afraid that they might take him away from you. He reminds me of the famous Muberid.[3] Maybe his work is even more beautiful. More passionate, more sincere. Have you heard about Muberid, Mullah-Yusuf?"

"No."

"He became rich and respected with the same talent that you have. And no one in our kasaba has ever heard about you. Not even those who come to the tekke. Our people take their talents to Constantinople or Egypt, and others bring us back stories about them. We don't know how to do anything, we don't care, or we don't trust ourselves."

PART 2

"Glory in this place is modest, no matter what the reason," I said, refusing to submit to his reproach. "I wanted to send him to Constantinople, but he didn't agree."

The young man became flustered, as he had the first time, but with less fear than before.

"I do it for myself," he said softly. "And I didn't even wonder whether it's any good or not."

Hassan laughed: "If your words are sincere, I should stand up in your honor."

He watched the youth as he walked away, flustered by this praise.

"There are still shy and sensitive men in the world, my friend. Don't you think it's strange?"

"They'll always be around."

"Thank God. There are too many of us who don't even know what that is anymore. We should preserve such people, as seeds. It seems that you're not very interested in him," he added unexpectedly.

"He's quiet, closed."

"Shy, quiet, closed. May Allah help him."

"Why?"

"Your dervish trade is strange. You sell words, which people buy out of fear or habit. He doesn't want to, or doesn't know how to sell words. He can't even sell silence. Or talent. And he doesn't care about success. What, then, does he care about?"

It was no use; Hassan was difficult to stop when someone aroused his attention. Often it was for no reason, or for some reason that was important only to him.

"Why are you asking about him so much?"

"I'm not asking. We're just talking."

"You have an uncanny ability to sense unhappy men."

"Is he unhappy?"

I told him everything I knew, or almost everything, about the plain, the boy, about his mother, and while I was talking it became clearer and clearer to me that the youth was a victim. As I was. I did not know whose suffering was greater. His had begun very early in life, and mine near the end. I did not say it, but I myself sensed that I pitied his misfortune too much: I was also talking about myself, creating my double.

Hassan listened, looking to the side, without interrupting me, excited, but sober enough to guess the core of the matter:

"It seems you understand him only now. He needed to be helped."

"He doesn't want anybody's help; he doesn't let anybody get close to him; he doesn't trust anybody."

"He'd have trusted love. He was a child."

"I loved him. I was the one who brought him here."

"I'm not accusing you. We're all like that. We hide our love and thus stifle it. A pity, both for you and him."

I knew what he was thinking: he could take the place of my brother now. But no one could take the place of my brother.

I had not helped Yusuf! And who had helped me?

I had been speaking about myself, but all he heard was the boy's name. By telling about him I pushed myself aside. Was it because Yusuf was young? Or because I was proud and strong? No one pities the strong.

"And now? How is he now? Do you two keep silent about everything?"

"Unhappy people are too sensitive. We might hurt each other."

There was no use talking about what was hard to explain, that I loved the memory of the plain, but hated his cold detachment and gloomy silence, which killed all hope. I simplified that complex relationship, telling only part of the truth, that we were somewhat estranged but that the bonds between us were still strong, because a man cannot easily walk away from someone he has helped. He tries to keep a pretty memory of himself. Yusuf and I were like the closest

PART 2

257

of kin, so our disagreements were like family problems, they always bordered on love.

"You can also hate your family," Hassan said with a laugh.

He did not surprise me. He had been serious for too long.

I answered with a joke:

"We haven't gotten that far yet."

From then on they saw each other more often. Hassan came to the tekke or invited him to his home. They ran around taking care of Hassan's business, wrote out contracts and settled various accounts, and in the evening took walks along the river. Mullah-Yusuf changed visibly: I knew, Hassan's straightforwardness hovered around him like a mist. He still wore his obedient, lost expression, with which he separated himself from others, but he was no longer dejected and difficult. It was as if that distant boy were coming back to life, although slowly, still hidden in shadows.

He would become restless if Hassan did not show up. He looked at him, beaming, when he finally did appear, and rejoiced at his serenity and friendly words. He never left, as he had before, when Hassan and I would begin a conversation; he stayed with us, almost forgetting the due respect, with the right that this new friendship gave him. And Hassan was content with his silent devotion and the joy with which the boy met him.

And then everything changed. Too quickly, too suddenly. Hassan stopped coming to the tekke, and did not invite Yusuf anymore. They no longer saw one another.

I asked him, surprised:

"What happened to Hassan?"

"I don't know," he said nervously.

"How long has it been since he came?"

"Five days already."

He looked depressed. Once again his expression became

insecure; a deep shadow covered his face, which had begun to cheer up.

"Why haven't you gone to see him?"

He bowed his head and answered with difficulty:

"I did. They wouldn't let me in."

I also barely managed to see Hassan.

The small woman, who looked at everyone absentmindedly, smiling quietly at her memories or expectations, with a flower in her hair, made up and perfumed (her husband certainly thought that it was for him, and was happy), let me in fearfully, asking me to say that I had found the door open; it would be easier for her to excuse herself for forgetting to lock it than for letting me in. They had not gone out for three days and nights, she said, without reproach. For her the world was cheerful.

I found him on his spacious veranda, with his friends. They were throwing dice.

The place was a mess, full of tobacco smoke, which drifted like fog in the half-darkness, since the thick curtains had been closed. Although it was morning they still had candles burning, and their faces were pallid and exhausted. Dishes and glasses all around them. And piles of money.

The expression on Hassan's face was stiff, uncomposed, almost malevolent.

He gave me a surprised look, showing no kindness at all. I was sorry that I had come.

"I wanted to talk to you."

"I'm busy now."

He was holding an ivory die in his hand and he tossed it on the carpet, preoccupied with the game.

"Sit down, if you want."

"I don't have time."

"What did you want to talk about?"

"It's not important. It can wait."

I left, insulted. And surprised. Who was this man? An empty babbler? The April sun? A weakling overcome by vice?

PART 2

I was in a bad mood, oppressed by the thought that there were no people who were always good. He squandered pretty words and forgot them immediately.

But when I reached the end of the long corridor, Hassan came out of the room.

For the first time I saw him slovenly, neglecting himself. As if he were someone else. His eyes were not serene or clear, but dim and sunken, worn out from drinking and lack of sleep. He blinked obscenely at the light.

We watched each other without smiling.

"Forgive me," he said gloomily. "You've come at a bad time."

"I see."

"It's not bad that you know everything about me."

"I haven't seen you for days. I wanted to find out what's happened to you."

"I've had business to attend to. Other than this."

"I've also come because of Yusuf. Has something happened? He came looking for you, but you didn't let him in."

"I'm not always in the mood for conversation."

"He's gotten used to you. He's come to love you."

"To love me—that's too much. To get used to me—that's nothing. And I'm not to blame for one or the other."

"You reached out to him, you brought him out of his solitude, and then you left him. Why?"

"I can't tie myself to anyone for my whole life. That's also my misfortune. I keep trying but I can't succeed. What's strange about that?"

"I'd like to know the reason."

"The reason is within me."

"Then nothing. Forgive me."

"You told me you loved him. Are you sure about that?"

"I don't know."

"Then you're not. Why did you bring him here if you didn't want to take him in?"

"I did take him in."

"You only did your duty, expecting his gratitude. But he isolated himself more and more and fortified his hatred."

"His hatred? Against whom?"

"Against everyone. Maybe even against you."

"Why would he hate me?" I asked, astounded by that possibility, although I had considered it before.

"You should've made a friend out of him or sent him away. As it is, you're both entangled, like two snakes that have swallowed each other's tails and can no longer separate."

"I was hoping you'd do what I haven't."

"And I'd like for someone else to do it, too. And so would everyone else. Therefore we do nothing. Is that all? They're waiting for me."

He smelled of liquor and tobacco. He was cross and bitter, ready to argue, disagreeable.

"Did Yusuf tell you all of this?"

He turned and left without a word.

It was good that I had also seen him like that.

Hassan was inconsistent. Hassan did not know what he wanted, or he knew but could not get it. Hassan had good intentions but was unbearable. Hassan tried but did not succeed, and maybe his misfortune truly lay in those hopeless beginnings, in building bridges that he never crossed. His was the curse of a desire that never went away, but was never fulfilled. He continuously searched with enthusiasm, and then gave up, empty and uninspired. It was as if he were drawn by ideas, and repulsed by people. That was a strange defect and a problem, not because he gave up, but because he always tried again. Which meant that the problem lay in him and not in others.

But I still sought a cause beyond him.

He was to blame for driving Yusuf away. And yet I asked myself, quite irrationally: Why? I did not realize that I was thus shifting the blame on someone else.

I tried to figure out why Hassan's enthusiasm had dwindled so quickly. What had Yusuf done? I had hoped that Hassan would tell me, but he only made accusations against himself. I tallied this self-accusation onto his account, but I continued to wonder: what had Yusuf done?

I asked myself, and asked Hassan on account of myself. The mystery tormented me, like darkness. I was obsessed. I connected it, like everything else, with my misfortune, which had engulfed me and become my food and air, the pith and marrow of my life. I had to solve it; everything depended on that. So I struggled feverishly, reconsidering every man, every event, every word that concerned me and my dead brother. Can anything that happens between people remain a complete mystery?

Their split forced me to go backward.

Everything happened over and over again in my memory, and all of it was familiar to me. But I kept churning up everything that had settled in my mind, again and again, until this painful game began to produce unexpected connections and vague hints of a solution. In my more rational moments it seemed that there was no purpose in those wearisome, tangled interrelationships, that I could gain nothing from my quest for hidden meanings in the most insignificant gestures or someone's words. But I could not abandon it; I gave myself up to it, as if to fate. When I put all the pieces together, I would see what I had discovered. It seemed like gambling; it was just as hopeless and just as impassioned. I did not expect a sure win, but the suspense had its charms, too. I was encouraged by the gold nuggets that I kept finding, which spurred me to search for the vein.

But maybe this was also a defense against the fear that might seize me. It was not far away; it danced all around me, like a ring of flames. I was trying to protect myself by pretending that I was doing something, that I was defending myself, that I was not utterly hopeless. It was not easy to bring to life within me people whom I had once met, and to induce them to speak their familiar words all over again. But in those ghostly movements, in that droning, whispering, and confusion, in that occasionally absurd linking of clues I managed to hold on to one idea, as a sailor does to his helm so that the waves of a storm will not carry him overboard.

And when I untied all the knots, when I made the choice myself, I would know whether I had fallen into the muddy current by accident or whether there were causes and culprits.

In my isolated world, bounded by the unstoppable sound of the rain, the cooing of pigeons, the grayness of a cloudy day, or the blackness of a pitch-dark night, witnesses settled into my room. They were clumsy at first, upset as I was, but I gradually managed to bring them to order, singling them out, one by one, as at an interrogation. I divided them into two kinds: important and unimportant. The unimportant ones were those who were obvious in their guilt before me. The important ones were those who had not said everything they knew.

And after I reconstructed what I could, in conversations between myself and their shadows and words, I found it necessary to check my suspicions and hunches—something I could not do with shadows and words that never changed. I set out among living people for the solution to the mystery.

I only had to wait a while, for everything to fall into oblivion. Fortunately, people easily forget what does not concern them. I tried to convince everyone that I had also forgotten, gotten over it, become afraid, or withdrawn into prayer. They could each believe whatever they wanted.

I called Mullah-Yusuf. In lonely nighttime interrogations I also made him repeat everything that he had said and done. I was nervous, because the conversation was important. I admitted that I had sinned before God and the world, as I had behaved absurdly in my misfortune, not at all worthily of the position that I held. I had been blinded by grief, and love, and that was my only excuse. I had forgotten that God had wanted it so, and that He had punished my brother, or me, or both of us, for our unknown sins. With someone else's hand, but with His own will.

He listened attentively, lacking the caution with which he usually guarded himself. Whether it was because of my calm speech and soft voice, or because the memory of his own misfortune began to hurt, he looked at me freely and openly. And yet, he was upset, almost irritated.

"What sins?" he asked, rebuffing me.

"We'll find out on Judgment Day."

"Judgment Day is far away. What will we do until then?"

"We'll wait."

"Is the hand with which God punishes us also guilty?"

That surprised me. He had never spoken so sharply or asked me anything so angrily. He interrupted my confession and began to talk about himself. He was thinking about the soldiers who had killed his mother because of her strange sins, and himself, because of no sin whatsoever. He himself hastened the arrival of what I wanted.

"I don't know, my son," I said calmly. "I only know that we'll each answer before God for everything we've done. And I know that not all men are guilty, but only those who indeed are."

"I'm not asking for those who commit evil, but for those who've had evil committed against them."

"You're asking for yourself. You've had evil committed against you. That's why I don't know what to tell you. If I say they're not guilty, I'd anger you. And it's not right to say that, either. If I say they are guilty, I'd be supporting you in your hatred."

"What hatred? Whom do I hate?"

"I don't know. Maybe even me."

He was sitting by the window, looking at his folded hands. Behind him there was the gray day and the cloudy sky; they resembled him. When he heard Hassan's words he suddenly turned around and gave me a bewildered, surprised, gruff, and truly hateful look. Then he shifted his gaze and said almost in a whisper: "I don't hate you."

"Thank God," I said, hurrying to calm him, afraid that he would leave, as he had before. "Thank God. I'd like to regain your trust if it's disappeared. If it hasn't, so much the better. I appreciate new friendships, they give us a love that we could never do without, but old friendships are more than love, because they are parts of our very selves. You and I have grown together, like two plants; both of us would be damaged if we were separated, our roots are tangled together, as are our branches. And yet, we could've done more than grow on the same clump of memory, each living his own life. We could've become close. I feel sorry now, because of everything that we missed. Why didn't we talk? We knew that we were both thinking about what happened; we can never forget it. I blame myself more than you. I'm older, more experienced. My only excuse is that I knew my love for you never changed. Your detachment kept me at a distance. You jealously kept your misfortune to yourself, as a mother monkey carries its dead young on its breast. One should bury the dead for one's own sake. I was the only person who could have helped you do that. Why didn't you ever ask me about your mother? I alone know everything about her. Don't wince; don't shut yourself up. I won't say anything that might hurt you. I loved both of you."

"You loved her?"

His voice was turbid, hoarse, threatening.

"Don't be afraid. I loved her as a sister."

"Why as a sister? She was a whore."

The expression on his face frightened me. I had never seen it before, it was sharp, merciless, ready for anything. But I knew that his rudeness and self-torment resulted from the sorrow that had been revived by this first conversation about his mother. I was also surprised by the ferocity with which he tore open his wounds. Was he really suffering so much?

Trying to calm him down, I said: "You're cruel because you're miserable. Your mother was a good woman. She was a victim, not a sinner."

"Why did they kill her, then?"

"Because they were stupid."

He said nothing, looking at the floor. I knew how hard it was for him, although I could only sense the horror of his torment with a shudder. Then he asked, giving me a hostile look, in one last hope that I would not be able to defend myself: "And what did you do?"

"I begged for her, in vain. And I took you away, to another village, so you wouldn't see. Afterward I wept, hidden, alone, sickened by the men, and yet pitying them, because they avoided each other's eyes all day long, out of shame."

"One day isn't very long. Who . . . How did they kill her?"

"I don't know. I couldn't watch. And I didn't want to ask."

"What did they say about her later?"

"Nothing. People easily forget what they're not proud of."

"And you?"

"I left soon. I was ashamed of them. And I pitied you, and her, for a long time. Especially you. We were friends; I never had a better one."

He shut his eyes and tottered, as if he were going to faint.

"May I go?" he said softly, without looking at me.

"Are you sick?"

"No, I'm not."

I put my hand on his brow, making that ordinary gesture with effort, I was almost unable to complete it, as I felt how my palm burned before it even reached him. And when I touched his hot skin, he barely kept from moving his head away, unnaturally tense, as if he were expecting a knife.

"Go," I said. "We've worn ourselves out with this conversation. We have to get used to it."

He staggered out.

I ordered Mustafa to get him some honey, sent him on walks, and tried to persuade him to begin another copy of the Koran. I even offered to order gold and red ink, but he refused. And he became stranger and stranger, more closed than before. It was as if my concern had truly become burdensome for him.

"You'll spoil him," said Hafiz-Muhammed, with ostensible reproach, but it was not hard to see that he was satisfied. The kindness of others moved him, although he himself never wanted to worry about anyone. For him kindness was like the sunrise: something to be watched.

"He looks worn out," I said, defending myself. "Something's happening to him."

"He looks worn out, indeed. Maybe he's in love."

"In love?"

"Why are you surprised? He's young. It would be best if he got married and left the tekke."

"Whom would he marry? The girl he's in love with?"

"No, not at all! Aren't there plenty of girls in the kasaba?"

"I see that you know something. Why are you letting me guess?"

"Well, I don't know very much."

"Say what you do know."

"Maybe it's not right for me to speak. Maybe it's only my opinion."

I did not press him. I knew that he was wrong, but I also knew that he would say it. His apparent hesitation was silly; he had begun the conversation in order to tell me everything. And God knows what he had seen and what he had imagined in his naïveté. I did not expect much from whatever it was that he had to say.

But when he told it, it seemed strange to me. He said that he had gone to see Hassan's father and seen Mullah-Yusuf in front of the gate to the kadi's house. He was standing there, indecisive, looking at the windows; he started toward the door and then stopped; then he went away from the house, slowly, looking back. He wanted something; he was expecting something; he was looking for someone. And when they met, Hafiz-Muhammed did not ask him anything, but the youth said that he had ended up there by accident, on a walk. And so, what he said made Hafiz-Muhammed suspicious and worried, because he had not ended up there accidentally and was not on a walk. And Hafiz-Muhammed would have preferred for the reason not to be what he thought. Therefore he had kept silent, until now.

"What did you think was going on?" I asked, unnerved, suddenly brought before the solution to the mystery.

"Well, I'm ashamed even to mention it. But his behavior was strange. And then, he lied to me to excuse himself, which means that he was guilty. I thought that he had fallen in love."

"With whom? With Hassan's sister?"

"So you see, even you have thought of it. And if it's not true, may God punish me for my sinful thoughts."

"Maybe," I said gloomily. "All sorts of things happen to people."

"Someone should talk to him. He'll torment himself needlessly."

"Do you think so?"

He looked at me with surprise, without understanding my question, without feeling its spite, and said that he felt sorry for the youth, that hopeless love would eat away at him like rust, and that would be a shame both for him and us. Shame before the world and before her, a married and honorable woman. And he, Hafiz-Muhammed, would pray to God to turn the boy from that path and forgive him for his sin if he had seen things falsely and if he had thought something bad.

When he had said everything, he was depressed; he regretted it. Yet if he had kept silent, it would have destroyed him.

If what this man had said were only true, this man who

saw sin even where there was none. But maybe there was? Why would that have been impossible?

I embraced that ugly thought and developed it in a moment. I gave it wings, discovering the splendid possibilities hidden in it. I remembered her lovely hands, how they had caressed each other unconsciously, eagerly clasping each other, and her cold eyes, which emanated an unspent strength, like deep water. I remembered the calm arrogance with which she took revenge for something. But I also remembered that everything had already happened before then, and that Harun had already been killed when she asked me to betray Hassan. She could not have known about my brother; maybe she had never heard his name, but I forgot that and remembered her as cruel, like her husband the kadi. For me they were two bloodthirsty scorpions, and my heart could not wish them good. And so, hatred cried out in me: if only that were true! In a moment of weakness I saw her submitting to Yusuf's youthfulness, and the kadi disgraced by the ancient justice of sin.

But I suppressed that thought quickly. I knew that it was shameful and humiliated me with a desire for petty revenge. And yet it also revealed something more important: it showed my powerlessness and fear of them. And fear and powerlessness give birth to base instincts. In my thoughts I left that battle for someone else and, if only for a moment, I secretly enjoyed their defeat. But what kind of a defeat was it, what kind of compensation when compared with what I had lost?

I grew ashamed and frightened. No, I said, determined, I don't want that. Whatever I decide, I'll have to do it myself, alone. No matter whether I forgive or get even. That's honest.

I called Mullah-Yusuf again, after my conversation with Hafiz-Muhammed. When he came in, I was examining Hassan's gift, Abu Faraj's book with the morocco binding and the four golden birds on the cover.

PART 2

"Have you seen this? A gift from Hassan."

"How beautiful!"

He ran his fingers over the leather and the outstretched wings of the golden birds; suddenly transformed, he looked at the wondrous initials and the ornamented words. This beauty, which excited him strangely, soothed the anxiety with which he had entered the room.

I knew that I would gain a significant advantage if I let him wait. I knew that he was afraid, imagining our conversation, that he was feverishly rummaging in the treasury of his sins—everyone has them. But I refused to take the advantage that his fear would have given me. I preferred his trust.

I said that I was intentionally resuming the conversation we had held, because he was still upset. And that was the worst condition any of us could ever be in (I knew from myself): when we can't make up our minds, but are crucified by our torments, and sometimes can't even determine exactly what they are, and when every breath of the wind rocks us, uprooting us. I'd like to help him, as much as I could, as much as he'd accept. I was doing this for him, but also for myself; maybe I was guilty before him. I'd neglected to bring him closer to myself and thus return his feeling of security. I had lost my brother, and he could replace him. I did not want for him to tell me what was happening with him: everyone has a right to his own thoughts, whatever they are, and it isn't always easy to speak them. We often spin like weathervanes, unsure of our positions, mad with insecurity. We vacillate between despair and the wish for peace and don't know what is ours. It's difficult to stop at either end, to embrace only one side, but that's what we need to do. Any decision, except the one that will disturb our conscience, is better than the sense of disorientation with which indecision bestows us. But the decision shouldn't be hurried; it should just be helped to develop. When the time comes. Friends can ease the pain of making a decision, but no more; they can never eliminate it. And yet we need friends, as one does a midwife at a birth. That's something else I know from my own experience. When I was feeling my worst, when I thought the only way out was to kill myself, God sent me Hassan, to lift me up and give me courage. His attention and kindness, and maybe I can even say: his love, returned my faith in myself and in life. Signs of that attention might seem trivial, but for me they were invaluable. My mad spinning stopped, my horror faded; I felt a warm wind of human kindness in the ice in which I was trapped. May he, Mullah-Yusuf, forgive me because that dear memory still excites me, but no one has ever offered me greater mercy in my life. I was lonesome, abandoned by everyone, left in the empty silence of my own misfortune, for injustice to be carried out against me to its end. I was on the verge of doubting everything that I believed, because everything was crumbling around me, burying me under. But you see, knowing that there's one good man in the world, a single one, was enough to reconcile me with everyone else. It might seem strange that I attach such importance to his deeds, which should be commonplace among us, and that I'm so grateful. But I've seen that such deeds are not commonplace at all, and that they make him stand out among other people. And at that, I was guilty, so his help has become even dearer to me.

Mullah-Yusuf raised his head.

Yes, guilty. I've done something bad to him, something very bad. It doesn't matter what, or why. I could find a reason, and maybe a justification, but that's not important. I needed his friendship, like air, but I was ready to lose it because I couldn't hide that lie from him. I wanted him to forgive me, but he did even more: he gave me still greater love.

"Did you do him any harm?" asked Mullah-Yusuf with effort.

"I betrayed him."

"And what if he'd begun to despise you? Or rejected you? What if he'd made your betrayal known?"

"I'd still respect him. He taught me once again that true generosity doesn't haggle. He helped me doubly and enriched himself doubly. I told Hassan that people like him are a real blessing, a gift sent to us by God Himself; and I really believe it. With some unknown sense he discovers who needs help, and offers it, like medicine. A wizard, because he's human. And he never abandons those he's helped; he's more faithful than a brother. Most beautiful is that his love doesn't even need to be earned. If I'd had to earn it I'd never have received it, or I'd have lost it long ago. He cares for it himself, he gives it away, without looking for a reason other than the need he himself feels, no other compensation except his own satisfaction and the happiness of others. I accepted the moral that he gave me: that he who gives, receives. I'm no longer vulnerable, his love has healed me, enabled me to support someone else. It's made me capable of love, I'll give it to you, Mullah-Yusuf, if it can be of any use to you."

I smiled silently and warmly, maybe I could barely remember everything that I wanted to tell him and that seemed important to me. And I was somewhat uneasy because of the thought that Hassan would not explain his friendship at such length. But everyone has his own way of doing things, and my task was more difficult.

Mullah-Yusuf was more withdrawn and unwilling to talk than during our first conversation. But he was not less upset. He sat in front of me on his knees, tense, feverish, in a constant effort to relieve the cramps in his fingers, which he dug into his thighs, helplessly closing and opening his burning eyes, raising them to me in pain. He could not hide that my calm words were raging within him, like storms. At one moment, when I thought that he would burst into tears, I wanted to let him go, so that I would not torture him or myself, but I forced myself to finish what I had begun. Our fates were being decided.

I said that Hassan's friendship and his gift, with which everything between us had started, had led me to reflections and decisions that saved me. The only thing that I had from my home, from my mother, was a kerchief with four golden birds embroidered on it, which I kept in a chest. Hassan had had them put on the cover of the book, and thus moved me, like a child, like a fool. Then I realized what was most important. Did he remember? I had also asked him once about the golden bird that meant happiness. Now I understood: that was friendship, love for another. Everything else can deceive us, but that cannot. Everything else can slip away and leave us empty, but that cannot, because it depends on us.

I could not tell him: be my friend. But I could say: I'll be yours. I had no one closer than him, than Yusuf. He'd be like a son to me, the son I'd never had; he'd be like a brother to me, the brother I'd lost. And to him I'd be everything he wanted but didn't have. Now we were equals; bad people had made us unhappy. Why couldn't we protect and comfort each other? Maybe it would be easier for me because the boy from the plain had always been in my heart, even when my own misfortune overshadowed everything else. And I hoped it would not be difficult for him, either: I'd be patient, I'd wait for the friendship, which—I knew very well—he'd once felt for me, to revive.

Had he bent over? Had he groaned? Had he suppressed a cry at the very edges of his dry lips?

It's futile, there's no saving us, you who were not meant to be my friend.

That was why I could tell him (I continued, mercilessly) even what I wouldn't say if I didn't care about him. Otherwise I'd have said differently, with different intentions, with the purpose of protecting the reputation of our order. As it was, this could be a friendly conversation, which concerned only him and me. It would not be easy for me to speak of it, or for him to listen to it, but it would be still worse if we kept silent.

Yes, he said, barely breathing, frightened, upset and curious, already stunned by what he had heard, and not sure whether there was more to come, since his attentiveness indicated that he was expecting something more all the time, something important, more important than anything else: the real reason for this conversation. I gave it to him, without revealing it, I wanted to let it reveal itself.

I told him: I'm not asking where he goes and what he does, I found out by accident, and I'm sorry I found out, if what I fear is true. (It seemed as if his eyes were going to fall out of his head; he looked at me as if I were a snake, spellbound; he hastened my words, but he was frightened by them.) What was he looking for in front of the kadi's house? Why is he getting pale? Why is he trembling? Maybe it's better to end the conversation if it's upsetting him so much, and yet this is precisely what makes me want to continue it, as it seems that this matter isn't trivial. I know a lot about him, I know or can imagine what's happening to him; and although all of it's shameful, his anxiety is a witness that his conscience is still strong and that it's reproaching him.

The youth's head sank lower and lower. He bent under the weight of the fear that was bearing down on him, as if his backbone were breaking.

He made a feeble attempt to repeat his story of how he had ended up there by accident, but I dismissed it with a wave of my hand, refusing even to talk about it.

He waited, breathless; I also waited, hardly breathing. Until the last moment I did not know if I would say the only thing that mattered, for which I would burn him alive, just to get him to admit to it. This accusation cried out within me, maddened, bloodstained, but I pressed my lips together, struggling to hold it back. If utter fear took control of him and made him deny everything, I would be left in the dark.

This way I had pressured him, pushed him to the limit, driven him mad: I almost expected him to bare his teeth, to start growling, to tear me to pieces so that he could see what I had hidden in my heart.

This strengthened my suspicions, but there was still no proof.

Now I needed to ease up, suddenly, and make everything seem silly. If an expression of relief appeared on his face, then I was on the right track. He was guilty.

Overcoming the turmoil within me and the deafening rush of my blood, I repeated Hafiz-Muhammed's naive assumption that he was perhaps in love with Hassan's sister. I'd have been sorry, since his heart, thirsting for love, would've been left black and shriveled by this sinful and hopeless desire. That would've finished him, alienated him from people, maybe even from me. And he shouldn't hold it against me; I was talking to him as I would to my own brother, who could no longer benefit from my advice. So I hoped he'd understand why I was crying, that he would understand maybe now, or later, when the greater part of his life was behind him, when he'd only have losses to think of, and would only fight to keep the love of those friends that he still had.

I really cried, shedding tears of sorrow and rage, upset as much as that confused youth. We only needed to conclude this horrible conversation with an embrace. But I could not go that far. And if he had done it, I fear that I would have strangled him, since I already knew everything.

I knew everything. When I came out of the wilderness of hints, which were a thousand raised knives, one of which would bring death (and he was expecting it), when I led him to clear ground, loosening the countless knots that I had mercilessly bound him with, when I freed him from his animal fear with my gentle warning, clear sky suddenly opened above him, unthreatening, and his tormented face glowed with wild surprise, with mindless joy at the sparing of his life.

Fool, I thought, watching him with hatred, he thinks he's escaped the trap.

PART 2

But then something happened that I had not expected, that I had not predicted. The joy of deliverance illuminated him only for an instant. It lasted only for a very short moment, and lost its initial strength and freshness immediately. He was struck by another thought almost simultaneously; all signs of liveliness disappeared from his face, and it became heavy with helpless grief.

Why? Was he ashamed of his jubilation? Had that sudden joy swept him off his feet? Did he feel sorry for me because of my childish naïveté? Or did he remember how dangerous his denial might be?

Slowly, with surprisingly slow movements, he bent down, all the way to the floor, as if he were bowing to me, as if he were falling. He could barely support himself with his arms; it seemed that they would not hold him up. Then he stood up, as if he were asleep. And he left the room, as if asleep, completely lost.

I had been cruel to him, and to myself as well. But I had not had any other choice. I wanted to find out. Hassan lived among different people, in another world, everything was revealed to him easily. But no one ever told me anything, and I had to turn my own soul and Yusuf's inside out to find the truth. That journey had been long, I had learned little by little, bit by bit. It took a long time for me to find out what two ordinary men tell each other in whispers during a short encounter on a street corner. I was stunned by the realization that occurred to me then: how much I was cut off from people, how lonely I was. But I put that aside, I would think about it later, when everything was over.

The rains stopped and warm, sunny weather followed, almost without transition. I went out in the street and walked along the river for a long time. I watched the mist rising from ground covered with lush grass; my eyes stopped on the wide, clear sky, the same one as above the plain and my village. I did not feel any desire to leave; my fear and the threatening roar of water rising in the darkness were no more; my powerlessness was gone. Here I am! I said to someone maliciously, knowing that there was a threat in the very fact that I was alive. I felt a need to move, to do something definite and useful.

I had a goal.

I went out among people, calm, quiet, armed with patience. I received with gratitude everything they might offer me—their rebukes, mockery, and information.

I did not act randomly. Even if I occasionally left my path and wandered in desolate places, I always found the direction that I sought. My landmarks were my own perseverance, someone else's words, hints, enjoyment at my misfortune, or surprise at the change in me. And I became more and more self-confident in my search for the solution to the mystery, both richer and poorer from those gleanings, from the alms that I received in others' words, from their hatred and compassion.

I spoke with the night-watchman, Kara-Zaim, guards, softas, and dervishes; with embittered, dissatisfied, suspicious people; with men who knew little on their own, but who, when put together, knew everything. I showed them the gentle face of a man who seeks neither revenge nor justice, but endeavors to establish his severed ties with the world around himself and to find peace in his love for God, which remains even when we have lost everything else. Many of them were distrustful, many cruel and inconsiderate, but I remained humble even when they hurled insults at me, and tried, with my head bowed, to recognize even the smallest particle of truth in the change of a voice, in a curse, in exultation, in feigned or genuine pity, even in generosity, which surprised me more than malice. And I remembered everything.

When I had completed that painful journey and learned even what was of no use to me, my naïveté died, from shame.

PART 2

Thus I learned the final lesson and reached the end. What I had been expecting should have happened. But there was nothing to happen anymore, and I no longer expected anything, either. I was defeated; that was all I had achieved. And among people there remained a nice story about a silly dervish who had calmly spoken with them about their lives and his own life, urging them to love and forgive, as he himself had forgiven, and who always consoled them and himself with God and the faith, and with the other world, which is more beautiful than this one.

When I returned from a visit to Abdulah-effendi, the sheikh of the Sinan tekke (I had visited him as well: it turned out that we were both suspicious of each other, and that we were both in the wrong, but God knows how much evil he had inflicted on me because of that empty suspicion, and how much I had on him), I saw Mullah-Yusuf in the garden, by the river. He started when I opened the gate and entered; he looked at me disturbed, with eyes that were glowing unhealthily.

He knew where I had been going and what I had been looking for.

We did not greet each other. I went to my room; it appeared dark and cold. I had imagined that it would be like a spacious, bright courtroom, when that hour came, but it was not even what it had been. It repelled me with its desolation. We had forgotten each other while I had been searching for the solution to the mystery. I had lost its favor, and I had found nothing in other places.

I stood by the window and, confused, watched the day gleaming with sunshine. That was all I could do, although I knew that it was senseless.

When the door opened I knew who had come in. I did not say anything. Neither did he. I thought I heard his heavy breathing by the door.

That uneasy silence lasted for a long time; he stood behind me for a long time, like my black thoughts. I had known that he would come, like this, uninvited. I had been waiting for this moment since long before. And now I only wanted him to leave. But he did not leave.

He spoke first, his voice was soft and clear: "I know where you've been going and what you've been looking for."

"Then what do you want?"

"You didn't search in vain. Judge me, or forgive me, if you can."

"Go, Mullah-Yusuf."

"Do you hate me?"

"Go."

"I could bear it more easily if you hated me."

"I know. You'd feel that you also have a right to hatred."

"Don't punish me with silence. Spit on me, or forgive me. It's not easy for me."

"I can do neither."

"Why did you talk to me about friendship? You already knew everything then."

"I thought that you did it accidentally, or out of fear."

"Don't send me away like this."

He was not begging humbly, he was demanding. It resembled the courage of despair. And then he fell silent, discouraged by my coldness, and went toward the door. But he stopped and turned around. He looked alert, almost cheerful.

"I'd like you to know how much you tortured me, speaking about our friendship. I knew it couldn't be true, and yet I wanted it to be. I wanted a miracle to happen. But miracles don't happen. It's easier now."

"Go, Yusuf."

"May I kiss your hand?"

"Please, go. I want to be alone."

"Very well, I'm going."

I went up to the window and stared at the sunset, not knowing what I was looking at. I did not hear him when he left; I did not hear the door close. He was quiet and humble again, pleased that everything had ended that way. I had let the rat out of the trap, feeling neither magnanimity nor scorn.

My eyes roamed over the hills above the kasaba and over the windowpanes gleaming with the sunset.

Well, that's it. And then what? Nothing. Twilight, then night, dawn, day, twilight, and night. Nothing.

I knew that this was not particularly clever, but it was all the same to me. I even looked at myself somewhat mockingly, as if I were someone else: it would have been better if my search had continued, uninterrupted; then I would have had a goal.

Then Hafiz-Muhammed came into my room, or rather he rushed in, excited and frightened. He was almost beside himself. I thought how he needed only to suffer an attack of coughing at that very moment, as he did whenever he was excited, so that I would have to solve the mystery of his frightened face on my own. Fortunately, he saved his coughing for later, and managed with difficulty to stutter that Mullah-Yusuf had hanged himself in his room. Mustafa had just taken him down from the rope.

We went downstairs.

He was lying on the bed; his face was reddish-blue and his eyes were closed, his breathing wheezy.

Mustafa was crouching beside him, giving him some water to drink, opening his tightly closed mouth with a spoon and the thick fingers of his left hand. With a nod of his head he signaled for us to leave the room. We obeyed and went to the garden.

"Unfortunate youth," sighed Hafiz-Muhammed.

"He's alive."

"Thank God, thank God. But why did he do it? Because of love?"

"Not because of love."

"He'd just left your room. What were you talking about?"

"He betrayed my brother Harun. They were friends and he betrayed him. He admitted that himself."

"Why would he betray your brother?"
"He was the kadi's spy."
"Oh, God in Heaven!"

It would have been easier for that honest old man, who fed his honesty with inexperience, if I had hit him in the face rather than enriched his experience with that filth.

He took hold of the back of a bench, feebly, sat down, and started crying softly.

Maybe that was best. Maybe that was the most sensible thing one could do.

PART 2

11

> The wide world became too small for them,
> they felt loneliness and anxiety in their hearts.[1]

MY RESTLESSNESS GREW, SPREADING BACKWARD IN TIME: I thought of how I had been surrounded long before then, how others' eyes had been lying in wait for my every move, waiting for one of them to be wrong. And I had not been aware of anything. I had been walking as if asleep, certain that my affairs concerned only me and my conscience. My spiritual son had been watching over me at someone else's order, leaving me only the empty conviction that I had any freedom. I had been a captive for years, God knows whose and of how many eyes. In hindsight I felt humiliated and confined, as I had lost even that free space I had imagined was mine, before my misfortune. They had taken it away from me, and it was no longer any use to return to memories. My misfortune had begun long before I became aware of it. Who had not been keeping an eye on me, who had not been listening in on what I said, how many paid or voluntary watchmen had not been following my movements and taking note of my deeds, making of me a witness against myself? Their numbers were becoming terrifying. I had gone through life without fears or suspicions, as a fool walks along a precipice. Now even a secure path seemed like a precipice.

The kasaba turned into a giant ear and eye that caught one's every breath and every step. I lost the ease and confidence with which I had met people. If I smiled, it looked as if I were trying to be flattering; if I made small talk, it looked as if I were trying to hide something; if I talked about God and His justice, I looked like an idiot.

I did not even know what to do with my friend Mullah-Yusuf. I say bitterly: my friend, but I think it would have been worse still if we had really been friends. As it was, I was not losing anything, as far as he was concerned. I know, I would have been better able to nurture my sense of injury if I could have complained: look at what my friend has done to me. But I did not want that. In that way I would have accused one man, and everything would have been reduced to an affair between him and me, since, hurt by the betrayal of a friend, I would have forgotten about the others. As it was, pushing him away from me and placing him with the rest of them, I increased both the guilt and my loss. I did that subconsciously, in the vague desire for the magnitude to be greater, like my pain, like my effort to get even. I say: my pain, but I did not feel any. I say: my effort to get even, but I did nothing. People had fallen deeply in debt to me, but I demanded nothing from them.

Mullah-Yusuf met me with fear in his sunken eyes; I smiled tiredly, completely black inside. Sometimes, but only sometimes, it seemed to me that I could strangle him while he slept or sat lost in thought. Sometimes I wanted to get him away from me, to send him to another tekke, to another town. But I did nothing.

Hassan and Hafiz-Muhammed were touched by my magnanimity and forgiveness, and surprisingly, I was pleased by their approval of what was not true. Because I had neither forgotten nor forgiven.

This returned Hassan to me, as well as the almost inexplicable satisfaction that his friendship gave me, a kind of inner glow, absurd, almost nonsensical. But I accepted it like a gift and wanted it to continue uninterrupted.

"It was smart of you to leave him alone," he said, not mentioning kindness, but rather benefit. Occasionally his approval sounded harsh. "If you get rid of him, another will come. This one's less dangerous, since you know who he is."

"No one's dangerous to me any more. I'll leave him alone and let him live the best he knows how. I can't even hate him. I even pity him."

"So do I. It's incomprehensible that someone can live only off misfortune—his own and that of other men. That he remembers his own and prepares that of others. Mullah-Yusuf surely knows what hell looks like."

"Why didn't you tell me when you found out?"

"It wouldn't have prevented anything. Everything had already happened. I wanted to let you look for it and get used to the idea. God knows what you'd have done if you'd found out with no warning."

"I thought that I'd do something when I found the man who did it. But I can't do anything."

"You're doing a lot," he said seriously.

"I'm not doing anything. I'm letting time pass. I've lost my bearings, there's no longer any joy in what I do."

"You shouldn't think that way. Do something, don't give up."

"What?"

"Go on a trip. Anywhere. Home, to Yohovats; change the scenery, people, sky. It's time for haymaking. Roll up your sleeves, take a place among the mowers, and work up a sweat. Wear yourself out."

"My home is a sad place now."

"Then come with me. I'm getting ready to go on a trip to the Sava. We'll stay in flea-infested inns or under beech trees. We'll travel across half of Bosnia, and go over to Austria if you want."

I laughed: "You think everyone likes to travel, just as you do. You even think it's medicine."

I had touched him in the right spot; his strings began to hum. "Everyone should be ordered to travel from time to time," he said, getting fired up. "Or even more: no one should be allowed to stop in one place any longer than necessary. A man isn't a tree, and being settled in one place is his misfortune. It saps his courage, breaks his confidence. When a man settles down somewhere, he agrees to any and all of its conditions, even the disagreeable ones, and frightens himself with the uncertainty that awaits him. Change to him seems like abandonment, like a loss of an investment: someone else will occupy his domain, and he'll have to begin again. Digging oneself in marks the real beginning of old age, because a man is young as long as he isn't afraid to make new beginnings. If he stays in the same place, he has to put up with things, or take action. If he moves on, he keeps his freedom; he's ready to change places and the conditions imposed on him. How can he leave, and for where? Don't smile, I know we don't have anywhere to go. But we can leave sometimes, creating the illusion of freedom. We pretend to leave, and pretend to change. But we come back again, calmed, consoled by the deception."

I never knew when his words would turn into mockery. Was he afraid of definite assertions, or did he not even believe in anything definite?

"Why are you constantly going away? To maintain the illusion of freedom? Does that mean that freedom doesn't exist?"

"It does and doesn't. I go in circles, I go away and come back. Free and bound."

"Then should I go or stay? Because apparently it doesn't matter. If I'm bound, then I'm not free. And if the goal is to come back, then why go away?"

"But that's the point of it all: to come back. To long for someplace else, to leave and to arrive again at the place where you started. If it weren't for the place that you're tied to, you wouldn't want it or any other world, either; you wouldn't have anywhere to depart from, because you'd be nowhere. And you're also nowhere if that's the only place you have. Because then you don't think about it, long for it, or love it. And that's not good. You need to think, to long for something, to love. So get ready to go. Leave the tekke to Hafiz-Muhammed, get rid of them and let them get rid of you, and prepare to arrive, on a calm horse, with sores on your backside, at the gates of another empire."

"That doesn't exactly sound like a triumph."

"Sores are sores, you old dervish."

"But the place is a little inconvenient."

"The place is like any other. You can't ride on your head, someone might think it strange. It would seem like rebellion. So are we agreed?"

"Yes. I'm not going anywhere."

"God help me! You're like a capricious girl, with whom you never know how you stand. All right, you bearded, capricious girl, it seems you're firmly resolved to remain indecisive. But if you change your mind, if you get bored wrestling with a single thought, as with the devil, come and get me. You know where I'll be."

I did not want to go anywhere outside of the kasaba. I had wanted to go away, once before, to wander off on unknown paths. But that had been empty dreaming, a powerless desire for liberation, a thought of what could not be.

I no longer had it anymore. This place bound me with the misfortune that had befallen me. It had pinned me here, like a spear. I had few thoughts left, few movements, few opportunities. I sat in the garden, in the sun, or in my room, over a book, or I walked along the river, knowing that I was acting according to habit, without enthusiasm, without enjoying it. But more and more often I caught myself feeling comfortable in the warmth of the sun, with my readings, with the reflections in the water. Life became ordinary, even beautiful, tranquil. It seemed that I really was forgetting; a quiet reigned within me. But then, unexpectedly, for no apparent reason, unaccompanied by any thoughts that might have summoned it, a fiery stab would pierce through me, like a hidden, torturous pain, like a cramp. "What's that?" I would wonder, acting surprised, afraid to acknowledge that undesired commotion, burying it with trifles that were within reach of my hands or thoughts.

But I was expecting something.

I was in an indefinite and unstable mood, like a man who is neither healthy nor ill, and who is disturbed more if the symptoms of his illness come and go than if they continue uninterrupted.

I was drawn out of that painful condition by hatred. It revived and steadied me, flaring up one day, in one moment. I say that it flared up, because until then it had been smoldering like a banked fire, its flames darting about, fiercely powerful, searing my heart with their heat. It must have been inside me for a long time. I had been carrying it like a spark, like a viper, like a tumor that had only then begun to spread. And I did not know how it had remained hidden until that moment, or why it had rested and kept silent, not even why it appeared in circumstances that were not any more favorable than they had been earlier. It had ripened in the silence, like every other emotion, and it was born strong and powerful, nurtured by the long wait.

Surprisingly, it was nice to think how it had appeared so unexpectedly, but I had also felt it within myself earlier, and pretended not to recognize it. I was afraid that it would grow stronger, but now I had grown stronger through it, holding it in front of me like a shield, like a weapon, like a torch, intoxicated with it, as with love. I thought I knew what it was, but everything that I had until then thought was hatred was only its empty shadow. This feeling, with which I had been overcome, lived within me like a dark and terrible power.

I will tell, slowly, without haste, how that happened. It really happened like an earthquake.

12

> Do not think them dead
> who are killed on the path of God.[1]

HASSAN AND I WENT TO THE GOLDSMITH HADJI*-SINANUDDIN Yusuf. He dragged me along everywhere he went; even then I knew that we were friends and that I liked to be with him. This was no longer a need for protection, but rather a need for human intimacy, without any other benefit.

In the Kuyunjiluk[2] we ran into Ali-hodja, who was in old, torn clothes, and worn-out slippers, with an unsightly felt skullcap on his head. I did not like to meet him; he was usually unpleasant. He hid behind feigned insanity so that he could say what he thought. And he did so rudely.

"Do you agree to a conversation that won't benefit you?" he asked Hassan, without looking at me.

"Yes. What are we going to talk about?"

"Not about anything."

"That means about people."

"You know everything. Because nothing matters to you. This morning I asked for your sister's hand."

"Whom did you ask for her hand?"

"Her father, the kadi."

"The kadi isn't her father."

"Then he's her aunt."

"Fine. What did you say to her aunt?"

"I said: Give her to me for a wife; it's a pity for her youth and beauty to go to waste for no reason. She'll never get married if she stays with you like this. And I'll take a dowry along with her; it all belongs to somebody else anyway. I'll take upon myself at least a thousand years of your hellfire, so you'll have it easier. Leave me alone, he said, go your own way. I'm going my own way, I said, why don't you let her do the same? Do you really hate her so much? I thought that of all the world you at least did not hate her. And you, where are you going?"

"To Hadji-Sinanuddin Yusuf, the goldsmith."

"Go. I'm not going with you. I don't know what he's like."

"You don't know what Hadji-Sinanuddin is like?"

"No, I don't. He thinks only about the prisoners, he takes them food every Friday. He'll become poor because of them. He gives them everything."

"Is that so bad?"

"What would he do if there were no more prisoners? He'd be unhappy. The prisoners are his passion, as hunting and drinking are for others. But should one make human misfortune one's passion? Maybe one should, I've never thought about it."

"Is it so bad to get used to doing good?"

"Should good deeds become a habit? They just happen, like love. And when they do, they should be hidden, so we can keep them. Just as you do."

"What do I do?"

"You take alms for the prisoners to Hadji-Sinanuddin, but you hide it. It's happened to you, but you're ashamed to show your love. That's why you're going alone."

"I'm not alone. Don't you know Sheikh-Nuruddin?"

"How could I not know Sheikh-Nuruddin! Where is he?"

"Here, with me."

"With you? I don't see him. Why doesn't he say something, so that I can at least hear him?"

"You don't want to see me, but I don't know why. Are you angry at me?"

"So you see—he's not here," said Ali-hodja, trying in vain to find me next to Hassan. "There's no trace of him. There's no Sheikh-Nuruddin."

He left without saying goodbye.

Hassan smiled awkwardly, certainly because of me.

"He's harsh with people."

"Harsh and malicious."

"A strange man."

"Why didn't he want to see me?"

"Because he was making sense. He needed to do something idiotic to make up for that."

No, it had not been idiocy. He had wanted something, intended something. There's no Sheikh-Nuruddin, he said. Maybe because I was no longer what I had been. Maybe because I had not returned the blow that had been dealt to me. Or because I had done nothing that a man should. And so, I did not exist.

"What do you think of him?" I asked Hassan. I did not want to reveal how hurt I was that Ali-hodja had not wanted to see me, and it did not occur to me that I was revealing myself by not forgetting him. Fortunately, Hassan wanted to make it up to me, but he did so awkwardly. I knew, because he was wasting too many words, and because he was speaking seriously.

"I don't know. He's just and sincere. Only he goes to extremes. That's become his *passion*, as he puts it. And his vice. He not only defends justice, but he attacks with it; for him it's become a weapon, not a goal. Maybe he's not even aware that he's become the voice of the many who keep silent, and he takes pleasure in daring to do what they don't, bringing to them their own unspoken words. They recognize him as a disfigured version of their need to speak, who wouldn't exist if they dared to fulfill that need. He's natural and unavoidable because he has his roots here, unconstrained and extreme because he's alone. And that's why he's rude, and that's why he goes to extremes. He's convinced himself that he's become the conscience of the town, and he pays for that pleasure with his poverty. Maybe he occasionally brings some freshness, like the wind, but I don't believe he does a great service either to sincerity or justice. With him they seem perverse. They resemble vengeance and cruel satisfaction, but never a virtuous need that people should aspire to have. He's turned into his own enemy, and become the opposite of everything he might ever have wanted. Maybe he's even a warning, but he's not a landmark. Because if we all acted and thought as he does, if we spoke openly and rudely about everyone else's deficiencies, if we flew in the face of anyone whom we don't like, if we demanded that people live the way we think is good, the world would be more of a madhouse than it is now. Cruelty in the name of kindliness is terrible; it would bind our feet and hands; it would kill us with hypocrisy. Cruelty based on power is better—that we can at least hate. Thus, we set ourselves apart and at least preserve hope."

I did not wonder whether what he was saying was true or sincere. I knew that he was on my side, that he was protecting me from an injust attack: he could tell what was bothering me. Not with anything else—mockery, severity, or a complete rebuttal—could he have calmed me so much as with these eloquent reflections, superbly adapted for my ears. Their effect was convincing because it was not petty and it left with me the right to complete the thought and to defend myself. Malicious joker! I thought angrily about Ali-hodja. Rabid, stray dog! He's placed himself above the whole world and spits on everyone equally, both the good and the bad, both on sinners and victims. What does he know about me that he could use to judge me so?

But my anger was not long-lasting or serious. I soon forgot about Ali-hodja, and the pleasant warmth of Hassan's words remained within me. I did not even think any longer about what he had said, I knew that it had been nice and that I was content. He had offered his hand to me again and had defended me. And that was much more important than the stupid whims of a wicked hodja.

While Hassan told Hadji-Sinanuddin Yusuf about that encounter and conversation, I thought about what a good and considerate man he was, and how lucky I was to have found him. They laughed: Hadji-Sinanuddin did so softly, Hassan loudly, showing his pearly, straight teeth. And they talked, without trying to be clever or serious, almost exuberant, like children, like friends who enjoy each other's company.

Hassan exaggerated in distorting what the hodja had said. He told how Ali-hodja had not wanted to come because he was afraid of Hadji-Sinanuddin. Caring for prisoners was Hadji-Sinanuddin's pleasure, like hunting, like gambling, like love. A world without prisoners would be Hadji-Sinanuddin's grief. What would his kindness feed on then? He could not live without them, and if they disappeared he would be unhappy and lost. He would beg the authorities: Don't destroy me; send someone to prison! What will I do without prisoners?! If there were no one to imprison, he would suggest that they arrest his friends, so that he would be able to care for them. That would be the best way of proving his love for them.

"I hope that you, too, would do me the favor," the old man said and laughed, going along with Hassan's joke, indifferent to what Ali-hodja had really said about him. And he immediately turned the conversation to Hassan: "And what did he say about you? That you're not capable of good or evil? It seems that that's what he said, isn't it?"

"I'm bad without personal benefit, and good only when I'm irresponsible. Sort of a sinful angel, an immoral virgin, an honest criminal."

"Sinful and noble-minded, calm and irritable, reasonable and stubborn. All of that. And impossible."

"You don't exactly value me much."

"No," said the old man beaming. "I don't."

His eyes said: I don't value you, I love you.

It was quiet and pleasant in that tidy shop, freshness rose up from the floorboards, which were still wet from having just been washed. The quiet warmth of a summer day drifted in from the stone frame of the open door, and one could hear the light tapping of the smiths' hammers, as if in some children's game, as if in a dream. Before my eyes there was the vaulted half-darkness of the stone shop, greenish with the shade of a thick treetop out in the street, like the tranquil reflection of deep water. I felt good, comfortable, safe. While Hassan was talking about Ali-hodja, I knew that he would not say anything about me, I was not worried about a betrayal or a slip of the tongue. Peace was settling down on me, like pollen, like summer dew, because of those two men. They were two shady trees, two clear springs. Maybe it is a deception, or my memories are turning into odors, but it seems that I really did smell a freshness and a faint scent wafting from them. I do not know which, of pines, of woodland grasses, of a spring breeze, of a Bairam morning, of something dear and pure.

For a long time I had not experienced the kind of quiet tranquillity that those two men bestowed on me.

Their luminous serenity, their friendship without exclamations or ornamental words, their pleasure from everything they knew about each other—all of these things made me smile as well, not particularly cleverly, and awoke in me a dormant or desired goodness, as when we watch children. I became transparent, light, without a trace of the malignant burden that had oppressed me for so long.

"Let's get you married, so you'll settle down," the old man said tenderly and reproachfully. It was certainly not the first time he had said this. "Come on, you evil man!"

"It's too early for me, Hadji. I'm not even fifty yet. And I've got a lot of highways ahead of me."

"Haven't you had enough, vagabond?! Our sons stand by our side when we're strong, and leave us when we need them."

PART 2

"Leave sons alone; let them go their own way."

"I'm doing that, vagabond. Am I not even allowed to be sorry?"

Then I stopped smiling. I knew that his son lived in Constantinople. Maybe it was because of him that he had begun to take care of prisoners, to forget his sorrow at not seeing him for so many years. Maybe that was why he had become attached to Hassan: he reminded him of his son.

"There you have it," said Hassan and turned to me, reproaching the old man jokingly. "He's sorry because his son finished school and doesn't hammer out other people's gold in this shop; because he lives in Constantinople and not in this stale kasaba; because he sends him letters full of respect, and doesn't ask for money to squander on gambling and women. Tell him, Sheikh-Nuruddin, so he won't persist in this foolishness."

My tender feelings suddenly disappeared. What Hadji-Sinanuddin answered, or could have answered—that happiness in another world is suspect, and that love is more important than everything, and warmth, among those who would give you their own blood—could remind me of my father and brother. It might have, but did not. That Hassan had spoken to me, for the first time in the whole conversation, for no reason, out of courtesy, so I would not be left out, reminded me that I was superfluous there, that the two of them were enough for each other.

A moment before I had been sure that Hassan would not mention the injustice that Ali-hodja had inflicted on me; I had known he would spare me. But now I realized that there was no place for me in their conversation. I was sobered by his belated attention, which spoiled everything.

It was difficult to deprive myself of the pleasure with which I had been filled, and of that pretty memory, which I would have liked to keep, but I could not stifle my doubt. He had repeated Ali-hodja's words about himself and Hadji-Sinanuddin, making them sound even worse than they had really been. And left out what had been said about me. Was it only out of courtesy?

Why did he say nothing? From what did he want to spare me, if he really thought it was idiocy? He did not think it was idiocy; that was why he kept silent about it. He knew well why Ali-hodja had not wanted to see me. I no longer existed for Ali-hodja or the kasaba. There's no trace of him, he had said. He's no more, Sheikh-Nuruddin is no more, his human dignity is dead. What's left is only the empty shell of a man who used to be.

If he did not think this way, why could he not joke about that as well, as he did about everything else?

Or he wanted to spare my sensitivity. If that were true, I had still come out ahead, although it hurt.

While I tried to free myself from the tight ring around my heart, missing what the two of them said, I saw a man pass by in the street, and because of him all my thoughts changed abruptly. I forgot Ali-hodja's scorn and Hassan's unexplained silence about everything. Is-haq the fugitive had passed by the shop! Everything was his, the gait, the confident bearing, the even steps, the fearlessness!

I said something, to excuse myself for leaving so suddenly, and ran out into the street.

But Is-haq was not there. I turned into another street, looking for him. How had he gotten into the kasaba? In broad daylight, undisguised, unhurried—how did he dare, what did he want?

Before my eyes I saw his face, as I had seen it from the darkness of the shop, dazzling and clear, as it had been that night in the tekke garden. It was he, I was more and more certain. I recognized every feature, now, in hindsight: it was he, Is-haq. Without wondering why I needed him, or why it was important for me to see him, I started after him. It is a pity that people do not leave an odor behind, like skunks; it is a pity that our eyes cannot see through walls when our desires get out of hand. I wanted to call out his name, but he had none. Why did you turn up here, Is-haq? I did not know whether it was good or bad, but it was inevitable; he had said: I'll come one day, and so, he came. Today was that one day, and everything came to life in me again, the pain, the distress, as before. I thought it had died and begun to decay. I thought it had sunk deep within me, unreachable, but there, it had not. Is-haq, where are you? Are you an idea, are you the seed or the flower of my unrest? I had seen him that night, in the garden; I had seen him just before, in the street. He was not a phantom. But I could not catch up with him.

I returned to the shop, defeated.

Hassan gave me a look but asked nothing.

"I thought I saw someone I know."

Fortunately, they could not see my confusion. They had certainly finished all of their business while I was looking for Is-haq, and were continuing their conversation—a different one, admittedly, in a different tone, with different words. I did not care; their friendship had become disagreeable to me. It seemed like immaturity. Or a pretty lie. What was happening to me was real; it was more serious, more important.

I shut out the world again, the path that led to people was overgrown in an instant. I thought of Ali-hodja, of Is-haq, of myself. I was upset and glum.

It did not concern me, but I heard their conversation again, without understanding it.

"No, I won't," Hassan said, refusing to do something. "I don't have the time or desire to do it."

"I thought you were courageous."

"When have I ever said I'm courageous? It's no use to egg me on. I don't want to get involved in that. And you'd better not get involved, either."

"Hot-tempered, hard-headed, impossible," the old man concluded softly.

But that was no longer love.

That was better, I thought faintheartedly, subconsciously justifying my detachment. That was better—no sweet words, no empty smiles, no deception. Everything is nice as long as we do not ask for anything; and it is dangerous to test our friends. Men are loyal only to themselves.

While I thus, flinging dirt at others, gave vent to my restlessness, with neither pleasure nor malice, the shop grew dark, and the blue shadows turned black.

I turned around: the musellim was standing in the stone doorframe.

"Come in," Hadji-Sinanuddin said to him, without getting up.

Hassan rose calmly, without haste, and motioned for him to sit down.

I moved aside, for no reason at all, thus revealing my anxiety. I saw him from up close for the first time since Harun's death. I had not known how this encounter would be, and I did not know now, as I watched him uneasily, shifting my gaze to him, from Hassan, from Hadji-Sinanuddin, from my own hands. I was confused and frightened, not by him, but by me, because I did not know what would happen, whether my wounded self would thrust me at him in the worst moment and in the worst way, or whether my fear would make me smile submissively at him in spite of everything I felt, because of which I would despise myself for the rest of my life. I was losing my composure; I felt a cramp in my bowels and a painful rush of blood into my heart. I took the tobacco box that Hassan offered me (had he sensed my anxiety?) and, barely raising the lid, began to gather the slender yellow fibers, spilling them onto my lap with trembling fingers. Hassan took the box, filled a chibouk* and offered it to me; I smoked, I drew in the sharp smoke, for the first time in my life. I held one hand with the other, and waited for him to look at me or say something to me, feeling that I was damp with sweat.

He wouldn't sit down, he told Hadji-Sinanuddin; he just stopped in on the spur of the moment. As he was passing by, he remembered that he wanted to ask him something.

PART 2

(The rush of my blood abated, I breathed more easily, and gave him furtive glances. I thought that he was even gloomier than he had been before, even uglier, although I did not know whether it had ever occurred to me that he was gloomy and ugly.)

It was none of his business, but he had been told that Hadji-Sinanuddin would not pay the seferi-imdadiya, the war tax, which had been decreed by an imperial order; and because of that others were also reluctant to pay. And if respected men, like Hadji-Sinanuddin, did not perform their duty, what could be expected from the others, spendthrifts and loafers, who did not care about their country or their faith, and who would let everything go to ruin if only their piasters remained untouched in their coffers? He was hoping that this had been an accident, that Hadji-Sinanuddin had forgotten or neglected to do it, and that he would do it as soon as possible, immediately, so there would not be any unnecessary trouble, which would not be of any benefit to anyone.

"It wasn't an accident," Hadji-Sinanuddin answered calmly, without fear or defiance, having patiently waited for the musellim to say everything he wanted to. "It wasn't an accident, and I didn't forget or neglect to do it. Rather, I don't want to pay what isn't due. The rebellion in the Posavina[3]— that's not war. So why should we pay a war tax? And the imperial decree you mentioned doesn't apply in this case. We should wait for the Porte's response to a petition that has been sent by the most distinguished men. And everyone thinks the same; no one has been influenced by anyone else, so if there's an imperial decision for it to be collected, we'll pay."

"Hadji-Sinanuddin Aga wants to say that it's safest to obey the imperial will. And if we pay now, we'll be doing it of our own free will and against the law, and free will and lawlessness create disorder and discord," Hassan cut in. He stepped between them from the side. His face was serious, his arms folded on his chest; he was politely ready to explain all the details to the musellim if he had not understood.

But the musellim was not one for jokes and was not hindered by this ostensibly naive interpretation. Without showing impatience at this interruption or anger at his open mockery, or even scorn, for which a man of his position never has to seek a reason, he looked at Hassan with his heavy motionless eyes, which even his own wife would not call gentle, and turned to Hadji-Sinanuddin:

"However you want, it doesn't matter to me. I just think that sometimes it's cheaper to pay."

"I don't care whether it's cheap, but whether it's just."

"Justice can be expensive."

"And injustice as well."

And they took a long look at each other. I could not see the musellim's expression, but I knew what it was like; and the old man even smiled, kindly and good-naturedly.

The musellim turned and went out of the shop.

I wanted to go outside as soon as possible, the air that he had breathed would suffocate me, I would be driven mad by what the two of them would say, making fun of him.

But these men kept surprising me.

"So?" asked the old man, not even watching the musellim leave. "Have you changed your mind?"

"No."

"Hassan never retracts his words, just like the emperor. I can't get anything done today."

He laughed, as if Hassan's refusal made him happy, and brought the conversation to a close: "When will you come again? I'm beginning to hate both my obligations and those of others; they keep me from my friends."

Not a word about the musellim! As if he had not been in the shop, as if a beggar had come in, asking for alms! They had forgotten him, immediately, as soon as he crossed the doorstep.

I was baffled. What kind of elegant, noble-minded pride was this, that so utterly rejected everything it despised? How many years and generations have to pass for a man to stifle his desire for mockery, spite, and reproof? I did not notice that they were doing it on purpose, or restraining themselves. They had simply erased him.

It was almost as if they had insulted me. Was it possible to ignore that man in such a way? He deserved more. He had to be thought about. He was impossible to forget, impossible to erase.

"How was it that neither of you said anything about the musellim when he left?" I asked Hassan in the street.

"What's there to say about him?"

"He threatened and insulted Hadji-Sinanuddin."

"He can ruin you, but he can't insult you. You have to watch out for him, like fire, like any possible danger. That's all."

"You speak like that because he hasn't done anything to you."

"Maybe. And you were upset. Were you frightened? You spilled the tobacco."

"I wasn't afraid."

He looked at me, surprised probably by my tone.

"I wasn't frightened. I just remembered everything."

I had remembered everything. God knows for which time, but differently than ever before. I had been upset when he came in, and while he was talking with Hadji-Sinanuddin, I could not sort out my thoughts, or stop any of them. They rushed through my brain, spooked, flustered, confused, burning with memories, hurt, rage, pain—right until he threw his cold, concentrated glance at me, heavy with scorn and condescension, unlike the way he looked at both of them. Then, in that brief moment when our eyes met, like the points of two sharp knives, it might have happened that fear prevailed in me. It had already appeared, and it flooded me, quickly, like a river rising over its banks.

I had experienced difficult moments before. Within myself I had been clashing with contradictory opinions, reconciling rash impulses with cautious reasons, but I did not know that I had ever, as at that moment, turned into the battlefield of so many opposing desires, that such hordes of unexpected wishes had charged and tried to break out, held back by cowardice and fear. You killed my brother, blood-thirsty rage shouted in me, you insulted, destroyed me. But at the same time I knew it was not good that he saw me precisely with those men, who despised and resisted him. So I found myself by accident, without my own will, on the opposite side, against him; but I would have preferred for him not to know it.

It seemed that it was this very fear that had been decisive. It was brushed aside by my shame for myself, the worse and gravest shame that gives birth to courage. My distress subsided; the mad rush quieted down; thoughts no longer flew through me like birds over a fire. I was aware of only a single thought, a calming quiet began, in which angels sang. Angels of evil. Exulting.

That was the joyful moment of my transformation.

Afterward, almost lit up with this new fire from within, I would watch his stout neck, his slightly hunched shoulders, his stocky figure. I did not care whether he would turn around; I did not care whether he would look at me with a smile or scorn. I did not care; he was mine. I needed him; I tied myself to him with hatred.

I hate you, I whispered passionately, averting my gaze, I hate him, I thought, watching him. I hate, I hate. Those two words were enough for me; I could not say them enough. That was a delight, young and fresh, lush and painful, like longing for love. It's he, I said to myself, not permitting him to get very far away from me, not allowing myself to lose him. He. As one would think about a beloved girl. Sometimes I let him get away, like a game animal, so I could follow his tracks, and then I would approach him again until he was in the sights of my eyes. Everything that was disjointed, confused, and scattered in me, everything that sought an exit and solution calmed down, abated, gathering strength, which increased continuously.

My heart found something to hold on to.

I hate him, I whispered deliriously, walking down the street. I hate him, I thought, saying the evening prayer. I hate him, I said, almost out loud, as I entered the tekke.

When I woke up the following morning, my hatred was awake and waiting for me, with its head raised, like a snake coiled in the folds of my brain.

We would no longer be apart. It had me, and I had it. Life had acquired meaning.

At first I was pleased with this delirious, somewhat dreamy state, similar to the first moments of a fever; all I needed was that black, horrible love. It almost resembled happiness.

I had become richer, more defined, more generous, better, even smarter. The dislocated world settled back into place, and I again established a relationship with everything. I freed myself from the dark fear of life's meaninglessness. I could make out the desired order ahead of me.

Go back, sentimental memories of childhood. Go back, slimy powerlessness. Back, terror of ineptness. I was no longer the flayed sheep driven into thorny underbrush. My thoughts were no longer groping in the dark, blindly. My heart was a glowing cauldron that boiled with an intoxicating potion.

I looked everything in the eyes, calmly and openly, fearing nothing. I went everywhere I thought I would see the musellim, or at least the top of his turban. I waited for the kadi in the street and followed after him, looking at his narrow, hunched back, and went away slowly, alone, exhausted by my hidden passion. If hatred had a smell, I would have left the scent of blood behind me. If it had a color, my footprints would have been black. If it could burn, flames would have leaped from all of my orifices.

I knew how it had been born, and when it grew stronger

it no longer needed a reason at all. It became its very own reason and end. But I did not want it to forget its origins, so that it would not lose its strength and heat or neglect those to whom it owed everything, and thus become everyone's. It should remain faithful to them.

I went to Abdullah-effendi again, the sheikh of the Mevlevi tekke, and asked him to help me find my brother's grave. I've come to him, I said humbly, because I don't dare to go myself and ask those who have power to show or not to show mercy; they'll refuse me, and then all doors will be closed to me. Therefore I have to send others in my place, and I'll nurture my hopes until I find them. I've come to him first, I trust in his goodness and will hide behind his reputation, since my own is no longer high, and God Himself knows that this happened through no fault of mine. I would be greatly obliged to him, because I want to bury my brother as God has commanded, so that his soul may rest in peace.

He did not refuse me, but it seemed to him that because of my misfortune I knew less and was not as worthy. He said:

"His soul has found its peace. It's no longer human. It's crossed over into another world, where there's no sorrow, unrest or hatred."

"But my soul is still human."

"Are you doing this for yourself?"

"For myself as well."

"Do you grieve or hate? Beware of hatred, so you won't sin against yourself and others. Beware of grief, so you won't sin against God."

"I grieve as much as is human. I'm wary of sin, Sheikh-Abdullah. I'm in God's hands. And yours."

I had to listen to his teaching calmly and to win his goodwill with my dependence. When they think they are above us, people can even be generous.

I was not powerful enough to have the right to be impatient; nor weak enough to have reason to be furious. I made use of others, letting them feel superior. I had a signpost and a mainstay; why should I have been small-minded?

He helped me; I was granted permission to enter the fortress and find the grave. Hassan went with me. We also took servants, with an empty coffin and shovels.

We were taken to the fortress graveyard by a guard, or servant, or gravedigger: it was hard to say what that silent man was, unused to conversation, unused to looking people in the eyes, timidly curious, angrily obliging, as if he were continuously torn between the desire to help us and the desire to drive us out.

"There it is," he nodded toward an empty clearing above the fortress, with cankers of fresh earth and wounds of sunken graves, overgrown with brambleberry and weeds.

"Do you know where the grave is?"

He gave us a furtive glance, without a word. That might have meant: "Of course. I buried him."

Or also: "How could I know? Look how many of them there are, without markers or names."

He walked between the graves, which were scattered without order. They had been dug hastily and without respect for the dead, like potato pits. He would stop over one of them, look for a moment at the sunken earth and shake his head: "Nikola. The highwayman."

Or: "Bekir. Masha's grandson."

Over others he was just silent.

"Where's Harun?"

"Here."

I went alone among the filled pits to find my dead brother. Maybe I would recognize him from my excitement, from my sorrow, from some sign; maybe the rush of my blood would warn me, or a tear, a shudder, a strange voice; maybe we are not always the helpless captives of our five senses. Could the mystery of the same flesh and blood not somehow speak?

"Harun!" I called silently, waiting for an answer from within myself. But there was no answer or sign, none at all, no excitement, not even sorrow. I was like clay, the mystery remained dumb. I was only overcome by a feeling of bitter desolation, of a peace that was not mine, of some distant meaning, more important than anything known by the living.

Solitary among the graves, I forgot about my hatred.

It returned when I joined the men again.

They stood over a pit, which was the same as others.

"Is that it?" asked Hassan. "Are you sure?"

"It doesn't matter to me, take whoever you want. But this is him."

"How do you know?"

"I know. He was buried in an old grave."

And indeed, the servants found two sets of bones, put one into the coffin, covered it with a shroud and started down the slope.

Whom have we taken? I wondered in horror. A murderer, a killer, a victim? Whose bones have we disturbed? There are many dead here, Harun is not the only one buried in someone else's grave.

We walked behind the servants, who carried on their shoulders the coffin and someone's bones under the green cloth.

Hassan touched my elbow, as if he were waking me.

"Calm down."

"Why?"

"You've got a strange look on your face."

"Is it sad?"

"I wish it were sad."

"A few moments ago, in the graveyard, I waited in vain for something to give me a sign when I came to Harun's grave."

"You ask too much of yourself. It's enough that you grieve."

I still did not understand what he had wanted to say, but I did not dare to ask. I was afraid he might figure out what was happening inside me. He was not trying to return me to sorrow for no reason.

At the bazaar, in the streets, people approached us. I could sense more and more feet behind us. The rumble of their steps grew louder, the human barrier thicker. I had not expected them to show up in such numbers. I had done this for myself, not for them; but you see, what was mine was being taken away from me and becoming theirs. I did not turn around to look at them, yet in my excitement I felt the throng carrying me forward, like a wave. I grew with it, I became more important and powerful; it was the same as I, it was myself magnified. They grieved, they condemned, they hated with their silent presence.

This funeral was a vindication of my hatred.

Hassan said something softly.

"What did you say?"

"Don't speak. Don't say anything over the grave."

I shook my head. I would not speak. It had been different then, in the mosque. They had followed me as I returned from the gates of death, and we had not known, neither I nor they, what was supposed to happen. Now we knew. They did not expect words from me, or condemnation; something had matured in them, and they knew everything. It was good that I had done this. We would not bury this former man to confirm his innocence; we would do more: we would sow these bones as a reminder of injustice. And anything, whatever God decided, could sprout up from them.

Thus my hatred became nobler and deeper.

In front of the mosque the servants placed the coffin with the green shroud on the meytash.* I performed the abdest, stood in front of the coffin and began the prayer. And then I asked, not out of duty, as I always had before, but defiantly and triumphantly:

"Tell me, people, what kind of man was the deceased?"

"A good man!" a hundred voices responded with conviction.

"Do you forgive him all of his trespasses?"
"We forgive him."
"Do you vouch for him before God?"
"We vouch for him."

Never had the testimony for a dead man before his eternal journey been more sincere and defiant. I could have asked ten times, and they would have answered louder and louder. Maybe we would have begun to shout, threateningly, fiercely, foaming at the mouth.

Then they carried that long-dead corpse away on their shoulders, passing the coffin to one another, paying their respects, for the sake of a good deed and spite.

We buried him next to the tekke wall, at the spot where the street opens toward the kasaba. To be between me and other people, a shield and warning.

I had not forgotten, Muslims had at one time buried their dead in common graves, to be equal in death as well. They had begun to separate when they had become unequal in life. I also set my brother apart so that he would not mix among others. He died because he had resisted; let him fight on in death.

When the people went away, each throwing a handful of earth into the grave, and I was left alone, I knelt by the swollen mound, someone's eternal dwelling, and a reminder of Harun.

"Harun!" I whispered to that earthen dwelling, that guardian mound. "Harun, brother, now we're more than brothers, you gave birth to me as I am today, so I can remember; through me you were reborn and set apart to serve as a marker. You'll meet me in the morning and evening, every day; I'll think of you more than when you were alive. And let everyone forget, since human memory is short. I won't forget, neither you nor them, I swear by this and the next world, brother Harun."

Ali-hodja was waiting for me in the street, out of respect for my conversation with the dead man's shadow. I would

PART 2

have preferred not to meet him, especially now, when I was upset after the funeral, but I could not avoid it. Fortunately, he was serious and kind, although strange, as always. He expressed his sympathies and wished me patience, me and all the people, because of the loss, which was a loss for everyone, although it was also a gain, because the dead can be more useful than the living. And we need them that way—they don't grow old or quarrel, they don't have their own opinions, they silently agree to be our warriors, and will commit no betrayal until they are called under different banner.

"Can you see me?" I asked him. "Do you know who I am?"

"I see you, and I know who you are. Who doesn't know Sheikh-Nuruddin?"

He did not scorn me; I was no longer only air for him.

What hopes did he have for me, now that he acknowledged my existence?

Hassan and the goldsmith Sinanuddin paid to have a memorial of hard stone erected above the grave and a pretty iron fence around it.

Coming back from the nighttime prayer, on the first Friday after the funeral, I saw a candle burning in the darkness above Harun's grave. Someone was standing beside it.

I came closer and recognized Mullah-Yusuf. He was praying.

"Did you light the candle?"

"No. It was here when I came."

Someone's hands had placed it there, and lit it for the memory of the murdered and for the repose of his soul.

From then on, on the eve of every holy day there were candles burning on the memorial.

I always stop in the darkness and look at those small, trembling lights, excited; at first I was moved, now I am proud. That is my former brother, that is his pure soul shedding the light of the flames, that is his shadow luring strangers to light those tender little fires in his memory.

After his death he became the love of the kasaba. During his life hardly anyone had known him.

For me he was a bloody memory. During his life he had only been my brother.

PART 2

13

> A beautiful word is like a tree, its roots are deep in the ground, its branches rise up to the sky.[1]

MY DEVOTION TO MY DEAD BROTHER GAVE HASSAN'S FRIENDSHIP back to me. Maybe in his words and deeds there was even some hidden intention, a wish to stop me on the path that he suspected I was taking. Or maybe I am mistaken; maybe my sensitivity saw what was not there. But, however that might have been, I could have no doubts about his friendship.

Nor could he have any about mine. I began to love him. I knew because I could no longer do without him, because I never reproached him for anything he did or said, and because everything about him had become important to me. Love is probably the only thing in the world that does not need to be explained and whose reasons need not be discovered. And yet I will try to do that, if only to mention one more time the name of the man who brought so much happiness into my life.

I bound myself to him (a good word: bound, like on a ship or a cliff, in a storm), because he was born to be a friend to people, and because he had chosen me of all of them. But I continually and repeatedly felt joyous that I could have such a friend in him, a man who seemed so wild and scornful.

I had always thought that a friend is someone who himself needs someone to turn to, a half looking for its complement; he is unconfident, somewhat languid, necessarily boring (although dear), since his company grows stale, like that of one's wife. But Hassan was a whole person, always fresh and always different, clever, daring, restless, confident in everything he undertook. I could not add or take anything away from him. He was himself with or without me, and he did not need me. And yet I did not feel inferior. Once I asked him how was it that he had bestowed his friendship on me, of all people. Friendship is not chosen, he said, it happens, who knows why, like love. And I haven't bestowed anything on you, but on myself; I respect men who remain magnanimous even in their misfortune.

I was grateful to him for that admission, and I believed it was true.

But his friendship was also precious because of the hatred that was growing within me. I do not know; it surely could have lived on its own, but this way it was better. One side of me was black, the other white. That was how I was, divided and yet whole. Love and hate did not mix, did not bother each other. They could not kill each other. I could not do without either of them.

I entered Hassan's life by the right of friendship and because he let me; but if I had hoped or feared that everything about him would become clear and familiar, I was mistaken. Not because he would have hidden anything from me, but because he was a deep and shadowy well, whose bottom could not be seen easily. And not because he in particular was like that, but because people are like that in general, unfathomable as soon as we get to know them better.

He took his father into his house. He showered him with attention that was somewhat strange, joyful, somehow carefree, as if he did not worry much about the old man's illness. He treated him as if he were healthy. He told him about everything, about the bazaar, people, business matters, weddings, even about girls who got better-looking each year—maybe only because he was getting older—but if that were true, then it was a pity his father could not see them; they would seem like heavenly houris* to him. The old man pretended to frown, but it was obvious that he was content. He had had enough of being left to his illness and being prepared for death. "In front of children and old men people speak only stupidities," he said angrily, probably thinking of the large, dark house in which he had lain. "Only this stubborn son of mine treats me like a man, because he doesn't respect me, thank God."

Hassan laughed and responded to him in the same measure, as if he had before himself a friend and a healthy man.

"Since when don't I respect you?"

"For a long time now."

"Since I left Constantinople and came here? Since I became a vagabond and a cattle drover? You're unjust, father. I'm a small man with an ordinary mind and modest abilities. Schoolchildren would never learn about me."

"You're more capable than many in high positions."

"That's not difficult, father; there are many idiots in high places. And what would I do with such a position, and that position with me? Like this, I'm content. But let's drop this conversation; we've never managed to finish it. Let me ask you for some advice. I'm having to deal with one man, he's unpleasant, conceited, stupid, dishonest, uncouth. He looks down on me, and I can tell he despises me. He almost expects me to kiss his slippers. And it's not enough for him that I say nothing about his stupidity and dishonesty. Rather, he's angry that I don't tell him he's clever and honest. And worst of all, he believes that himself. Please tell me, what should I do?"

"Why are you asking me? Tell him to go to hell; that's what you should do."

"Father, I told him to go to hell, then, in Constantinople," Hassan said, laughing, "and came here to be a cattle drover."

They loved each other with a strange, whimsical affection, but it was truly tender, as if they wanted to make up for the time when their hardheadedness had kept them apart.

The old man demanded that Hassan marry ("I can't until you do," Hassan made fun of him), to give up cattle driving and the long journeys, and not to leave him. He even tried trickery, claiming that he was seriously ill, that his last hour might come at any time and that it would be easier for him if his own flesh and blood were beside him, so that his soul might depart without difficulty. "Who knows who'll go first," Hassan answered. But he agreed to the sacrifices that love imposes; without much enthusiasm, of course, especially because of his journeys. It was autumn, the time for traveling, he had gotten used to it, as storks do. The swallows had already flown south; soon wild geese would begin honking high above, flying their courses, and he would look into the sky at their formations and imagine the strange pleasures of his wanderings. He was kept from one love by another.

Important changes occurred in the house. Fazli, the stocky stablehand and husband of the black-eyed beauty Zeyna (the younger one's lover), became the old man's faithful nurse. It turned out that his enormous hands were capable of the most tender movements and the most careful attention. Hassan would leave small sums of money in his father's room, since he knew the man and was afraid his devotion might fade.

Hassan ended the dangerous love affair resolutely. Its apparent strength gave out more easily than even the most cynical imagination could have predicted. Its strong fortress fell victim to the eternal traitors against love.

After he had recovered enough for death not to seem too near, his father would not agree to give all of his estate to the wakf, but the wakf was nevertheless large, and along with the caretaker (one honest and reasonable clerk from the courthouse had agreed to accept a caretaker's bird in the hand rather than two of the kadi's in the bush—then it became clear to me who had informed Hassan of Harun's misfortune), they also needed to find an assistant. Hassan called his younger stablehand in his room and offered him that respectful and well-paid position, if he would never again come into his house, except on business, to see him, and if he would never and nowhere meet with Zeyna, except accidentally, and even that should pass in silence. If he agreed and kept his word, he could take advantage of the opportunity that had been given to him; but if he agreed and did not keep his word, he could start looking for another line of work at once.

Hassan was prepared for the youth's resistance and complaints. He even considered relenting a little, to let everything go on the way it had been, because he regretted putting such a hard choice before him. But the youth agreed immediately. He was quick and capable. Hassan felt sick.

Then he called the woman, to explain everything to her. But the youth told her himself, that they could unfortunately no longer see each other, that he was leaving to follow his destiny—she already had hers. He hoped she would not have bad memories of him; he would only have good memories of his life in that house. And so, that was how God wanted it to be.

Someone needs to keep watch on him, thought Hassan with disgust.

Zeyna stood by the door, silent, a pallor showing through her darkly tanned skin. Her lower lip trembled, like a child's; her arms hung powerlessly beside her full thighs, lifeless, lost in the folds of her shalwars.*

She remained like that even when the youth had left the room. That was how she was when Hassan came to her and put a string of his mother's pearls around her neck. "So you'll take better care of my father," he said, not wanting to compensate her for her sorrow openly, and leaving her unsuspicious before her husband.

For two weeks she walked around the house and yard with the pearls around her neck, sighing and waiting, watching the sky and the gate. Then her sighs stopped, and she began to laugh again. She had gotten over it, or hidden it.

Her husband grieved longer. "It's really empty here without him. And he, the ingrate, has forgotten us," he would say reproachfully, long after the youth's departure.

Hassan was discontent with both them and himself. He had done everything for things to happen that way, but it was as if he would have preferred for them to end differently. "Look: I got involved in order to untie this knot," he said, laughing. "But what have I achieved? I incited the young man's selfishness and made her unhappy and free from restraint. I've hung this embittered woman round her husband's neck, and I've convinced myself once again that I act wrongly whenever I do something planned. Damn it, nothing is so screwed up as a good deed done on purpose, and nothing so stupid as a man who wants something his own way."

"Then what isn't screwed up or stupid?"

"I don't know."

A strange man, strange but precious. He was somewhat mysterious to me, but he was to himself as well, as he continuously revealed and sought himself. Only he did not do it with effort or an ill-temper, as others do, but with a certain childlike openness, with the ease of scornful doubt, with which he usually questioned himself.

He liked to talk and he did that well; the roots of his words were deep in the ground, and their branches spread out into the sky. They became a need and pleasure for me. I do not know what it was in them that filled me with joy. I barely remember some of his stories, but they intoxicated me with something unusual, bright and beautiful: stories about life, but more beautiful than life.

"I'm an incorrigible babbler. I love words; it doesn't matter which, it doesn't matter about what. (I am writing down, at random, things that he said one night, while the kasaba slept in the darkness.) Conversation is a link between people, maybe the only one. That's what an old soldier taught me, we were captured together, thrown into a prison together, chained together and bound to the same iron ring on the wall.

"'Shall we talk or be silent?' asked the soldier.

"'What's better?'

"'It's better to talk. That way it'll be easier to rot in this dungeon. It'll be easier to die.'

"'Then it's the same.'

"'Well, you see, it isn't. We'll think we're doing something, that something's happening. We'll hate ourselves less, and what must be will be; it's not in our power anyway. Two enemy soldiers met in the woods once, and what could they do? They began to do what they knew and what their trade was. They fired their muskets and wounded each other, drew their sabers and cut each other up; they fought all morning long, until they broke their sabers, and when their knives were all they had left, one of them said:

"'Wait, let's take a rest. You see, noon has passed. We're not wolves, but men. Look, you sit over there, and I'll sit here. You're a good fighter, you've worn me out.'

"'You've done the same to me.'

"'Do your wounds hurt?'

"'Yes.'

"'Mine too. Put some tobacco on them, it'll stop the bleeding.'

"'Moss is also good.'

"So they sat down, talked about everything, about their families, their children, and their hard lives. Everything about them was similar, much was the same. They understood each other, and grew close. Then they stood up and said with satisfaction: 'Hey, we've really had a good talk, like men. You see, we've even forgotten about our wounds. Now, let's finish what we've started.' And they drew their knives and did each other in.'

"That friend of mine from the dungeon ring was cheerful, and he made me laugh with this sarcastic parable. He made me laugh and gave me courage. Maybe someone else would've said that the two soldiers in the woods parted as friends. And that would've been a shameful lie, even if it had happened that way. Like this, the story's bitter ending was truthful, maybe mostly because I was afraid they would be portrayed better than they were. But again (I've never been able to explain this conclusion to myself convincingly), maybe it was precisely because the end was so cruelly truthful that I was left with a childlike idea, a stubborn hope that they nevertheless made peace with one another. And if not those two soldiers, then maybe some others, because it almost happened that way even in this story. Although that wasn't important for my soldier; he talked so he wouldn't be alone. He'd seen enough of the world, and experienced almost everything. And he knew how to make his tales interesting, lively, somehow intimate; he savored them, dispelling my fear that it'd be harder for me with him than if I were in prison alone. I'd wake up at night and listen to his breathing.

"'Are you asleep?' I'd ask him. 'Tell me something, if you're not.'

"'What are we going to do when we tell all of our stories?'

"'We'll tell them again, in a different order, backward.'

"'And when we tell them backward?'

"'Then we'll die.'

"'Content, like those two soldiers.'

"'Content, like two fools who've done their duty.'

"'You're bitter,' he said, without reproach.

"'And you're not?'

"'No, why should I be? You see, I went to war of my own free will, which means I agreed to be wounded, captured, killed. The easiest thing of all has happened. So why should I be bitter?'

"As soon as his soft voice began to flow the night would

become less empty. He built a bridge of cobwebs between us, a bridge of words. They fluttered above us in an arch; they rose and dropped, like the waters of a river. He was the source; I was the mouth. A secret was woven between us, and the beautiful madness called conversation worked a miracle: two dead logs that lay side by side suddenly revived, and were not completely separated. When they exchanged us for enemy prisoners, we parted without regret. He'd always find people to listen to him, because he needed them; and I also began to find them. People became closer to me, through conversation. Not all of them, of course. Some are deaf to the words of others; they're a misfortune both for themselves and for everyone else. But one should always try. You'll ask: Why? For no reason. So there'll be less silence and emptiness. At the very beginning, when I'd just gone into trading, I heard about a woman in Vishegrad, the widow of a landowner. She had no one but her son, a young man of twenty. You can imagine how she loved him. He was her only son, all her life lay in him. When the young man died at war, his mother went out of her mind. At first she didn't believe it. Then she locked herself in her room, started eating only black bread, drinking only water, and sleeping on the bare floor; and every evening she placed a heavy black stone on her breast. She wanted to die, but she didn't have enough strength to kill herself. And as if from spite, death would not visit her. For twenty years she lived that way, on black bread and water, with the heavy stone on her breast, only skin and bones; she turned grey inside, then black, and then hardened, like an old rind. She couldn't have looked worse if she had hung from a beam, but she lived on. I was particularly shocked by the black stone that she put on her breast every night; it somehow made me appreciate most how much she suffered. And it was the stone that led me to her. Her house was large, with an upstairs, but it was dilapidated and had not been whitewashed for a long time. The property around the house was spacious, surprisingly nicely cultivated. There was only one old woman in the house; she served the widow for years, and grew weak herself. She told me that they had no help. The property was large; the estate manager took care of everything, but the widow didn't want to settle accounts with him. She didn't want to take the money; he took it for himself and gave the two of them just enough to stay alive. But God would not take her and stop her suffering. I lied to the widow and told her that one of my friends, who had also died, had spoken of her son, and that because of this I had come to see her, as it seemed to me that I had known him as well. I lied, because it was the only way I could get her to talk to me. About her son, of course. She'd kept silent for years. For years she'd waited for death, for years she'd thought of him, poisoning herself with anguish. And now she could speak about him. I got her started. I forgot what I'd said in the beginning (lying is very risky); I talked about him as if I'd known him. But there was no way I could make a mistake. She didn't even realize I'd been just a kid when he died, maybe she even thought her son was much younger than I, since he hadn't changed in her memory. I told her that he'd been handsome, intelligent, kind and generous to everyone, tender toward her, that he'd stood out among thousands. I portrayed her very thoughts and couldn't overdo it. All of my praise was weak and insufficient for that mother. She spoke softly, hoarsely, but each word came from her dry lips like a kiss, caressed, coddled, scented with love, wrapped in the fine cotton of her long memory. I was new, a stranger; it was worthwhile to tell me everything about him, to make up for her stubborn silence. But subconsciously she wanted to explain to me why she grieved so much, ceasing to grieve while she spoke, because she saw him at his best and alive. I think it was the first time she really succeeded at it. Alone, and with someone she knew she revived only enough to see his shadow, knowing that he was dead. Now she forgot about death, she repressed within herself everything except for that distant time in which there had been no misfortune. I knew this wouldn't last long, that she'd come upon the thought of death. I kept expecting its black cloud to cover her. I would see it by the darkness on her face, but no matter, she was delivered at least for a moment. After that I visited her whenever I was in the area, going on a journey, or coming back, and the woman found more and more images in her memory, and her son became smaller and smaller, younger and younger, always the same and always alive. She shifted him backward into the past from the black hour that had ended his life. She would wait for that moment of resurrection, as for a feast, as for the Bairam; she would wait for me for days. She had the guest room heated if it was winter, for the first time in so many years. She had food prepared, which she didn't eat, she had moth-eaten mattresses covered with yellowed bedsheets, for me, if I agreed to stay for a few more days and extend her holiday. She didn't change her life much; she continued to eat only black rye bread and to drink water, and continued to sleep on bare floorboards, with the black stone on her breast, but in her eyes there was no longer only the thought of death. I persuaded her, and she agreed, to request the withheld income of her property from the estate manager, to erect a mekteb for the village children, and to help them with food and clothing, because that was certainly what her son would've done. She had the mekteb built, brought in a hodja, and helped the poor villagers so their children wouldn't go ragged and hungry to school. She did a good deed, and alleviated her suffering."

"And so, everything ended well and everybody was happy, like in a fairy tale," I said, mocking Hassan's narrative.

It seemed that this tale and its moral was intended for my ears, to serve as an example for me: I was probably supposed to gather children and boys around me, and to instruct them how to lead a happy life. It sounded naive and unusual for him, the opposite of everything I knew about him. But he had studied well in the school of the old soldier from the dungeon.

He smiled. Not quite victoriously, but not faintheartedly, either:

"Well, not exactly everything ended well. The villagers welcomed the help for the children. They began to drink, and drank up her money and then even their own. Their wives felt that as well, because their drunken peasants' hands became harder and quicker to strike, and so the village women cursed the widow. And the village men cursed her as well, because she'd taken the children from the cattle and work in the fields. The children rarely went to the mekteb, and the teacher wasn't one of the best, so they barely learned anything. And what they did learn they'd forget after a year or two, so that everyone in the village asked: What kind of school is this? You work your butt off studying, and forget everything in a year. The widow had lived for twenty years waiting for death, and died in the spring three years after we met, waiting for me in the wind and sleet, because I was held up on my trip and had to stay longer than I planned."

"So everything turned out badly?"

"No. Why? She died waiting for a friend of her son, don't you understand? Full of pretty words, eager to speak about her love; she wasn't thinking of death. The villagers ended up where they began, without liquor or assistance, since her heirs divided the estate. And there were only nice memories of the widow in the village; everything else was forgotten. There remained a story: in this house there once lived a strange and good woman. No one, of course, is the better for it, but it's nice."

I was disturbed by that story: it was harsh and unusual, like life, and elusive, like life. And by Hassan's scornful acceptance, or calm rejection of the painful swirling of life, to which man must adapt if he is not to go crazy.

I laughed, to alleviate any possible bitterness, and any awkwardness in his moral: "Stick to something, for God's sake, define who you are, find some solid ground. You're unsure in everything you do."

"You're right, I'm unsure in many things. Is that bad?"

"It isn't good."

"So, it's not good, and it's not bad, either. And to be sure is good. Can it also be bad?"

"I don't understand."

"Is there anything you're completely sure about?"

"I'm sure that God exists."

"But you see, even those who don't believe in God are also sure. And it might be better if they weren't."

"Yes. But what then?"

"Nothing."

But I already regretted that I had asked, without noticing the trap of his treacherously shrewd logic. What a clever and dangerous idea that was! And he had led me to it playfully.

He was well versed in his uncertainty.

I was not bothered because he was like that. Nothing about him bothered me anymore. I had come to love him so much that I admitted that he was right even when we disagreed. He was dear to me, even when I thought he was wrong.

A single day without him seemed empty and long to me. I ripened in his shadow peacefully.

His father was waiting, without fear, for everything that might befall him, obsessed with his newly revived love.

For the two of us Hassan was the most important man in the world.

That was why I was saddened to hear that he was going away.

I went to his house. I had not seen him for a whole day and night. He was playing backgammon with his father, sitting beside his bed.

The old man was getting angry, throwing the dice on the black and white triangles:

"Ugh, curse you, just look at how you roll! Fazli," he complained to the servant, "it seems I'm not having any luck."

"Did you blow on the dice, Aga?"

"I did, but it didn't help. Is Zeyna here? If she could only put them between her breasts for a bit."

"How shameful, father!"

"What can I do that's shameful anymore? Is it shameful, Fazli?"

"No, Aga. God forbid."

"Father, it'd be better to rub them against the dervish's sleeve."

"Really? You won't mind, Ahmed-effendi? By God, it helps."

"I'm glad you've come," said Hassan to me, laughing.

"I haven't seen you since yesterday."

"Wait with that conversation," said the old man grumpily, "until I win. My luck is picking up."

"My father has recovered."

"Do you mean to say I'm in a bad mood?"

He really did win, and was tired and beaming with happiness. He resembled a child. He resembled Hassan.

"I'm going away, to Dubrovnik," Hassan informed me, smiling at his father as if he had done something wrong.

"Why are you going?"

"On business. My friends are going, too, so we'll go together."

"That Catholic woman is going, so he'll go, too. And he's just making up the part about business."

"I'm not making it up."

"You are. If it were because of business, I could talk you out of it. But I can't because of her; she's more important."

"My father is imagining all sorts of things."

"Am I? If I've grown old, I haven't forgotten everything. And if I can't figure out some things, that's another matter."

"Is there really anything you can't figure out?"

"There is."

The old man was speaking to me, as if he were angry at Hassan.

"There is. I can't figure out why he's going on a trip with

PART 2

the woman and her husband together. Who's the fool here? My son or that Catholic man?"

"Or both," Hassan said with a laugh, not offended in the least. "It seems you don't acknowledge friendship."

"Friendship? With women? My thirty-year-old child, where have you been living? Only pederasts can be friends with women."

I intervened in this awkward conversation, which only made Hassan laugh:

"Maybe he's friends with her husband."

"Ahmed-effendi, we can't hold it against you—you can't know about these things. With them a husband always accepts his wife's friends, never the other way around."

"Father, you'll have an attack of asthma."

"Unfortunately for you I won't. It's a clear day today, and the air is fresh. You can't scare me. I told him: if you don't care about her, don't waste your time; if she doesn't want you, find another. If you love her and if she loves you, take her away from him."

"With my father everything is simple."

"And why is he going with them? What the hell is he going to do with them? Who knows? All I know is that he's taking armed men with him, so his friends won't be attacked by highwaymen. But can't he himself be attacked by highwaymen? And with me everything is simple! It's simple with you, my wayward son: you don't understand anything."

"How true is what you've just said, father! From time immemorial sons have been less reasonable than fathers, and so reason should have completely disappeared. But luckily, sons become reasonable as soon as they become fathers."

"Will you ever become reasonable?"

"Father, sons are a bother."

"Don't mock me, I know. How long will you be away?"

"Fifteen days or so."

"Why so long, my unfortunate son? Do you know how long fifteen days is?"

"Maybe even longer."

"Fine, go. If you don't care, neither do I. In fifteen days you might have to come to my grave. No matter, go."

"You told me that you're feeling better."

"At my age better and worse stand side by side and alternate, like day and night. Even a candle is brighter when it's burning out."

"Do you want me to stay then?"

"To stay? First, you're lying. Second, I'd pay dearly if you did stay. It's too late now, go. Don't stay away any longer. Fifteen days, it's a lot for me and enough for you. And take more men; I'll pay for them. I'll feel better if I know you're safe."

"Sheikh-Ahmed will come visit you while I'm gone."

"The best gift that God could give you is this good and sensible man. But it's not bad for him to take a little rest from you. And for the next fifteen days we won't say a single word about you."

And we spent the entire fifteen days talking about him.

His departure left both of us with a feeling of emptiness. We made up for it with his name. It was harder for the old man because he regretted every day that he lost his newly regained son, who had chased away his thoughts of death. His nagging was love, grumpy and passionate, but it was also a turning away from the approaching shadow. A black bird was circling above him. Now he knew it, and was afraid. Had he felt better before, without love?

I was also sorry about his departure, because he had accustomed me to his being around, and I really needed him now.

At that time my life was divided into what had already happened and what was going to happen, which was unknown to me. I was lying in wait, like a hunter, alert and patient; but I was not sure that someone else was not also lying in wait for me, that I would not be caught as well. Having a friend beside me would have soothed my shudders at the silent steps that fate was sending me. I was horrified

PART 2

by the feeling that darkness and mystery were behind everything I could not see, a mystery that would be revealed to me. But I was also quietly jubilant, because what I had been waiting for was going to happen, because I had been chosen to carry out a will stronger than my own. Yet I was not only a tool or someone else's hand, and I was not a stone or a tree. I was a man, and sometimes I feared that my soul could be weaker than my desires, or that my swollen hatred might tear me apart, like a ripe seed tears the membrane in which it grows. If Hassan had been there I could have waited calmly; if Hassan had been there I could have calmly matured into action, so that the green banner of the faith would be unfurled above the kasaba, and not a shroud over me.

We waited for the return of the only man we cared about. Ali-aga did not hide that he was restless. He began to scold his son. His old, aggressive nobility had apparently not slackened, but this awkwardly concealed tenderness soon turned into a helpless lament.

"To hell with him and that Dalmatian woman. She means more to him than his own father. And if she were only good-looking—she's just skin and bones! But let him be, let her drag him all over the wide world with those shifty eyes of hers, if he's that stupid. Fifteen days, my unfortunate son! Rainstorms might move in, cold weather might hit them, highwaymen might attack them. It's no use talking to a fool. Father, you just sit over there in your corner, leaning against the wall like a chibouk, and wait. Let your heart skip a few beats every time the door opens or someone comes up the stairs a little quicker, be jarred out of your sleep by black dreams and bad feelings. It'll cost me a year of my life even if I survive. And he promised he wouldn't go anywhere; he promised but couldn't keep his word. Have a son to your own detriment, to make things harder for yourself. Oh, forgive me, God, for talking nonsense."

Fazli offered to invite the old man's friends for a game of backgammon or to talk. He wanted to take the stallion out in the yard, under the windows, and asked Ali-aga if he wanted him to go to the mountains for spring water, which cleanses and strengthens the blood. The old man refused everything, and only requested that he put his pillows on the divan by the window, and kept looking at the gates, as if Hassan might come back earlier. Or maybe it was easier for him to imagine his return that way.

How had he spent so many years without his son? I wondered, surprised by this love and grief at their parting. And I remembered Hassan's strange explanation, that it was precisely their stubborn feud that justified that love and made it what it was. If it had existed forever and always, it would have worn itself out and slackened. But had there not been any desire for it, either, it would have withered away. I was not moved by this love in the beginning; I was cool toward it, even ill-disposed. What do you want, old man? I asked myself angrily. Does the whole world have to see this love of yours? And is showing it as you do really so difficult? It's easier to sigh and whine than to keep silent. What is your love, anyway? Senile tenderness, fear of death, the desire to keep your lineage alive, selfishness that feeds on someone else's strength, the authority of parental blood. And why? For the pleasure of petty tyranny and helpless appeals for his son's arms when everything else is gone.

But there was no use trying to defend myself with attacks and disdain. That love stunned me. I would catch myself thinking about my own father and trying to bring him closer to myself. Would it have been possible for me to await his words with joy, to be worried about his illnesses, to renounce everything that was dear to me for him? Father, I whispered, growing accustomed to my role, trying to wring all the pain of life from myself, to induce the need for love with compassion; father, papa. But I could not find any other words. There was no tenderness between us. Maybe I was even impoverished because of this: the attachment to another is nevertheless the sunny side of human nature.

Maybe I embraced Hassan's friendship with such eagerness only to satisfy that human need, stronger than reason.

At first the old man received me with suspicion. He tried to make small talk, but he choked on unnecessary words; he was not able to lie. I was surprised how much Hassan resembled him, only he was polished, refined, softened.

"You're a strange man," he told me. "You don't say very much, you're secretive."

I hurried to explain that it was probably an inborn trait that I had developed further in my order. And if I appeared strange, it was probably a consequence of everything that had happened to me.

"You're hiding behind words. I can't see what's inside you. So tragedy has struck you. They couldn't have hit you any harder, but I didn't hear a word of either condemnation or grief from you. And you were talking about your own brother."

"What happened is too hard for me to speak about. I can only tell it to someone who's like a brother to me."

"Have you found someone like that?"

"Yes."

"Sorry, I'm not asking for myself."

"I know. We're both attached to him; you more closely, by blood and fatherhood, I by friendship, which is stronger than anything a man can feel without sin."

Had it been necessary, I could have tricked him easily, because his son's name lulled his cunning and experienced caution to sleep. But I had no need to, that was really how I thought. As for my solemn words, I spoke them for the old man, to make things nicer and to soothe his fears of people who hide themselves.

He was trying to figure me out because of his son, and he accepted me because of him as well. His cunning and confidence had the same roots.

Hassan's absence led us to begin to invent a fairy tale about him. Once upon a time there was a prince.

And surprisingly, Hassan himself spoke most often about his own defeats, without regret, laughing. But by the effect of such contrary thoughts (he noticed this very keenly) his defeats never looked serious or convincing. The magic of his easygoing sincerity even turned them into victories that he did not want to discuss and did not particularly care about.

Later I tried to distinguish between the fairy tale and reality, but as much as I knew the truth I could hardly free myself from that spellbound state, in which we often trap ourselves, wishing for our own heroes.

According to what was not the fairy tale, it seemed that there was nothing unusual about him. Having passed in school through the fire of religious fervor, and still as a young man having learned Avecena's natural and critical philosophy with some free-minded, poor thinker, of which there are many in the East, and whom he often mentioned with affection and scorn, he entered into life with a burden that most of us bear: with the example of great men before his eyes and the desire to follow in their footsteps, but without any knowledge of petty men, who are the only ones we meet. Some get rid of these useless models more quickly, some more slowly, others never. Hassan adapted badly. He was oversensitive about everything concerning himself and his homeland and convinced of human values that he thought would be recognized everywhere. Finding himself in the rich imperial city, with its intricate connections and relationships between people—necessarily merciless, like among sharks in the deep sea, falsely polite, hypocritically polished, interwoven like the threads of a spider's web—the inexperienced honesty of one young man was drawn into a genuinely vicious circle. With his outdated attitudes, by which he tried to make his way through the Constantinople wilderness, with a naive belief in honesty, he resembled a man who goes into battle empty-handed against skilled pirates armed to the teeth. With the benevolent serenity, honesty, and knowledge that he had gained, Hassan entered

PART 2

that den with the confident steps of an ignoramus. But as he was not stupid, he soon realized what a bed of coals he had stepped onto. He could either have agreed to everything, or remained unnoticed, or left. But he, unusual as always, rejecting Constantinople's cruelty, began more and more to think about his kasaba, and to contrast its quiet life with that commotion. They mocked him and spoke scornfully about his remote, backward region. "What are you talking about?" he would ask with surprise. "Not an hour's walk from here there are regions so backward you can hardly believe your eyes. Here, in your back yard, not far from this Byzantine splendor and wealth, which has been hauled in here from the whole empire, your own brothers live like beggars. But we belong to no one, we're always on some frontier, always someone's dowry. Is it then surprising that we're poor? For centuries we've been trying to find, trying to recognize ourselves. Soon we won't even know who we are, we're already forgetting that we've even been striving for anything. Others do us the honor of letting us march under their banners, since we have none of our own. They entice us when they need us, and reject us when we're no longer any use to them. The saddest land in the world, the most unhappy people in the world. We're losing our identity, but we cannot assume another, foreign one. We've been severed from our roots, but haven't become part of anything else; foreign to everyone, both to those who are our kin and those who won't take us in and adopt us as their own. We live at a crossroads of worlds, at a border between peoples, in everyone's way. And someone always thinks we're to blame for something. The waves of history crash against us, as against a reef. We're fed up with those in power and we've made a virtue out of distress: we've become noble-minded out of spite. You're ruthless on a whim. So who's backward?"

Some hated him, some scorned him, others avoided him; he felt an increasing loneliness and longing for his homeland. One day he hit one of his countrymen, who was telling jokes about Bosnians, and went out into the street, saddened and ashamed of both that man and himself. Then, by a market he overheard the woman from Dubrovnik and her husband. They were speaking his language. Never had a human language seemed so beautiful to him; never had anyone been more charming than that slender woman of noble appearance and the plump merchant from Dubrovnik.

It had already been months since Hassan had done anything, and his idleness and the pointlessness of his roaming around that big city had begun to gnaw at him. But his father kept generously sending him money, proud of his son's imperial service. And while the Dubrovnik merchant was attending to his own affairs, Hassan accompanied his wife to the most beautiful places in Constantinople, listening to the most beautiful language from the most beautiful lips, forgetting his silly problems; and it seems the woman did not try to avoid him, either. What had most attracted this gentle noblewoman of Dubrovnik, educated in the Lesser Brethren Monastery,[2] to the young Bosnian was not his good looks, polish, and education, but his being all that and yet a Bosnian. She had thought that people from those remote regions were rude, crazy, wild, and pigheaded; that they had a courage that reasonable men would not always think too much of, and some silly pride because of their faithful service to those who were not their friends. But this young man was neither rude, nor wild, nor uneducated. He was equal in bearing to any Dubrovnik aristocrat, a pleasant interlocutor, a useful escort who was delighted with her (that increased the value of all of his qualities), and so restrained that she had doubts when she watched herself in the mirror at home. She was not thinking of love at all; she was just used to men courting her. She waited with anxiety and unease for that to happen, but when it never did, she was surprised and began to watch him more closely. Hassan, very young and honest, did not know about glib words that would oblige neither him nor her, and was not thinking of love, either; the delight he felt at their encounter was enough for him. Yet love thought of him: he soon fell for her. When he discovered this for himself, he hid it from her, trying not to give himself away, even with a single look. But the woman realized it at once, as soon as a passionate fire appeared in his eyes (she had to admit that they were beautiful), and she began to protect herself by strengthening their friendship, acting like a sister, without inhibitions. Hassan sank deeper and deeper into this love, or rose higher and higher on its wave; and no one should have been surprised by that, as she was beautiful (I say this by the way, because with love that is unimportant). She was gentle and sweet (and with love that is important), and she was the first creature to chase away his murky restlessness and convince him that there are things that a young man cannot forget and remain unpunished.

He helped the Dubrovnik merchant with a Bosnian, the son of the goldsmith Sinanuddin, to finish more quickly the business for which he had come, to get permission and privileges for trade with Bosnia. Thus he acquired his friendship but shortened their stay, happy about the man's trust, which seemed to pardon the sin of his love, and unhappy about their approaching departure, which would leave him more dejected than he had been before. And whether the Dubrovnik merchant really felt any trust, or just tied Hassan's hands with it, since he knew how people are, or whether he trusted his wife that much, or just had no imagination, or did not care, it is hard to say, but he was not important in their silly love. I say: silly, and I say: love, because it was both one and the other. Frightened or encouraged by her approaching departure, Hassan told Maria (that was her name: Mayram)[3] that he loved her. Whether it was because of the paleness that appeared in her face, even though she had not heard anything she did not know, or because of his naïveté, Hassan said what a wise and experienced man would never think of saying. He said he was sorry, because of her husband, since he was his friend, and maybe that would offend her as well, since she was a virtuous woman, but he had to tell her that, and did not know what would happen to him when she left. Thus the woman was also forced to hide behind her husband and her virtue, and to return him to the harmless position of a family friend. It seems that then, miraculously, as if Hassan's naïveté had defeated her austerity, she fell in love with him. But that Franciscan protégée's Catholic sense of marital faithfulness and her deep fear of sin buried her love in the most secret part of her heart, obliging him as well not to force her to uncover it, he who was overjoyed since he knew of its existence. As he had told her everything about himself, revealing what he had not revealed to anyone, she suggested that he come along with them, by boat, to Bosnia, by way of Dubrovnik, since in any case nothing was keeping him in Constantinople. She wanted to show both of them that she was not afraid of him or herself. It was sort of "la route des écoliers," she said, and explained, since he knew no French, that it was the roundabout way by which children go home from school, longer but safer. She even tried to protect herself with French, because she sensed his delight at her knowledge of that strange language, created for women. She forgot that he would have been delighted even if she spoke Gypsy. Just as she forgot that delighting him was a poor way of protecting herself. On the boat they saw each other less than Hassan had hoped. The merchant could not take the rough seas, and he spent almost the entire trip lying in bed, suffering and vomiting. Hassan saw all of it. He smelled the heavy stench, because of which the cabin had to be aired for hours, so that the very moment when everything had been cleaned and aired out, it would be soiled and stunk up again. And the poor man was yellow and blue, as if he were dying. "Maybe he'll die," Hassan thought with fear and hope, but afterward he felt remorse at such a cruel thought. Maria, with some unbecoming sense of sacrifice and sufferance, spent most of the time with her husband, cleaning and airing the cabin, comforting him and holding his hand, supporting his head when he retched, which did not decrease his suffering, just as that ugly sight did not increase her love for him. When he fell asleep, she would go up on deck, where Hassan was impatiently waiting to see her swaying, slender figure, and then with fear she would count the minutes until her duty would call her into the stinking cabin again, where—moved by her own sacrifice—she would think of the fresh sea air and the tender voice that spoke of love. They did not speak about their own love, but about that of others, and it was the same. She recited European love poetry and he Eastern, and they were the same. They had never made such use of the words of others, and that was the same as if they had invented their own. Shielded from the wind behind the captain's cabin or behind boxes and bundles on the deck, they shielded themselves with poetry as well, and it was then that poetry found its full justification, no matter what else may ever have been said about it. And when the woman became aware of her sin, when she felt that everything was too beautiful, she would punish herself with her husband and her sacrifice. "Maria," the young man whispered, taking advantage of her permission to call her by her name, which seemed like the greatest mercy to him, "will you come out this evening?"

"No, my dear friend, too much poetry at once isn't good, it could become oppressive. And the wind is also chilly. I'd never forgive myself if you caught a cold."

"Maria," said the young man, breathless. "Maria."

"Yes, my dear friend?"

"Then I won't see you until tomorrow?"

She let him hold her hand and listened to the beating of the waves and the pulsing of his blood, maybe wanting to forget about time, but then she woke up:

"Come into our cabin."

And he went into their cabin, to choke in the rancid air

and in those narrow confines, and to watch in amazement the devotion with which Maria nursed her husband. He was afraid it might make him seasick as well.

As they drew near to Dubrovnik, on the last night, she squeezed his hand (he unsuccessfully tried to keep hold of it) and said:

"I'll always remember this trip."

Maybe because of Hassan and the poetry, or maybe because of her husband and his vomiting.

In Dubrovnik he was a dear guest in their house twice, among numerous aunts, relatives, acquaintances, friends, and both times he could not wait to escape from those strange people, who in the streets hardly noticed his Eastern dress but who looked at him in the salon of Master Luke and Madam Maria as if at a wonder. As if there were something indecent in those visits of his, and so he was also flustered and unnatural. And when he encountered a coldness in Maria's attention, because of which she appeared almost completely different, distant, feigning smiles, it became clear to him that her house was where he could see how far apart they really were. There they were two strangers, with everything between them, and not since yesterday. The habits and customs there, the ways people spoke and also kept silent, and what the two of them had thought about each other earlier, without even knowing each other—all of that created a chasm between them. He realized that in this city Maria was shielded and protected by houses, walls, churches, sky, the smell of the sea, and by people. But this side of herself, it was not the same anywhere else. And he was the one from whom she was protected, maybe from him alone. And maybe even he from her. Because he shuddered at the thought of living in this wonderful place, either alone or with her, and a sorrow like he had never felt crept into his soul. He took his leave gladly when he came across a merchant caravan that was about to leave for Bosnia from Tabor in Ploche.[4] He was still happy

PART 2

when he saw the snows on Mount Ivan,[5] the Bosnian fog, and when he felt the biting wind from Mount Igman.[6] Filled with joy, he entered the dark kasaba nestled tightly between the mountains, and kissed his countrymen on the cheek. The kasaba seemed smaller to him, but his house was larger. His sister told him politely that it would be a pity for their mother's house to stand empty. She was afraid he would move into his father's larger house. He fell out with their father at once, maybe mostly because the old man felt personally deceived and shamed, since he had been spreading word about his glory and successes in Istanbul, to spite his son-in-law, the kadi, whom he could not stand. The locals interpreted his return as a failure, since no one with any common sense would have come back to the kasaba from Constantinople or left a high imperial position if he did not have to. He got married, because of Maria, because of his memories, because of the empty chambers of his mother's house, at the insistence of others. He barely endured a single winter with his wife, a stupid, garrulous, greedy woman. He freed himself of her and her family, giving them the estate near the town and some money, ostensibly lending it to them. And then he began to laugh. His homeland was not the land of dreams; his countrymen were not angels. And he could no longer change them for the better or worse. They gossiped about him, were suspicious of him, and tried to provoke him. His in-laws robbed him blind, taking advantage of his wish to get rid of his wife as soon as possible. He was the talk of the town for a long time; they welcomed him because he chased their boredom away. He remembered how in Constantinople he had spoken about the dignity of his countrymen, and laughed. Fortunately for himself, he did not hold anything against anyone or complain. He took everything that happened to him like a cruel joke. Others are even worse, he would say, and it seemed to me that he was defending his earlier enthusiasm more than the truth. After two or three years he began to love them again. He got used to them and they to him, and he began to value them in his own way, scornfully but without malice, respecting life the way it was more than the way he wanted it to be. "They're a clever people," he told me once, with the strange mixture of sarcasm and seriousness that so often perplexed me. "They get their idleness from the East, and their nice life from the West; they're in no hurry, because life itself is in a hurry; they're not interested in seeing what tomorrow will bring, what's destined will come, and few things depend on them; they come together only when they're in difficulties, and therefore they don't like to be together often; they hardly trust anyone, but they're most easily deceived with pretty words; they don't look like heroes, but they're most difficult to frighten with threats; for a long time they won't pay attention to anything, they won't care about what's happening around them, and then, all of a sudden everything matters to them, they mess with everything and turn everything on its head; then they doze off again, and don't want to remember anything that's happened; they're afraid of change because it often brings them misfortune, and they easily get annoyed with one man, even if he's done them good. A strange people. They'll talk behind your back and love you; they'll kiss your cheek and hate you; they'll ridicule noble deeds and remember them for generations; they live by spite and generosity and you never know which will prevail or when. Bad, good, gentle, cruel, lethargic, tempestuous, open, closed—they're all of that and everything in between. And on top of everything, they're mine and I'm theirs, like a river and a drop of water, and everything I've said about them I might as well say about myself."

He found a thousand things to criticize about them, and yet he loved them. Loved and scolded them. He began to drive caravans to the East and West, partly out of spite, to show his scorn for the positions he had held, angered by the reproach of distinguished people, and maybe most of all to take a rest from the kasaba and his countrymen, so he would not begin to hate them, so he would long for them again, so he would see bad things in other countries as well. And it was this continual circling, with one point on the earth that gave meaning to that motion, which made it leaving and coming back and not just roaming around, which meant freedom to him, real or imagined, it was all the same in the end. "Without that point which you're bound to, you wouldn't like any other place, either; you wouldn't have anywhere to go, because you'd be nowhere."

This thought of Hassan's, which was not entirely clear to me, this inevitability of attachment and the effort of liberation, this necessity of love for your own and the need to understand others—was this a grudging reconciliation with his small domain and the fulfillment of a desire for a larger one? Or a change of standards, so that his own would not become the only ones he knew? Or maybe it was a pitiful, limited escape, and a more pitiful return. (It was hard for me to understand that, because I have a different way of thinking: there is a world with the true faith, and one without it; other differences are less important, and I will find my place wherever I might be needed.)

In the spring, the year after Hassan's return from Constantinople, Master Luke came to the kasaba with his wife, the woman from Dubrovnik, and everything started all over again, with new vigor and new restrictions.

The kasaba was not suitable for their love, either. Wherever they were, one of them was always an outsider. Even if they broke down the barriers of the Latin mahal and the Muslim kasaba, their own barriers remained. The woman certainly could no longer deceive herself with friendship. But except for glances and kind words, she did not allow herself anything more—or so it seemed, at least. At confession she probably even admitted penitently to her sinful thoughts of love for Hassan. And Hassan left on his trips, and came back with a desire that had grown during the long months of his absence. Was it this strange love that gave meaning to his wanderings? Was it because of this that he felt doomed to be bound to one place and strove continuously to liberate himself?

This was only part of the truth about Hassan—what I had heard, learned, figured out, filled in, assembled into a vague whole. A somewhat wearisome story about a man with no real home or country, with no real love, with no real ideas, who had taken the uncertainty of his path in life as human fate, without complaining that it was so. Maybe there was a pleasant serenity and courage in such reconciliation, but that was failure.

This realization was invaluable, I saw that he was no stronger than I.

But I was charmed then, and I preferred to invent fairy tales about my great friend: Once upon a time there was a hero. With his knowledge and mind he overshadowed all the muderrises in Istanbul; if he had wanted he could have been the Constantinople mullah or the imperial vizier. But he loved his freedom and allowed his unrestrained tongue to speak his thoughts. He flattered no one, never told lies, never said what he did not know, never kept quiet about what he did, and was not afraid of great and powerful men. He liked philosophers, poets, loners, good men, and beautiful women. He left Constantinople with one such woman, went to Dubrovnik, and she followed him to the kasaba. He despised money, high positions, and power; he scorned danger and sought it in dark side roads and desolate mountains. If he ever decided to, he would do what he desired and people would hear about him far and wide.

It is really funny how by making small adjustments, skipping over details, omitting a cause, and slightly altering real events, defeats can be turned into victories, failure into heroism.

Only I must admit that Hassan had no part in the creation of this fairy tale. We needed it, but he did not. We always want to believe that there are people capable of extraordinary feats. And in a sense he was like that; he was capable of them, at least according to the way he took everything that happened to him. He would compensate for his losses with a smile, and created his own inner riches. He believed that there were not only victories and defeats in life, that there was also breathing, and watching, and listening, and words, and love, and friendship, and ordinary life, which depends greatly on us and no one else.

Well, all right, it exists, I guess it does, in spite of everything, but it is fairly silly and seems like the thought of a child.

Three days before Hassan's return, Ali-aga grew so restless that he could neither talk, nor play backgammon, nor eat, nor sleep.

"Has there been any word of highwaymen?" he asked constantly, sending me and Fazli to inquire with caravan drivers in inns, and we would bring good news, which he did not believe, or he would interpret it according to his worries:

"If they haven't been attacking for some time, that's even worse. They've grown bolder. No one pursues them, and they might attack the road at any time. Fazli!" he ordered his servant suddenly, without turning around as his daughter, the kadi's wife, entered the room—this was more important to him. "Find ten armed men, get some horses, go out to meet him. Wait for him in Trebinye."[7]

"He'll get angry, Aga."

"Let him get angry! Find some reason. Go and buy figs, or whatever you want, just don't come back without him. Here's some money. Spare no expense, override the horses if you have to, but get there in time."

"And what about you, Aga?"

"I'll wait for you, that's what I'll do. And no more questions, get moving!"

"Do you have enough money?" his daughter asked. "Should I give you some?"

"No, I've got enough. Sit down."

She sat down on the divan by her father's feet.

I wanted to leave with the servant. The old man stopped me, as if he did not want to stay alone with his daughter.

"Where are you going?"

"I was going to go to the tekke."

"The tekke can do without you. When you fall ill like this, you'll see that everything can do without us."

"Only there are some things we can't do without, even when we fall ill," said the woman calmly, without a smile, reproachfully alluding to Hassan.

"Why are you surprised? Have I already died, and can I do without everything now?"

"No, you haven't, God forbid, and I'm not surprised."

I felt uncomfortable, because of her. I still remembered that conversation and our treacherous scheme, and I averted my gaze, so our eyes would not meet. She was calm, beautiful, and confident as she had been during that conversation, which I could not forget. As she was in memories that kept coming back against my will.

I looked away, but I still saw her. Something glowed within me, and I felt uneasy. She filled the whole room, changed it, and everything became strangely exciting. Sin had occurred between us; we both shared the secret, like adultery.

But how could she be so calm?

"Do you need anything?" she asked her father with concern. "Is it hard for you to be alone?"

"I've been alone for a long time. I've gotten used to it."

"Couldn't Hassan postpone his trip?"

"I sent him. On some business."

She smiled at that lie.

"I'm glad he's with friends. It's easier when one has company. They'll help him out, and he them. I found out only today that he'd left, and I hurried over to see how you are."

"You could come even when Hassan isn't away."

PART 2

"I didn't get out of bed until a little while ago."

"Are you sick?"

"No."

"So why were you in bed?"

"Lord, do I have to say everything? It seems you're going to be a grandfather."

Her pearly teeth gleamed as she smiled: she did not show either unease or shame.

The old man propped himself up on one elbow and looked at her with surprise, a little disturbed, or so it seemed to me.

"You're pregnant?"

"It seems so."

"Are you, or does it just seem so?"

"I am."

"Ah. Congratulations."

She went up to him and kissed his hand. And she sat again at her place by the old man's feet.

"I'd hope so, for you as well. You'd certainly like to have a grandson."

The old man kept looking at her, as if he did not believe her. Or maybe he was too excited by the news.

He said in low voice, defeated: "I'd like to. Oh, how I'd like to."

"And Hassan? Will he get married?"

"I don't think so."

"A pity. You'd like a child from your son more than from your daughter."

She laughed, as if she had said that jokingly, although she never spoke a single word without reason.

"Daughter, I want a grandson. From you, or from him, it doesn't matter. If he's from my daughter then it's more certain he's from my blood; there can be no mistake. I've already begun to fear that I won't live to see him."

"I prayed that God wouldn't leave me childless, and so, thank the Lord, it helped."

Of course, prayers help a lot with that!

I listened to their conversation, stunned by her cold deliberateness, surprised by the ruthlessness hidden under the peace of her pretty face, delighted by her masculine confidence. There was nothing of Hassan or Ali-aga in her, and nothing of her in them. Had their father's blood failed in her, or had it only given her what could not develop in either of them? Or was she taking revenge for an empty life, for a lack of love, for the demise of her girlish dreams? She had become cruel because of her disappointed expectations and was now calmly settling accounts with the whole world, without regret or remorse, mercilessly. How calmly she looked at me, as if I were not there, as if we had never had that shameful conversation in the old house. She either scorned me so much that she had forgotten everything, or she was no longer capable of shame. I had not forgiven her for my dead brother; I did not know how to deal with her within myself, she was the only one that I had not placed on either side, neither among my few friends nor among my hated enemies. This was perhaps because of the stubbornness with which she thought only of herself, because no one else mattered to her. She lived for herself, perhaps without even knowing that she was inconsiderate. Like water, like a cloud, like a storm. But perhaps also because of her beauty. I do not have a weakness for women, but her face was hard to forget.

When she left, the old man kept looking at the door for a long time. Then he turned to me.

"Pregnant," he said thoughtfully. "Pregnant. What do you say to that?"

"What could I have to say?"

"What could you have to say? You could congratulate me! But don't do it now, it's too late. You didn't do it; that means you don't believe her. Wait, it's not clear to me either. For so many years my esteemed son-in-law hasn't been able to sow his seed, and his old age, for sure, hasn't made him

PART 2

any more virile. Hopes and prayers don't help much here. Only if someone younger, God forgive me, had jumped our fence. I couldn't care less, it's all the same to me. I'd even prefer it that way, so the kadi's rotten lineage won't be continued, but it'd be hard to believe for anyone who knows her. She won't submit to anyone; she's too proud and there'd be too much danger in that. Only if she killed him afterward. And we haven't heard that anyone's been killed. So why did she come to tell me this? This can't be hidden, we'll know whether she is or isn't. She was sure she'd make me happy. Was I happy?"

"I don't know. You didn't give her a gift."

"So you see. I didn't give her a gift, you didn't congratulate me—something is wrong."

"You must've gotten excited, and forgotten because of that."

"Well, I did get excited. But if I'd really believed it I wouldn't have forgotten. She worried me more than she made me happy. I don't understand."

"Why did she worry you?"

"She wants something, but I don't know what."

The next day, when I came from the afternoon prayer, he received me with an unusual liveliness and a forced cheerfulness. He offered me apples and grapes that his daughter had sent him. "She asked me what to prepare for me, and I sent her a gift, a string of gold coins."

"It was good of you to do that."

"Yesterday I was confused. And last night I didn't sleep, I thought and thought. Why would she lie to me, what could she get from that? If it was because of my estate, she knows she'll get some of it. I can't take it with me. And maybe my wretched son-in-law, the kadi, flared up before his last gasp, like a candle, and did the only honest thing in his life. Or Allah granted it in some other way; I thank him no matter what it was. But I believe it's true, I can't think of any reason why she would lie."

"Neither can I."

"You can't either? So, you see! Maybe I can still be tricked by parental love, but you can't."

He believed it because he wanted to, but Hassan would have enough trouble because of his father's happiness or whatever it was he felt.

I intended to stay longer with Ali-aga. He was upset by the news from his daughter (which I did not believe, but I would not have told him that) and by Hassan's approaching return. My heart would also miss a beat whenever I remembered it. But Mullah-Yusuf came and called me to the tekke: the Miralay* Osman-bey* was waiting for me. He was passing through with his troops, and would like to spend the night in the tekke.

The old man listened with interest.

"The famous Osman-bey? Do you know him?"

"I've only heard about him."

"If there isn't enough room there, and if the Miralay-bey agrees, invite him in my name to come here. It's spacious, and there's room for both him and his escort. It would be an honor to have him as a guest in our house."

He offered his customary hospitality, but expressed himself in a solemn, old-fashioned way. He had a weakness for famous people. That was why he had been angry with Hassan for not becoming one.

And then he suddenly changed his mind:

"But maybe it's better if he stays in the tekke. Fazli has gone to meet Hassan, and Zeyna has enough to do caring for me. I wouldn't be able to receive him properly."

I knew why he had changed his mind; it was because of Hassan. I calmed him down.

"I don't believe he'd come. Imperial officials go to the tekke when they don't want to offend anyone somewhere. Or when they don't trust anyone."

"Where will he bivouac his troops?"

"I don't know."

PART 2

"Don't tell him anything. Maybe Hassan wouldn't even like it if the Miralay spent a night in our house. I wouldn't, either," he added, magnanimously agreeing with his son. "If you need any bedding, food, or dishes, let me know."

"May some of the dervishes spend the night here, if need be?"

"All of you may."

In the street I met Yusuf Sinanuddin, the goldsmith. He was going to see Ali-aga, as he did every evening, but when I saw him he was standing on a corner as if he were listening to something. He started walking when he saw me.

"You have a famous guest," he told me, strangely absent-minded.

"I've just heard."

"Ask him how he feels. He gained his fame fighting against the enemies of the empire, and now he's going to kill our people. In the Posavina. Old age is ugly. If he'd only died on time."

"It's not for me to ask him that, Sinanuddin-aga."

"I know it's not, and I wouldn't either. But it's difficult not to think about it."

He stopped at the gates, it seemed to me that he was trying to hear something.

I sent Hafiz-Muhammed and Mullah-Yusuf to spend the night at Ali-aga's. I took Hafiz-Muhammed's room and gave my own to Osman-bey. We put the guards in Mullah-Yusuf's room.

I was surprised how old, white-bearded, tired, and reticent the miralay was. But he was not rude, as I had expected. He apologized for disturbing me, but he did not know anyone in the kasaba, and it seemed most convenient to come to the tekke; most convenient for him, though certainly not for us. But he hoped we were used to unexpected guests, and he would stay only that night and continue his journey early the next day. He could have spent the night with his troops in the field, but at his age he preferred to stay under a roof. He thought about going to the local goldsmith, Hadji-Yusuf Sinanuddin, whose son was a friend of his, but he did not know who would like that and who would not, and therefore he decided to do this. Although he had news to pass on to Hadji-Sinanuddin about his son: immediately before he had left to come here, Hadji-Sinanuddin's son had been named the imperial silladar.* I could pass word of it on to him; it might make him happy.

"Of course he'll be happy!" I said, almost stunned. "No one from the kasaba has ever risen to such a high position."

But the officer had expended all his words and attention, and fell silent, tired, without a smile, eager to be left alone.

I went to my room and stood by my window, awake and extremely upset.

The imperial silladar, one of the most powerful people in the empire!

I did not know why I was so excited by that news. Before, I would not have cared. I might have been surprised or gladdened by his good luck. Maybe I would even have pitied him. But now it was almost like poison. Good for him, I thought, good for him. The time had come for him to pay back his enemies, and he certainly had them. And now they waited in fear for his hand, which had become as heavy as lead overnight, to fall on them, a hand pregnant with many deaths. It seemed impossible, like a dream, like an illusion, too nice. God, what inconceivable happiness—to be able to act. Man is pitiful with his vain thoughts, with his wishes for the stars. His powerlessness humiliates him. Silladar Mustafa was not sleeping tonight, just as I was not: everything inside him was stirred up by the happiness he had not yet grown accustomed to. Below him was Istanbul, all in moonlight, quiet, plated with gold. Who else was not sleeping tonight, because of him? He knew all of them, by heart, better than his own kinsmen. "How are you?" he asked softly, patiently. "How do you feel tonight?" Destiny had not elevated him for their sake, to punish or frighten them. He had more

PART 2

important matters to attend to, but it was precisely because of those matters that he could not leave those men alone. Oh, and because of hatred, for sure. It was impossible that he did not feel it. It was impossible that he had not hidden it within himself, carrying it like fog, like poison in his blood. It was impossible that he had not been waiting for this night as if it were sacred, to pay them back for all their evil and for his earlier powerlessness.

There were two sides to me that night. I knew how greatly the silladar was rejoicing; I even felt his triumph myself, as if it were mine. But I also felt worse because my desires were nothing but air and light, which shone and burned within me alone, comforting and torturing me.

I wanted to howl into the night: Why he, of all people? Was he the one who needed most to get even? Was my desire really less than his? To which devil would I have to sell my miserable soul in order to have such luck shine on me?

But I was torturing myself to no avail. Fate is deaf to laments, and blind when it chooses its executors.

If it had not been night I would have gone to the goldsmith Yusuf Sinanuddin, to tell him the good news about his son. He still did not know; he had no inkling of it. It had been left for me like a valuable, to keep and enjoy, although it was not mine. It would not have bothered me that it was night; he would have been grateful to me even if I woke him up. He would have forgotten that he had spoken reproachfully of the miralay, and hurried off to thank him. I did not go. Maybe I would not even have been able to, because of the guards by the door. It would have been unpleasant if they stopped me or sent me back; it might have seemed suspicious and been dangerous for me. And I did not want to go to the miralay's room to ask for permission. He would have been surprised: Is it really so important and urgent?

Indeed, why was it so important to me?

I had become excited out of envy, out of hatred, out of a vicarious experience of someone else's happiness. And there was no other reason, since it was none of my business. I was not in a hurry to take the news to those whom it concerned. I stayed in the tekke.

I could not have dreamed how important that trivial decision would prove to be.

If I had gone to Hadji-Sinanuddin and told him what I had learned, if only to make him happy, or to stay up all night talking together, my life would have taken a different direction. I am not saying that it would have been better or worse, but it would have certainly been different.

Under the weight of its sleep, the kasaba smoldered quietly in the autumn moonlight. There were no sounds, none at all: the people had all died, the birds had all flown away, the river had dried up, life had burned out. But somewhere far away it was still humming, somewhere things were happening that people here desired. We were surrounded by emptiness and darkness. What did we have to do to leave the emptiness of that long night? O God, why did you not keep me blind, and let me rest in that dark, calm sightlessness? And why are you now holding me crippled in the trap of powerlessness? Free me, or put out the useless ray of light inside me. Release me, it does not matter how.

Fortunately, I did not lose my senses, although my prayer seemed like raving. My weakness did not last long, and before sunrise a dawn began in me. My darkness slowly faded, a single thought began to form, vague, uncertain, distant, but ever closer, clearer, more definite, until it illuminated me like the morning sun. A thought? No! A revelation from God.

My anxiety was not unfounded. Its cause had been planted inside me, although I did not yet comprehend it. But the seed had sprouted.

Quicker, time, my moment has come. My only one, since tomorrow it might already be too late.

In the early dawn there was a restless clatter of horses' hooves in the street. The miralay left his room at once, as if he had not slept at all. I went out as well. In the dim morning light he looked old and blind, because of his swollen eyelids, gray, exhausted. How had he spent that night?

"Please excuse the smoke in the room. I smoked a lot. I couldn't sleep. And neither could you; I heard you walking around."

"If you'd called me, we could've talked."

"A pity."

He said that in a dead voice, and I did not know whether it was a pity that we had not talked or would have been if we had wasted any time talking.

Two soldiers lifted him onto his horse. He rode away down the empty street, hunched in his saddle.

On my way back from the mosque I saw Mullah-Yusuf in front of the bakery, talking with the night-watchman and the baker's journeyman. He hurried to catch up with me, explaining that he had not come to the mosque because he had said the morning prayer with Ali-aga and Hafiz-Muhammed. And then he had been stopped by those two men, who told him that some Posavina rebels had escaped from the fortress the night before.

Three guards rushed by in the street. The musellim certainly had not slept that night; neither had the kadi. Many of us had spent it sleepless. We had each been in a different place, but fate had spun a strong thread between us. It had taken care of everything and now gave me the final solution. I had been waiting, knowing that it would come, and when I caught sight of it, my knees started trembling, my stomach began to hurt, my brain glowed red-hot. But I did not let go of what I had caught.

We stood next to Harun's grave. I looked at the tombstone covered with drops of wax from burned-out candles, and said a prayer for my brother's soul.

Mullah-Yusuf also raised his hands, whispering a prayer.

"I often see you praying over this grave. Do you do that for others or for yourself?"

"Not for others."

"If you do it for him and for yourself, then you're not completely corrupted."

"I'd give everything to forget."

"You inflicted a great evil on both him and me. On me more than on him, because I've been left alive to remember and to hurt. Do you know that?"

"Yes."

His voice was tired, sunken somewhere deep in his throat.

"Do you know about my sleepless nights, about the darkness you pushed me into? You've driven me to think about how to destroy you and the evil in you, to wonder whether I should hand you over to the law of our order or strangle you with my own hands."

"You'd be right if you did, Sheikh-Ahmed."

"If I'd known what's right, I'd have done it. But I didn't. I left everything to God and you. Yet I knew that there are others who are more guilty. You were a pawn in their hands, a trap with which they caught idiots. I felt sorry for you. And maybe you felt sorry for us."

"I did, Sheikh-Ahmed. God is my witness, I did and still do."

"Why?"

"That was the first time someone suffered so much because of my obedience. The first time I know of."

"You say you're sorry. Is that just a word?"

"It's not just a word. I thought you were going to kill me. I waited nights on end, listening for your footsteps, certain that your hatred would bring you to my room. I wouldn't have lifted a finger to defend myself. I swear to you by the name of God, I wouldn't have opened my mouth to call anyone."

"If I'd asked something of you then, what would you have said?"

"I'd have done it, anything."

"And now?"

"Now, too."

"Then I ask you: will you do everything, truly everything I tell you to? Think before you answer. If you won't, go your own way peacefully, I won't so much as reproach you. But if you agree, you mustn't ask anything. And no one must know, only you and I, and God, who showed me the way."

"I'll do it."

"You're answering too quickly. You haven't thought about it. Maybe it won't be easy."

"I thought about it a long time ago."

"Maybe I want you to kill someone."

He looked at me horrified, caught unaware; his words of agreement had slipped out too quickly. His memory and that grave had made him obedient. He said: everything, but he had his limits. And now he did not want to back out.

"Let it be so, if it's necessary."

"You can still back out. I want a lot. Later there'll be no turning back."

"No matter. I agree. What your conscience can do, let mine accept as well."

"Good. Then, swear before this grave, which you dug: may Allah condemn me to the worst torments if I say anything to anyone."

He repeated that, seriously and solemnly, like a prayer.

"Be careful, Mullah-Yusuf, if you say anything, now or later, and if you don't do it, if you betray me, nothing will be able to save you. I'll be forced to protect myself."

"You won't have to protect yourself from anything. What do I need to do?"

"Go to the kadi, right now."

"I don't go to the kadi any more. All right, I'll go."

"Tell him: Hadji-Yusuf Sinanuddin helped the Posavina rebels to escape from the fortress."

The youth's blue eyes widened with fear and astonishment. It seemed that he would not have been less surprised if I had asked him to kill someone.

"Do you understand?"

"Yes."

"If he asks who told you, you heard it by chance, from strangers in the inn, or someone whispered it to you in the darkness, or you can't tell who it was. Make up something. Don't mention me. And tell them not to mention you, either. The name you're giving them is enough."

"They'll kill him."

"I told you not to ask anything. They won't kill him. We'll take care that nothing happens to him. Hadji-Sinanuddin is my friend."

He did not look very intelligent with the expression of utter bewilderment that showed on his face. He tried in vain to make some sense of everything he had heard.

"Go."

He kept standing there.

"And then? Afterward?"

"Nothing. Come back to the tekke. You don't need to do anything else. Make sure that no one sees you with the kadi."

He left, as if blind, without knowing what he was bearing or what purpose he was serving.

I had released their own arrow. It was bound to strike someone.

Yellow, shriveled leaves were falling from the trees, the same ones I had touched the previous spring, wishing for their sap to flow into me, wishing to become unfeeling like a plant, to wilt every autumn and to bloom every spring. But you see, it happened differently, I had wilted in the spring and was blooming in the autumn.

It's begun, brother Harun. The long-awaited hour has come.

PART 2

14

■ ◻ ■ ◻ ■

Say: The hour of truth has come![1]

I COULD HAVE LOOKED AT THE CLOCK AND KNOWN EXACTLY: now Mullah-Yusuf is at the kadi's; now the guards are in front of Hadji-Sinanuddin's shop; now it's all over. I had taken into account their acquired habits, their feeling of security, and their wish for revenge. And so I knew I had not thrown out the bait in vain. Acquired habits lead to repetitions of actions; a feeling of security takes away one's common sense; the wish for revenge hastens decisions. If they failed to do anything, I could just as well expect the end of the world.

But surprisingly, the bazaar was quite calm; the everyday hum of isolated words, clattering of horses' hooves, striking of clocks, banging, and shouts rose above it; people worked or talked, numbed by the ordinary.

Even the pigeons walked calmly on the cobblestones.

I had not set anything in motion. What had happened? Where had I gone wrong?

Had I expected too much from these people? Would they keep silent, as they had when I had been imprisoned? Had I made a mistake in trying to bait them like that? Had their common sense been awakened? Had Hadji-Sinanuddin already been taken from his house and did these people still not know about it? Or did they not care?

But that was impossible. I was different; our dervish order leaves us in the lurch when misfortune strikes us, because we are each an insignificant part of a greater whole, helpless when we are abandoned. But Hadji-Sinanuddin's name was synonymous with the bazaar; if something happened to him, everyone else would feel threatened as well. They were also a whole, in which everyone was important in and of himself. And if danger loomed over one of them, it loomed over all of them, like a cloud.

Or had I been in too much of a hurry, urged onward by the miscalculations of my impatience?

Or did no one dare to strike at him?

Or had Mullah-Yusuf deceived me?

Or had the whole world been turned upside down?

I walked slowly down the street, between the protruding storefronts, listening to the calm hum of life, which had never been harder for me to bear.

Moments before I had been cheerful and confident. I had been steering events, and had thought that I was above them. Things and people looked smaller; I felt as if I were hovering over them. I was experiencing that for the first time, and that sense of superiority felt natural to me—I barely noticed it while it lasted. It emanated from me like a scent, like strength, like a right to something that I was not even proud of, because it was inseparable from me, one of my traits. But now everything appeared strange and distant; people and life were not below me but around me, locked, closed, like a wall, like a dead end. I do not know whether there are victories in life. There are certainly defeats.

I could not determine how long that inner dejection lasted, or whether I noticed the change immediately, as soon as it occurred, or whether my senses warned me when everything began to appear strange.

At first I heard silence. In the space directly around me the voices suddenly died; the scraping, tapping, and hammering stopped. And then that stillness began to spread farther. It resembled astonishment, or a tightened throat. This lasted only for a moment, and no matter how strange and horrible it was—as if the blood of some giant body had stopped circulating—I knew what had happened. I breathed a sigh of relief.

Harun, I haven't gone wrong! It's cost me a lot of effort, but I've figured people out.

Then the voices came back, only different from before, different from every other day, muffled and dangerous; at first they resembled a deep sigh, and then a stifled growling. I heard surprise, fear, and anger in them. I heard dull thunder, as before a storm, before the end of the world. I heard everything I wanted to hear.

My sense of ease and confidence returned.

I started after the bazaar shopkeepers, mixing among them, feeling the heat and the sharp odor of their bodies (that was the smell of sudden astonishment and a still undetermined rage; in battle the smell of men is pungently sweet, like blood), I listened to their barely intelligible questions, which were like incantations, mad murmurings, the gurgling of deep water, or underground rumblings. The words were not important, but rather their high-pitched snakelike hissing, their dull, guttural, unnatural voices, which had transformed them into something unfamiliar and dangerous, something they could no longer even remember.

We pressed through the bazaar, in a single direction, with our heads raised toward something in expectation. We pressed forward, shoulder to shoulder, crammed together, but without seeing one another, squeezing out those who were weaker. And there were more and more of us; we were each indistinguishable, transformed into a multitude, melting into its fear and strength. With difficulty I resisted a strange and powerful need to become a senseless, enraged fragment. I heard my own growling and felt dizzy from some danger that had also threatened me. I was reviving my sense of superiority, to keep from succumbing to the ancient need to rush madly ahead with one's threatened tribe.

Hadji-Sinanuddin's shop was wide open, empty.

We ran down a second street, then a third, and in the Kazazi[2] we stopped in front of a mob that had gathered there. I made my way through with difficulty.

In the middle of the street, in the open space between the people who had stopped and those ahead who were parting to make way, some guards were leading away Hadji-Sinanuddin.

I edged my way forward with my shoulders and stepped out ahead of those who were in front, who had stopped out of fear. I could no longer be one of many; my time had come.

I went out into the open space, excited, aware that a hundred fervent eyes were watching me, and started after the guards.

"Stop!" I shouted.

The mob sealed off the street.

The guards stopped and looked at me in surprise. Hadji-Sinanuddin looked at me as well. His face was calm. I thought he gave me a smile, like a friend; or maybe I just wished that he had smiled, in my excitement, to encourage me. And I really was excited, because of the people, because of him surrounded by the guards, because of the importance of what I was doing, because of those whom I hated, because of everything I had spent an eternity waiting for.

In the silence, which I had expected, but which still broke over me like a wave of boiling water, the guards took off their muskets and aimed them at the crowd. The fifth one, unfamiliar, unarmed, asked me angrily: "What do you want?"

We stood facing each other, like two wrestlers.

"Where are you taking him?"
"What do you care?!"

PART 2

"I'm Sheikh Ahmed Nuruddin, a slave of God and a friend of this good man whom you're taking away. Where are you taking him? I ask in the name of these people, who know him; I ask in the name of the friendship that binds me to him; I ask in his name, since he can't defend himself now. If any wrong has been spoken about him, it's a lie. We're all his guarantors, we're all witnesses that he's the most honorable man in the kasaba. If you imprison him, who should remain free?!"

"You're a grown man," he said threateningly. "And I shouldn't tell you what to do. But it'd be better if you didn't get involved."

"Go home, Sheikh-Ahmed," said Hadji-Sinanuddin, surprisingly serene. "Thank you for your friendly words. And you, good people, go home. This is some mistake, and will certainly get straightened out."

That is what they all think: a mistake. But there are no mistakes, only things we do not know.

The human cluster broke up, and the guards led Hadji-Sinanuddin away. I watched them go from where I was standing. They had also taken me away like that, and Harun, only no one had come out to say anything nice about us. I had spoken, and I knew I was superior to them. I was not troubled by feelings of guilt about the imprisonment of a good man, since if he had been anything else none of this would have made any sense; none of it would have served anything. Even if he were killed, it would serve a goal greater and higher than the life or death of a single man. I was going to do everything in my power for him, and God's will could decide. Fortunately, the one thing that would have been most senseless—for them to have released him immediately—did not happen.

The people followed after Hadji-Sinanuddin and the guards, and when the last of them were rounding the corner I saw that Mullah-Yusuf was standing in front of one of the empty shops. I did not call to him, but he came up to me, as if spellbound, fear showing in his timid eyes. What was he afraid of? It seemed that his eyes and thoughts were not following after Hadji-Sinanuddin, but had stopped where I was. Stiff and horrified, they did not dare to avoid me.

"Have you been here the whole time?"

"Yes."

"Why are you looking at me like that? You're afraid. What happened?"

"Nothing."

He made an effort to smile, but it resembled a spasm, a cramp. And his face, which had begun to lose its freshness, was again frozen by that fearful expression he had been trying in vain to hide.

I started down the street, and he followed me, my shadow.

"Why are you afraid?" I asked again, softly, without turning around. "Something unforeseen hasn't happened, has it?"

He hurried to catch up with me, so as not to miss a single word of what I was saying. Not out of love.

"I did everything as you said. I promised and did it."

"And now you're sorry?"

"No, I'm not sorry, I'm not sorry at all. I did what you ordered me to do, you saw that yourself."

"So what's the matter?"

I turned to him, maybe too rashly, surprised at his unsure voice and stuttered words, angry at myself because it mattered to me and I was asking him. But I wanted to know if anything had happened that he was afraid to tell, since now any mistake at all would be dangerous. But when I looked at him so suddenly—maybe because of my unexpected movement, or because of the threat in my voice—he flinched, stopped involuntarily, as if he were trying to evade a blow, as if frozen with fear, and his face turned into a mask of horror. Then I knew: he was afraid of me. I was convinced by his open mouth, which his stiff muscles could not give any shape to or move; by his cramped body, which betrayed itself in a moment, caught unawares and terrified. All of it lasted only briefly, very briefly, and then his contracted veins allowed the impeded flow of blood to resume, his mouth regained its normal shape, and the small blue circles in the middles of his eyes began to move.

"You're afraid of me?"

"No. Why should I be afraid?"

Rage was coming over me, there was nothing I could do to stop it.

"You sent people to their deaths, but now your guts are cramping up because you've seen that I can also be dangerous. I can't stand this fear of yours, it's the path to betrayal. Be careful. You agreed yourself, you can no longer go back. Until I send you away from here."

That burst out of me unexpectedly, as if from some need to ease my burden, to vent my anger after long hours of tension. This murky sludge—that earlier my common sense and caution had not allowed to move—flowed out of me, violently. Maybe it was not wise or cautious for me to act that way, even then, but as I flogged the youth with words that had been conceived in me long before, I felt them gushing from my veins irresistibly, filling me with a pleasure that I could hardly have had any inkling of. When the first wave of that discharge weakened and when I saw what a stunning effect that open burst of hatred and scorn had left upon the youth's face, it occurred to me that his fear could be useful: it could bind him to me more strongly than love.

His astonishment at seeing before himself a man completely different from the earlier Sheikh-Nuruddin gave me pleasure as well. This youth had helped that calm and gentle man to be killed, a man who had believed in a world that does not exist. This present man had been conceived in pain, and only his face was the same.

He thought I was taking revenge. I did not care. I was the only one who knew that this new Sheikh-Nuruddin was very similar to the young dervish who had swum across a river with a bare saber in his teeth, to attack the enemies of the faith. He was similar to that crazy dervish who had been different from today's because he had not had cunning or wisdom, which can be given to us only by a difficult life.

I wish you eternal peace, you inexperienced young man of long ago, who burned with pure flames and a need for sacrifice.

And I wish eternal peace to you, honorable and noble Sheikh-Nuruddin, who believed in the power of gentleness and God's word.

I light a candle to each of you in my memory and in my heart, you who were kind and naive.

Now he who bears your name continues your work, renouncing nothing of yours, except your naïveté.

Until then, time had been a sea that swelled slowly between the great shores of duration. Now it resembled the swift current of a river that carried moments irretrievably away. I could not lose even a single one; a different possibility was tied to each of them. I would have been afraid to think like that before; I would have been driven mad by that violent roar and unstoppable motion. But now I was forced to catch up with it. I had made up my mind to do this, because I had no time to lose. But I did not act rashly. I had measured out every moment that would appear out of the future's darkness, as well as the deed with which I would impregnate it so that what I wanted would happen, when everything would be linked in a chain of causes and effects.

I knew what Ali-aga would say to me when he heard, and yet I went to him first. But he had already heard everything; the story had preceded me. And I listened to what I had thought I would hear the next day or in the afternoon, only it was more juicy than I had expected. Yellow, ghostlike, thin, he propped himself up a little in his bed; he cursed, threatened, and swore. And I should've told them the same thing, he said, and mentioned their mothers, although that was admittedly unsuitable for me, because of my rank and position. But no matter, I'd acted like a man; that was to my credit, and I'd told them what one honest man should say on behalf of another.

I stood and waited for him to reel off that mass of words; he would get even more upset. They could all get as upset as they wanted. And I thought about how everyone was worried about Hadji-Sinanuddin, how they were all upset and indignant, while no one had been saddened or angered when they took me away; no one had said what one honest man should say on behalf of another. Who was not honest, I or they? But maybe one should not talk about honesty; everyone thinks that his concerns are honest. And I did not belong to them: I did not belong to anyone; I had to do everything on my own. On my own, as before, but now they would be my army, and I would not be obliged to them at all. I did not belong to them, nor did I care about them. I had sent one of them to his doom, and now they would try to save him, unaware that they were working for me. And for justice, because God was on my side; and they could be as well, unwittingly.

It had been my duty to do that (I said this to the old man, belittling what I had done), and it would be my duty to do even more. If we did not defend justice there would not be any justice. I did not want to rise up against the authorities, but I would be struck by God's punishment if I failed to speak out against the enemies of the faith, and they were anyone who undermined its foundation. If we did not stop them they would be encouraged by our fear, and would do more and more evil, scornful of both us and God's law. But could we allow this? Did we dare to tolerate this?

I don't know much about the enemies of the faith, Ali-aga said, but we can't allow good people to be tyrannized. And it's our own fault that we let all sorts of criminals and good-for-nothings push us around. We look down on them, we stopped caring about them, and so they became bold and forgot who they are. But be that as it may, we wouldn't have woken up had they been smarter. "Send for the kadi," he ordered me, forgetting all propriety, just like any other man whose wealth gives him the right to dispose of other people.

I was afraid he would say that, and I had prepared for it in advance, not knowing what the kadi might do. It would be good if the kadi refused to come; he would enrage both the old man and the bazaar shopkeepers. But if he agreed, if the old man frightened or bribed him into releasing Hadji-Sinanuddin, everything would end miserably before it even began. Therefore I opposed his intention, because of the small possibility that I would have ended up looking ridiculous. The only thing left for me to do would have been to wait hopelessly for another opportunity.

I asked calmly, confident of my reasoning: "Why do you need the kadi? His own safety is more important to him than anything you might offer or threaten him with. If he releases Hadji-Sinanuddin, he'll be accusing himself."

"What do you want? For us to wait and look into a crystal ball? Or to pray?"

"We should send a letter to Constantinople, to Hadji-Sinanuddin's son, Mustafa, telling him to do everything he can to save his father."

"By the time the letter reaches him it'll be too late. We have to get him out before then."

"Let's do both. If we can't save him, then let them at least not escape punishment."

He gave me an anxious look, as if he were stunned by the possibility of his friend's demise.

"An honest man such as he could do no evil. So what can happen to him?"

"That's what I thought about my brother. And you know what happened to him."

"That was different, for God's sake!"

"What was different, Ali-aga? That Hadji-Sinanuddin isn't small and insignificant like my brother, that he's got someone to stand up for him? Is that what you want to say?

Maybe it's true, but both the kadi and the musellim know that. So why did they imprison him? To release him when you make threats? Don't be naive, for the love of God!"

"What do you want? Revenge?"

"I want to stop evil."

"All right," he said, wheezing. "Let's do both. Who'll write the letter?"

"I've already written it. You can also put your seal on it, if you want. And we need to find someone to take it, as quickly as possible. And someone needs to pay for that. I don't have any money."

"I'll pay. Give me the letter."

"No. I'll take it."

"You don't trust anyone, do you? Maybe you're right."

The post station was a strange place. I remembered it for its smell of horses and manure, for the strange men who show up from nowhere and leave for somewhere, for the absent gazes in the empty eyes of travelers who send their thoughts ahead like an advance guard, or drag them behind themselves like luggage; they are lost, like exiles.

But surprisingly, now they all looked at me, curiously and suspiciously.

"Is the letter important?" the postmaster asked.

"I don't know."

"How much money did Ali-aga send?"

I showed him.

"It seems important. Do you want me to make a deal with the courier?"

"I have to tell him who to give it to."

"However you want."

He brought the courier into the room and left.

The courier was in a hurry.

"A letter with no name? It'll cost more than that."

He looked at me impudently with his small eyes. His face had been roughened by the wind, sun, and rain, and there was something merciless in the expression of that man, who galloped along distant roads bearing messages concerning the fortunes and misfortunes of others, unconcerned with their tears and happiness.

"I'm not the one paying. I'm just delivering it for someone else."

"I don't care. I need to be paid in full now. And the tip when I come back."

"Half now, half when you get back. And you'll get the tip from the man you're taking it to."

"That's never certain. If the news is good, they forget to pay it because they're happy. If the news is bad, they get angry and forget anyway."

"The man you're taking the letter to occupies a high position."

"That's even worse. People like that think it's an honor for us to serve them. I need to be paid in full now."

"It seems that you're blackmailing me, my friend."

He was holding the letter in his palm, as if trying to guess how heavy it was.

"Maybe I am. How much do you think I'd get if I gave it to someone else?"

"Who else?"

"The musellim, for example."

I stiffened with fear, and could feel myself breaking out in a sweat under my shirt. No one can ever anticipate everything; we rely on luck more than we think. All of my calculations and preparations had been in vain—the greed of a courier could ruin me at the outset. He had sniffed out my inexperience immediately, and I had nothing that could have instilled fear in him.

In the fear that came over me my first thought was to get hold of the letter at any price: my hands were already trembling, ready to grab the courier by his neck. Fortunately, I succeeded in regaining control of myself, I even smiled, and said calmly: "Do what you want. I don't know what's in the letter, and I don't know whether it'll be worth it for you."

"I'll think about it."

"Listen to me, friend. Maybe you're joking, but I don't trust you now. Give me the letter."

"I'm joking, you say? I'm not. I wanted to see whether it's dangerous, to know what I've got. Now I know, it's dangerous. You told me yourself."

"What did I tell you?"

"Everything. You froze when I mentioned the musellim. You know very well what's in the letter. Here it is, take it. Another courier is leaving in five days. You'll have to pay him even more."

I paid what he wanted, and gave him the silladar's name, thinking with relief how stupidly he had been joking with both of our lives.

I left, tired, almost exhausted by the horrible thought that I should not let him get away alive with that dangerous letter. But I had given the letter back to him when I saw that he was only playing a cunning game.

And yet I had done that too easily, freeing myself rashly from some inner pressure. I was seized by doubt as soon as I went out into the street. Had I myself admitted my guilt and caused my own ruin? Had I left evidence against myself in the uncertain hands of the courier? Before this I had thought foolishly: I'll do everything on my own. But how can a man do everything on his own?

Twice I decided to go get the letter from him but turned back around, without any real determination to leave the game. And yet the third time, when my fear drove me to it, I went as far as the yard of the post station, to stop everything, to tear up that incriminating piece of paper. But the courier was not there. He had gone to the bazaar; no one knew why.

Now I could only wait. I walked the neighboring streets, restless, fearful, angry at myself, not knowing whether I should keep walking stupidly in circles or hide, so unsure of myself that I felt like a frightened child. "I shouldn't have done this," I thought, reproaching myself, not knowing exactly where I had gone wrong. Should I not have tried anything, or just not have sent the letter? Not to have tried anything meant giving up on everything, not to have sent the letter meant not doing anything, reconciling myself, but that was what I did not want. Then where had I gone wrong? Or was I so nervous about the chance occurrences that I had forgotten to include in my calculations, but that are apparently decisive in life? Or about my inevitable dependence on many people, none of whom I could trust?

And then, probably from fatigue, I felt myself calming down wearily and surrendering to the wait. Nothing depended on me any more, and I could not change anything. God would decide what was going to happen. But that was not right. Not that it mattered, but that was not right. I had not even considered the courier. He was so unimportant, how could he destroy me now? But no one can consider all the couriers in life.

Before noon I tried to find him again, without knowing why I was doing it; so much time had passed that he could have done whatever he wanted. But I could not find him, he had departed on his long journey.

If he had shown them the letter, everything would soon be over. I had nowhere to run.

I did not have the strength to wait. Those two hours of uncertainty had worn me out. I left for the musellim's office, to rid myself of this nightmare. And as soon as I made up my mind to do that, I felt relieved. The end would be the same, whether they found me or whether I gave myself up. And yet everything was different, as I was going to meet the outcome myself. My courage returned, and a more cheerful mood, because I had changed the game, taking the decision upon myself. Maybe facing the threat in this way seems petty and resembles self-deception, but that is the point. To act, not to wait. To be a player, not a victim. Maybe that is the essence of courage. Had it taken so many years for me to discover such an important secret?

PART 2

I told the guard who I was and requested to see the musellim. The guard should not say: some dervish, but should remember my name and rank. It was important.

If he agreed to receive me, I could tell him all sorts of things. I could have sought mercy for my friend, Hadji-Sinanuddin. Or explained why I had asked the guards to release him. Or warned him of the agitation that reigned in the bazaar. Or told him countless things that in no way obliged me but showed my goodwill.

I was not quite calm, but I knew this was better than anything else I could have done: I was not trying to hide or run away, I had come to talk to him of my own will, with good intentions and a clear conscience.

If he had seen the letter, they would lead me in at once, and everything would be explained very quickly. And even if he had seen it, there was still hope. The letter was Ali-aga's, I had only written it. And I had come to tell that to the musellim.

And while I waited, thinking about everything he might ask, it occurred to me that—in addition to this unpleasant waiting and conversation full of half-truths, and even lies—I would have to do all kinds of other things that are not pretty, for a deed that was. Maybe I would be forced to do things that I would have been ashamed of in an uneventful life, for justice, which is more important than all of our petty sins.

But I could still stop myself, if that was God's will.

O God, I whispered to myself eagerly, looking at the grey sky over the kasaba, heavy with snowy clouds, God, is what I'm doing good? If it's not, shatter my firmness, weaken my will, make me uncertain. Give me a sign, make the branches of the poplars sway with only a breath of wind; it wouldn't be a miracle in this autumn weather. And I'll give up, no matter how great my desire to do this.

Not a single poplar on the riverbank stirred. They stood still, silent and cold, hanging by their thin tops from the cloudy sky. They reminded me of the poplars of my home, above a bigger and prettier river, under a sky bigger and prettier than this one. This was not an opportunity to delve into my memories; they came like a flash, like a sigh. And disappeared. And what was left was the gray day in front of me, and the heavy clouds over my head, and some kind of muddy sludge within me.

Would Is-haq's shadow appear? This was his time.

The guard returned. The musellim could not see me.

"Did you tell him who I am? You didn't forget to mention my name, did you?"

"Ahmed Nuruddin. The sheikh of the tekke. He says he's busy. Come again some other time."

He did not know about the letter.

Suddenly all the shadows disappeared. I forgot about the poplars, the gray day, my sorrow, my memories. I had been right: I should not wait for anything, I should go out to meet everything. If one is not stupid or cowardly, he is not helpless, either.

The kadi's servant-girl was standing in Ali-aga's yard, wearing her best clothes. Zeyna told me in a whisper that the kadi's wife was with Ali-aga; she had had to go to get her twice. The aga had demanded that she come no matter what, Zeyna did not know why.

I stopped at the very bottom of the stairs. Above, through the open door, I could hear a conversation. I would not have listened in on it had it not surprised me and had I not needed to know what it was about. The old man demanded from his daughter that the kadi come to him no matter what. He absolutely insisted on it.

"It's important," I heard him wheeze. "He's done something stupid; he or someone else, but he'll also be guilty. Tell him to come, or tell him to release the man. So I can get some peace as well."

"I don't interfere in his affairs. They're not my concern. Least of all now. And it'd be better if you didn't, either."

PART 2

"Do you think I want to interfere? I don't. And I can't. I'm old, powerless, sick. How can I worry about others? But I must. It's what everyone here expects from me."

Was that Ali-aga's voice, tearful, weak, dripping with self-pity? Were those his words? God almighty, will I never learn anything about people?!

"You don't have to, you want to. You've grown accustomed to being listened to. You like it that way."

"I don't. I won't anymore, I don't have the strength for anything. I don't even have the strength to admit it to anybody. Help me, tell him to release him, for me. So it won't be said that I forgot my friend, though I did forget him. This small amount of breath left in me, it's for you. And Hassan. How can I tell them that?"

"Very well, father. We'll talk about it some more. We're not on opposite ends of the world."

"It's urgent. Very urgent."

"I'll come tomorrow."

"Come early, to tell me what he says. Night is good for talking."

What was this? The first crack had appeared where I thought the rock was hardest. I felt scorn for his weakness, which he hid, and also shame, as if I had caught him doing something disgraceful.

I went back down to the entryway, so it would look as if I had just arrived.

She raised her hand to lower her veil, but changed her mind when she saw that it was me. I asked how her father was; she answered, briefly, and wanted to pass. I had to keep her; I was not so timid as I had once been.

"Just two words, if you're not in a hurry."

"I'm in a hurry."

"This spring we began a certain conversation, which we should finish. My brother, of course, is dead, but I'm alive."

"Let me pass."

"I'm a friend of your father's. A very good friend."

"What do I care?"

"I'll help you to get what you want, so your father won't forget you on his deathbed. But you persuade the kadi to release Hadji-Sinanuddin. Otherwise, don't hope for anything. I'm offering to make a deal with you. You have the most to gain."

"*You're* offering to make a deal with *me*?"

"Yes. And don't dismiss what I'm saying too quickly."

A shadow of hatred or scorn darted across the woman's bright eyes. I had insulted her, but that was what I wanted. Now the kadi would not release Hadji-Sinanuddin, even if he had been intending to do so.

It was not easy for me to be rude, and her anger struck me like a whip. I would have been in dire need of God's mercy had she deigned to be my enemy.

I entered Ali-aga's room, thinking more of the lightning in that woman's eyes than of her beauty. Where were her closed thoughts going, too hot to stay at rest? What would be the result of her scornful silence? She could have been a good wife and a good mother, but what was she since she was not?

"Did you send the letter?"

I looked at the old man absentmindedly, still blinded by the woman's scorn.

"Did your daughter come by?"

"She comes every day. She's worried because I'm eating so little. Did you talk to her?"

"Does she ever talk to anyone?"

"Well, I think so. Don't you like her?"

"I pleaded with her on Hadji-Sinanuddin's behalf. So that she'll persuade the kadi to release him."

"And what did she say?"

"Nothing."

"She's strange sometimes."

"How are you feeling? You look fine."

"I'm feeling so well that—God forgive me— soon I

PART 2

might like for my friends to be thrown in prison every day."

This voice was strong and confident. Had I not, moments before, heard a different one, frightened and tearful?

What kind of game was he playing? With whom? With himself, for others? Or with others, for himself? And what was he? A bundle of habits? A fictitious image? An extended memory? Was what others expected of him more important than his own powerlessness? And both of these things existed within him, and could be decisive. His old pride drove him to get involved, but everything he was today resisted it. His deathbed weariness urged him to close his eyes, but he gave people the illusion of his past strength, its shadow. Does every man end that way, fighting with his former self?

What would prevail?

"The courier blackmailed me," I said, sitting down by his feet. "He turned brazen when he saw there was no name on the letter."

"Why didn't you tell him to . . . I'm sorry. You should've paid him. He'd have softened up at once."

"I got rather frightened. And that made me wonder whether it was right for me to burden you with this problem, and to persuade you to get involved."

"I don't know what you're talking about."

His voice sounded impatient, almost insulted. "You can persuade a fool, or a silly child, but not me. The only thing you mentioned was the letter. I said we had to do more. Or has my memory completely failed me? And what have you burdened me with? I can't get up, but fortunately, I can still speak. And no one can free me from my worries about a friend. That's a question for my conscience."

"It might be dangerous."

"Nothing can be dangerous for me anymore. Or, if you will, everything is dangerous. Death is hiding behind the door, waiting. When I'm doing something, I don't think about it; it doesn't concern me. I'm alive."

He spoke confidently and it sounded convincing. Like

what he had just been saying, a little before. Yet one of those two men must have been more like him, closer to his thoughts and desires.

But anyway, it did not matter. I would reassure him in what I needed, trusting him. I told him flatteringly:

"I'm glad to hear you say that. I value courageous and noble people."

"And you should. If you find them. However, old men are neither courageous nor noble. And I'm not, either. Maybe I'm only cunning, and that comes with longevity. What can they do to me, like this? Will they imprison or kill a man who already has one foot in the grave? People are stupid; they'll save a useless old man, but destroy a youth who has his whole life before him. Therefore I'll take everything upon myself, all of it. I'll take this advantage; it occurs only once in your lifetime."

He laughed and coughed.

"Spiteful, isn't it? To be a hero without any danger. Spiteful and funny."

I did not know whether it was funny, nor was I sure that they would spare him. But let it be the way you want, old man. I'd be sorry if you perished, but I'd be more sorry if I failed. Neither of us is important anymore.

Surprisingly, until then he had not asked me, even once, why Hadji-Sinanuddin had been imprisoned, or if he was guilty. I told him that I had heard that he was somehow involved in the escape of the Posavina rebels, and that his arrest was the beginning of a campaign against distinguished men, due to their increasing refusal to submit to the dictates of the emperor and the vali. The occasion for this was the unpaid war tax. Knocking out their teeth was supposed to inspire fear, after the rebellions in the Posavina and Krayina, so that their misdeeds would not serve as an example to anyone. And that was how it should be. And for this very reason, to avoid a greater disturbance, to avoid something that no reasonable man would desire, those who spread discord and discontent should be removed, those who practice oppression, under the guise of law, and whose misbehavior might lead others to shameful and bloody deeds. If Hadji-Sinanuddin's misfortune would help God to remove them from our midst, even that misfortune would not be in vain, and neither would our worries.

He dismissed Hadji-Sinanuddin's apparent wrongdoing with a wave of his hand, either because he did not think it serious, or because he did not believe it. As for the campaign, he said that it was always a matter of human fear, which was quite understandable, because things never get better, only worse. Or it only seems so to us because what is is always more difficult than what was, and a paid debt is always easier than one hanging over your head. He did not believe that anyone had really heard about the campaign, since if they really were going to do that, they would never tell about it. And if they'd really told about it, they weren't serious;they were only trying to frighten people. As for the authorities, they're always hard to put up with, and they'll always try to force us to do what we don't want to. What would happen if they disappeared? In his lifetime more kadis, musellims, kaimakams had been removed, deposed, or killed, than he could count. Had anything changed because of that? Not much. But people still believed that things would be different and wished for change. They dreamed of rulers who were good, but who was that? As far as he was concerned, he dreamed of bribable ones, he liked them the most because there was a way to them. Worst are the honest ones, who need nothing, who have no human weaknesses, and know only about some higher law, which is almost incomprehensible to ordinary men. No one can do more evil than they can. They create enough hatred to last for a hundred years. And these of ours? They're nothing. Petty in everything. They can't be evil or good. They're as moderately cruel as they are considerate. They hate the kasaba, but they're afraid of it. Therefore they're resentful and take revenge whenever they can. Or whenever they think they can. They'd be terrible if they dared to do what they want, but they're always afraid of some mistake. And they can make a mistake either if they ease up or go to extremes. They're best softened with threats, if those are spoken quietly and not revealed completely, since they can't rely on their own grit. They always depend on chance and someone higher up, and they can always end up as change in someone's transactions. All in all, nothing but wretches, and therefore something very dangerous. All he wants is to help Hadji-Sinanuddin, and he couldn't care less whether they stay in power or go to hell.

His opinion was somewhat different from mine, but it would not make any sense to argue with him, if he was not in my way.

He requested that Mullah-Yusuf spend the night at his place. None of his servants was around.

The youth lowered his eyes, to hide his joy, when I told him to stay there.

A hazy evening, heavy and motionless clouds, silence above the kasaba.

People had been expecting something all day long, straining their ears, their eyes wide open, too detached for ordinary matters and conversation. It was too quiet after the morning's excitement; too dull, as if hostile armies had withdrawn to their camps, awaiting night or morning, for a battle to begin. And that very silence, that motionlessness, the empty battlefield, without a cry, or a curse, or a threat, created a tension that grew ever greater. The end would come when everything burst. They looked at each other, they looked at the passersby, they looked down the street, they waited. Anything could be a sign. I also looked down the street. It had not yet begun. But I waited; we waited; something was going to happen, soon. The foundations of the old kasaba were breaking; the wind moaned in the heights, barely audibly; the whole world was creaking.

Birds cried and darted across the black sky; the people were silent. My blood ached from waiting.

15

■ □ ■ □ ■

The truth is mine. I speak the truth.[1]

IT TOOK ME A LONG TIME TO FALL ASLEEP THAT NIGHT. When I did I kept dozing off and waking up in short intervals, continuing the same thought both asleep and awake. I was unable to separate those two states, and was convinced that I had not slept a wink and that I would sit up all night like that, half-dressed, so events would not catch me unprepared.

I was not able to think coherently, maybe because of my fitful sleeping, which broke my train of thought and disturbed its order, or because of the impatience that drove me to get to what was most important as quickly as possible. So I continually imagined encounters with those three men, mostly with the kadi. Slowly, without haste, I followed their every expression of surprise, fear, and hope, prolonging that moment as much as I could, that beautiful moment when everything would be torn asunder: the root had just been pulled up, but no one was fully aware of it, they did not yet feel lost or humbled, they were still living according to their old habits. Their fear—that was what was beautiful. Not any reconciliation with their fall. Fear, uncertainty, a ray of hope, restlessness in their eyes. Or even better (I returned them to the game, and made them begin again): everything was over for them, but they did not know it, they could not believe it and stood upright, arrogant and confident, as they had then, as they always had until now. I would not have liked to see them destroyed; my hatred waned whenever my thoughts—even involuntarily, without obeying me—went farther than I wanted. And for hatred, as well as for love, one needs living people.

I was roused from my sleep by the heavy sound of shooting somewhere in the kasaba. Had it begun?

The dark night still dragged on. I lit a candle and looked at the clock on the wall. It would soon be dawn.

I got dressed and went out into the corridor.

Hafiz-Muhammed was standing in his doorway, with a short fur coat over his shoulders. Did he never sleep?

"I heard you getting dressed. Where are you going so early?"

"What's all the shooting?"

"This isn't the first time they've started shooting. Why do you care?"

"Isn't it because of Hadji-Sinanuddin?"

"Why would they start shooting on account of Hadji-Sinanuddin?"

"I don't know."

"Don't go out. We'll find out in the morning."

"I'll be right back."

"It's dark, dangerous; there are all sorts of people about. Merciful God, has his misfortune hit you so hard? Must you also perish because of your kindness?"

"I have to see."

"What are you expecting?"

I walked, keeping close to the fences and walls. When some soldiers ran by I hid in the darkness. Since I had gotten out of prison I had been suffering from an irrational fear of quick footsteps and excited running; I was afraid of anything that happened suddenly. Now I wanted to know what was happening. I wanted to go there, to see it, to take part.

To take part in what?

Indeed, what was I expecting? What was I hoping for?

All my hope lay in the letter that the courier had taken to Silladar Mustafa in Constantinople. If a katul-ferman* did not arrive soon, or at least a letter about the removal of the guilty parties, then there was no longer either filial love or honesty in the world. But that was not worth thinking about, because in that case life would be worth less than a copper piaster.

But even if there was none of that any more, I trusted in the arrogant pride of powerful men. It could not fail. Would the imperial Silladar's vanity let some petty kasaba scum drag his father from prison to prison? He would resist such shame even if he were up against someone stronger; and as for the locals here, there would be hell to pay, without a doubt. His temper was certainly not angelic, nor his hand light, since he had succeeded in rising to such a position.

He was going to take care of everything for me. All I had to do was wait, and that would be best and safest. But there was no way I could avoid the bazaar shopkeepers. As soon as I had chosen Hadji-Sinanuddin as the bait, I had gotten them involved as well. They might ruin everything, but what else could I do? If Hadji-Sinanuddin were released too soon, without any fuss or harm, everything would have been in vain. Nevertheless, I had expected them to do more, something more serious. I did not know what. Maybe their messenger had already gone to the vali with their complaint. Maybe they would pay some ruffians and ex-soldiers to go and break out the prisoner. Maybe they would incite the janissaries* to remove the authorities from power. Hardly anyone knows their dealings, but I hoped that this would not pass quietly. As many people as possible needed to hear about it. And I did not want anything to happen without me. I had to get even.

At the stone bridge I met the night-watchman.

"Where are you going so early, Sheikh-effendi?"

"I read my clock wrong."

PART 2

"My God, see what life is like? Those who can sleep don't, and those who are always sleepy are condemned to roam around all night."

"What's going on?"

"All sorts of things! Something new is happening all the time. Only nobody tells me anything, so I don't know."

"A few moments ago someone was shooting somewhere."

"Fortunately, it wasn't in my area."

"Could you ask around a little?"

"It's none of my business."

"I'll pay you."

"You didn't even pay for what was more important to you. Or is this more important? Wait, don't get mad. I'll tell you for free. I asked the night-watchman from the neighboring area. He doesn't know, either. And if he doesn't know, nothing might as well have happened. There's no one else for me to ask."

Lights began to appear in the windows; the houses were opening their eyes.

After daybreak Mullah-Yusuf brought me two pieces of news: first, that Hassan had returned earlier that morning, he had been traveling all night; and second, more strange, that all the shops in the bazaar were closed.

Indeed, the stores and shops were bolted shut, their shutters lowered, their padlocks securely fastened. Not even on the most solemn holy day was it so empty.

A young tailor, a newcomer, was hurriedly closing some wooden shutters, looking around fearfully.

"Why are all shops closed?"

"I don't know. I came early, and was going about my work when I looked out and saw that none of the shops were open."

He checked the door, put the key in his pocket, as if he were hiding it, and went hastily down the street.

Two merchants came up, walking unhurriedly, like sentries, and calmly watched the tailor go away.

I asked them:

"Didn't you tell him the bazaar would be closed?"

"Who'd have told whom?"

"You mean you didn't all make an agreement?"

They looked at each other, surprised:

"Why would we make an agreement?"

"Then why did you close your stores?"

"I thought: 'Let's not open up shop today.' That's probably what the others are thinking."

"But why?"

"Why? What do we know why?"

"So you really didn't all make an agreement?"

"Come on, Effendi. How could the whole bazaar come to an agreement?"

"But don't you see? Everything's closed."

"Yes. And that's exactly why it's closed."

"Why?"

"Because there wasn't any agreement."

"Fine. So it's not because of what happened yesterday?"

"Well, it's also because of what happened yesterday."

"Or because of the shooting this morning?"

"Well, it's also because of the shooting."

"Or because of something else?"

"Well, it's also because of something else."

"What's going on in the kasaba?"

"We don't know. That's why we're staying closed."

They looked past me, serious, distant, worried, elusive.

"And what happens now?"

"Nothing, with the help of God."

"But if it does?"

"Well, there you are—we've closed our shops."

Does our dervish reasoning seem as incomprehensible to such shopkeepers as theirs does to us?

And I would not say that they were insincere or overcautious. They just sensed some approaching danger: when that happens, everyone has his own language.

I told Hassan about this conversation. A peculiar impression had been made on me by those two merchants, who had turned into strangers overnight, because of what I had started. Should they not have become closer to me? I asked Hassan that, differently: should we not have thought more alike, since we were both troubled by the same thing?

Hassan was getting dressed in his room. He had bathed for the second time already—he was tired, he said, they had been in a hurry, because of his father. His friend from Dubrovnik was exhausted, he would certainly sleep for two days and nights. Hassan did not seem tired, but rather absentminded; the lost serenity of his expression made him seem dreamy and detached. He was illuminated from within by something like moonlight, a silly happiness, something not very clever that blinded him to the world around him. He answered: yes, of course. But it seemed that he did not understand me at all, as I had not understood the merchants.

"You're not really back in the kasaba yet," I said, somewhat confused, somewhat amused by his absentmindedness.

"What? Oh, yes! Well, I'm here, I already know what's going on: my father is seriously ill, Hadji-Sinanuddin is in prison, and Miralay Osman-bey has left to butcher the Posavina rebels. Is there anything else?"

He smiled happily, as if those things were the most cheerful pieces of news that he could ever have heard.

"How can Ali-aga be seriously ill? Last night he was fine."

"He's been upset by Hadji-Sinanuddin's arrest."

"We're all upset. We're afraid for him."

"Why? They'll release him. Men who love money have already been found. Imagine, such people do exist!"

For him there were no grave matters that morning. He laughed and said: "For his whole life he cared for prisoners, until he became one himself. Strange, isn't it: to become the object of one's passion."

"We're very sorry for him."

That was a reproach. I wanted to draw him away from

his strange thoughts. But he would not let anything bother him.

"I also feel sorry for him. And I think how all his life he's sought God's reward by doing good for others, but now the others are doing the same with him. Maybe that serves him right."

I knew he did not like tender displays of emotion, but this was too harsh. Maybe I was asking too much of him. Today he could think only of his own happiness.

"How was your stay in Dubrovnik?"

"Nice. It's still summer there."

I wondered that it was not spring.

In the yard the gates opened and Hassan went up to the window.

The servant Fazli, who had come in from the street, signaled for him to come down.

"Can you stay with my father?" he asked me.

"I don't have much time."

"Stay for just a little while. I'll be back soon."

Ali-aga was the same as the night before; he was even livelier.

"Where's Hassan gone off to?" he asked me.

"I don't know. He said he'd be back soon."

He asked me what was going on in the kasaba and was surprised to hear that the bazaar was closed. He also asked me to persuade Hassan to stay at home, for him: who knows what can happen when one's ill?

"Why did you tell Hassan you're feeling worse?"

"It's true. I am feeling worse."

"Since when? Last night you were as good as ever. I was about to tell Hassan, but I didn't get the chance."

"Don't you have something better to talk about? I felt better, but now I feel worse, and I'd like to have him by my side. What's so strange about that?"

"Nothing. In fact, you want to keep Hassan by your bed until all of this is over. Isn't that right?"

PART 2

"It's better for him. You know how rash he is. He'll do what you'd never expect. Look and see if he's come back."

Then everything became clear to me—his strange behavior, his whimpering before his daughter, his request that the kadi release the prisoner, his bad condition that morning. All of it was because of Hassan, to shield him from danger, to keep him from doing something hasty. Therefore he tried to bind his son with his illness, therefore he had been playing that strange game that I could not understand. He wanted to save Hadji-Sinanuddin as quickly as possible, so that Hassan would not do it himself. His love had endowed him with fear, resourcefulness, and imagination.

I calmed him down:

"Don't worry about Hassan. He won't do anything hasty."

"Why not?"

"He's only thinking about his woman from Dubrovnik. Larks are singing in his heart. I can almost hear their chirping."

"Do you think I can't? That's what I'm afraid of, my friend."

"What?"

"Those larks. It's because of them that he might do something stupid. At such times all men are good and pity others."

"Yes, they feel pity, but they don't do anything. Love is selfish."

"Come on, dervish, what do you know about love? I stuck my neck out because of him. Is that selfishness?"

I wanted to ask the old man, and I would have to at some point, how far he would go for his son, and what he would betray. And what would his love turn into if his son ever perished? That would be the deepest hatred I know of.

This love was the only thing that existed in his life, it and nothing else. Even on his deathbed, waiting to breathe his last, he still cherished it. And maybe it also sustained him, kept him alive. Maybe that was the deep and complex cunning of old age, the fear of death turned into love, so that the last buds would flower in his aged heart. A son's heart is like a bush of flowers that you do not have to dung so it will flourish; a father's love is just one of those many flowers. Maybe it is even an obstacle, a bother imposed by duty. But it is an old man's only anchor.

I say: maybe, because I do not know.

The kasaba was quiet. As if it had begun to die, breathing more slowly, living more and more faintly.

I sat in the yard of the mosque, on a stone beside the fountain, while people walked through the bazaar and in the streets, singly or in groups. They walked as if asleep, absorbed, barely conscious, unhappy about something, feeling betrayed and empty. They walked and waited for time to pass, or for a time that would come, enshrouding me with their drowsy circling and the thick web of their footsteps.

I asked: "What's going on?"

No one heard me.

Had Hadji-Sinanuddin's arrest upset them so much? With what strange bonds were they tied to each other, in what kind of closed circle, unknown and inaccessible to me, did they live? What had happened to them? They were not enraged, they were not even depressed: they just seemed detached from everything. As if they viewed the kasaba and the world with some dead curiosity, sleepy but persistent, and were waiting. They had lost their own features, and acquired new ones, common and indistinct.

I had to do something, because it seemed to me that the germ was growing, invisible; but time was empty and separated me from myself and from them, although I did not know where I belonged.

It was as if I had strayed into an unfamiliar region, among unfamiliar people.

I hid my eyes from them and watched the narrow stream

of water that splattered against the stone and sprayed into swarms of droplets, colorless, because the sun was not shining: I thought I would be calmed by what lives on its own, and forever. But my anxiety was growing.

Then I saw them stop, listen to something I could not hear, and then start off in one direction.

"Where are you going?" I asked one of them.

"That way."

"Why?"

"Everyone else is."

Shouting reached us from the Kurshumli mosque.[2]

The people came alive and started walking faster.

The streets were crowded. I could not see anything; I could not hear what was going on. I tried to push my way through and was suddenly drawn into the surging mob, as if into a whirlpool. It pushed and pulled at me, forward and backward, from one wall to the other, refusing to leave me to myself, not even for a moment, holding me firmly in its embrace, hot, restless, close, unpleasant. It was ugly and silly, as if the devil himself had made sure to entangle me in hundreds of vines of human legs and arms, and in this way to separate me from everything that was happening. Squeezed into the mob, I could push, like them, I could shout and make threats, but I could not make decisions. So irreversibly enmeshed, I was one of many, a senseless and terrible power that became lost in it.

Then something strange happened: I forgot how impossible and unacceptable my situation was, and for entire moments my roots and the fanned embers of my memory would return me among them, rendering us equal. I was no longer a captive. I was not offended at being shoved back and forth; the smell of sweating bodies was not unpleasant. I forgot that I had to make my way through them, to go somewhere, to get to the right place, to decide something. The right place for me was here, I was the same as they, excited by our numbers, excited by the shouting, excited by our common strength. I was shoulder to shoulder with the others. I raised my arms and threatened someone who was not there, freed from all fear, convinced that the time had come for all sins to be paid, even ancient ones passed on through blood. And I shouted, loudly, like the others. What was I shouting? I do not know. Maybe: death to them! That was what I thought. Or I added my featureless voice to theirs, like a scream, like a threat, to make it stronger, since I was a part of them. But no! I was myself, with a hundred voices, a hundred arms, a hundred heads. A thousand problems gnawed at me; they belonged to everyone but were also mine. I howled: Aaah! Thinking: revenge! Thinking: blood! Thinking: the end! The end of what? Oh, of everything that is wrong, that is inhuman. I knew that, without even thinking. Bright skies were opening in front of me.

And then I was aware of myself again. I tore myself from our common roots, I was able to feel people's elbows and sweat, and was angry at their howling and because I could not get out. "Let me through!" I shouted, hating them, captured and incapacitated, completely foreign to them.

Then I heard what they were shouting, what they were complaining about, whom they were threatening. No one mentioned Hadji-Sinanuddin; no one remembered him, not even by chance. They only mentioned what concerned *them*, only what bothered *them*. And there were very many things that bothered them, shortages, high prices, fear, injustices great and small, empty promises, wasted years, betrayed hopes, unrelenting nights, premature old age, small loves, great hatreds, uncertainty, humiliations, all that misery called life.

Much of that rubbish had been accumulating; they had gathered it, and now were shouting out their discontent, like at a market, angrily showing those riches of theirs. They gave them away like gifts—whoever wanted them could take them—or they offered them in exchange, for hatred or blood.

During a pause, between two cries, as if between two shots on a battlefield they would tell in a few words, breathless, how a guard had been killed on the watchtower—not with a gun or knife—and how he had remained standing, dead; how in the Karanfil mahal[3] a child had been born with one eye on his forehead. They wanted something fateful to hover above this anger of theirs.

It became unbearable. Warmer and warmer, denser and denser, crazier and crazier, the mob pulled at me; the mob spun me around, like a current; I was just a splinter, a speck; they whirled me in eddies; I dug my elbows into someone's ribs; I shouted, and the others shouted; I stepped on someone, the torrent roared; I staggered, I too would be trampled under; I grabbed onto someone's neck, like a drowning man; now the water rushed in another direction, we would all drown; it roared down another street, the watergate gave way. I was breathing more easily. I rushed behind the others; I tried to stop them, to calm them down. I was overcome by fear; they no longer knew where they were running or what they wanted. They were rocks in a landslide; they were a wild torrent.

Shots could be heard in front of the musellim's office.

"What's that?"

"The guards are shooting."

No one stopped.

When I got there, breathless, a young man lay dead on the cobblestones, his thin cotton shirt stained with blood. A few men were standing around him in a circle, and someone, whose face I could not see, was kneeling beside him, trying to raise his head.

The mob broke into the building, and one could hear things being overturned and smashed.

The musellim and his guards were not there; they had fled.

I went up to the man who was kneeling over the bloody youth. I was sorry to see that they were both dressed in peasant clothing.

"Is he dead?"

In his left hand he was holding the youth's head, as he would that of a child, and looking with fear into his face, which was white as a sheet, expecting it to regain its ruddiness, expecting its mouth to quiver, expecting everything to be as it had been a few minutes before.

They were both young.

"Was he your brother?"

"We came to the market," he said confusedly, beckoning to us with his restless eyes, which still lingered in the past; he did not dare to approach this moment. "To buy salt."

"Lay him back down on the ground."

"And nails. We're building a house."

"Lay him down. He's dead."

"And I say to him: we came for nothing, the shops are closed. And he says . . ."

He gently touched the dead face with his thick, plowman's fingers, and began to call to him softly: "Shevki! Shevki!"

Father will be angry that they've taken so long; Father will scold you because you won't be going home with him. Get up, Shevki, wake up.

Shevki, where are you?

Where are you, Harun?

Where are you, all you lost and murdered brothers?

Why do they separate us when we are separated anyway? Is it so that we will realize it? Or so that we will begin to hate, if we did not know how to love?

"They've killed your brother. Do you want us to bury him here?"

Now he was warming his cheek with his whole palm.

"Take him with you. Let him at least have a decent funeral."

He carried the corpse away. As he would a child, a folded kerchief, a sheaf of wheat, taking long steps on the cobblestones of the bazaar, a habit from plowing fields, still looking into his brother's face with mad hope.

PART 2

I walked in front of the youth's corpse and said prayers aloud.

I heard people shouting; there were many of them; their rage had not waned.

At the corner by the courthouse I stepped aside, so that everyone could see the corpse in the young man's arms.

They formed a semicircle around him and watched him silently.

I said a prayer and left for the mosque.

Behind me, behind us, there was a howling, a shattering of glass, the banging of loud blows.

I did not turn around.

Near the mosque I met Hafiz-Muhammed and asked him to take care of both brothers, living and dead; I started down the street.

"Where are you going?"

I dismissed his question with a wave of my hand. I truly did not know.

"Hassan was looking for you."

It was as if that name bathed me in light. The time I had spent without him had worn me out. That day, then, at once—I needed him more than ever. But I would wait a little longer.

I walked, following a street uphill, to feel myself climbing, to exhaust myself with that effort. I wanted to withdraw. I had been tense since the morning, taking part in every passing moment.

I left time to continue without me; it could finish whatever it wanted on its own.

I had to get away from the bazaar, right at that moment, to move away, as if from a fire, so I would not be guilty, so I would not be a witness.

I was trying to detach myself.

It was late autumn; the plum trees were leafless and black, and the rocky peaks of the mountains were covered in fog. The wind howled in the gaps between the mahal's houses.

Soon there'll be snow, I said to myself.

And it did not matter to me.

I tried to walk like someone out on a leisurely stroll.

I haven't been here for a long time, I thought.

And I did not care.

I saw: some children were playing tipcat. Strange, I thought, the children are playing tipcat.

And you see, that mattered to me.

The children were playing. But below, in the bazaar, their fathers were going on a shameful rampage.

I looked: in the valley the kasaba, calm and tranquil. People were passing through the streets, tiny, unhurried, innocent. From that distance, from up there, they resembled the children. But they were not children. Never had I seen their faces so maddened, their eyes so cruel. I could not recognize them for their bloodshot eyes and their bared teeth; they looked like the disfigured masks worn by the infidels on Christmas. This was their terrible holiday.

I did not want to think about them, I did not want to think about anything. Time was flowing; time was taking care of everything without me. I could neither stop nor hasten it.

Time was dripping down like the rainwater, drop by drop.

I took shelter under the eaves of one of the mahal's dilapidated mosques, next to its wall.

And the children scattered.

An old hodja with a white beard, stooped over the cane in his trembling hand, came slowly toward the mosque, unreal in that silence, alone, without a single believer behind him. They were all below in the kasaba, but he did not care. His old age saw things that are more important. In front of the mosque he gave the call to prayer: it was a futile, barely audible call to someone who was not there.

That meant it was noon.

I had been on my feet since the early morning. I began to

feel weary, as if that realization of time's passage were weighing down on me.

Leaning with my back against the wall of the mosque, I looked in front of myself into the ever denser showers of rain, which separated me from the world, and listened to the weak murmur of the hodja's prayer. His was a voice from the beyond, hopelessly sorrowful, utterly lonely, and it was worse that I heard it, because it was speaking about my loneliness as well. I could not help him, I was separated from him by the wall; he could not help me, either.

Alone. Alone. Alone.

Alone, like one under suspicion.

But why would I be guilty? What could I have done to prevent anything? No one could have stopped them that morning. Their time, which was meant for evil, had come, like a phase of the moon, stronger than my will, stronger even than theirs. I could have tried to persuade or to dissuade them—it would not have mattered.

What was happening below? Or had already happened? I did not know, I did not care. The wind had been sown, and therefore a whirlwind was being reaped.

Had anything really needed to happen? By now everything must have already quieted down. They had all gone home, frustrated and ashamed, they would bring home to their wives the little rage and bile they still had left. I was trying to detach myself for no reason, trying in vain to direct my distracted attention to the autumn, to the leafless plum trees, to the rocky mountaintops, to the imminent snow. It was all in vain, because my thoughts were below, in the kasaba. Maybe nothing had happened, and what I had done had not had any consequences.

Yet if I felt anxiety, and maybe even shame because I had shown the murdered youth to the enraged mob, I had not reconciled myself to the possibility that nothing had happened. I had wanted it to happen, and had agreed before God to accept my share of the guilt.

This dilemma was painful, but it also gave me satisfaction: my conscience was alive even when *they* were in question.

A dervish is as cruel as a hawk and as sensitive as a spinster. Hassan had said that once, mockingly, as always. Maybe he was right, because my feeling of nausea would not go away.

As dark and light shadows were thus passing over me, as I denied the guilt which I did not want to give a name, five horsemen approached in the street, at a gallop, wearing long raincoats, with muskets strapped to their saddles.

I recognized the musellim and his men.

He also recognized me and stopped his horse, watching me with surprise and malice.

At first I was frightened because of the unexpectedness of our encounter, and because that place was so isolated. No one could have helped me; no one would have even seen if something happened to me. And that day was a day of evil deeds.

He must have also been more than a little surprised, seeing me in a place where he would never have dreamed of finding me. Did he think I was his fate, or a game animal flushed out in front of him? I was an attractive target, pinned there against the white surface of the mosque's wall.

Surprisingly, my fear passed quickly. I looked directly at him, upright with hostility. I knew everything, I remembered everything again, as if it had happened only a moment before. I did not even remember it: it had been ready within me, like an instinctive obstacle, like disgust that one does not think about. I also looked at his four escorts; they had attacked me in the narrow street leading to the tekke, back then, when everything began. And I did not know what I could have done had they come at me as they had before, but all of those eyes, aimed at me like guns, did not frighten me this time. My saving hatred gave me strength, like wine.

If the musellim had so chosen, I would have been his

sacrificial lamb in a moment. If only he had known how much he would regret that missed opportunity!

"We'll see each other again, dervish."

I thought: with the help of God, but I said nothing. I could not have spoken anything other than harsh words, but then I would never have seen him or anyone else again.

They turned their horses and galloped away past the mosque.

They were fleeing the kasaba!

Had I had time, I would have gone out in the street and watched the musellim disappear, cursing him and savoring the moment that would bring us together again. But I did not have a moment to lose; my wait had come to an end. The musellim had fled. So it had *happened*. I had not sown the seeds in vain.

My awkwardness, regret, and shame disappeared. I had nothing to be ashamed of, or to regret. I could be proud; I could be happy that I was not on the side of evil. God had passed his verdict, and the people had carried it out: my hatred was not just mine. I was not alone. I had no doubts. I was cheerful, like every true believer who knows he is on God's side.

I hurried down into the kasaba, meeting an occasional passerby who was strangely flustered, left behind as if by accident after the mad rush that had set those streets ablaze.

There was no one in the bazaar. Or in front of the courthouse. The door had been smashed open, all of the windows shattered, papers scattered along the walls.

Ali-hodja was squatting and collecting records, documents, verdicts, and countless notes that had amassed like testimonies of sins and cruelties. Men record everything they do. Maybe they do not consider themselves cruel?

I bent over and began sorting through them. The crime that concerned me most had been recorded there.

"What are you looking for?"

"I want to see what they wrote about my brother."

"Why? To justify your hatred? I'm going to burn all of it. You're all like wolves; you'd rummage through this trash to find reasons for new crimes."

"If you want to insult me, that's easy. You need only to be inconsiderate."

"I'm not trying to insult you. I'm just saying things that are unpleasant. Because I'm sick."

"Why?"

"Have mercy on me, go away. I'm sick of people. Leave me alone."

I left him alone; that was most sensible. Protected by his madness, he was stronger than all of us.

I went into the courthouse. There was no one there, just as when I had gone there on account of my brother. There was also the same silence that begins to buzz in your ears, like a soft, high-pitched hum. There was the same restlessness because of invisible human shadows that hid in the nooks and corners. Only the stuffiness was gone, the wind rushed in freely through the shattered windows and the gaping doorway.

From the kadi's room I could hear a quiet conversation—someone was with him.

I stepped into the ransacked courtroom and stopped in the empty doorframe, upset: the kadi was lying on the floor, dead.

No one told me, but I knew he was dead. I had known even before I arrived there. I had known even while I was waiting under the eaves of the old mosque up in the mahal. That was why I had gone to the edge of the kasaba, so it would happen while I was not there.

Several people were standing in the middle of the room. They looked at the kadi with compassion. I was not sure whether I belonged in their dolorous group.

I crossed through the room and stopped above the corpse. I bent over and lifted the gown that had been thrown over his head.

PART 2

His face was yellow, as always; only his forehead was blue and bloody. Surprisingly, his eyelids were lowered, and there was no expression on his face. He was hidden from everyone, as he had been in life.

"Wretch," I thought, feeling neither hatred nor exultation. "You did me much evil. May God forgive you, if he wishes."

Death had separated him from me; not even ugly memories could keep him here. But that was all I could think. No regret, no memory, no forgiveness. He was no more, that was all.

I did not want to give him a farewell kiss, as is our custom. It would have been unnecessarily hypocritical: those men knew what he had done to me.

I said the prayer for the dead, I could do that much.

Then I heard footsteps and turned around. The kadi's wife was approaching the corpse.

I stepped aside to give her room, without spite, even without curiosity. I had hated him while he was alive, and I would have thought it strange if someone felt sorry for him. But it was somehow distasteful that even his wife would grieve for him, lying, for the sake of propriety, just to fulfill nice customs.

She removed her veil, paying no attention to us, and knelt over the corpse. She looked at him for a long time, without moving at all, without a sigh, without a word, and then bent down and kissed him on the shoulder and forehead. After carefully wiping his face with her silken scarf, she kept her hand on his yellow cheek. Her fingers were trembling.

Was she really grieving for him? I had expected a sorrowful posture, deep dejection, even tears, but in no way had I expected trembling fingers on the corpse's face. I was stunned by the tenderness with which she wiped away his blood, as if he were a child, softly, to keep from hurting him or causing him any pain.

When she stood up I approached her.

"Do you want him to be taken home immediately?"

She turned her head toward me abruptly, as if I had hit her. Only later did I remember that her eyes were shaded with kohl and full of tears. Had it been easier for her when she heard than when she saw him? But at that time I paid no attention to it, because I was surprised by the glance with which she pushed me away, scorched me, stabbed me. It was the glance of a mortal enemy.

I was perplexed by both that threat and that unexpected sorrow. Maybe it had not been so dead in their empty house, maybe it would only be that way now. Not knowing why, with no real reason, I pitied both her and myself. I felt empty and lonely, just like her. Maybe because of the fatigue that had descended upon me, like twilight.

Later I remembered that she seemed beautiful, more beautiful even than on that evening in her large house, because of her eyes, glistening with tears, and because of her expression of utter hatred. One of her hands, upset, forgotten, emerged from under the folds of her chador* and stopped in mid-escape, startled by the silence.

I felt a desire to place my forehead under that hand, which was searching for something, and, with closed eyes, to forget my fatigue and the present day. To make peace with her. And with the world.

I was still caught in that gloomy mood when I went out into the street, into the gray rainy day dappled with wet snowflakes, oppressed by a mass of black clouds that had covered the world.

The wind whistled through me; I was an empty cave.

How can an empty heart be healed, Is-haq, you phantom, whom my powerlessness has conjured up again and again?

I walked aimlessly, stood in front of the inn for a long time watching a caravan that had just arrived, and I did not know whether it was good or bad to be a traveler. I stopped at Harun's grave and had nothing to tell him, not even how it felt to be a victor.

I should have gone into the tekke, to spend some time alone, to regain my strength. But I could not even make up my mind to do that.

Then Mullah-Yusuf found me, and my apathy vanished; it was as if the fog had risen. While the more important part of my work had still been ahead of me, I had not thought about him. Now he surfaced, as if from underwater, an unpleasant reminder of himself.

Hassan is looking for me, he said, and wants me to come to Hadji-Sinanuddin's house.

I had also forgotten about Hadji-Sinanuddin. Was he really at home already?

He told, briefly—more because I asked than because he himself wished to tell—how in the morning Hassan had found out that the musellim had sent Hadji-Sinanuddin under guard to the Vranduk fortress,[4] from which hardly anyone ever returns, and raced off in that direction with his men. But they would have worn out their horses in vain had not the river swept away some bridge in front of the fortress; thus they caught up with the guard and kidnapped Hadji-Sinanuddin. They hid him in a village, and sent for him as soon as they heard what had happened.

I would have been more interested in this story if it had been told to me in different circumstances and by another mouth. Now I looked at the youth suspiciously. He seemed cold and restrained. He spoke hesitantly, as if none of it were any concern of mine.

In a fury that was hard to control before him, I said: "I don't like the way you're looking at me. I don't like the way you're talking to me."

"How am I looking? How am I talking?"

"You're keeping yourself at a distance. And you're keeping me at a distance. It'd be good if you forgot what you know."

"I've forgotten it. It's not my affair."

"Not so! It is your affair, but you should forget it. None of what I've done is mine alone."

He surprised me with his response, and drove me to rearm myself with the caution and firmness that had left me a little while before.

"Let me leave the tekke," he said abruptly, making not a request, but a demand. "As long as you look at me, I'll continually remind you that I might betray you."

"You'll also remind me of the pain you inflicted on me."

"So much the worse. Let me go away, let's forget one another. To free ourselves from fear."

"Are you afraid of me?"

"Yes. As you are of me."

"I can't let you go. We're both bound by the same chain."

"You'll ruin both our lives, yours and mine."

"Go into the tekke."

"No one can live like this. We're following on each other's heels, like death. Why didn't you let me die?"

"Go into the tekke."

He went in, dejected.

PART 2

16

> On that day we will ask hell: are you full?
> And hell will answer: are there any more?[1]

SNOW, RAIN, FOG, LOW CLOUDS. THE FORERUNNERS OF WINTER have been threatening for a long time now. And winter will be endless; it will last almost until Saint George's Day. I thought about how the mufti must have already been suffering in advance: for six months he would worry and wait, for six months he would freeze. I could not understand why he did not leave this place. I ordered that he be supplied with beech or oak wood, that his chimneys and stoves be rebuilt so the rooms could be heated from the outside, from the corridor, day and night; and that juniper branches and elecampane be burned in his rooms.

I also became sensitive to the cold. In my and Hafiz-Muhammed's room a fire crackled pleasantly in an earthen oven with red and blue tiles. I also hired a new servant. Mustafa could not get things done and was already unbearably quarrelsome—he grumbled and growled like an old bear. And I could no longer stand a cold room, as I once had, especially when I would return from the courthouse, wet and shivering, full of dampness like a cleaning rag.

Many things in my life had changed, but I kept my old habits. I allowed myself a few more comforts, but really very few, and more simplicity in my dealings with people; perhaps because I was not threatened and because the honor and rank of kadi gave me a pleasant feeling of security. And more power, which I did not want. But I could see it even in Hafiz-Muhammed's look, when I went into his room in the evening to ask him how he was and whether he needed anything.

My duties as kadi do not leave me much time for anything else, and it has been a long time since I have looked into these notes. But when I remembered them one evening and read through a few pages, I almost doubted my memory. Could it be that I had really written this, and that I had really thought this way? I was surprised most of all by my faintheartedness. Could I really have doubted in divine justice so much?

At first I was surprised by the offer of some prominent townspeople to give me the rank of kadi. I had never intended or desired to attain it. I might have even refused in other circumstances, but then it seemed like salvation to me. Because suddenly, after everything that had happened in the bazaar, I felt tired and exhausted, unpleasantly aware that I was in a trap; and not only I and not only since yesterday. Men are too vulnerable, they need protection.

Surprisingly, I grew accustomed to my new position quickly, as if a long-awaited dream of mine had come true. Maybe this was the golden bird from fairy tales. Maybe somewhere within me I had secretly been waiting for such an act of confidence for a long time, forever. That I had not allowed this vague ambition to manifest itself was because I had certainly feared disappointment if it did not come true, and suppressed it in a dark and hidden place in my soul, as I did with all other dangerous desires.

I had raised myself above fear and the ordinary, but I was no longer surprised by that. Who considers his happiness undeserved?

On the first night I stood by the window and looked at the kasaba, the way I imagined the silladar had, and, listening to the excited rush of my blood, I watched my enormous shadow in the valley. From below, tiny people turned their eyes up at me.

I was happy, and yet I was not naive. I knew I had been helped by many accidents that had fallen into place like beads on a string after the first incident that had caused everything, my brother Harun's misfortune. Well, they were not exactly accidents: that blow had given me strength and set me into motion. God had wanted it that way, but He would not have rewarded me if I had sat with my hands tucked in my belt. And they had chosen me and no one else, because I was partly a hero, partly a victim, partly a man of the people, not too much of anything but rather everything with a moderation acceptable to both the people and the town leaders. And what had apparently prevailed was their certainty that they would be able to control me easily and do whatever they wanted.

"You again think you'll be able to do exactly what you want," Hassan told me.

"I'll do what the law and my conscience command me to do."

"Every man thinks he can outwit everyone else, because he's sure he's the only one who's not stupid. But thinking like that is truly stupid. And so, we're all stupid."

I did not feel insulted. This blunt remark confirmed for me that something was bothering him. I did not know what it was, but I hoped it would pass. It would have been a pity if it lasted too long, a pity both for him and me. I needed him unhurt, untroubled, and not plagued by bitter thoughts. I would also have liked him this way—I would have liked him no matter how he was, especially since I was his equal. But he was dearer to me as my lighter side. He was nonchalance itself, a free wind, a clear sky. Everything I was not, but that did not bother me. He was the only man who did not respect my position and missed me the way I had been. And I tried to be as close as possible to the image that he saw. Sometimes I even believed I was like that. I tried to find him after my encounter with the dead kadi; he was indispensable to me, he alone; I wanted to see only him. He was the only one who could drive away my strange fear. I became attached to him, once again, forever. I would bring him back to myself whenever it was necessary. I did not know exactly why, maybe because he was not afraid of life. My new position gave me security, but it would also bestow loneliness upon me. The greater the heights, the greater the emptiness. For that reason I wanted to keep his friendship. He would be my army, a warm refuge.

Soon that need became even stronger.

I set about this difficult office, thinking it a shield and weapon in a fight that I had been forced into. But it was not long before I had to defend myself. Although no bolts of lightning had struck yet, an ominous thunder could already be heard.

Upon receiving the imperial decree with which the grateful Silladar Mustafa compensated me for my help and confirmed my office, I decided I would consult only my conscience in everything I did. I immediately felt a chill wind around me. Those who had put me in this position suddenly fell silent when they saw that I would not relent. But rumors that I was guilty in the death of the former kadi began to be heard more and more frequently. I tried to find the people who spread them, but I might as well have tried to catch hold of the wind. Had someone spoken of this, thinking that no one would be held responsible? Or had they known earlier, and had need of it only now? Maybe they would not even have chosen me if I had been totally unblemished.

I do not know whether I would have relented, either, hardheaded as I was and confident of protection from higher up, and I do not know whether *they* would have agreed to any kind of compromise anymore. We began to hunt each other.

PART 2

I was also disturbed by the musellim—or rather both of them, the former and the current one. The former one sat in his village, threatening me and sending letters to Constantinople. The current one, who had already held that office before and knew how unsteady such a position is, cunningly let everything go by him, and did not reproach anyone who might have been able to harm him in any way. I found out that he had even let his predecessor know he should hide before he sent soldiers to make a sham search for him. And no one held it against him.

I avoided the townspeople. Partly because I scorned them, but more because I remembered well how much evil and destructive rage they carry within themselves. I did not know how to talk with those people any more, since I no longer knew who they were; and they sensed my dislike of them and gave me dead looks, as if I were an object.

I would go to see the mufti. Everything was as it had been before, when I had tried to save my brother, playing the fool before him. Only now I did not consider it necessary to humble myself, at least not too much. He asked: Which musellim? Which kadi? Or he began to talk about the Constantinople mullah, as if he were the only man in the world whom he knew. And once he even called my brother Harun forth from his memory, by some belated connection, as if in the cruellest of jokes, asking me whether he had been released from the fortress. Malik looked at him as at a treasury of wisdom. In the end he would send me away with an impatient wave of his yellow hand, and I stopped visiting that wretch, who would have been an ordinary fool had he not been the mufti. Malik spread the word that the mufti could not stand me. And everyone believed it, because they wanted to.

I had decided to refuse my pay, but had to give up that nice idea. I surrounded myself with trustworthy people, so I would not be groping in the dark, but they troubled me again and again with ugly rumors that they heard or made up. Everyone did this, and we knew everything about each other, or thought that we did. I paid Kara-Zaim to tell me what he heard at the mufti's office. God only knows who of my people were eavesdropping on me for others!

Only Mullah-Yusuf, whom I kept with me because of his pretty handwriting and out of caution, remained silent and went quietly about his work. I believed that he was loyal to me, out of fear. But I watched over him, too.

I was living as if in a fever.

Less and less at ease, I got involved in a business that was fairly ugly though understandable. In search of protectors, I began writing letters to the vizier's assistants, to the vizier, to the imperial silladar, sending gifts and complaints. The gifts were useful, but the complaints were annoying. I knew that but I could do nothing else—it was as if I were losing my common sense. I gave warnings that the path to godlessness must be stopped, calls for the imperiled faith to be saved, cries for them not to abandon me in this place that was so important to the empire. And no matter how much I felt the harmfulness of those oaths and curses, with which I could offer neither alliances, nor more powerful friendships, nor substantial benefits (so I even discovered how helpless and alone I was), I felt an indescribable satisfaction at sending them into the world and awaiting a solution. Just as a besieged military leader with no troops left sends calls for help and awaits reinforcements.

Do I even need to say that none of this helped me?

It only broke the neck of the former musellim, because upon my request that the lawlessness be stopped, the vali's defterdar* arrived and, after he summoned the musellim for a talk, sent him under guard to Travnik, where he was strangled.

I was accused of this death as well. In return the vali bound me to obedience, which had been denied to him here for a long time. I accepted, in an effort to save myself.

I considered backing out and leaving everything, but I

knew that it was too late. They would destroy me as soon as I stepped out from behind this bastion.

(I know I am telling things too quickly and confusedly; I know how much I am skipping over, but I cannot do otherwise. Everything has closed around me, like a hoop, and I do not have the time or patience to write slowly and meticulously. I did not hurry while I was calm; now I am rushing and condensing things, as if a fire were closing in on me. I do not even know why I am writing; I must resemble a lonely, dying man who scratches a sign of himself into a rock with a bloody fingernail.)

And Hassan keeps drifting farther and farther away. At first I thought Mullah-Yusuf had told him about Hadji-Sinanuddin, but I became convinced that the reason was something entirely different. It was not even because of the lady from Dubrovnik: she had fled our harsh winter, and he knew that springtime would bring her back to the kasaba.

To both his and my misfortune he went away to get some relatives in the vicinity of Tuzla,[2] who had suffered in the revolt, like many others. Miralay Osman-bey had done his work well; he killed, burned people's houses, drove them from their land, sent them into exile, and the people met the winter in great misery. Hassan brought back his relatives, women and children, and took them into his house. From then on he was a completely different man, difficult, tiring, boring. He told about uprooted lives, burned ruins, unburied corpses, and especially about children next to gutted houses, hungry, rattled, with a living fear in their eyes because of everything they had seen.

His careless superficiality had disappeared, as had his scornful ease, his cheerful glibness, his ability to construct bridges out of airy words. All he did was talk disturbedly about the tragedy in the Posavina, and he did that uneasily, without his earlier playfulness, confusedly and gravely.

He called the victims, who lay murdered under the black soil of the Posavina or dragged themselves along distant roads into exile, suicides and Bosnian fools. Our enthusiasm, he said, is just as dangerous as our lack of common sense. What did they think, if they thought anything at all? That they could hold out against the imperial troops, who need neither courage nor enthusiasm, because they're armed and ruthless? Or did they hope that they'd be left alone, as if anyone would ever leave a spark to turn into a fire, however dilapidated the house might be? Haven't we had enough of our mindless strength, and our heroism, which leaves only desolation behind? Do fathers dare to determine the fate of their children thus, bequeathing them suffering, hunger, unending poverty, fear of their own shadow, cowardice for generations, the destitute glory of sacrifice?

Or he talked completely differently, saying that nothing was so humiliating as cowardly acquiescence and petty common sense. We're so subordinated to someone else's will, above and beyond our own, that this is becoming our destiny. The best of men, in their best hours, try to escape from that powerlessness and dependence. The refusal to admit weakness is already a victory, a conquest that will one day become more enduring and widespread, and then it won't be an attempt but rather a beginning, not defiance but rather self-respect.

I listened and waited for him to get this out of his system, because I knew that neither his enthusiasm nor his bitterness ever lasted long. Only one mad passion endured, his love for the woman from Dubrovnik, but it was really so inexplicable that it seemed more like a need for love than love itself. He never tried to reach his potential, to figure out who he was, or to define himself; he tried everything but finished nothing, allowing himself to be a continuous failure. He would also fail at kindness.

Once he showed me the cripple Jemail, who was pulled by his children from place to place in a cart and who would hobble into his tailor's shop on two canes, dragging his lame, withered legs. When he was seated he astonished everyone with his beauty and strength, his masculine face, the warmth of his smile, his wide shoulders, strong arms, and wrestler's build. But as soon as he stood up all of his beauty disappeared, and he would hobble toward his cart, a cripple whom it was impossible to watch without pity. It was he who had crippled himself. While drunk, he had stabbed himself in the thighs with a sharp knife until he severed all of his tendons and muscles; and even now, when he drank he would drive the knife into the withered stumps of his legs, not allowing anyone to approach him. No one could restrain him, either; his arms were still incredibly strong. "Jemail is the true image of Bosnia," Hassan said. "Strength on mutilated legs. His own executioner. Abundance with no direction or meaning."

"So what are we then? Lunatics? Wretches?"

"The most complicated people on the face of the earth. Not on anyone else has history played the kind of joke it's played on us. Until yesterday we were what we want to forget today. But we haven't become anything else. We've stopped halfway on the path, dumbfounded. We have nowhere to go any more. We've been torn away from our roots, but haven't become part of anything else. Like a tributary whose course has been diverted from its river by a flood, and no longer has a mouth or a current; it's too small to be a lake, too large to be absorbed by the earth. With a vague sense of shame because of our origins, and guilt because of our apostasy, we don't want to look back, and have nowhere to look ahead of us. Therefore we try to hold back time, afraid of any outcome at all. We are despised both by our kinsmen and by newcomers, and we defend ourselves with pride and hatred. We wanted to save ourselves, but we're so completely lost we don't even know who we are anymore. And the tragedy is that we've come to love our stagnant tributary, and don't want to leave it. But everything has a price, even this love of ours. Is it a coincidence that we're so overly softhearted and overly cruel, so sentimental and hard-hearted, joyful and melancholy, always ready to surprise others and even ourselves? Is it a coincidence that we hide behind love, the only certainty in this indefiniteness? Are we letting life pass by us for no reason, are we destroying ourselves for no reason, differently than Jemail, but just as certainly? Why are we doing it? Because we're not indifferent. And if we're not indifferent, that means we're honest. And if we're honest, then let's hear it for our madness!"

His conclusion was as unexpected as all of those reflections were strange. But it was convenient, since it could explain anything a man might or might not do. I did not suffer from that historical and patriotic illness, as I was bound by faith to eternal truths and to the wide expanses of the world. His point of view was narrow, but I did not argue with him, since I had more important worries, since he was my friend, and since I considered his views in fact to be heretical but harmless, because they vitiated themselves. Some things were even explained for me by this imaginary pain, which was a kind of poetic explanation of his failure, or the excuse of a big, clever child, aware that he is squandering his life to no end. In fact, as he was rich and yet honest, what else could he do? He had not acquired his wealth himself, and accordingly did not respect it, but he did not want to deprive himself of it, either. For this reason he artificially arranged for his life to fit him badly, imagining these small, interesting lies so he could calm his conscience.

And I was mistaken about that, as I was about many other things concerning Hassan.

Once more, a long time has passed since I have written anything down. Life has become troublesome.

And as it became more troublesome, I thought more and more about Hassan's sister. I remembered her strange look and the hand that had betrayed her sorrow. She did not want to let me enter her house when I went there to refute the ugly rumors about me. Then I sent her a message that I would propose to her, if she would agree. She refused, without explanation. I learned that she was indeed pregnant. And that she sincerely mourned her kadi. I had thought she saw him through my eyes, but apparently she found something in him that no one else did. Or he had been as tender to her as he was cruel to everyone else, and that was the only side of him she knew. Her widow's grief would pass, but I had approached her too early. A pity. Marriage to her would have defended me from accusations better than anything, and I would have entered into a prominent family, which would have served as protection for me. But you see, Aini-effendi could still get in my way, even from the grave.

My good Hassan has gone completely out of his mind. I explain this by the fact that everything that can enter the human mind can become a passion. This is not really an explanation at all, but there is no other. He went to the Posavina a few times, thinking only of what went on there. I heard that he was going to buy some of the land confiscated from the Posavina rebels. I asked his father if it was true. The old man gave me a cunning smile.

"It's true, we're buying it. It's a good deal; it'll be cheap."

"Do you have money?"

"I do."

"Then why are you borrowing it?"

"You know everything. I want to buy a lot of it. That's why I'm borrowing. Never in my life have I gotten such a good deal."

"You're going to buy poor people's property?"

"Yes."

He laughed, cheerfully, like a child. This would put him back on his feet. He had also lost his senses, out of love for his son. The reasons were different, but the consequences the same. They would destroy themselves.

"This will cure you of your illness," I said, also laughing, as cheerful as he was, more than I had been for a long time.

"I can feel myself recovering."

"You'll be healthy and poor. Is that happiness?"

"I'll be healthy and I won't have anything to eat. I don't know whether that's happiness or not."

"Who'll feed you? Your son or your daughter? I can also send you the food from the tekke. One can live that way, too."

"I'll stand in line in front of the imaret."*

We laughed like lunatics. We laughed, as if all of it were the best of jokes, as if it were something clever and profitable. We laughed because a man was destroying himself.

"So you know, you old fox?" he asked me. "How did you find out? Why don't you believe I'm getting a good deal?"

"I know. How could the two of you do anything intelligent? Especially if your son persuaded you? It's not intelligent, but it's good."

"It's true, my son persuaded me. And then it's both intelligent and good. If you had a son, you'd know that."

"I'd know how joy can be created from loss."

"Is that really so little?"

"No."

Surely they would not be left destitute, buying confiscated property in order to settle it with poor people, who had been driven from their homes. Ali-aga's common sense would overcome both his own and his son's enthusiasm, but the damage would be great, since Hassan would make sure to do as many foolish things as possible once he had already begun. He did everything on the spur of the moment, in a fervor that was short-lived. Now he was sure that this was the only thing he should do, and by the time he grew weary of it, by the time he got bored with it, and that would happen quickly, he would already have gotten his father and himself deeply into debt.

I have never had anything, and have never wanted to have anything, but my peasant blood has retained a fear of careless spending. It leads to a dead end. And this seemed like drunkenness, when one lacks moderation; like an excess of zeal and hot-bloodedness, when one is difficult to stop; like senseless enthusiasm that does not consider consequences; like Jemail, who was his own destroyer. And yet, behind everything that my mind could not accept I sensed a certain abundance of serenity and a barely tangible reason for profound joy. Because it was absurd, because it was ridiculous, because it reminded me of a joke: let's do something unusual. Because it was hard to find an explanation for it.

They would surely come to their senses, when it was all over, and they would see how expensive generosity is. But everything would turn out so well that they would not have an opportunity for regret. They would be blinded by pride because of praise from people whom it had not cost a single piaster.

And I realized more and more what a difficult and complicated task it is to be in power. I wasted time with tedious matters, defending myself and attacking others, doing whatever it took to stay afloat, instilling fear in others and enduring it myself. I felt my power become greater and greater, along with my difficulties, since I no longer needed to soften my blows. But with a strange melancholy and inexplicable envy I thought of Hassan's face, of the joy with which he always renounced certain support, of the hope he inspired in people's hearts. This was nothing very serious, but again, it seemed as if I had missed some sort of opportunity.

Then a few important events occurred.

(If I were more idle, as I once was, I would feel the need and the desire to think about how they were in fact similar to others, but gained importance because they concerned certain people. And so events are not important in and of themselves, but rather because of our interest, which singles them out from among the others. Or something like that. There is a certain pleasure in such slow, deliberate thought, as if we are above things. But now I have been engulfed by them, and I can manage only to record them.)

In the Posavina, on the day the auction of the confiscated property was to take place, Hassan encountered an unexpected obstacle. The town crier announced that a representative of the vizier would buy all the property, and that was nothing other than an order for no one to enter into the bidding. But this was an obstacle only in my opinion; in Hassan's it was not. Ignoring the vizier's wish, he bought a few pieces of property; the rest, the vast majority of it, was taken by the vizier's representative, for nothing. Hassan even left some money, so that a few houses could be repaired as much as was possible and so that food could be bought for the families who would settle there. He returned to the kasaba, satisfied.

"Why did you have to lock horns with the vizier?" I asked him, joking, because I did not believe that the vizier's anger would last long. "Do you really fear no one?"

It was the old man who answered. He was walking slowly around the room with a fur-lined coat over his shoulders:

"God a little bit, the sultan not at all, the vizier about as much as my bay horse."

"What do I have to fear?" asked Hassan, parrying my blow. "I've got you. Hopefully you'd protect me."

"It would be better if you never even needed anyone's protection."

"A dervish will never give you a direct answer," the old man said, laughing.

Hassan answered seriously: "He's right. It's better if I don't ever need anyone's protection. I should be my own shield. It's not right for me to burden a friend with troubles that I create myself. If you can't swim, you shouldn't jump in the water hoping someone will pull you out."

"But that someone wouldn't be a friend if he didn't do it. You understand friendship as freedom; I understand it as obligation. My friend is the same as I. If I protect him, I protect myself. Do I really need to say this?"

PART 2

"No. And my father is dragging out a needless conversation, so he won't have to tell what he did to me. Did you know that he hid gold from me? A thousand ducats! I found them when I returned, in a chest under lock and key."

"I told you about it myself."

"You told me about it after I'd already found out."

"Why would I hide them? And from whom? The money is yours, do what you want with it. I'm not going to take it to the grave."

God bless his bones, the old man's mind still works!

"And even if I did hide it, is that really something bad? But I didn't, I forgot about it. Is that so unexpected from an old mind?"

From his lack of persistence, from the smile he wore as he listened to the old man's naive defense, not even trying to extract some more convincing explanation, from their mutual spirit of cheerful tolerance, in which they resolved this apparent argument, I would have said that Hassan was not even discontent with the way everything had turned out. They had done their good deed and still had some ducats left. And their relatives no longer bothered them in the house.

But no matter, others would not have done even that much. And such generosity, with moderation, which maybe even stemmed from pity, was somehow closer and more familiar to me. It was more human; it had limits that I could perceive. It did not frighten me with a suicidal nature, or offend me with immoderation. Irresponsible generosity is the extravagance of a child who gives away everything he has, because he does not know the value of any of it.

On the second day of the Ramadan Bairam I was visited in the tekke by Piri-Voivode, the man who followed the movements of suspicious people, and for him that was everyone. He handed me a letter by one Luke of Dubrovnik, a friend of Hassan's, which had been sent to the Dubrovnik senate. It had been in the hands of some Dubrovnik merchants who had left the kasaba that morning with their loads of merchandise.

"Why did you take this?"

"Read it, and you'll see why."

"Is it important?"

"Read it, and you'll see if it is."

"Where are the merchants?"

"They've gone. Read it, and tell me whether they should have."

The devil himself had hung that man around my neck, that stubborn, incorruptible, distrustful idiot who would surely watch his own mother with suspicious eyes. Understanding nothing, but accusing everyone of everything, he buried me in reports, remembering them and later inquiring as to how each of them had been resolved. Half of my troubles, and I had enough, came to me from him, and I had already begun to think, considering him a form of divine punishment, that everyone must have his own Piri-Voivode. Only mine was the worst. I even suspected that he had been assigned to me on purpose, as a subordinate who would watch over me (and they could not have chosen anyone better). He was not anyone's man; he served nothing other than his own stupidity, and that was enough to drive me into a rage three times a day. Yet he was invulnerable. At the beginning I would try in vain to bring him to his senses; later I despaired of it. He hardly listened to me, holding his head high, arrogant and scornful, or sincerely surprised, doubting my intelligence and honesty, and torturing me further with his unbearable conscientiousness. The only thing left for me to do was to strangle him when I finally lost control of my anger, or to flee head over heels when I could no longer bear it. Worst of all was that you could find a thousand reasons to call him a fool, but not a single one to proclaim that he was dishonest. Within him there raged the principle of some monstrous justice and the passionate desire for all people to be punished, for anything. And all of my severity was insufficient for him. Others accused me of cruelty; he reproached me for leniency. My enemies agreed with both one and the other.

He told how highwaymen had attacked the Dubrovnik merchants at the foot of the mountain, and before they could fight them off one of their horses got away, galloped off toward the kasaba, and wandered into some village. The Dubrovnik merchants looked for it in vain, and left without having found it, because they were in a hurry to cross the mountains before dark. Piri-Voivode learned of the horse and found it at once, making the peasants give back everything that they had taken (and I am sure that they would have given him even their own possessions, not just someone else's). That was how he found the letter, and took it to the saraf* Salomon so he would read it to him, since he did not know the Latin alphabet.

My head began to spin from that intricate tale and its barely tangible thread of events, to which no reasonable man would have paid any attention, but Piri-Voivode brought it to completion, chasing shadows and fishing a spy's report out of it!

He stood in front of me and waited. I read the letter and learned what I already knew, that foreigners write about what they see and hear in other lands. Everyone knows it and everyone does it, but everyone is astonished when someone is caught in the act. I read the letter and breathed a sigh of relief: there was nothing about Hassan that might have cast some suspicion on him, or about me that might have insulted me. The Dubrovnik merchant wrote mostly about the vizier and the way the land was ruled. Parts of it were accurate, to be sure, but they were not pleasant to read. ("Chaotic administration has indeed sapped the strength of the land. . . . You should see what imbeciles they are, those kaimakams and mutesellims: you would be surprised how it is possible that those men, who do not at all even belong to upright society, can have power. . . . A net of spies, consisting of officials and secret informants, is spread out as if this were some land in the Occident. . . . The vizier has introduced a state of lawlessness, and equated himself with the empire, and whoever does not accede to his demands is an enemy. . . . In general he appoints, shuffles and dismisses his officials and rules the land according to his own whim; he has made it known on several occasions that he does not know the laws. . . . He is odious to Muhammedan and Christian alike. But the government cannot rid itself of him so easily, because in the last seven years he has amassed quite a lot of ducats, and supports himself in Constantinople with them. . . . All of his family are in with him. . . . With the help of this immoral, cruel, and treacherous gang he sits on the backs of the people, so that no one dares utter a word. . . . This system of terror and police, of course, has naturally made Bosnia the dead limb of the empire, since no one believes his neighbor any more, or a father his son, a friend his friend, since all of them fear Osman's black men and are happiest if no one notices them . . ." The purchase of the confiscated lands in the Posavina was also mentioned, as well as the price at which they were bought, a trifle, and the names of the friends and *lovers* of the vizier's entourage, and everything that they took, acquired, and seized. The Catholic man had not sat here in Bosnia with closed ears and eyes!)

"Terrible," I said because of Piri-Voivode, who was waiting with interest for my reaction.

"He should be arrested."

"It's not easy to arrest a foreigner."

"Can a foreigner do anything he wants?"

"No. I'll consult the mufti."

"Consult him. But the man should be arrested first."

"Maybe. I'll see."

He went out, very discontent.

What a mess! If he had not been nosing around where he should not have, I would at least not have had to worry about this. I had not known anything about it and it had been no concern of mine. Now I knew about it and it had to concern me. But whatever I did, I might make a mistake, and my conscience, on which I had relied so much, could not help me at all. It is moments such as those that make a man's hair turn gray prematurely.

The mufti would not even hear of discussing business matters on the Bairam. He did not really want to ordinarily, but it was not his opinion that was important to me—rather his name.

The musellim was not at home. I was told that he had gone to the bazaar. I found him in his office. On the Bairam! He already knew everything.

"He has to be arrested," he said without hesitation.

"And if we're making a mistake?"

"We'll apologize."

I was surprised by his resolve, it was very unusual. It would have been best not to do what he advised me, because he did not wish me well—that I knew. But if I obeyed, the responsibility would not lie with me alone.

"It looks as though that's best."

I agreed, though I was not convinced.

Piri-Voivode freed me from that worry, but saddled me with another. He came to tell us, bitter because it had happened, and satisfied that his suspicions had been confirmed, that the Dubrovnik merchant had fled the kasaba with Hassan's help. They had gone on foot to the outlying fields, and there Hassan's men had been waiting with horses for the merchant. Hassan had come back alone.

"Unfortunate," said the musellim, shaking his head.

Everything about him seemed worried, his voice, his hunched shoulders, the hand stroking his beard, everything, except a barely visible smirk on his thin lips. It would be strange if he did not report to the vali that he had been in favor of arresting the man, but that, unfortunately, he did not make the decisions.

Piri-Voivode was already clearing himself of any guilt and making accusations: "I said he should have been arrested."

"Unfortunate," the musellim repeated, driving a nail into my forehead.

And yet I myself knew just how unfortunate it was. The Dubrovnik merchant was no longer guilty, since he was gone. The culprits were those who were still here. Hassan was guilty. And I was guilty, because I was his friend, and because I had let the merchant escape. Guilty for the deeds of others, for their loyalties and stupidities. Guilty before the vali, who was my protector.

We sent for Hassan at once, and I was afraid that he would be scornful, hot-tempered, and insulted that we were questioning him. And I could not warn him and persuade him to be cautious since rashness would not help him. I only hoped that he would understand both our positions, and I calmed down completely when I heard how he answered. It's true, he said, the Dubrovnik merchant has gone home; he was in a hurry. He received news that his mother is on her deathbed. He lent him his men and horses, because there were no rested horses at the post station. And he saw him to the fields, as he always sees off his friends. They talked about ordinary things, so ordinary he can hardly remember them, but he'll try if it's really necessary, although he can't see how that could be of any importance. His friend did not tell him about any report ("A spy's report," the musellim explained). He thinks it very strange, since the man was involved only in business, and wasn't interested in anything else. And he persuaded Hassan to send caravans and goods to Dubrovnik, instead of Split[3] and Trieste, if he ever took that up again. He didn't leave with the other Dubrovnik merchants, because he received the letter from home only after they had already left (that's easy to check: the man who had brought the letter is still in the inn), and he packed up and left, taking only the most important things with him.

When we showed him the report, he looked it over and

shook his head, expressing surprise that his friend would write it. He doesn't know, of course, because they've never corresponded, so he can't recognize the handwriting. But it's possible to recognize someone's thoughts, and that's exactly what he doesn't see here. But if it's truly his, and from everything it seems it is, then the man has two souls, the latter of which he's never showed him before. He laughed, reading the report, and said that he would be sorry he came out looking like a fool, if any harm could come from this letter. But fortunately, none can, since what's written here could be written by anyone about anyone else's land, and no one's surprised by such things any more. It's not his place to give us any advice, nor is it his habit, but he doesn't think there's any reason to stoke up a fire if there's no need to, or to put it out when it's already gone out on its own. Scandal and insult have been avoided, because scandal isn't what's done, and especially not what isn't done, but rather what's spread by word of mouth. All that's left are a few thwarted intentions. So then there's no insult here either, unless we're looking for it. And thus, some good can even be extracted from all of this. No, he certainly doesn't condone such behavior—although for a long time he's not thought that people are angels—but he doesn't want to say anything bad about his friend, because that wouldn't be nice. Nor does he want to excuse him, because that's no longer any use to anyone. He can only speak for himself and, although he's not guilty, he's ready to express his regret, both to us and to the vizier, that he was involved in such an idiotic affair, which has caused us more worry than it's worth.

I listened to him with interest. I doubted that he did not know the reason for the merchant's flight, but he gave the impression that his conscience was clear, and it must have been, because neither the letter nor the vizier's reputation were of any concern to him. He had a calm and convincing answer to everything. Maybe I alone detected a scornful tone in what he said, because I followed his every word attentively, glad that he was successfully casting suspicion away from himself. Once again I realized how much I cared about him, and how much I would be hurt if he got into trouble. I would not easily have let anyone take out his revenge on him, but I was glad that he acquitted himself. I preferred that to what I might have been forced to do.

I did not worry much about my standing with the vizier: he needed me.

On Friday, after the noon prayer, Mullah-Yusuf informed me that the vali's defterdar was waiting for me in the court-house. What the hell had brought him here in such bad weather?

I stopped by the musellim's office. He had gone home a little earlier, he had come down with a fever, they told me. I knew which fever that was, it saved him from anything unpleasant, but knowing this did not make me feel any better.

The defterdar met me politely, giving me the vali's greetings and saying that he would like to take care of the reason for his visit immediately, and that he hoped it would not take long. He was tired from the long journey on horseback, and he would like to bathe and get some rest as soon as possible.

"Is the matter really so urgent?"

"One might say it is. Today I still have to report to the vali about what's been done."

He said everything at once, without hesitation, stressing at the start that the vali had been angered and offended by the letter (this was intended for me, to warn me about the gravity of the entire affair), and that he was disappointed with me as well, because I had allowed the Dubrovnik merchant to escape when I could have prevented it. (Those words had left here long ago and were evidently returning to their birthplace!) He had written the Dubrovnik senate and requested that the guilty party be punished for lies and the insult he had inflicted on him, thus also insulting the land that he, according to the emperor's mercy, governed. If the guilty party were not appropriately punished, and if he were not informed of it, along with the due apology, he would be forced to forbid all trade and contacts with Dubrovnik, because that would mean there was neither friendship nor desire on their part to maintain good relations, which were beneficial to both of us, but more to them than to us. He was likewise sorry that our hospitality, which we do not refuse anyone with good intentions, was repaid with loathsome fabrications about both himself and the most reputable people in the province, which showed how little love for the truth and how much hatred there was in the heart of the aforementioned merchant. Therefore, if they acted as was proper, and if our relations remained healthy, which he desired with all of his heart, and which was certainly the desire of the honorable senate, they could send a real friend, both ours and theirs—and there were certainly such men around, since our relations had not begun yesterday—a man of polish, who would respect the customs and rulers of the land receiving him, and who would neither spit on our welcome nor behave in an undignified manner, to both his own disgrace and the disgrace of the republic that sent him, nor associate with the worst kinds of people, who are found everywhere, and also here, who certainly did not have good intentions for themselves or the land that bore them, and whose services the aforementioned merchant had bought in a shameful manner, which was in any case known to the honorable senate.

"You must know who the vizier is thinking of."

"I don't."

"You do."

He was plump, soft, round, wrapped in a broad silk garment. He resembled an old woman—like everyone who for years hangs around those in power.

"The vali wants him arrested."

"Why arrested? He acquitted himself. He's not guilty."

"You see, you figured out who I'm talking about."

Yes, I figured it out, I knew everything as soon as I heard you'd arrived. I knew you'd want his head, but I won't let you have it. I'd give you anyone else, but you can't have him.

I told the defterdar that the honorable vizier's wish had always been my command. Had I not done everything he asked of me? But now I begged him to give up his idea, for the sake of the vizier's reputation and justice. Hassan was loved and valued by everyone, and they would not be happy if we arrested him, especially since people knew that he was not guilty. If the vali was not informed about this, I would go to explain everything to him and to ask him for mercy.

"He's informed about everything."

"Then why is he demanding this?"

"Isn't the Dubrovnik merchant guilty? Then Hassan is as well. Maybe even more. We can expect a foreigner to be an enemy of this land, but not one of our own. It's unnatural."

I wish I would have been bold enough to ask: Are the vizier and this land one and the same? But in conversations with men of power one must swallow all reasonable arguments and accept their way of thinking, which means that one is already defeated.

I maintained that Hassan was not an enemy and that he was not guilty, but it was no use. The defterdar dismissed it all with a wave of his hand, saying that we had believed his impudent story blindly.

"Didn't he maintain that the Dubrovnik merchant couldn't get fresh horses at the post station? But they didn't even go there."

"Who said that? The musellim?"

"It doesn't matter who said it. It's true; we checked it out. And not only that, there are other lies in his story. Have you talked with the man who apparently brought his friend the letter from Dubrovnik? No, you haven't. Hassan lied, and he's guilty, and therefore an arrest is in order. And as to why the vali wishes for you to do it, that's so it won't be said that he commits violence, because it's not violence, and he doesn't want to meddle in your affairs. Everyone must take care of his own affairs, each according to his conscience."

"According to which conscience? Hassan is my best friend, the only one I have."

"So much the better. Everyone will see that it's not a matter of revenge, but justice."

"I beg you and the vizier to spare me in this case. If I agreed, I'd be doing something terrible."

"You'd be doing something smart. Because the vali wonders how it is that they could find out about everything so quickly."

And so, with his limp hands he began tightening a stiff noose around my neck.

"Do you mean to say the vali suspects me?"

"I mean to say it would be best for a judge if he didn't have friends. Ever. Not a single one. Because people make mistakes."

"And if he does have one?"

"Then he has to choose: either his friend or justice."

"I don't want to sin against either my friend or justice. He's not guilty. I can't do this."

"That's your business. The vizier isn't forcing you to do anything. Only . . ."

I knew that *only*. It flew around me like a black bird, surrounded me like a ring of spears pointed at me. I knew that, but I told myself resolutely: I won't let you have my friend. This was a courage that brought me no relief. The shadow around me turned blacker still.

"Only," he said, shivering, rubbing his fat hands to warm them, "you probably know how many men there are who don't like you, and how many complaints have been sent to Constantinople, all of which demand your head. The vizier has kept most of them. He's your defense; without his protection, the hatred harbored against you by other men would've destroyed you long ago. If you don't know that, you're a fool. And if you do know, how can you be such an ingrate? And why did the vizier protect you? Because you have pretty eyes? No. Because he thought he could rely on you. But if he sees he can't, why should he protect you any more? Authority isn't made of friendships, but alliances. And by the way, it's strange that you're severe with everyone, but gentle only with the vali's enemies. And the vali considers the friends of his enemies to be his enemies as well. If the vali and the land have been insulted, and you don't want to defend them, then you too have gone over to the other side."

"Read this," he said and handed me a piece of paper.

Barely making out the words and barely understanding their meaning, I read a letter written by the deputy of the Constantinople mullah, in which he asked the vali why he so stubbornly defended the Kadi Ahmed Nuruddin, who had incited the rebellion at the bazaar and, out of personal hatred, brought about the death of the former kadi, an honorable alim and judge, which had been proved by the charges of his widow and the testimony of witnesses. And other charges had been made by the most respected men, embittered by Ahmed Nuruddin's self-will and desire to seize all power, whereby he had sinned against the sharia* and against the high imperial wish that authority, which is given to the Padishah* by God and which he transfers to his servants, should nowhere be in the hands of a single man, because that is the path to oppression and injustice. But if none of that was true, and if the vali had a different opinion and other reasons, he should contact the mullah's deputy, so that he would know how to act accordingly.

The letter stunned me.

I had known about intrigues and complaints, but I was seeing proof of them for the first time. It was as if an arrow had flown past, barely missing me. I was afraid.

"What do you have to say?"

What could I have said? I was silent. Not out of defiance.

"Will you write the order?"

O, Allah, help me, I can neither write it nor refuse to write it. It would be best to die.

"Will you write it?"

What are they trying to make me do? To condemn a friend, the only being that I have kept for my unsatisfied and hungry love. What will I be then? A worthless man who's ashamed of his own self, the loneliest wretch in the world. He's preserved everything that's human in me. I'll kill myself if I hand him over. Don't make me do this; it's too cruel.

I told that merciless man: "Don't make me do this. It's too cruel."

"You won't write it?"

"No. I can't do it."

"However you want. You've read the letter."

"I have, and I know what to expect. But understand me, good man! Would you ask me to kill my father or brother? And he's more than either of them to me. He means more to me than my own self. I hold on to him like an anchor. Without that man the world would be a dark cavern for me. He's all that I have, and I won't give him up. Do whatever you want with me, I won't betray him, because I don't want to extinguish the last ray of light within me. I'll die, but I won't give him up."

"That's pretty," the defterdar mocked me, "but not smart."

"If you had a friend, you'd know that it's both pretty and smart."

Unfortunately, I did not say that or anything similar. Later I thought how it might have been honorable if I had.

But everything happened completely differently.

"Will you write the order?" the defterdar asked.

"I have to," I said, looking at the letter, looking at the threat in front of me.

"You don't have to. Do what your conscience tells you."

Ugh, leave my conscience alone! I'll do what my fear tells me to do, what my terror tells me to do, I'll bid farewell to my nice ideas about myself. I'll be what I must: scum. May shame fall over them, they've made me become something that's always disgusted me.

But at the time I did not even think that. I felt bad, I felt that something terrible was happening, so inhuman it was simply inconceivable. Only that, too, was suppressed, obscured by a fear that overcame me, like a daze, and a wild gurgling in my blood that stifled me with agitated heat. I wanted to go outside, to get a breath of fresh air, to escape the black haze, but I knew that everything had to be resolved immediately, at that moment, and that then I would rid myself of all of it. I would climb a hill, the highest crest, and would stay until evening, alone. I would not think, I would breathe. Breathe.

"Your hands are shaking," the defterdar said in surprise. "Are you really so sorry?"

I felt sick to my stomach, I wanted to throw up.

"If you're so sorry, why did you sign?"

I wanted to reply to that mockery, to say something, I did not know what, but I kept silent, with my head lowered, for a long time, until I caught myself, and began to ask, stuttering:

"I can't stay here any longer. I need to go somewhere, anywhere. Only far away."

"Why?"

"Because of people. Because of everything."

"You're absolutely worthless!" said the defterdar calmly, with profound contempt, although I did not know and was unable to wonder why he despised me. It did not even hurt; I just kept repeating those ugly words to myself like a prayer, without understanding their real meaning. The only thing living inside me was a feeling of utter peril, as before a hunt. Everything had closed around me; there was no way out. But it was not as if it did not matter: I was afraid.

"Who'll go to get Hassan?"

"Piri-Voivode."

PART 2

"Let him take him to the fortress."

I went out into the corridor and ran into Mullah-Yusuf. He was returning to his room from somewhere.

When he looked at me, his eyes froze, only for a moment, for a single moment, and it hit me: he had been listening to our conversation. And he knew. If he left, he would inform Hassan. It was he who had told him about the merchant. How had it not occurred to me?!

"Don't go anywhere, I'll need you soon."

He bowed his head and went into his room.

We waited, silently.

The defterdar dozed on the divan, but opened his eyes at every noise, raising his heavy eyelids quickly.

When Piri-Voivode returned, I knew that it was all over. I did not dare to ask the defterdar what would happen to Hassan. I no longer had the right to do that, nor did I have the strength for such hypocrisy.

I was left alone. Where could I go, anyway?

I did not hear when Mullah-Yusuf came into my room; his steps were silent. He stood by the door and watched me calmly. I saw for the first time that he was not uneasy before me. Because now we were equals.

He was the only one I had left. I hated him, found him repulsive, and feared him, but still, at that moment I wanted him to come to me, for us to be silent together. Or for him to tell me something, or I him, anything. For him to place his hand on my knee, at least. To look at me differently, not the way he was. Even to reproach me. But no, he had no right to that. Even at the very thought of it I felt resistance, even rage, and I knew I would accept either a tender word, or nothing. I was on the verge of becoming a broken man or a beast.

"You said you'd need me."

"I don't anymore."

"May I go?"

"Do you know what's happened?"

"Yes."

"I'm not to blame. They made me, they threatened me."

He was silent.

"I had no choice. They put a knife to my throat."

He kept silent, completely hostile, not allowing me to approach him.

"Why don't you say something? Do you want to show your condemnation? You have no right to that. Not you."

"It would be good if you left the kasaba, Sheikh-Ahmed. It's terrible when people shun you. I know very well."

No, he should not have talked like that to me. It was worse than a reproach; it was cool advice from afar, scornful exultation. But still, it was as if my heavy heart expected something, anything, be it comfort or insult, that would bring it back to life. Maybe insult was even better; comfort would have completely exhausted me.

"You're absolutely worthless," I said, choking as I repeated the words that were hurting me so much. "It was precisely because you know so well that I thought we'd speak differently. You're not very clever; you chose a bad time for your revenge. No, people won't shun me. Maybe they'll watch me with fear, but they won't scorn me. And you won't, either, you can be sure of that. They forced me to sacrifice my friend; why would I care about anyone else?!"

"That won't make it any easier for you, Sheikh-Ahmed."

"Maybe it won't. But it won't be easier for anyone else, either. I'll remember that you're also to blame for his suffering."

"If scolding me will cause the burden to fall from your heart, just go ahead."

"If the merchant hadn't escaped, Hassan would now be sitting peacefully at home. And it wasn't a fortune-teller who told the merchant what was going to happen to him."

"He knew the letter had been taken. Did he really need anything else?"

"You're the one who knows that."

PART 2

"Are you asking or accusing me? It seems it's really hardest for those who stay here."

"You didn't stay. You were kept here. And now get out!"

He left without turning around.

It was no use. Misfortunes come like jackdaws, in flocks.

The next day we slept through the morning prayer, both the defterdar and I. The defterdar did so because of his long journey and a job well done; I because of a sleepless night and sleep that overcame me just before dawn. But I was the first one to hear the terrible news, and that was proper, since it concerned me more than anyone else. And it was proper that I heard it from Piri-Voivode; it was revolting, as he was himself.

At first I did not understand what he was telling me, it was so unlikely and unexpected. Later it seemed just as unlikely, but I understood.

"We carried out your order," that hateful man said. "The dizdar was a little surprised, but I told him it was none of his business. It's his place to obey, just as it is mine."

"Which order?"

"Your order. About Hassan."

"What are you talking about? About what happened yesterday?"

"No. About what happened last night."

"What happened last night?"

"We gave Hassan over to the guards."

"Which guards?"

"I don't know. Guards. To take him to Travnik."

"Did the defterdar give you the order?"

"No. You did."

"Wait a minute. If you're drunk, you should go sleep it off. If you're not . . ."

"I never drink, Kadi-effendi. I'm not drunk, and I don't need any sleep."

"If only you were, it would be better for both of us. Did you actually see that the order was from me? Who brought it?"

"Of course I did! It was written by your hand, stamped with your seal. Mullah-Yusuf brought it."

Then I sat down—my legs could no longer hold me up—and listened to a pretty tale of others' impudence and my misfortune.

Sometime after midnight Mullah-Yusuf had awakened him and showed him my order to the dizdar of the fortress, to hand over the prisoner Hassan to the guards in the presence of Piri-Voivode; accompanied by Mullah-Yusuf, they would take him to Travnik. It was also written in the order that the aforementioned Hassan's hands should not be untied, and that he should be taken out of the kasaba before dawn. The guards remained on horseback at the fortress gates; the two of them went to wake up the dizdar and handed him my order. The dizdar grumbled, complaining that if he had been told of it earlier, he wouldn't have sent the prisoner to the lower dungeons. This way everybody would have to wait a little, and he would miss a night's sleep—he didn't know when it was night and when it was day anymore. But Piri-Voivode told him what he mentioned a little before, that it's their place to obey, and then Mullah-Yusuf also started complaining that this was our work and not his, and there, he even had to do things he didn't want to, since it was important, and the vali wanted it done and didn't want anyone to hear of Hassan's departure; people here are crazy, as we'd recently seen, and it'd be better if everything were done quietly and unnoticed. He also added that he'd asked me to send Piri-Voivode with Hassan and the guards, since he wasn't skilled at riding; he'd get sores before they reached Travnik, but I'd said that I couldn't give up Piri-Voivode at all, I needed him here, he's like my right hand, for which Piri-Voivode is very grateful. (Never say you've met the most stupid man in the world; it can always happen that someone else will surpass him!) When they brought Hassan, whose hands were bound, he requested that they untie him, asked where they were taking him, and called them cowardly night-owls, complaining that they'd woken him from the sweetest sleep. But when Mullah-Yusuf calmly explained that they were only acting according to orders, he asked him when he would finally grow up and begin to think with his own head and not according to orders; it's about time, he's surely of age. Or is it that he's planning to take after Piri-Voivode? Hassan didn't recommend this at all, because Yusuf would never reach such perfection, and he could only become a smaller Piri-Voivode. Piri-Voivode did not understand that, but he thought it was some kind of insult. After that Hassan thanked the dizdar for the comfortable lodging and the complete silence with which he had been surrounded; he'd liked it so much that, out of gratitude, he wished the dizdar the same. Piri-Voivode cut off that chatter and ordered them to move out. "You're right," Hassan said, "you've got so much work, it'd be a pity to lose any time." When he saw the guards he asked: "What do I have to do, agas and effendis, to leave you nice memories of myself? Will I ride or trail behind you on foot?" "Stop your babbling!" a stout guard responded, raised him onto a horse, and also tied his legs with a rope. "Greetings to my friend the kadi," he shouted back as they started out.

"And they left at a trot."

"How do you know?"

"Now it doesn't matter what I know. And it seems it's not yet clear to you."

"What should be clear to me?"

"That they escaped. And that you helped them."

"But I saw your order."

"I didn't give any order. Mullah-Yusuf wrote it."

"And the guards? They even tied him up."

"They probably untied him in the first street they turned into. They were certainly his men."

"I don't know whether they were his men or not, but I do know the handwriting was yours. And your seal. I've received more than one order from you. I know your every letter. No one else could've written that."

"I'm telling you, you fool, that I didn't know. I've just heard everything from you."

"Oh no, that's not true. You knew everything. You planned it out. You wrote the order. For your friend. Only why did you have to ruin *me*? Why me? Couldn't you find someone else? I've been serving honorably and honestly for twenty years, and now I'm your sacrificial lamb. Mullah-Yusuf will also confirm that."

"Mullah-Yusuf won't ever come back."

"So you see, you know!"

It was useless to say anything, as far as he was concerned I was the only culprit.

The defterdar came in, wiping his fat face with a silk kerchief, red from excitement, but he spoke in a soft and seemingly calm voice.

"What's this, dervish, have you begun to mock us openly? Well, that's fine. You've made your move; now it's someone else's turn to make theirs. But tell me, what were you counting on? Or doesn't it matter to you?"

"I didn't do anything. I'm as surprised as you are."

"Then what's this? Your order, and your seal."

"That was written by my clerk, Mullah-Yusuf."

"Tell me about it! Why would your clerk do that? Is he related to that Hassan? Or a friend, like you?"

"I don't know."

"He wasn't his friend," Piri-Voivode cut in. "Mullah-Yusuf was the kadi's man. He obeyed him in everything."

"You're not exactly smart, Ahmed Nuruddin. Whom were you trying to fool with this bold game?"

"If I'd put my name on that order, then I'd really be a fool. Or I wouldn't be here. Isn't that clear to you?"

"You thought that we're a bunch of fools and that we'd believe your little fairy tale."

"I'll swear on the Koran."

PART 2

"I'm sure you will. But the matter couldn't be any clearer. Hassan is your friend—your best and only friend—you said so yourself. Yesterday I saw how much you care about him. And your clerk didn't have any personal reason to free the prisoner. He was only obeying you, as your trusted man. As he's also fled, you have to lay all the blame on him. All right: if such a case came before you, what would your verdict be?"

"If I knew the man, as you do me, I'd believe what he says."

"What a convincing argument!"

"I told him, too: you wrote everything. For your friend."

"You shut up! They had you right where they wanted you, like a sprig of basil in their vest pocket. You're just the one to decorate all this mess. The vali will be overjoyed."

Thus I found myself in a strange position. The more I tried to acquit myself, the less they believed my story, until it became unconvincing even to me. People now associated my name with friendship and loyalty; some with condemnation, others with approval. I would have taken one and refused the other, but it seems that they always go together. I accepted the more agreeable of the two. Hafiz-Muhammed almost kissed my hand; Ali-hodja called me a man who was not afraid to be one; the townspeople looked at me with respect; strangers brought gifts and left them with Mustafa, for me; and Hassan's father, Ali-aga, sent me his particular gratitude through Hadji-Sinanuddin. I could not fend off this quiet admiration. And so I began to grow accustomed to the idea and to accept people's grace silently, as a reward for the greatest betrayal that I had ever committed. Was friendship really so far beyond people's suspicion? Or were they touched because it was so uncommon? It resembled a bad joke: I had done all sorts of things in life, both kind and beneficial, in order to gain people's respect, but it had been brought to me by a shameful deed, which everyone considered noble. I knew I did not deserve any of their respect, but it suited me, and sometimes I was pained by the thought that I should have in fact acted that way. Of course, nothing would have been any different, except within me. And still, it was better this way (not good, but better); people respected me as if I had done that deed, and I was sure I would clear myself of the charges, because I knew I had not done anything. But when a letter arrived for the mufti from Hassan and Mullah-Yusuf, from somewhere near the western border, in which they acquitted me, telling the whole story, people became firmly convinced that I was in league with them (because why would they defend me if I had done them wrong?). I viewed the letter as evidence I would use to convince everyone of my innocence. I hoped that I would now find enough witnesses on my behalf, if it came to interrogations.

But it did not come to interrogations. Everything was settled in my absence, although the final part could only be settled with me.

Toward evening Kara-Zaim came to find me. He was upset, more on his own account than on mine. Maybe he would not even have come if it were not time for me to pay him his monthly salary; then he usually brought me news he considered important. He also thought this news was important, and this time he was right.

First he wanted to raise the amount, because he had had to pay the mufti's servant. He had found everything out from him.

"Is it so important?"

"Well, I think it is. Did you know that the courier arrived this morning from Constantinople?"

"I know. But I don't know why."

"On account of you."

"On account of me?"

"Swear you won't give me away. Put your hand on the Koran. Like that. They're going to imprison you tonight."

"Did he bring any kind of order?"

"It seems he did. The katul-ferman."

"So they're going to strangle me in the fortress."

"So they're going to strangle you."

"What can I do? That's fate."

"Can you flee?"

"Where can I flee to?"

"I don't know. It's just a thought. Don't you have anyone to help you? Like you did Hassan."

"I didn't help Hassan."

"It's all the same to you now. You did, and let it remain at that. You did, you helped him; don't tear down your own monument to yourself."

"Thank you for coming. You've exposed yourself to danger for me."

"What can I do, Sheikh-Ahmed? Poverty drove me to it. And you should know I'm sorry."

"I believe you."

"You've helped me a lot. I came to life with you. My wife and I speak of you often. And now we will even more so. Do you want to kiss one another farewell, Sheikh-Ahmed? We were once on the same battlefield. They left me cut up and you in one piece, but you see, fate wants you to go first."

"Let's kiss one another farewell, Kara-Zaim. And speak well of me now and then."

He went away with tears in his eyes, and I was left in my dusky room, stunned by what I had heard.

I could not doubt it, it was certainly true. I had been trying in vain to deceive myself with crazy hopes: it could not have turned out differently. The vali had raised a floodgate, and the torrent was carrying me away.

Helpless, I repeated: death, the end. And I did not fully comprehend it, as I once had in the fortress dungeons, when I had waited for it with indifference. Now it seemed far away to me, incomprehensible, although I knew everything. Death, the end. And suddenly, as if my eyes had been opened by the darkness threatening me, I was struck with the terror of nonexistence, of that nothingness. So that is death, so that is the end! A final encounter with our most horrible fate.

No, never! I want to live! No matter what happens, I want to live. Even if only on one leg or on a narrow precipice until death, but I want to live. I must! I'll fight, I'll bite with my teeth, I'll run until the skin falls off the soles of my feet. I'll find someone to help me, I'll put a knife to someone's throat and demand that they help me—I helped others!—and even if I didn't, it doesn't matter, I'll run from the end and from death.

Resolute, with the strength that stems from fear and from the desire to live, I started for the door. Calmly, only calmly, so rashness or a nervous look won't give me away. Night will fall soon; the darkness will hide me, I'll run quicker than a greyhound, more quietly than an owl; dawn will find me deep in some forest, in some distant region. I just shouldn't breathe so noisily, as if I were already on the run, and my heart shouldn't beat so wildly; it'll give me away, like a bell.

But suddenly I collapsed. My courage disappeared, along with my hope. And strength. It was all in vain.

Piri-Voivode was standing in front of the courthouse, and three armed guards were walking in the street. For me, I knew.

I left for the tekke.

I did not turn around to look at the courthouse. Maybe I had been there for the last time, but I felt nothing. I did not want to, nor could I think about anything. I was empty inside, as if my insides had been pulled out.

In the street, by the bridge, a youth came up to me. "Forgive me. I wanted to go into the courthouse, but they wouldn't let me see you. I'm from Devetak."

He laughed when he said that, and explained immediately. "Don't be angry because I'm laughing. I always do that, especially when I'm nervous."

"Are you nervous?"

"Well, yes. I've been repeating what I'll say to you for a whole hour."

PART 2

"Have you said it?"

"I've forgotten everything."

And he laughed again. He did not look nervous at all.

From Devetak! My mother was from Devetak, I spent half of my childhood in that village. The same hills had surrounded us; we had watched the same river, the same poplars along the bank.

Had he brought my home in his laughing eyes so that I would see it once more, before the end?

What did he want? Had he left his village, as I once had? Was he seeking paths in life wider than those in Devetak? Or was fate playing a joke, to remind me with him of everything, before my great journey? Or was he a sign, a reassurance sent to me by God?

Why did this village boy, who is closer to me than he thinks, appear now, of all times? Has he come to take my place in this world?

Piri-Voivode and the guards were following us. They were waiting at every turn; they would leave me only one way out.

"Where are you going to stay tonight?"

"Nowhere."

"Let's go to the tekke."

"Are those your men?"

"Yes. Don't pay any attention to them."

"What are they protecting you from?"

"It's just a custom."

"Are you the most important man in the kasaba?"

"No."

When we went in, he sat down on the carpet in my room. The feeble candlelight shimmered over the depressions in his bony face, and there was an enormous shadow behind him on the floor and the wall; I watched how he ground the plain tekke food with his protruding, iron jaws, maybe even unaware of what he was eating, because he was wondering how this encounter would end. But he was not worried, either, or unconfident. I had been all of that, then. I remember my first meal. I hardly got three bites down; they almost choked me.

We were different, and yet the same. That was I, different, made of different matter, beginning the same path all over again.

Maybe I would do everything the same again, but everything around me is growing dark with sorrow.

"You surely want to remain in the kasaba."

"How did you know?"

"Aren't you afraid of the town?"

"Why would I be afraid?"

"It's not easy here."

"But is it easy where we are, Ahmed-effendi?"

"Do you expect a lot?"

"Half of your good fortune would be enough for me. Is that a lot?"

"I wish you more than that."

He laughed cheerfully.

"May God hear your words. And I've had a good start. I didn't think in my wildest dreams that you'd receive me like this."

"You've come at a good time."

"At a good time for me."

Maybe. Why should this path be the same for everyone?

I watched him with interest, maybe even with tenderness, as if I were watching myself, as I had once been, inconceivably young, without experience, without thorns in my heart, with no fear of life. I could barely keep myself from taking him by his bony, hard, confident hand, and reviving the past with closed eyes. Just one more time, if only for a brief while.

In my look he saw a sorrow that had nothing to do with him. He asked, freed by my unexpected attentiveness.

"You're looking at me strangely, as if you recognize me."

"I'm remembering a youth who also came to the kasaba, long ago."

PART 2

"What happened to him?"
"He grew old."
"Let's hope that's the worst of it."
"Are you tired?"
"Why do you ask?"
"I'd like for us to talk."
"We can, of course—the whole night, if you wish."
"Who's your father?"
"Emin Boshnyak."
"Then we're related. And closely, too."
"Yes, we are."
"Well, why didn't you say that?"
"I was waiting for you to ask."
"How old are you?"
"Twenty."
"You're not twenty."
"Almost nineteen."

I was choking with excitement. We talked about him, about the old hodja, about people I knew, skirting around the only thing that really interested me. Not that I wanted to find out—I wanted rather to talk, to touch everything again, since it had already happened that fate sent him to me on this of all nights, to immerse myself in thoughts about what had been reality only once, and was now only a shadow. But that is all I have. The rest is not mine. The rest is horror.

"How are my father and mother?"
"Well, they're all right. It could be worse. Harun's death hit them hard. And the rest of us, too. Now they've calmed down a little, but they're still bitter. They take care of what they have to, and then sit and look into the fire. It's sad."

He laughed. His laughter was resonant, cheerful.

"Forgive me. It slips out, even when I'm feeling depressed. And so, they live on. People help them where they can. And they still have some of what you sent."

"What did I send?"

"Money. Fifty piasters. For us that's real wealth. And they don't need much. They eat like birds and mend what they have. That's not the worst of it."

Who had sent fifty piasters? Hassan, certainly. This is the night of unnecessary tenderness, the night of good tidings, before the very worst. It has not visited me for a long time, and never will again.

Why did I hesitate to go to the end? After tonight there will be no tenderness. There will be only the inevitable.

"And your parents, how are they? How is Emin?"

"They're healthy, thank God. But they live a meager life: either the river floods, or the sun scorches everything. Only my father is good-natured, and that makes everything easier. It's one misfortune to be poor, he says, and yet another to grieve about it. So this way even the one seems smaller."

"And your mother? Does she know you've come to me?"

"Yes, of course she does! My father says: he's got enough to worry about—meaning you. But my mother says: he won't cut his head off—meaning mine."

"Has she grown old?"

"No."

"She was beautiful."

"Do you really remember her?"

"Yes."

"She's still beautiful."

"I was coming back from the army then. It was twenty years ago."

"You'd been wounded."

"Who told you?"

"My mother."

Yes, I remember. Tonight I have been remembering everything. I was twenty years old then, or a little older, I came back from the war, from captivity, with fresh battle scars, newly healed or still tender, proud of my heroism, and sorrowful because of something that remained unclear to me after everything. Maybe because of a memory that I repeated over and over again, because of the solemnity of our sacrifice, which had elevated us to the heavens, so that afterward it was hard to walk the earth, empty and ordinary.

But one day stands out against the others.

I saw that image even in my sleep, when one early morning we decided, knowing that we were surrounded and that there was no way out, to die like soldiers of God the Divine. There were fifty of us in a wooded clearing, above a desolate autumn plain, over which smoke rose from the enemy campfires. They obeyed me; I was sure they all thought as I did. We performed the abdest with sand and dirt, since there was no water. I made the call to prayer, without lowering my voice; we said the morning prayer. We stripped down to our white shirts so we could move more easily, and, with our sabers unsheathed, went out of the forest just as the sun broke over the plain. I do not know how we looked, wretched or terrible: I did not think about that; I only felt a fire in my heart and limitless strength in my body. Afterward I thought I could see that line of young men in white shirts, with bare muscles, with sabers that reflected the light of the early sun, marching shoulder to shoulder in the plain. That was the purest hour of my life, the greatest self-forgetfulness, an alluring flash of light, a solemn silence in which all I could hear were my own steps, miles away. Kara-Zaim was surprised when I said that; he thought he was the only one who knows what a warrior feels (there is nothing I desire now so much as that feeling, but it cannot come back). They were afraid of us, and evaded us for a long time, waited to ambush us for a long time. There were many more of them than us, and a bloody massacre ensued that caused many a mother to wail, both ours and theirs. I was the first, and the first to fall, cut up, stabbed through, battered, but not immediately, not quickly. I carried my bloody saber in front of me for a long time, stabbing and hacking at anything that was not wearing a white shirt, and there were fewer and fewer white shirts. They turned crimson, like mine. The sky above us was a crimson sheet, the earth below us a crimson threshing floor. We saw crimson, we breathed crimson, we shouted crimson. But then everything turned black, turned into peace. When I woke up there was nothing more, except for a memory in me. I would close my eyes and relive that great moment, not wanting to know anything of defeat, of wounds, of the slaughter of fine men, not wanting to believe that ten of us had given up without a fight; I denied what was—it was ugly. I feverishly tried to preserve my image of our great sacrifice, in all of its flash and fire, trying not to let it fade. Afterwards, when the illusion vanished, I cried. In the spring I returned home from captivity, on muddy roads, without my saber, without strength, without joy, without my former self. I was holding on to a mere memory, like a talisman, but even that became weak; it lost its color and freshness, its vivacity and former meaning. I trudged silently onward, through the mud of the gloomy plains; I spent the nights in silence, in village bowers and inns; I walked in silence, in the spring rains, guessing my direction like an animal, driven by the desire to die in my homeland, among the people who had given me life.

I told the youth in simple, ordinary words, how it was when I came into the village that spring, twenty years ago. I told him for no reason, for myself, as if I were talking with myself, because it did not concern him. But without him I would not have been able to tell it. I would not have been able to talk with myself. I would have thought about tomorrow.

He watched me seriously, with surprise.

"And if you'd been healthy and happy, you wouldn't have come home?"

"When everything is lost a man seeks refuge, as if he were returning to his mother's womb."

"And after that?"

"After that he forgets. He's driven to it by his restlessness. He wants to be what he was not, or what he was. He runs away from his fortune and looks for another."

PART 2

"Then he's unhappy, if he thinks his fortune is always somewhere else."

"Maybe."

"And those flashes of light on the battlefield? I don't understand that. And why is that the purest hour in one's life?"

"Because a man forgets himself."

"What does he get from that? And what does anyone else get from it?"

He would never know anything of our enthusiasm. I do not know whether that is good or bad.

"And what happened then?"

"Didn't your mother tell you?"

"She says you were sad."

Yes, I was sad, and she knew it. She knew it even before she saw me. They had heard I was dead, and I felt that way, as if I had come back from the dead, or worse, as if I were going to die, from desolation, from some dull tranquillity, from misery, from darkness, from my horror at not knowing what had happened. I had been somewhere, flashes of the sun and crimson reflections pained me, because they flared out of the darkness, as during an illness. Something collapsed—there, where I had been and here, where I was supposed to be, it was washing away like a sandy bank when the water rises, and I do not know how I managed to float to the surface, or why.

My mother tried to heal me with charms, throwing a piece of hot lead into a cup of water over my head, because I kept silent when I was awake and screamed when I was asleep. They wrote amulets for me, in case I had fallen under a spell, took me to the mosque and said prayers, asking God and men for medicine, still more frightened that I agreed to everything, and that I did not care.

"Did your mother tell you anything else?"

"Yes. That you flirted with each other. My father always laughs when we talk about it. You're both happy, he says.

He, my father, because everyone thought you were dead; you, because you hadn't died. Because if my mother hadn't heard that you were dead, she wouldn't have married him. Like this everyone is all right, and all three of you are happy."

He knew a lot, but not everything. She waited even when she had heard; she would still have waited, God knows how much longer. She did not get married; they married her off. A few days before I arrived. Had I slept less, had I traveled nights as well, had I not been so exhausted, had the plains been smaller and the hills lower, I would have gotten back in time; she would not have married Emin, and I might not have left the village. And none of these painful things would have happened, not Harun's death, not this last night of mine. But maybe they would have, because there has to be a last night and there has to be something painful, always.

He wanted to know more.

"Was it hard for you when my mother got married?"

"Yes."

"And that's why you were sad?"

"Well, that, too. And because of my wounds and exhaustion, and because of my dead comrades."

"And then?"

"Nothing. You forget, you get over everything."

What did he want me to say to him? That I had not forgotten or gotten over it? That I did not care? His expression was tense as he looked at me; something within him remained unsatisfied. His laughter was forced, as if he were hiding some thought. Was it a son's jealousy about his mother's virtue, which he does not want to doubt? But something was disturbing him.

"Do you love your mother a lot?"

"Of course!"

"Do you have any brothers or sisters?"

"No."

"Did you talk about me often?"

"Yes. My mother and I. My father listens and laughs."

"Whose idea was it to send you to me?"

"My mother's. My father agreed to it."

"What did she tell you?"

"If Ahmed-effendi won't help you, she says, then no one will."

"Your father agreed. And you?"

"I did, too. You see, I've come."

"But you're not happy about it."

He blushed, his sunburned cheeks blazed with fire, and he said with a laugh:

"Well, I was surprised. Why you and no one else?"

"Because we're related."

"That's what they say."

"I told Emin, when your son grows up, send him to me. I'll look after him. I should be able to do that much."

I lied, to calm him down.

He was more sensitive than I thought. It seemed inappropriate to him that they were asking me. He thought it a little strange.

I did not think it was strange. And so I found out now, at the end of everything, that she has not forgotten me. I do not know whether I am happy, because it is sad. She mentioned me often; that means she was thinking about me. And she has entrusted her only son to me, so I will help him, so he will not remain a poor villager. She loves him, certainly, she loves him enough to agree to let him go, just to get him out of the dirt and insecurity of their village. Maybe I am also to blame that those people send their children to the kasaba. My renown leads them to do it.

You'll regret it, beautiful woman, when you hear.

I do not know what she looks like now, but I remember her for her beauty. And for an expression on her face of grief, such as I have never seen since, and which I could not forget long afterward, since I was the cause of that grief. It was because of this woman, the only one I ever loved, that I never married. It was because of her, whom I lost, because of her, who was taken away, that I became hardened and more closed toward everyone: I remember feeling as if I had been robbed, and I would not give others what I could not give to her. Maybe I was taking revenge upon myself and people, involuntarily and unwittingly. Her absence hurt me. And then I forgot, I really forgot, but it was all too late. It is a pity that I did not give my unspent tenderness to someone, to my parents, to my brother, to another woman. But maybe I say that without reason now, settling accounts. Because I also left her to go off to war, without sorrow, and I regretted it only when it was too late for me to change anything.

On the morning of the third day after my return, tired of my parents' attention and worry, I wandered away from our house and ended up on a plateau overlooking the village, the forest, and the river, on a rocky waste, above which there were only eagles flying in circles. With my palm I touched the slab of a large tombstone; it was the only thing between the wastes of the earth and sky, soothed by the centuries and undiscovered by anyone. I strained to hear a voice from that stone, or grave, as if beneath it were hidden the secret of life and death. I sat on the cliff's edge, above the endless forests and crags and listened to the snakelike hissing of the mountain wind, in a twofold wasteland of loneliness and nonexistence, like the ancient corpse under the slab. "Hey!" I cried to it, far away, into the void of time, and my voice tumbled over the jagged rocks. A lonely voice and a lonely wind.

Then I went down into the forest, I beat my brow against the bark of trees; I battered my knees against their gnarled roots, stopped in the open arms of the bushes, embraced the beech trees, and laughed. I fell down and laughed, got up and laughed. "Hey!" I cried to that distant, lonely corpse, who had wanted to be in the heights, even if shut inside a grave. "Hey!" I cried and laughed as I ran away.

I skirted her village, so I would not see her; I went down

to the river; there was no loneliness there. I brought it down from above, I brought it from afar. I went along the level shore and walked in the shallow water, stepping in and out of it, as if drunk, enthralled by the soft gurgling of the swift current; I stood in the water up to my knees and imagined that I was sinking deeper and deeper into a whirlpool: deeper and deeper, the water was up to my chin, to my lips, over my head. Above me the current was rippling, around me there was a greenish silence, the swaying grasses wrapped around my legs. I was also swaying, like a blade of grass; small fish swam into my mouth and out of my ears; crayfish caught my toes with their claws; a large, slow fish brushed against my thigh. Peace. Indifference. "Hey!" I cried, silently, and sat down in the grove between the path and the river, between life and death.

There was no one. No one passed through that small valley between the two villages. Everyone was out in the fields or working around his house. This solitude hurt pleasantly; it made me sorry, but I would not have traded it for anything. The ground smelled of the warm moisture of spring. Turtledoves landed in the poplars, pigeons were bathing in the shallow water, ruffling their feathers, splashing red and green droplets of water all around. A cowbell rang sluggishly somewhere in the distance. A familiar place, familiar colors, familiar sounds. I looked around: it was mine. I smelled the air: it was mine. I listened: it was mine.

Mine was also what was empty, what was not there.

I had yearned to go there. I had sniffed at the wind, like a wolf; my desires had found a direction, and there I was. I had come. I did not find the miracle that I had hoped for, but it was good, it was beautiful, it was quiet. Quiet, as during sleep. Quiet, as during convalescence.

I ran my palm through the soft grass, freshly sprouted, tender as a child's skin, and forgot about the awakening earth.

While I had been hurrying back from the army, I had

thought of my homeland, of my family's house, and of her, sometimes.

But then I was thinking only of her.

It would have been better if you'd waited for me, I whispered to myself; it would have been easier for me. I don't know why, but it would have been easier. Maybe you're more important than my homeland and my family's house, now that you're gone. If only you didn't exist, it would be easier; it would be better. Without you the distant, foreign lands hurt more, and the empty roads, and the strange dreams that I have even when I'm awake, that I can't chase away without you.

I was not sorry; it did not matter. But I called to her shadow, her absent face, to say goodbye, one last time, to leave her once again.

And I succeeded in summoning her, in creating her out of the green bushes, out of the water's reflection, out of the sunlight.

She stood, distant, entirely shadows. If a breath of wind came up, she would disappear.

I desired that, and dreaded it.

"I knew you'd come," I said. And immediately, without stopping:

"It's too late, there's nothing left, except in my thoughts. And let there not even be that."

"Allah be with you," I said in farewell. "I won't let you haunt me like a ghost. You'll always be standing between these hills, like the moon, like the river, like an alem* on a minaret, like a shining apparition. You've filled this place with yourself, like a mirror, filled it with fragrance, like a bed. I'll go out into the world. You won't be there, in that other place; not even your image will be within me."

"Why are you holding your head in your hands?" she asked me. "Are you sad?"

I'll go away, I said and closed my eyes, lowering my eyelids like visors, like gates, to capture her fleeting image. I'll

PART 2

go away, so that I won't have to look at you. I'll go away, so I won't think about your betrayal.

"Do you know how I felt? Do you know how I feel now?"

I'll go away, so I won't hate you, so I'll stop caring. I've scattered your image along distant roads: the winds will carry it away; the rains will wash it away, I hope. My hurt will erase it from within me.

"Why did you leave last autumn? A man should never leave when he has a reason to stay."

"I had to."

"You left me. What were you seeking in the world? You've come back sad. Is that all you accomplished?"

"I'm sad because of my wounds, my fatigue, because of my dead comrades."

"You're also sad because of me."

"I'm also sad because of you, but I didn't want to tell you that. I traveled for days and weeks to see you. In the evening I'd lie down under a tree in a forest, hungry, my legs bruised, frozen by the icy rains, and I'd forget about everything, talking with you. I walked endless roads, and I'd have been frightened at how many of them there were and what kinds of horrible distances there are in the world, had I not held your hand in mine and walked by your side, feeling your hip next to mine, hardly waiting for a level road, to close my eyes, for you to be closer and clearer to me. Why are you crying?"

"Tell more of how you thought about me."

Her cheeks were pale, her eyelashes cast deep shadows under her eyes, her bent knees trembled on the ground, her hands rested beside them, she touched the grass with her palms, as I had a little before.

"Why did you come?"

"Do you want us to go out into the world together? I'll leave everything and come with you."

She had been the wife of another for three days already, she had the traces of another's hands on her body, another's lips had brushed the bloom from her skin.

I told her that, in anguish.

"But just because of that," she answered foolishly, incomprehensibly.

I grabbed her by her arms, like a drowning man. She belonged to another man. I did not care; she had been mine, forever. I did not know what forever is; I only knew about that moment, the only one that mattered, which erased time and my sorrow. My quivering fingers dug into her like nails; no one could take her away from me alive; I held her pinned to the ground in that beastly grip. The river became silent; the only sound was that of bells within me, unknown and unrung until then, all of my bells, as if they were sounding an alarm. People would gather around; they did not concern me; they did not exist. Oh, my dream, which has become a victim.

Then the bells stopped; the world returned, I regained my sight and saw her reborn, strangled, white on the grass, which was green, like bile; she was transformed into a white river pebble, grown into the ground, a bear's foot bloomed from her armpit, snowdrop bloomed from between her thighs, catkins from a poplar drifted over her light skin, I did not know whether to leave her to be buried in them, or to lay her into a deep whirlpool, or to carry her away and place her in the stone grave above the forest. Should I have lain down beside her and turned into spring grass and willow branches?

I left without turning around. I do not know whether she called to me, and I remembered her as strange, like that tombstone.

"Hey!" I cried occasionally, through the expanse of time, calling to that white spring grave, but no echo ever came back from the distance.

And so I forgot.

And I believe that I would not have remembered now, if tonight, tonight of all nights, her son had not come. And maybe my son, too.

I know, like every fool, I could say: if what happened

hadn't happened, my life would be different. If I hadn't gone off to war, if I hadn't fled from her, if I hadn't called Harun to the kasaba, if Harun hadn't . . . It's ridiculous. What would life be then? If I had not left her, if it had not seemed easier to me to run away than to defy the whole world, maybe this night would not have even come, but I would certainly have begun to hate that woman, thinking that she stood in the way of my happiness, keeping me from succeeding in life. Because I would not know what I do now. Man is damned, and regrets all the paths he never took. But who knows what would have awaited me on others?

"You're lucky to have left the village," the youth said to me dreamily.

"Go to bed, sleep. You're tired."

"You're lucky."

"I'll wake you early. I'm going on a journey."

"Are you going far away?"

"Hafiz-Muhammed will look after you. Do you want to stay in the tekke?"

"I don't care."

Neither did I. Let him make his own decision, let him try it. I cannot help him. No one can help anyone.

He wanted to kiss my hand; they must have advised him enough to do it, so he would win my goodwill and show a gratitude he did not feel. I did not let him.

He left, tired—it is a long way from the village to the kasaba (and even longer from the kasaba back to the village)—maybe a little surprised that everything had ended well, and maybe saddened that he was going to stay. We passed each other coldly, like strangers.

I thought almost with disgust how it could have been different. I could have embraced him. We could have kissed one another on the cheek. I could have given him clever advice, held his knotty hand in mine, my eyes full of tears, whispering sorrowfully: my son. I could have tried stupidly to find my own features in his face, I could have moved him with the final image of myself, which would remain in his memory. It was really better if he remembered something nicer and more sensible.

Yes, I stood over him, with a candle in my hand, as he slept a deep sleep given only to the young and to idiots, and I tried in vain to find tenderness within myself. The light leapt across the hollows of his face, his bony breast breathed peacefully, his stark mouth, similar to mine, was smiling at something he had left but was still bound to. I thought: he'll take my place here, and in life, my bones, perhaps, I as I once was; life goes on. But nothing stirred within me; that forced thought remained cold, and I did not bend down to kiss him or touch him with my palm. I am not capable of tenderness.

But still, I wish you luck, young man.

Somewhere in the darkness the night-watchman has called out midnight. My last midnight, my last day: my end will meet its beginning.

I know this, but surprisingly, everything that must happen seems far away and completely unreal. Deep within myself I do not believe it will happen. I know it will, but something within me is smiling, resisting it, denying it. It will happen, but it is not possible. I do not know enough yet. There is still too much life in my heart, and I refuse to accept it. Maybe because I am writing this: I have not despaired, I am rejecting death.

But when I set down my reed a while ago, I could not take it up again into my numb hand for a long time, because of weariness, or a lack of will. Because of a cowardly thought that came to me—that what I am doing does not make any sense. And since I was left defenseless, the world around me came to life. But that world is silence and darkness.

I got up and went to the open window. Silence, darkness. Complete, final. Nothing anywhere, no one anywhere. The last vein had stopped pulsing, the last flicker of light gone out. Not a sound, not a breath, not a trace of light.

PART 2

O world, wasteland, why do you have to be like this right now?

Then, somewhere in that deafness, in that death, a voice sounded out, serene, young, clear, and began singing a strange song, dreamy and soft, yet fresh and resistant. Like the song of a bird. And it ended as suddenly as it began. Maybe the voice had been strangled, like a bird.

But it has remained alive in me, moved me, excited me, alarmed me. That ordinary, unfamiliar human voice, which until now I would not even have noticed. Maybe because it appeared in the silence, from the other world; maybe because it was not frightened, or because it was, because it was calling to me, with sympathy and assurance.

I have begun to feel a belated tenderness. You who are singing in the terrifying darkness, I hear you. Your frail voice sounds like a lesson to me. But why now?

Where are you, Is-haq, you renegade, did you ever exist?

Golden bird, you are nothing but an illusion!

In the next room Hafiz-Muhammed is keeping his vigil. Maybe he has found out and is waiting for me to call for him or to go to him, giving me time to settle accounts with myself and to ask God for mercy. He is surely shedding his helpless, aged tears at the sorrow of this world. He pities all men. He fails to love them in one way, and I in another. That is why we are lonely.

But maybe he would pity me more than others, maybe he would pick me out of this general misery and accept me as the last man would the last man.

Should I say to him: Hafiz-Muhammed, I'm alone, alone and sad, give me your hand and be my friend, only for a while. Be my father, my son, a dear man whose nearness gladdens me; let me weep on your sunken chest, and you weep as well, for me, not for all men. Put your moist palm on top of my head: it won't last very long, but I need it; not long, since I can already hear the first roosters crowing.

The first roosters! Those malicious heralds, they goad

time onward, spur it along to keep it from falling asleep, hastening our misfortunes, rousing them from their lairs so they will wait for us, with their hair bristling. Be silent, roosters! Stop, time!

Should I shout into the night, to summon people, to look for help?

It is no use. The roosters are merciless; they are already sounding the alarm.

I am sitting on my knees, listening. In the silence of this room, from somewhere in the wall, from somewhere in the ceiling, from some unseen space I hear the striking of the kudret-clock,* the unrelenting step of fate.

Fear is flooding over me, like water.

The living know nothing. Teach me, dead ones, how to die without fear, or at least without horror. Because death is senseless, as is life.

> I call to witness the ink, the quill, and the script,
> which flows from the quill;
> I call to witness the faltering shadows of the sinking evening,
> the night and all she enlivens;
> I call to witness the moon when she waxes, and the
> sunrise when it dawns.
> I call to witness the Resurrection Day and the soul
> that accuses itself;
> I call to witness time, the beginning and end
> of all things—to witness that every man always suffers loss.

With his own hand wrote Hassan, son of Ali:

I did not know he was so unhappy.
Peace to his tormented soul!

1962–1966

PART 2

NOTES

Chapter 1

1. "In the name of God, Most Gracious, Most Merciful!"—the opening line of each of the *suras* (chapters) of the Koran.

2. This passage consists of several lines that belong to different *suras* (S. lxviii, 1; S. lvi, 75; S. lxxiv, 33–34; S. lxxv, 1–2; S. ciii, 1–2).

3. *Mevlevi*: Muslim mystical order, founded in the thirteenth century in Konya, Anatolia, by the Persian poet Jalal ad-Din ar-Rumi, whose popular title *mawlana* (Arabic for "our master") gave the order its name. The Mevlevi are also called "dancing" (or "whirling") dervishes on account of their ritual prayer, which is performed while spinning on the right foot to musical accompaniment.

Chapter 2

1. S. xvi, 61.

2. *Saint George's Day.* An important Christian holiday (old style 23 April, new style 6 May); for the South Slavs it celebrates the passage from winter to summer. Among the numerous activities performed on the eve of this day was the ritual of bathing in rivers, especially at water mills, as a symbol of the awakening of new natural forces. Saint George's Day, which had pagan proto-Slavic origins, had become deeply entrenched in the Christian tradition of the South Slavs by the time of the Turkish conquest, and was later cel-

ebrated by Bosnian Muslim Slavs even after their conversion to Islam.

3. Selimović alleges that he drew this and the following quotations from works by the Islamic thinkers and poets Abu Faraj, Ibn Sina, al-Ghazzali, and Jalal ad-Din ar-Rumi, although he never specifies the exact sources. Indeed, a basic assumption of al-Ghazzali's philosophy is the dichotomy between certainty and doubt; similarly, in his *Metaphysics* Ibn Sina talks of death as the decay of matter, not of the soul.

4. *Dawud*: David in the Judeo-Christian tradition.

5. This passage is another instance where Selimović quotes inexactly from the Koran, grafting passages together (cf. for example, S. xxxiv, 13; S. xvii, 81; S. xxix, 6; S. xli, 30; S. lxxxix, 27–30).

6. In the contemporary Bosnian vernacular the capital of Turkey is variously referred to as either Carigrad (Constantinople) or Stambol (Istanbul). Selimović uses both names, and the translators have remained faithful to the original in this respect.

7. *Wallachia*: Region in present-day Romania, between the Transylvanian Alps and the Danube.

Chapter 3

1. S. xliii, 88.

2. *Lovage*: European herb (*Levisticum officinate*), formerly cultivated in gardens and used as a domestic remedy.

3. *Sinan Tekke*: Hadji Sinan Tekke in Sarajevo, built between 1638 and 1640.

4. *Bayramiyya order*: Mystical order founded in Ankara sometime during the fourteenth and fifteenth centuries by Hadji Bayram-i Wali.

5. *Ahriman*: Evil spirit in the dualistic doctrine of Zoroastrianism.

6. *Asaf*: Asaf Ibn Barahija (Hebr. Asaf b. Berkjab), leg-

endary vizier of King Solomon; in Islamic legend he is a symbol of wisdom.

7. *Anka-bird*: Large legendary bird, which is said to have received its name from its long neck. The name of the biblical "Anakim" is derived from the same root. Some Arabic authors suggest both the griffin and the phoenix.

8. *Ibn Arabi*: Celebrated mystic of pantheistic doctrine (1165–1240). His works were thought by many to border on heresy.

Chapter 4

1. S. liii, 24.
2. *Constantsa*: City and port on the Black Sea, located in present-day Romania. A well-known center of learning and calligraphy since the ninth century.

Chapter 5

1. S. xlvii, 24.
2. These three lines come from S. xxxvii, 109, 120, and 130 respectively; Ibrahim, Musa, Harun, and Ilyas are Abraham, Moses, Aaron, and Elijah in the Judeo-Christian tradition.
3. *Dubrovnik*: City-republic on the southern end of the Adriatic coast in present-day Croatia; a strategic treaty with the Ottoman Empire protected the city's liberty and established it as a major trading center linking Europe with the Ottoman Empire.
4. *Latin mahal*: Christian quarter in Ottoman Sarajevo, built by merchants from Dubrovnik.
5. *Avicenna*: Ibn Sina (Selimović uses the Latin transcription of the name, from Hebr. Aven Sina, 980–1037), for centuries considered the most important Muslim scholar. Some of his opinions are strongly influenced both by Neoplatonic and Aristotelian works.

6. *Krayina*: Northwest Bosnian borderland between Austro-Hungarian and Ottoman Empires.

7. *Travnik*: Administrative center of Bosnia during the Ottoman occupation, the seat of the vizier.

8. *Abu Faraj*: Arab historian and poet (897–967); his most important work, on which he apparently worked for fifty years, is the *Book of Songs*. It is this work that Selimović undoubtedly has in mind here.

Chapter 6

1. S. xxii, 73.

2. *Smyrna*: City in Western Turkey (modern Izmir), the chief port in Asia Minor.

3. Hassan's words may echo several verses from the Koran. See, for example, S. xi, 93, 121.

4. A slightly modified version of S. ix, 20, 24.

5. S. v, 101.

6. This exact line is presented as a quotation from the Koran, but it is not.

7. A generic version of a common Koranic line; see, for example S. lxxvii, 15, 24, 37; S. lxxxiii, 10.

8. S. lviii, 7, 10.

9. A generic version of a common Koranic line; see, for example S. iv, 144.

10. S. ix, 25.

11. A similar idea, although differently expressed, can be found in S. xlix, 2.

12. S. xliv, 29.

13. S. xci, 10.

14. S. xviii, 94.

15. This is not an exact quotation from the Koran.

16. No verse in this form exists in the Koran, although the idea that it embodies is common throughout.

17. S. xiv, 34.

18. This line is not an exact quotation from the Koran.

19. The concept expressed here is Koranic, but this exact line probably occurs nowhere in the book itself.

Chapter 7

1. S. xli, 30.
2. *Antioch*: Important city of the classical world, now the capital of the southern Turkish province of Hatay (modern Anatakya).

Chapter 8

1. The original verse from the Koran reads as follows: "My God, I have no one besides myself and my brother" (S. v, 28). It is not clear whether Selimović made the change intentionally or if there is a misprint in the original edition of the novel. The Serbo-Croatian *sebe* (myself) differs from *tebe* (you) only in the initial letter.
2. *Hussein-effendi of Mostar*: Hussein Čatranja, born in Mostar; wrote poetry under the name of Husami. In one of his poems he speaks of Shahin the acrobat who, accompanied by his apprentices, crossed the Neretva River in Mostar on a tightrope in 1669. Six lines of the poem have been preserved. However, the quoted lines are essentially Selimović's.
3. *Adem*: Adam in the Judeo-Christian tradition, the first man.
4. Probably an echo of S. xvii, 26.
5. S. xx, 25, 29–32.
6. *Quabeel*: Cain in the Judeo-Christian tradition, the elder son of Adam.
7. S. v, 34.
8. *Nuh*: Noah in the Judeo-Christian tradition.
9. This verse is probably an echo of S. vii, 85 or S. xxvi, 117–18.
10. *Baqara Sura*: second chapter of the Koran, "The Cow."
11. S. ii, 285–86.

Chapter 9

1. S. xi, 55.
2. *Waqiah Sura*: Al-Waqiah (The Event) is the fifty-sixth sura of the Koran.
3. S. lvi, 1–7.
4. *Spider Sura*: El-Ankabout, the twenty-ninth sura of the Koran.
5. S. lvi, 8–34.
6. S. lvi, 41–44, 51–55, 60.
7. S. lvii, 13–14.
8. A common image of paradise in the Koran; see, for example S. ii, 25; S. iii, 15; S. iv, 13 and elsewhere.
9. S. iv, 59.

Chapter 10

1. S. xci, 10.
2. *Sava*: River in northern Bosnia that served as a natural border between the Austro-Hungarian and Ottoman Empires.
3. *Muberid*: It is not quite clear to whom Selimović is referring. Al-Mubarrad (826–892) was a celebrated Arab philologist and poet. One of his minor works was copied by the famous calligrapher Ibn al-Bawwab (d. 1022). Thus, Selimović's *Muberid* might refer to the artistic endeavors of two different men.

Chapter 11

1. S. ix, 118.

Chapter 12

1. S. iii, 169.
2. *Kuyunjiluk*: Coppersmith section of the Sarajevo bazaar.

3. *Posavina*: Region in northeastern Bosnia, along of the Sava River.

Chapter 13

1. S. xiv, 24.
2. *Lesser Brethren Monastery*: Franciscan monastery in Dubrovnik, established in the fourteenth century.
3. *Mayram*: Muslim version of the name Mary, the mother of Christ.
4. *Ploche*: Eastern suburb of Dubrovnik, located outside the city walls; *Tabor* refers to the sixteenth-century building in which all travelers to the city had to be quarantined for six weeks.
5. *Mount Ivan*: Mountain forming a natural border between Bosnia and Herzegovina.
6. *Mount Igman*: Mountain to the west of Sarajevo.
7. *Trebinye*: City in eastern Herzegovina, located eighteen miles inland from Dubrovnik.

Chapter 14

1. S. xvii, 81.
2. *Kazazi*: Silk-weavers' section of the Sarajevo bazaar.

Chapter 15

1. S. xxxviii, 84.
2. *Kurshumli Mosque*: Kurshumli (from Turk. *kursun*, "lead") is an attribute of buildings with leaden roofs. Sarajevo's largest madrasah (built in 1537–38) bears the name Kuršumlija, but there is no mosque of the same name. The Turkish traveler Evliya Celebi, who visited Sarajevo in 1660, mentions two mosques with leaden roofs: the Ferhad Bey Mosque and the Gazi Husrev Bey Mosque. The latter is located across the street from the Kuršumlija Madrasah.

3. *Karanfil mahal*: "Carnation quarter"; seventeenth-century Sarajevo was divided into 104 mahals, of which twelve were Christian, two were Jewish, and the rest Muslim. The local eighteenth-century writer Mula Mustafa Baseškija in his *Chronicle* mentions by name each of the one hundred mahals that still existed in Sarajevo in his time. One of them was called the *Sunbul mahal* (Hyacinth quarter). Selimović, not being a native of Sarajevo, might have simply confused the names of the flowers.

4. *Vranduk*: Town and fortress in central Bosnia, fifty-five miles north of Sarajevo; in the eighteenth and nineteenth centuries the fortress served as a jail for political prisoners.

Chapter 16

1. S. l, 30.
2. *Tuzla*: City in northeastern Bosnia.
3. *Split*: City and port on the Adriatic coast, now in Croatia.

GLOSSARY

abdest   Muslim ritual of washing the face, arms, and legs, rinsing the mouth and nose, and rubbing the neck, ears, and top of the head before prayer

aga   Originally an officer, later a gentleman or landowner

alem   Copper crescent that decorates the top of a minaret

alim   Learned man, Islamic religious scholar

Bairam   One of the two most important Muslim religious holidays; the Ramadan Bairam (*Eid-al-Fitr*) follows after the month of fasting, Ramadan, and lasts for three days; the Kurban Bairam (*Eid-al-Adha*) comes two months and ten days after Ramadan; the holidays are set according to the lunar calendar

bey   High-ranking official in provincial service; in Bosnia often a title of respect, regardless of the occupation of the person so addressed

chibouk   Long-stemmed tobacco pipe

chador	Women's ankle-length coat, worn outside the house
defterdar	Officer of finance, accountant-general of a province, or secretary
dervish	Member of one of various Muslim religious orders
dizdar	Commander of a fortress
effendi	Title of respect, initially used for government officials and members of learned professions; later as an equivalent of "sir" or "master"
fakir	Muslim religious mendicant
hadji	Title given to one who has made a pilgrimage to Mecca
hafiz	Honorific title, earned by one who knows the Koran by heart
harem	House or part of a house allotted to women in a Muslim household; usually designed for maximum seclusion
hodja	Muslim man of religion; teacher
houri	Nymph in the Muslim paradise
imaret	Originally a hospice for the accommodation of pilgrims and travelers; here, a free kitchen for the poor

janissary	Soldier of an elite corps of Ottoman troops; janissaries were usually taken as small boys from Christian families and raised as Muslims
kadi	Muslim judge who interprets and administers the religious law of Islam
kaimakam	High administrative official, vizier's deputy
kasaba	Provincial town in the Ottoman Empire
katul-ferman	Death-warrant
kiblah	Direction (of Mecca) to which Muslims turn at prayer
kudret-clock	Invisible clock whose bells announce important events
madrasah	Islamic theological seminary
mahal	Section of a town or city
mekteb	Religious elementary school
meytash	Stone pedestal on which the shrouded body of a deceased person is placed during the funeral prayer
mintan	Type of coat with long, narrow sleeves
miralay	Rank in the Ottoman military, equivalent to colonel

muderris	High-ranking teacher in a *madrasah* (Islamic theological seminary)
muezzin	Man who proclaims the hour of prayer
mufti	Highest religious official in a province
mullah	Ottoman scholar, versed in theology and Islamic law
musellim	Chief executive officer in a district; also called *mutesellim*
padishah	Persian title, equivalent to "Great King" or "Emperor"; in Europe used to designate the Sultan of Turkey
Porte	Title of the central office of the Ottoman government
saraf	Banker or money changer in the East
shalwars	Wide trousers worn by men and women in the East
sharia	Islamic religious law
sheikh	Muslim religious and spiritual leader
sherbet	Cooling drink of the East, made of fruit juice and sweetened water
silladar	High official at the Porte, in charge of the arsenal
softa	Student at an Islamic university

sura	Chapter of the Koran
tekke	Complex of buildings housing a Muslim religious order
vali	Civil governor of an Ottoman province; here used synonymously with *vizier*
vizier	Here, the sultan's deputy, governor of an Ottoman province
wakf	Endowment that serves Islamic religious, cultural, educational, and humanitarian purposes
yasin	Chapter of the Koran that is recited as a prayer for the dying or deceased
zaqqum	Mythical tree that grows in hell
zurna	Type of woodwind instrument

SELECT BIBLIOGRAPHY

Translations into English

Ćurčija-Prodanović, Nada. "Lightness and Darkness" (excerpts from *Four Golden Birds*). *The Bridge*, no. 2 (1966): 29–38 (N.B.: Selimović first proposed to call *Death and the Dervish* by the title *Four Golden Birds*). Also in *Matica Iseljenički kalendar* (1971): 203–11.

Koljević, Svetozar. "Death and the Dervish" (excerpts from *Derviš i smrt*). In *New Writing in Yugoslavia*, edited by Bernard Johnson, 250–83. Baltimore: Penguin, 1970.

Rosslyn, Felicity, and Svetozar Koljević, trans. "Wild Horses." *Books in Bosnia and Herzegovina* 3, no. 5 (1984): 273–78.

Selimović, Meša. *The Island*. Translated by Jeanie Shaterian. With an Introduction by George Vid Tomashevich. Toronto: Serbian Heritage Academy, 1983.

Bibliographies of Yugoslav Literature

Mihailovich, Vasa D., ed. *First Supplement to A Comprehensive Bibliography of Yugoslav Literature in English, 1981–1985*. Columbus, Ohio: Slavica, 1988.

———, ed. *Second Supplement to A Comprehensive Bibliography of Yugoslav Literature in English, 1986–1990*. Columbus, Ohio: Slavica, 1992.

Mihailovich, Vasa D., and Mateja Matić, eds. *A Comprehensive Bibliography of Yugoslav Literature in English, 1593–1980*. Columbus, Ohio: Slavica, 1984

Secondary Sources

Butler, Thomas J. "Between East and West: Three Bosnian Writer-Rebels: Kočić, Andrić, Selimović." *Cross Currents* 3 (1984): 339–57.

———. "Literary Style and Poetic Function in Meša Selimović's *The Dervish and Death*." *Slavonic and East European Review* 52 (1974): 533–47.

Eekman, Thomas. *Thirty Years of Yugoslav Literature (1945–1975)*. Ann Arbor: Michigan Slavic Publications, 1978. Pp. 104–10.

Egerić, Miroslav. *Derviš i smrt Meše Selimovića*. Belgrade: Zavod za udžbenike i nastavna sredstva, 1982.

Gluščević, Zoran. "Izmedju dogme i ništavila." *Književnost*, no. 11 (1981): 2030–55.

Buñevats, Maritsa Kosanovich. "Meša Selimović: Origen y elección." *Quimera* 96 (1990): 36–43.

Makarova, N. G. "Osobennosti manery povestvovanija v romane Meši Selimoviča 'Derviš i smert.'" *Vestnik Moskovskogo universiteta*, 9th ser., no. 5 (1991): 74–77 (iz studenčeskix rabot).

Mihailovich, Vasa D., et al., eds. *Modern Slavic Literatures: A Library of Literary Criticism*. Vol. 2, *Bulgarian, Czechoslovak, Polish, Ukrainian and Yugoslav Literatures*. New York: Ungar, 1976. Pp. 675–78.

Palavestra, Predrag. "Kritičko značenje alegorijske forme." *Savremenik*, no. 4 (1983): 275–80.

———. *Posleratna srpska književnost, 1945-1970*. Belgrade: Prosveta, 1972.

Peco, Asim. "Fremdwörter als stilogene Elemente im zeitgenössischen jugoslawischen Roman." *Zeitschrift für Slawistik* 28, no. 4 (1983): 594–602. Also available in Serbo-Croatian: Asim Peco, "Funkcionalnost turcizama u romanu *Derviš i smrt* Meše Selimovića." *Naš jezik* 25, no. 3 (1981): 118–28.

Petrović, Miodrag. *Roman Meše Selimovića*. Niš: Gradina, 1981.

Popović, Radovan. *Život Meše Selimovića*. Belgrade: BIGZ, 1988.

Prohić, Kasim. "Činiti i biti: U potrazi za apsolutnim: zategnuti luk transcendencije." *Život* [Sarajevo] 66, nos. 11-12 (1984): 333–44.

Radulović, Milan. "Otvorena trilogija Meše Selimovića." *Književnost* 38 [75], no. 12 (1983): 2044–59.

Thiergen, Peter. "Zum Eingangskapitel von M. Selimovićs *Derviš i smrt*." In *Studia phraseologica et alia: Festschrift für Josip Matešić zum 65. Geburtstag*, edited by Wolfgang Eismann and Jürgen Petermann, 497–510. Munich: Otto Sagner, 1992.

■ □ ■ □ ■

WRITINGS FROM AN UNBOUND EUROPE

Words Are Something Else
DAVID ALBAHARI

The Victory
HENRYK GRYNBERG

The Tango Player
CHRISTOPH HEIN

Balkan Blues: Writing Out of Yugoslavia
JOANNA LABON, ED.

Compulsory Happiness
NORMAN MANEA

Zenobia
GELLU NAUM

The Houses of Belgrade
The Time of Miracles
BORISLAV PEKIĆ

The Soul of a Patriot
EVGENY POPOV

Estonian Short Stories
KAJAR PRUUL AND DARLENE REDDAWAY, EDS.

Death and the Dervish
MEŠA SELIMOVIĆ

Fording the Stream of Consciousness
In the Jaws of Life and Other Stories
DUBRAVKA UGREŠIĆ

Ballad of Descent
MARTIN VOPĚNKA